Praise

"Apple Gidley has the most delicious authorial voice. She draws you in with the intimacy of her writing, and the engaging nature of her characters. This is also a subject and setting I've never encountered in a novel before and it's so interesting."

JANE JOHNSON, AUTHOR OF *SECRET OF THE BEES*

"There is a marvellous arc to this absorbing story of resilient, plucky Australian Annie Cutler, from her nursing in wartime New Guinea, to the Cold War blockade of Berlin, to the regeneration of postwar London and finally to the tranquillity of a rural community. Told from the female point of view throughout, *Annie's Day* pulls no punches about the horrors of a theatre of war unjustly neglected in fiction, but this is also a novel about hope in the face of loss and adversity—the hope to go forward and to love again."

KATHERINE MEZZACAPPA, AUTHOR OF *THE MAIDEN OF FLORENCE*

"An eye-opening insight into the little-recorded wartime experiences of nurses from the Australian Army. Moving and enlightening, I heartily recommend it to all those interested in WW2 history."

DEBORAH SWIFT, AUTHOR OF *LAST TRAIN TO FREEDOM*

"Totally absorbing. A deeply moving tale of love, courage, hope and endurance."

LIZ HARRIS, AUTHOR OF *JAIPUR MOON*, PART OF THE COLONIALS SERIES

About the Author

A nomadic life has seen Anglo-Australian Apple Gidley live and work in twelve countries—the cultures and experiences of which influence her writing. Her roles have included editor for a global charity magazine, honorary consul, and dive bum, among others. After ten years in the Caribbean, Apple relocated to Cambridgeshire, England in 2023, where Bella, a ten-year-old rescue cat, has become her de facto, real-time editor.

Currently researching her next historical novel, which takes place in places Apple does not know well, will ensure her itchy-feet get to travel some more.

applegidley.com

Annie's Day

Apple Gidley

Annie's Day

Print Edition
ISBN: 978-3-98832-180-0
Published by Vine Leaves Press 2025

Cover design by Jessica Bell
Interior design by Amie McCracken

You know that place between sleep and awake … the place where you can still remember dreaming? That's where I'll always love you. That's where I'll be waiting.

J.M. Barrie

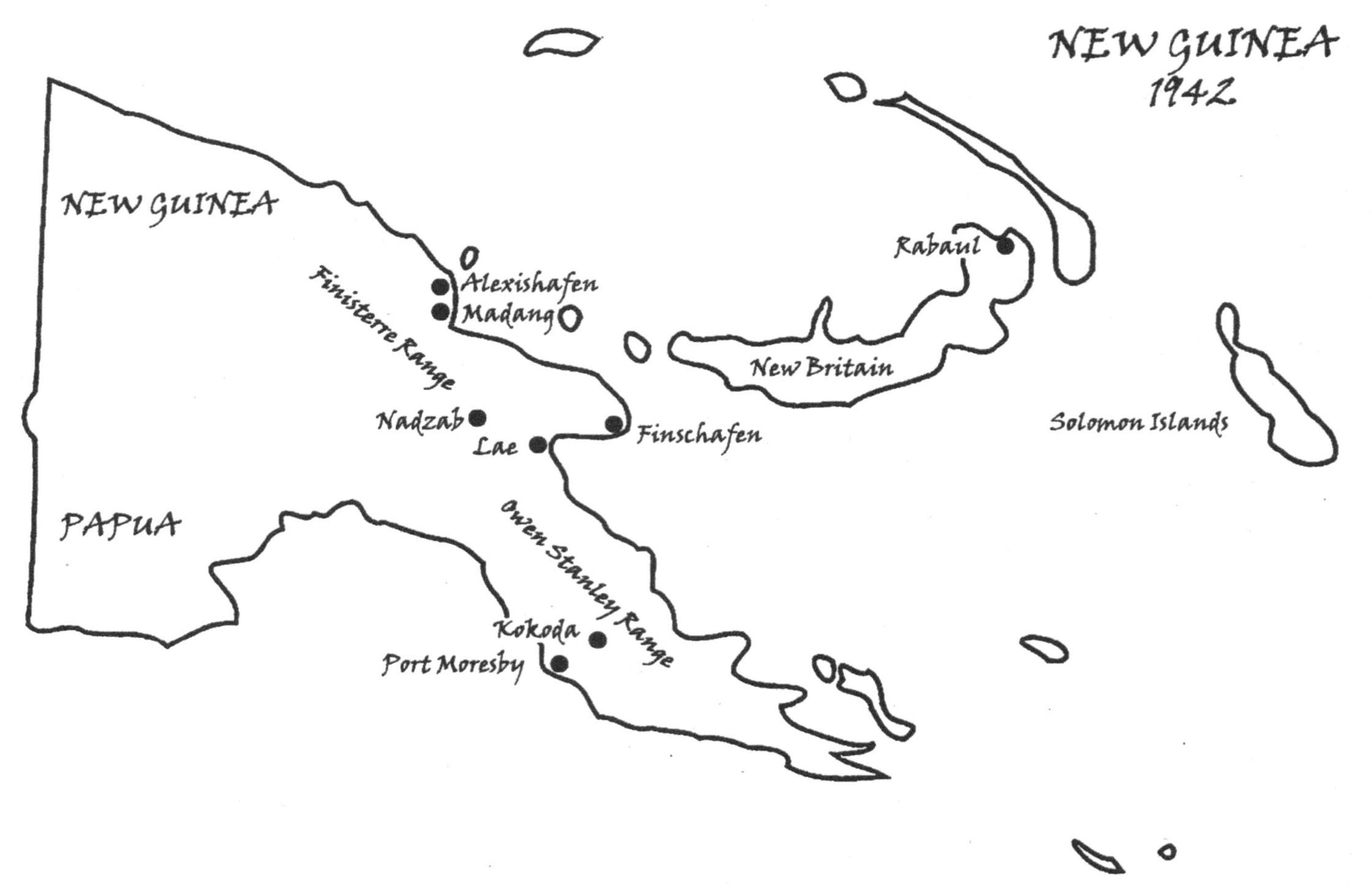
NEW GUINEA
1942
NEW GUINEA
Alexishafen
Madang
Finisterre Range
Rabaul
New Britain
Solomon Islands
Nadzab
Lae
Finschafen
PAPUA
Owen Stanley Range
Kokoda
Port Moresby

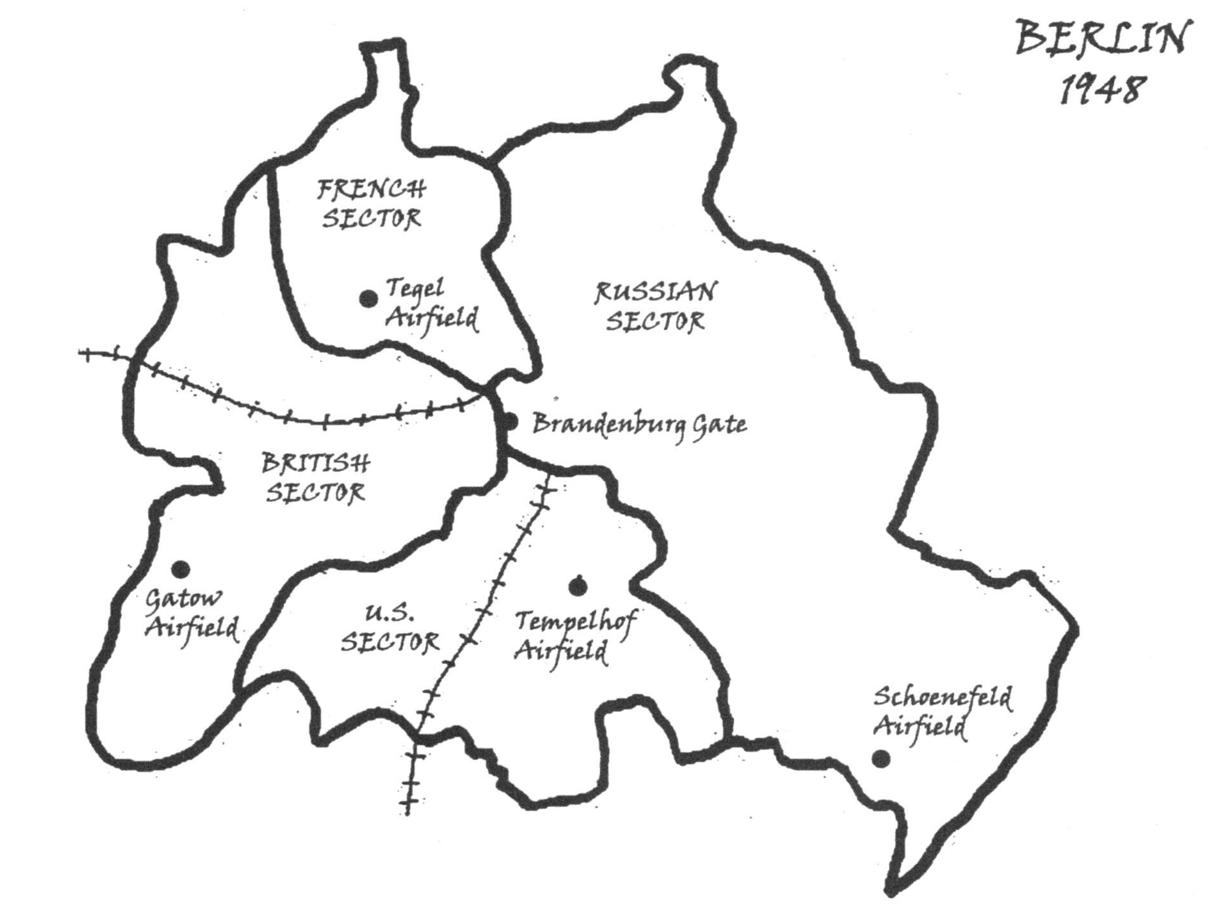
BERLIN
1948
FRENCH SECTOR
Tegel Airfield
RUSSIAN SECTOR
Brandenburg Gate
BRITISH SECTOR
Gatow Airfield
U.S. SECTOR
Tempelhof Airfield
Schoenefeld Airfield

For my grandchildren,
Ava, Harley, and Max

and

In Memory Of
their great grandmother,
Ida Arundel Girling, née Morse
CMF N108172 (April–August 1941)
AIF NFX76282 (August 1941–November 1946)

Author's Note

Historical fiction draws on many sources and, inevitably, there will be some discrepancies. Examples, in *Annie's Day*, include differing reports regarding the number of nurses (53 or 59) aboard the Empire Star, and whether they were tendered out to the ship. Evacuees boarding the Vyner Brooke were, so I made an assumption that the nurses were, too. Reports also differ about whether the Empire Star sailed alone or as part of a convoy when escaping Singapore. The number of people killed and wounded whilst on the way to Batavia (Jakarta) also differs.

The massacres, both at St. Stephen's College in Hong Kong, and on Bangka Island happened; so, too, the sinking of the hospital ship, Centaur, by the Imperial Japanese Army Air Service in the waters near Brisbane in 1943. The US Liberator plane disaster in New Guinea is fact, as are the military manoeuvres described. The events leading up to and including the Berlin Airlift are also true.

Real people, mainly military, are interspersed throughout, particularly with regard to manoeuvres in New Guinea, and during the Berlin Airlift. Within the Australian Army Nursing Service, three must be named: Margaret Anderson and Veronica (Vera) Torney, who were decorated for their bravery aboard the Empire Star, received the George Medal, and a Military MBE respectively. Vivian Bullwinkel, who survived the horrors of war with incredible fortitude, continued her nursing career after the war, and received many honours, including the Order of Australia, and the Florence Nightingale Medal from the Red Cross.

A word of warning. Some words and terms might be deemed derogatory now, but they are true to the era, and have only been used in dialogue, in a manner consistent with that time. An example is Fuzzy Wuzzy Angel used by the Australian military and nurses in New Guinea, with affection, to describe the incredible bravery of native bearers bringing the injured down from the mountains.

Apple Gidley
Cambridgeshire, 2025

Chapter 1
Cambridgeshire, September 2003

Red-tipped spears streaked down with a malevolence heightened by the black backdrop, followed by a thunderous juddering crump. The jolt woke Annie. Sun peeked through loose-weave curtains, and she stretched her hand over the tangled sheet, feeling only cool space. She turned her head on the down pillow. Nothing. The dream had been so vivid.

"Get a grip." Her voice a mutter, she rolled across the mattress and levered over the side. "Bugger off!" She glared at the blinking light on the medical alert, the one she had promised to wear. She ignored the cord dangling from the bedside table, a silent reminder of her frailty, and wriggled into fluorescent green slippers—a present from her grandsons—and grinned down at the persimmon pink of the frilly flowers at the toe.

"Righto, a quick shower." Annie snorted. Nothing happened quickly these days. She jiggled the latch and prised the bathroom window open to gaze out at the grey-green gum tree—a reminder of a life so long ago that some days it didn't seem hers. The tree towered above, trying to surpass the church steeple on the other side of a garden wall held together with ivy and stinging nettles. A hint of September hung on the wisp of wind that rustled the eucalyptus leaves. If she shut her eyes and clicked her heels, she'd almost be back in Australia.

Showered and dressed in tatty jeans and a purple sweatshirt, threads hanging from the frayed cuffs, she stabbed an enamelled bamboo chopstick through the silver knot on top of her head then, holding the rail, made her way downstairs. The thought of coffee almost lured her from the first task of the day. She quickened her step. If she didn't open the garage doors soon the neighbours would think she'd snuffed it.

Most of the time she appreciated their care, but sometimes it rankled. Occasionally she'd like to lounge around in pyjamas and not worry about concerned faces peering through a window, or banging on the door or, God forbid, actually using the key they had for emergencies. Not that there had ever been one. Well, not with her.

After heaving the garage door up and over, Annie paused to admire the bed of lobelia, the blue mimicking the sky, then bent, her left knee grating, to retrieve the newspaper stuffed through the letterbox. The older she got, the further away from her feet she felt. She left the front door open and, glancing up, saw her tall figure reflected back in the mirror above the hall table. David would have been appalled.

"For Heaven's sake, Annie," his mellow voice came from deep in her memory, "you're far too old to wear jeans—they look ready for the scrap heap."

"Along with me, you mean. I'll have you know slashes in the knees of one's jeans are the height of teen fashion."

"My sweet, you are not a teen," she imagined him saying, with a hug, "fortunately I love you any way you choose to dress, although do please hide should anyone come to the door."

Annie shook her head and waited for the kettle to boil. Some days she enjoyed wandering back, other times it became so painful she longed for sleep that would not come. Today would be happy. She jiggled the teabag. One of the few things to which David had really objected when they appeared on the shelves. His voice thrummed into her head again.

"Tea is an institution, succour in times of direst need. It should be made with reverence!"

"Oh, the pomposity of the man." Annie remembered swatting his hand as he had measured the exact amount into the warmed pot the first time he had been in her kitchen.

So long ago. She sighed and shoved bread into the toaster.

Taking her toast, slathered with butter and Vegemite, cholesterol be damned, she sat at the head of the table and dropped the newspaper beside the plate. "I'm in charge." The words often spoken to the boys made her smile. The dialogue in her head felt so real she couldn't help glancing at the children's chairs. "You can be in charge when you're as tall as me," had been David's stock phrase. He had treasured their sons, teasing them to manhood with a gentleness that had been missing from her childhood. His tone always calm and reasonable, unlike her every so often more acerbic responses to misdemeanours. She had wondered sometimes whether his manner would have worked with teenage girls. Probably.

The paper rustled as Annie flipped the pages, scanning scraps that caught her attention. Headline writing really was an art. She read the bold print, *Iraq still a threat to the world.* Another war. Every war promised to be the last. How could people fall for such nonsense? She could rarely remember jokes, or quotes, but David's voice again intruded. One of his favourites had been from Plato, *Only the dead have seen the end of war.*

Her eyes welled. "You're an ancient, and gibbering woman." She drained her tea and pushed back the chair to make room for Eartha Kitty. Annie twiddled the black cat's ears, and was rewarded with a purr. "Just you and me now. And I need to outlive you." Eartha slid off Annie's lap and stalked through the cat flap installed in the French doors. "Where's the loyalty?" she demanded. David had grumbled when she had come home with yet another bedraggled bundle of matted fur, rescued from the brambles that marked the village boundary. "Let me guess, a stray?" he'd asked. But he never meant it.

A flurry of wings and dropped seeds heralded Eartha's pounce. Sparrows and robins flew in a ruffle of indignation and cheeps to the branches of a gnarled apple tree. The cat struck a nonchalant pose as she tended her ablutions. Annie watched the mind games.

Everyone played them. Except David. He had been straight and sure. In his love of God, of her, of their boys. She had worried in the early days that his sureness would become claustrophobic. She had little belief in a Divine Being, although she accepted that deep faith sustained David in a way she could not. She had never resented his time spent with his God, rather marvelled that, after all he had seen, he could still believe.

She knew that for David to be truly complete, he needed both her and God. Although, Annie giggled, she had drawn the line after the birth of their first child.

"Thank God," he'd said, as he had been ushered into their bedroom by the district midwife.

"God had nothing to do with it. This is all my own work," she'd replied and, with an exhausted smile, held out the swaddled bundle with a shock of black hair and a wrinkly nose. "Meet your son, darling." They had cried a little and looked in awe at the twitching, sleeping infant. And now that bundle was fifty-one.

The phone jangled Annie from her reverie. The newspaper scattered as she got to her feet and, with exasperation, she kicked the pages out of the way and grabbed the receiver from the wall.

"Hello, the Old Vicarage."

"Hey, Granny Annie." A cheerful voice, so like his father's, rumbled down the line.

"Hello, my love, and, just for the record, I am not your grandmother. I am your children's grandmother." She pulled a chair over to the phone.

"Alright, Mumsie," her elder son teased, knowing she hated the name both boys used when her words had bewildered everyone.

"I don't know why I bother answering the phone when all I get is abuse."

"Okay, I'll start again," Jake said. "Good morning, Mother, how are you? Is that better?"

"Well, at least you got the description right, but plain old Mum will do, though perhaps less of the old." Annie stroked the creped skin at her neck.

"We thought we'd come over tomorrow. Pick you up and go for a pub lunch, if you're up for it."

"Oh, darling, that sounds lovely. Don't the boys have anything on?"

"Their game has been cancelled. It's one of the few free Sundays for the next couple of months so we thought we'd make the most of it."

"In that case, would you like to come over this afternoon? It won't take a moment to make up the beds." Annie did a rapid inventory of the rambling house. Had the sheets been washed since the last time they'd stayed?

Jake's voice brought her back. "Great in an ideal world. Sadly, Susie and I have a dinner we can't avoid, but we'll be over at tennish for coffee."

"Where are we going? Tiaras or tatty jeans?"

"Up to you, Mum. We could try The Swan. I heard it's been done up. And they've got a garden the twins can play in when they get fed up with us, or we with them."

"Perfect. Tiara then. Can you remind Susie to bring me a cutting of that mauve geranium, please?" She smiled at his chuckle.

"Great minds and all that. It's sitting in a milk bottle by the front door so she doesn't forget."

"Lovely. And, Jake, remind me to talk to you about Eartha." Annie felt hair trickling down her neck and caught the chopstick as it slid out.

"What's the matter with her?"

"I just want to make sure she'll be alright." Annie hurried on, "Now, you may have all day to talk but I have a busy schedule. Newspaper, coffee, water the plants, tea, pick up the apples, more tea ... and so on until I can have my whisky."

"Okay, I'll check Eartha out tomorrow, although you do realize I treat people, not cats."

"Very funny!" Annie could sense Jake's grin.

"Right, bye, Mum, enjoy the whisky."

"Good bye, darling boy, give my other boys a sloppy kiss." Annie smiled as she hung up. She leant back in the chair and watched Eartha through the front door, still glaring at robins from her hiding spot behind an old dragon jar overflowing with trailing nasturtiums. The bright orange show had been welcoming visitors every summer for as long as Annie could remember.

The colour reminded her of the Illawarra flame trees that sprinkled vibrant splashes of sunburnt orange amidst the panoply of greens as she had wandered around the Botanical Gardens in Sydney. Her mind in free fall as the previous years flickered across her memory like the jerky movements of a film showing at the World Newsreel Theatre on George Street.

"God knows we needed some brilliance in our lives then," Annie said to the loitering cat. She watched a bee flitter into the depths of a nasturtium, and thought back to the mood in Australia as war had come ever closer to their shores. Not that it hadn't affected countless families already. "Mother England!"

Annie remembered her father almost biting off the end of his pipe when the government had followed Britain's 1939 policy toward Nazi Germany and declared war, after Hitler had invaded Poland in September. She could still recall fragments of Prime Minister Menzies' speech. The first and last bits anyway. Any speech starting, 'Fellow Australians, it is my melancholy duty' was never going to be good when it ended, 'Australia is also at war.'

Chapter 2
Australia, 1939 - 1941

"Another generation of Australians to be slaughtered," Annie's father, Ian, said, looking at his grown children gathered around the radio in the homestead kitchen. A rare moment with the family before Joe, her younger brother, returned to university, and Annie reported back to the hospital, both in Sydney. He reached back and flicked off the wireless.

"But, Dad," Ernest, the eldest, replied, "we can't rely on others to defend us."

Ian waved his pipe, his words dismissive. "The Germans will never get to Australia."

"What if other countries join in?" asked Annie.

"And what would you know about war, missy?" Her father asked, a sneer curling his lip.

"It's not just men who go to war, Father," she answered, stung into a response but knowing he'd never listen.

"Well, none of you are going!" He glared at Annie and her two brothers. "Someone has to run the farm."

Pipe smoke swirled in the strained silence, hanging in the kitchen like a shroud.

"Too late, Father," Ernest said, his face grim, determined. "I signed up with the Citizen Military Forces yesterday."

Annie held her breath but the expected tirade didn't come. Instead her sturdy, rugged father deflated, as if muscles honed from years of mustering and throwing sheep had liquified.

"Bloody fool!" His quiet anger turned to certainty. "Joe, you will stay in Sydney, finish university. Annie, you'll be coming home. I'll need help."

Defiance crossed Joe's face and Annie knew he too would go to war, probably even before he finished his law degree. Well, if they were going, so was she. Annie glanced at the chair in which her mother had traditionally sat, longing, yet again, for her support. "No, Father, I won't. They'll need nurses."

The delayed onslaught erupted. Before she could whip out a retort, Ernest pushed her out to the screened verandah which formed one side of the homestead. "Let Joe calm him down. Good practice for his lawyering." He patted her shoulder, "Come on, we both need a ciggie."

She sighed and took the offered cigarette. "Have you really signed on? Before Menzies even announced war."

"Too right!"

"What did Gracie say?"

"Haven't told her."

"Oh, Ernie. Shouldn't you have talked to her first?" Annie exhaled, smoke lingering in the still air, an image of her older brother's skittish girlfriend drifting in front of her, "There'll be tears."

He shook his head. "There'd be tears either way. I'll tell her tomorrow."

"When do you start?"

"Three months basic training at Ingleburn, near Liverpool, at the end of the week."

"You know Joe will join up." Annie couldn't imagine her brother, the less sporty, more academic one, coping with the rough and tumble of military training.

"That's why I didn't tell him before. I hope he finishes his degree." Ernest drew nicotine deep into his lungs.

"Yeah, me too." She tilted her head toward the kitchen. "Sounds like he's calming down."

Ernest nudged her shoulder. "You know Dad loves you?"

"He's got a funny way of showing it."

"He just doesn't know how to talk to you, Annie."

"He never has."

"I suppose. Since Mum died, you're about the only female he sees."

"Apart from ewes." She sighed. "He didn't really talk to Mum either, Ernest. Do you think he ever wonders about her death? She died of exhaustion. Working the property with him. Keeping the house. Looking after us. Slave labour." She shivered.

"Ahh, don't be too hard on him. He does care." Ernest put his arm around Annie, his calloused fingers rough against her thin sweater.

She shrugged. "How did we all turn out like her and not him?"

"Postman!"

Their laughter dissolved across the home paddock and into a stand of gums beyond the stockyards. The screen door clicked, and they turned to see Joe, a smile crinkling his narrow face.

"Well, that took some talking."

"Something you've always been able to do." Annie jabbed her brother in the ribs. "You got away with everything, even when Ernie and I got hauled over the coals by Mum!"

"Hardly the coals. Mum couldn't stay cross for longer than it took to boil the billy." Joe grinned at his siblings. "You okay, both of you?"

"Yeah, fine." Ernest looked hard at his brother. "What about you?"

"What about me?"

"Don't give me that, mate. You know what I mean?"

"Will you finish uni?" Annie asked.

"Doubt it. Still got a year to go."

Annie shivered again, winter still a breath on the air, or perhaps an omen, and peered at her younger brother. "What's going on?"

"Wha'd ya mean?"

"Don't give me that, Joe." Annie repeated her brother's words, "I can always tell when you're hiding something. You've signed up too, haven't you?"

"Not technically." Joe shook out a cigarette and flipped his Zippo lighter.

"But something's going on." Ernest's voice was flat.

"Might be." Joe paused. "Look, I'm not being coy, or lawyerly, to use your word, Ernie, but I can't speak about things I'm not sure of yet. Leave it at that."

"I need another smoke." Annie reached for Joe's packet of Turfs.

—

Annie, blankets drawn up to her chin, lay awake a long time. She heard her father stomp down the verandah stairs and guessed he wanted to check the pregnant ewe he'd brought into the home paddock. As a child she'd wondered at his sixth sense in knowing which of his mob would have trouble lambing. All three of them had helped deliver lambs at some stage and, for a moment, she considered pulling on clothes and joining him. The thought dissipated as fast as it had appeared. He would not welcome her presence.

She yawned, and her thoughts turned to Ernest and Joe. She tried to forget the words her father had thrown around—cannon fodder. The image would not go away. She couldn't fight, but she could help mop up the aftermath. A surgical diploma would be more helpful than the midwifery one she'd just started, but the Australian Army Nursing Service would accept any additional training. She knew, from her talks with Iris, that they fell into the age range. And they were spinsters. Annie muffled a wry giggle. What a word. Sounded like a bunch of hags sitting at spinning wheels, not trained nurses with at least three years' experience. She fell asleep, to that image easing her dreams.

Annie stood at the Aga flipping eggs. The screen door to the back verandah slammed and she heard her father kick off his boots then pad into the kitchen. He looked tired. He might never have been an engaged parent but he'd always cared for the stock. "Morning, Dad, how's the ewe?"

His chair scraped against the floor as he pulled it out. "Triplets." He lit his pipe, the sweetness of the tobacco mingling with the smell of frying bacon. "All good." He cocked his head. "Joe not up?"

"He'll be in soon. He worked late on an essay."

"Good thing one of you got some brains."

Her shoulders tensed, but Annie kept her head down and her mouth shut. What was the point? Ernest had never had an option. Even going to agricultural college had been laughed out of the kitchen. She glanced again at her mother's chair. It had been she who persuaded her father that Annie should have a chance, not just hang around waiting for a husband.

Annie felt her eyes blur. Mum would've been proud. Then with Joe getting top marks at school, and the money from his godfather, there had been no question of her brother not going to university.

"Where's Ernest?" She asked, sliding eggs and bacon onto a plate.

"Out checking newborns in the top paddock," her father replied, smothering his eggs with a coat of mustard, "put his grub in the warmer." He looked up as Joe entered, rubbing his eyes. "I hope the lawyering business doesn't start as early as farming. You'd never make it to court on time."

"Morning to you too, Father," Joe said, winking at his sister, the gap in his teeth showing in his smile. "Morning, Annie. Any of that bacon for a poor, starving student?"

"Here you go." She handed him a full plate of bacon and toast but no eggs.

"Who doesn't eat eggs?" Her father asked around a mouthful.

"Me, Father. Never have, never will, so you might as well stop asking the question." He smeared butter on his toast. "Ernie still out?"

"Yeah." Annie saw a shadow cross the window. "But that's him now. He must've hitched Bessie to the paddock rail." She filled up another plate, then sat opposite Joe with her toast.

"No point letting her go, he's got fences to check after breakfast."

"Annie and I are going to need a lift into Armidale later." Joe looked at his father, "I thought Ernest could drive us in."

"There'll be bloody petrol rationing soon." Ian pushed back from the table and relit his pipe.

"That's right, Dad. Look on the bright side." Annie tried to smile.

Joe ignored them both, and continued, "We could grab a beer at Tatts before the train leaves."

Ian scowled. "Your sister can't go into a pub."

"I'm not, Father, although they do have a ladies bar now."

Her father sniffed. "No lady goes into a bar. Just remember that. War or no bloody war." Ian wiped his eyes, watery from coughing. "When will you be back?" His question did not include Annie.

"Dunno, Dad."

"What about you?" Ian nodded at his daughter. "How am I expected to manage without anyone here? Your duty is here, Annie. What would your mother say?"

Before she could respond, Joe leant over and touched her arm, then turned to their father. "Really, Dad? It was Mum who pushed for Annie to get her nursing qualification. Annie doesn't owe you a damn thing." He smiled at Annie. "Ma would be proud."

Annie gave Joe a grateful look and rose to take Ernest's plate out of the warmer as he came in and threw himself down at the table. "Thanks, Annie. A feast." Picking up his knife and fork, he looked around the table. "What have I missed?"

"Nothing new," Annie said. She turned from her father. "Do you think Gracie would like to come into town with us? We could pick her up on our way. She and I could have a cuppa at Nick's, while you and Joe go to Tatts."

—

Squeezed on the bench seat between Gracie and Joe, with Ernest driving the Ute, Annie wondered when she'd be back in Armidale. She'd finish her midwifery, sign up, then use precious leave to cadge a ride to Ingleburn to see Ernest before he shipped out. Life would be different. They might not see each other all the time, but each knew where the other was—could visualize them in their different roles. At home, at uni, at the hospital. War would change that. She sighed.

"You right, Annie?" Gracie asked, her smile pert.

"As rain, thanks."

Joe nudged her in the ribs and winked. Neither could see what attracted Ernest to the fidgety girl whose sole concern appeared to be her hair getting blown by the open window of the truck, although both made an effort for their brother's sake.

"Ernie?" Annie leant forward and looked at her brother concentrating on the road as they drove past the turn off for the golf club. "Before you drop us off at Nick's, can we drive past the school?"

"What for?"

"I dunno. Sentimentality. I'd like to pop into the Chapel."

"That's not a drive past, that's a drive through," said Joe.

"Have you got religion, girl?" Ernest asked with a grin, but he turned off the Bundarra Road anyway.

"Don't be daft, I just like the building."

"It wasn't even there when you went to NEGS," said Gracie.

"Doesn't mean I don't like it." Annie tried not to be defensive.

"You didn't have to go to services every day." Gracie sounded petulant.

"You've got to admit, it is a beautiful building."

"If I ever get married," Annie saw Gracie glance at Ernest from under her lashes, "I'm not getting wed there. I want a central aisle."

"Of course you do." Annie could feel Joe's shoulders tremble with suppressed laughter. "Thanks, Ernie," she said as they pulled up. "I won't be long." She waited for Joe to clamber down from the Ute.

"Do you want me to come in with you?" he asked, holding out his hand.

"Nah, I'm right." Annie paused and looked up at the blue-tinged brick, sombre in the afternoon light. She pushed open the heavy doors and waited for her eyes to adjust to the gloom. Gracie did have a point. The aisles leading to the transepts and altar on either side of the oak pews did not lend themselves to a floating bride. More to the rows of girls seated each morning. "You would've loved this, Ma." Annie smiled. "I don't think I ever really thanked you for talking Father into allowing me to come to NEGS. Or to go nursing." She sat down on one of the pews. It had been through her mother's friendship with the headmistress, Miss Dumolo, combined with Ma being an old girl at the school that Annie had won the small scholarship that had made her father cave. She could remember the arguments, the angry words, leaching through the kitchen wall to her bedroom, night after night. Her mother's determined voice saying, "If the boys can go to TAS, then Annie can go to NEGS. That's the end of it, Ian."

And it had been. Annie thought of Iris, the two of them meeting that first uncertain day, then continuing to nursing school together. The soft-spoken, red-headed girl even more apprehensive than Annie. She wondered if they'd share the next adventure. That had to be Iris's decision but, deep down, Annie knew her friend would follow her. She shivered. Light filtered through the stained-glass window behind the organ, throwing an inky glow across the pews in front of her. She didn't know what, or if, she believed, but there was something about the chapel that seemed calm. Perhaps it was the chancel lamp hanging above the altar, a glow in the cool half-light. Perhaps that was what religion provided. Certainty. Nah. She couldn't go with that. Too many persecuted for what they believed. She took one last look towards the simple oak altar, then went out to the truck. A trio of pupils, books clutched to their bodies, wandered past and looked at them curiously.

"All good?" Joe moved off the bonnet and stubbed his cigarette out on the sole of his shoe.

"Yeah, thanks. Just needed to say goodbye to Ma."

"Don't say that, Annie. You'll be back. We all will."

"Hope so. Right, come on. Tea and Gracie await me. I'd rather have a beer with you two."

"I know."

A couple of hours later, Ernest pulled the handbrake as they rolled to a stop in front of the station building. Another of Annie's favourites. Cast iron columns with filigree detailing held up the slate-covered, gabled roof like tiers of a wedding cake.

"Okay, kids, away you go." Ernest swung his long legs out of the truck, waited for Gracie to sidle across then helped her down. He pushed his hat back off his forehead and shook hands with Joe, their arms pumping a moment longer than normal, then he pulled Annie into one of his enveloping hugs.

"Look after yourself, Annie. Don't do anything silly."

"You galah, Ernie! I'll see you in Ingleburn, or Sydney. We both will, eh, Joe?"

"Too right." Joe gave Gracie a peck on the cheek, then watched Annie, towering over the petite girl, do the same. He picked up both their cases and, without looking back, marched into the station.

—

General Nursing and Obstetrics qualifications clutched firmly in gloved hand, Annie waited for Iris and Verna on Oxford Street, Paddington, so they could walk along to Victoria Barracks together. She smoothed down her waisted floral dress, then touched her hat. Not often intimidated, Annie felt a flutter of nerves. What had seemed an easy decision did not feel so comfortable now.

"G'day."

Startled from her doubts, Annie turned at Verna's voice.

"Are we up for this?" Her friend sounded buoyant.

"Of course," Annie said, "well, I think so. How are you feeling, Iris?"

"Fine." Iris paused, brown eyes down, red curls framing her face under a navy hat. "No, actually, not quite so fine."

"Remember how we felt, when we met, on our first day at Prince Henry Hospital?" Verna grinned, her fine blonde hair escaping the neat bun at the nape of her neck. "The anticipation of what we don't know is worse than the real thing."

"You sound like a damn textbook," Iris said, with a wan smile. "Slight difference," she added, "we weren't signing up to get shot."

"We'll be nowhere near the shooting, ducks," Annie said, "nurses are way behind the lines."

Verna nodded, blue eyes shiny with excitement. "She's right, Iris. And our boys'll need support."

"Righto then," Iris smoothed her gloves over her fingers and straightened her shoulders, "come on, anymore dilly-dallying and I might bottle out."

Reaching Queen Victoria Gate, they paused then, following directions given by the guard, linked arms and strode through. The imposing Regency style barracks sent a quiver down Annie's back and made her glad they had agreed to sign on together.

The imperative to defend Australia had filtered through to even the remotest cattle stations, and men, some in uniform, some in civvies, milled around the quadrangle. A few catcalls followed the women.

"They wouldn't dare do that if we were already in uniform," Verna said with a giggle.

"I wouldn't bet on that." Annie relaxed. No chance to change her mind now. She looked around the room lined with desks as they waited to be called forward, and wondered if Ernest had suffered the same qualms when he'd signed on at the Armidale Show Ground. She thought about Joe and couldn't imagine him in the hurly-burly of basic training.

When called, the women moved forward as one. Annie answered the brusque questions first.

"Name? Address—permanent? Education? Sign here." A pen was thrust into her hand.

Annie, her voice low, read aloud, "I, Annie May Cutler swear that I will well and truly serve our Sovereign Lord, the King, in the Military Forces of the Commonwealth of Australia until the cessation of the present time of war ..." Apprehension in her voice, she looked at Verna and Iris. "Hell's bells!" Annie's curse drew a glare from the sergeant standing nearby. She scribbled her signature and said, "Well, that's it then."

They watched the attesting officer scribble his signature below hers.

Verna signed without a murmur, but Iris, her face pale, hesitated.

"It's alright, ducks," Verna touched Iris's hand. "You don't have to."

"She's right," Annie chimed in. "You've got to be sure."

They waited, then watched Iris, her eyes watery, as the pen hovered over the form before she scratched her name.

"Thank you, ladies." The sergeant took the pen, turned and called, "Next."

Standing back in the quadrangle, still steadily filling with men and a scattering of women, they looked at each other, trepidation changed to composure.

"We're in!" Verna said with a grin.

Iris, now less subdued, nodded. "That was easy."

"It has a ring, doesn't it?" Annie asked, looking down at the paper in her hand. "The Australian Army Nursing Service."

"I suppose they just had to change the wording on the forms from reservist to serving." Verna stopped at the gates and looked back. "Do you think everyone signing on here will go to Cowra for training?"

"Dunno." Annie paused. "Just glad we'll be together."

Iris said, "You know, I was alright until the next of kin bit."

Annie giggled, "Listen to this bit, 'I will endeavour to up uphold the highest traditions of Womanhood and of the Professions of which I am Part.'"

"It's not funny, Annie," Iris said.

"I know. But I suppose we're going to have to laugh at things." Annie slung her arms around Verna and Iris as they walked back along Oxford Street, and sang, "Well, girls, we're in the army now, tra la!"

"Wonder where we'll be sent."

Iris clutched Annie's hand still around her shoulder, and squeezed. "God, I hope we can all stay together."

"Well," Verna said, ever practical, "we signed on together, we're training together, so we'll probably be posted together."

"I hope so," Iris said, "I'm not as strong as you two."

Annie hugged her close. "Rubbish, Iris."

"You're as tough as the boots we'll have to wear!" Verna added.

"First," Annie said, taking off her hat, "we have to learn how to march in those boots."

"And follow orders," Iris reminded Annie with a chortle.

"I've been doing that since we started nursing."

"Not always!" Verna grinned. "Come on, we deserve a cup of tea. My shout!"

Chapter 3
Singapore Burning, 1942

"G'day, I'm Florence Taylor. Bet you hoped there'd be a spare bunk."

Annie, Iris and Verna turned from cramming things into narrow drawers between the bunks to see a stocky uniformed woman with brown eyes and blonde hair standing at the door to their cabin on the RMS Aquitania.

"G'day, I'm Annie Cutler."

"Verna Sinclair."

"I'm Iris Mann. Do you want the top or bottom bunk?"

Florence's eyes danced. "Probably better for you if I'm on the bottom." She laughed.

"So, am I the interloper?"

"Yep!" Annie answered for the others. "We all trained together. What about you?"

"Royal North Shore."

"I did my midwifery there." Annie squinted at the woman, not recognizing her.

It did not take long to get to know each other in the confined space. Although Aquitania had been requisitioned as a troop ship and painted a cheerless steel grey, elements of the royal mail liner she had once been still showed—despite the three and a half thousand people aboard. Flo knowing Gracie's older brother, James, sealed the friendship.

"You're from the smoke, James is from the bush, how on earth do you know each other?"

"He did a stint at my hospital. Before he joined the medical corps. He plays a mean game of tennis."

Annie nodded. "Don't I know it. We grew up together. He and my brother, Ernie, were best mates."

Flo missed the slight shake of Verna's head. "Were?"

"Yeah. He died in Libya."

"I'm sorry, ducks." Flo looked up from the bottom bunk. "Was he a medic too?"

"Nope. Ernie was a Digger." Annie used the term coined for Australian soldiers in the Boer War, given because so many had been miners. She clambered into her bunk and faced the wall, willing sleep to ease her mind and stomach.

—

The Japanese landing on the Malay peninsula on December 7th the previous year, forty minutes before the raids on Pearl Harbour, had galvanized men, and women, from all reaches of Australia. And with the rapid enemy advance, the belief that the Far East was a cushy posting had dissolved.

Despite the Aquitania being full to bursting, the voyage from Sydney had not been too bad. Lectures on tropical diseases, interspersed with shifts in the ship's hospital helped pass the time, and lessened tensions that sometimes trickled around the nurse's cabins. The edict that nurses should always be in pairs whilst surrounded by so many troops had begun to grate and, despite being used to communal living, Annie began to crave solitude.

The authorities had deemed it too risky to sail the final leg to Singapore aboard Aquitania, even under the escort of HMS Canberra, because of Japanese long-range planes based in occupied Indochina. Instead, troops and medical personnel transferred over to seven smaller vessels at Ratai Bay in the Sunda Strait. From there it would take four days to steam on to Singapore.

The medical lectures stopped, and Annie found little to distract her from the constant seasickness. Long days made her doubt her stomach would ever be the same again. To relieve the tedium, the women spent hours on the deck of the lurching packet steamer, watching the Indonesian islands pass by.

"Look!" She pointed down at a squadron of flying fish, their iridescent wings glinting across the sea like strands of sequins on a flapper's dress.

"Something's chasing them," Flo said. "Poor sods, predators below the surface and diving frigate birds above."

"Bit like us. Subs below, bombers above. Hobson's choice!"

Standing next to Verna on their final day, Annie groaned, her knuckles showing white as she gripped the rail and kept her eyes focused on the horizon. "Singapore can't come soon enough. Even a bombed Singapore."

"You've chundered enough for the entire Navy," Verna said with a sympathetic grin.

Ships of every size clustered at anchor, or along the docks as they entered Keppel Harbour and edged their way to Collyer Quay. Annie peered over the side to watch grunting men heave hawsers over the capstans, before turning her gaze to the throngs covering every inch of the dock. The cacophony prevented idle chat, although most of that had ended as the ship drew nearer to the island and wisps of smoke became thick cords as the sight of buildings smouldering from the latest Japanese air raid came into view. Shouts ricocheted in strange tongues. Whistles blew. Bicycle bells tinkled, and horns blared.

"Have you ever seen so many coloured people?" Iris's voice trembled as she joined them, easing the uniform collar from her neck.

"I don't think I've ever seen so many people, full stop." Chinese in coolie hats jostled with Indian stevedores, sweat-stained cloth wrapped in swathes around their heads. Sola topees and sun hats protected the Europeans, military and civilian. "Or so many kinds of headwear." Troops, slouch hats on, lined the decks with their kitbags, and Annie took a step back as a sergeant brushed past to bellow at a couple of lads laughing and joshing.

"Some of them don't look older than Tom. I don't think my Mum could bear it if he went to war."

"He's only fourteen, ducks," Annie said, patting Iris on the shoulder, "no need to worry about that." She glanced over the railing again, her mind flitting to her brother, Ernest. A stab of pain followed, so real she sucked in her breath. If only he'd stayed home he might not be buried somewhere foreign. She didn't know where Joe was. Annie shook her head and forced a smile. "And anyway, I don't think we'll have much time to think, let alone worry. Mark the day, girls. Saturday, January 24th, 1942."

—

"I wonder where Bukit Panjang is?" Iris stumbled over the unusual words as they trundled along roads rutted by bombs and shells towards the 2nd/4th CCS in an army truck, their small brown regulation cases held still behind their knees.

Annie struggled not to snap. "I haven't the foggiest, Iris, but it's a Casualty Clearing Station so I imagine it'll be busy." She peered out from where the canvas flaps had been clipped back to allow a little air. "Looks like we're climbing."

The bombed roads and collapsed buildings shocked Annie. Even though she had seen Japanese planes flying high overhead whilst on their sea voyage, bombs clearly visible under the wings, the reality of them dropping had seemed remote. Now in the steaming heat, bodies crumpled where they had fallen. Cats slunk through the rubble. Rats would come out with the night. Despair creased the faces of many they passed, and a sense of urgency permeated the air. Annie shuddered.

The senior sister watched the nurses scramble down, straightening their uniforms as they formed in lines. She stood straight, but weariness etched her face.

"Welcome, I'm Sister King." An exhausted smile lifted the corners of her mouth. "I don't know how much you ladies know about Singapore but, as I'm sure you noted on the drive here, it is no longer a tropical paradise." Her voice quavered. "It's mainly our boys here. We have two hundred beds. All full. Your shifts have been assigned. Day staff will work a twelve-hour shift, those on night duty will cover two six-hour shifts, but often we just keep going." She turned, then stopped. "And, Sisters, don't get too comfortable. I doubt any of us will be here long."

"What does she mean?" Iris asked.

"Iris, really? I do not have all the answers." The minute the words spat out, tears trembled on Iris's lashes and Annie regretted her harsh tone. "I'm sorry, ducks. I guess we're all a bit on edge, and none of us know much." She patted her friend's arm. "Righto, let's see what's what, come on."

—

A sweet scent, she wondered if it was jasmine, drifted over Annie to mingle with the cigarette smoke. Tiredness and nerves kept at bay by a smoko. She yawned. Bombing raids had become a daily occurrence, and shelling—one of the first had landed on the Tan Tock Seng civilian hospital, a travesty that had angered everyone. The day before had been long as they moved patients and as much equipment as possible from their burning CCS unit to the Swiss Rifle Club at Bukit Tinggi.

Annie drew on the cigarette, her eyes narrowing as the tip glowed. A pinprick of red against the dark night, although a few stars shimmered between the leaves of the mahogany. She struggled to understand why Singapore town glittered in the distance, as if festooned for a party. Why hadn't a black-out been implemented? At least try to make it harder for the swarming Japanese planes. Cicadas set up their orchestra, a welcome change from the whine of plane engines overhead. Annie rotated the red and white Turf cigarette packet in her hand and said, "I wonder if we can get these here? I'm almost out."

"How would I know?" Verna blew a smoke ring and leant against the tree. "You're as bad as Iris!"

Annie's laugh was defensive. "No, I'm not!" She yawned. "So much for two hundred beds. I heard we've got over a thousand."

"Troops from the mainland." Verna coughed. "An Argyll and Sutherland Highlander came into my ward yesterday. He said they blew the causeway up after they'd crossed. He reckons only ninety came across, from about 880 when they went to Malaya. What's the date today? I've lost track."

"February 1st." Annie replied. "That explains the lads we admitted this morning. They came over last night from Johor, in boats. Do you think blowing the causeway will stop the Jap advance?"

"My bloke didn't think anything would. He said they're like ants—ploughing through everything."

Verna, her voice sombre, asked, "Annie, do you ever think about what happened on Christmas Day? In Hong Kong? At St. Stephens?"

"No!" A spasm rolled across Annie's shoulders. News had filtered out about the college being used as a hospital. Where patients had been bayoneted by the Japanese, before British and Chinese nurses were gang raped, before having their throats slit. Other captured medical personnel had later been dismembered and slaughtered like animals in an abattoir. "At least, I try not to. What's the point?"

"I do," Verna said. "Most of the time we're too busy to think, but now, out of the wards, away from the patients, I can't help it. Especially with the Nips just across the Straits."

"I try not to think about that either." Annie drew smoke deep into her lungs and stayed silent.

"What kind of person allows his men to behave like that?"

"I dunno, ducks. If the Japs wanted to force capitulation, I suppose striking terror is a good way to do it. I heard somewhere that the orders came from the Emperor's uncle."

"If they did it in Hong Kong, they could do it here. A white flag means nothing to them." Verna shuddered. "We're a hospital in a rifle club. In their eyes that would make us fair game. Except we've got no guns. Nothing. We wouldn't be able to save our patients. Or ourselves."

"I imagine there'll be a lot more horror stories when this is all over." Annie looked up as planes whined overhead. "That's why it doesn't help thinking about it now."

"Nope, 'spose not." Verna looked at her friend, then flinched as the crump of a bomb reverberated from further down the hill. "I wish I could be as calm as you, Annie."

"I'm not bloody calm. That's why I try my damnedest to find something odd or funny to think about instead."

"Like what?"

"Oh, I dunno." Annie paused. "Like during a raid this morning, I was dressing a boy's leg, and the major told me to get under the table."

"Did you?" Verna asked.

"'Course not!"

"What'd the major say?"

"Nothing. We just got on with it." Annie chuckled. "Don't think I'll be strung up for disobeying an order." Annie took one final drag. "Righto, smoko's over."

Verna sighed. "Wonder if we'll be evacuated? Feels like we've been here longer than twelve days, doesn't it?"

"Dunno, and yup." She stubbed her cigarette out on the tree trunk and put the butt into a little tin.

Verna did the same, then added in a quiet voice, "Anyway we couldn't leave our boys. That'd go against all our training."

"Too right," Annie said, tucking her hair back under the veil. "Come on, back to it."

—

As daylight broke after a night of pounding from shell bombardments, rumours flurried around the hospital that the Japanese had landed on the northwest coast of the island and had faced fierce resistance from the Australian 2/20 Battalion and Dalforce Company. The naval base had been shelled and abandoned. A sinister orange glow on the horizon suggested the oil terminal might also be ablaze. And they moved again. This time to St. Patrick's School where two concrete tennis courts covered with a marquee served as one of the wards.

"One lad couldn't stop crying last night. Do you know what he told me, when I sat with him?" Flo asked, her voice hoarse as she poured them two mugs of weak tea.

"What?" Annie yawned, longing for her bed.

Flo replied, her face pale. "He said that when they crossed one of the rivers on the mainland, they walked on bodies."

"Christ!" Annie gagged.

"How do you forget something like that?"

Annie rubbed her eyes. "I don't know. I suppose you lock it away somewhere then chuck out the key."

"There'll be a lot of padlocks needed."

"Yup." Annie sighed. "For us all. One way or another." She plunked the mug of now tepid brew on the mess table. "During the attack early this morning one bloke kept saying, 'Don't worry about that one, Sister, it's one of ours'. His chart says he's eighteen but he looks younger. I think he was trying to bolster us both."

"Did it work?"

"Nope, but we both pretended it did." Annie lowered her voice. "Have you heard the rumours?"

"Which particular one are you talking about?" Verna plopped down on the bench next to Flo. "This tea is foul."

"Shipping out."

"No, but I heard an officer on the ward muttering 'surrender'. Although that could have been the morphine talking. He's lost one leg, and likely to lose the other." Verna eased her tight veil, her action weary. "How can we be asked to leave them behind?'

Flo shrugged. "Maybe it won't come to that."

"I wish I'd never heard about Hong Kong." Verna pushed her mug away. "It plays around and around in my head. I'm hanging onto the fact there'd be a lot more of us in Singapore than there."

"I'm sorry, ducks, but don't be dotty. There's no safety in numbers. The bloody Nips don't care how many they slaughter, or who sees what they do, or how they do it."

"Christ!" Flo glared at Annie. "Do you have to be quite so blunt? And don't you dare speak like that in front of Iris."

"I'm not completely insensitive!" Annie snapped. "But we all know, even Iris, what they do. There's no point pretending. We do enough of that for the patients."

"Annie's right," Verna said, "It just scares the hell out of me. I don't know how brave I'd be."

"None of us do," Flo comforted her.

"Desert or surrender? What a choice."

Flo patted Verna's hand, still clutching the mug. "We wouldn't be deserting, we'd be following orders."

"Tell that to the boys we'd be leaving." Annie eyed her tea with distaste and yawned again. "Anyway, I can't believe Matron would let the generals bully her. Come on, drink up, we all need some sleep."

—

The citadel that was Singapore, despite declarations in London that it could never happen, continued to crumble under the relentless Japanese onslaught. The next day, February 10th, they heard the last RAF planes roar overhead to the perceived safety of Sumatra in an attempt to save what remained of their squadron.

Then the day the Australian nurses had dreaded arrived.

"What's going on?" Annie, one of the last to enter, slipped into the back of the hall between Florence and Verna. She could see Iris's red head nearer the front.

"Another move probably." Verna spoke out of the side of her mouth as Matrons Drummond and Paschke walked in.

"Good afternoon," Drummond began, her eyes drawn and weary, taking in the rows of nurses. "It's been a difficult few months. Thank you for your dedication. I know rumours have circulated about General Bennett not wanting nurses to evacuate because of the effect it would have on the men's morale. Something we supported." She paused, "However, despite my protestations, General Percival has ordered that all nurses leave Singapore. The Japanese are close to surrounding us and cutting off any exit."

A bubble of shocked and angry voices burst out.

"Leave our patients?"

"We can't do that."

"That's not right."

"I'm not going."

"What happened to 'patients first'?"

"Who's going to look after the men?"

"That's running away."

Matron Drummond let the babble subside. "There is a ship, the Empire Star, leaving within hours that can take 53 of you. The remaining 65 nurses will leave tomorrow morning on the Vyner Brooke. So, ladies, I need volunteers prepared to go now to step forward."

No one moved.

The matron, a proud smile lifting the tired lines on her face, sighed. "Sisters, despite the confusion with regard to ranks in the AANS, you will be court-martialled if you refuse an order."

Still no one moved. Verna clutched Annie's hand and squeezed as she reached for Flo.

"Very well." The matron looked at the women in front of her, took a deep breath, then gestured to one side of the room. "This side will leave, now." She again ignored the protestations. "Pack what you can. You will be transported to the wharf in an hour. The rest will board the Vyner Brooke during the night for a dawn departure." Her voice wavered. "You've done Australia proud. Now, quickly, girls, gather a few things and do not forget, despite what our orders are here, that the patient always comes first."

Shock mirrored in their faces as Annie, Florence and Verna looked at each other. Annie saw Iris turn, searching, then push her way towards them from the other side of the hall. They hugged, then moved away, their eyes brimming.

Chapter 4
En Route to Safety, February 1942

Eighteen days after landing in Singapore, Annie returned to the docks at Collyer Quay. Nurses, many with tear stains streaking their faces, sat hunched in the back of the truck, cases once again behind their knees. Leaving 'their boys' went against everything in their training.

The flap on the truck had been dropped but Annie, next to Florence and nearest the swaying tarpaulin, peeped through the slit. She wished she hadn't. Dogs, ribs showing, clambered over the wreckage snuffling at bodies lying where they had fallen. Shell-shocked Chinese, Malays and Indians wandered aimlessly amongst the rubble or stood outside the ruins of their homes and businesses. Some sobbed. A child's hand, detached from its arm, held a toy car. Annie closed her eyes.

"You right, love?"

Annie felt Flo pat her knee. She nodded then said, her voice soft, "I wish Iris was with us. She'll be terrified."

"She's stronger than you think, Annie."

"Maybe, but it's my fault she's here in the first place, Flo. I tried not to, but I pretty much talked her into joining up."

"Nonsense. She's not a fool. You need to stop feeling responsible for everybody. We'll all be fine. Meet up at The Queen's Club when we get back to Sydney, and exchange war tales."

Annie gave a weak smile. "Now who's trying to save everyone?"

If it had been chaotic when they'd arrived, bedlam now ensued. Women yanked children over debris and through the throng towards a chain link fence that tried to hold people back, in some sort of order. Husbands waved papers, and sometimes money, in a desperate attempt to get a berth for their families. Some families clung together, others, their shoulders stiff with resolve, stood rigid as they bade their farewells.

"Why the hell didn't all these women and children evacuate sooner? And there's someone with a dog in her arms." Verna bent to pick up a dropped scarf and, after handing it back to a weeping woman, rejoined the nurses as they waited to board a launch to take them out to their ship.

"Because the bloody bigwigs in London kept saying Singapore could never fall," replied Annie, thinking of another nurse she'd worked with in the last few days. "Thelma told me they'd had an easy time of it up in Malacca, lots of leave and partying, until the Japs landed and all hell broke loose." She could feel her uniform sticking to her back in the cloying afternoon heat. "Look at those kids over there, Verna. Not crying. Just waiting."

"Probably numb. They've seen, and heard, a lot in the last couple of weeks."

"We all have." Annie's mind filled with the bodies sprawled wherever they had been hit. "Yeah, but worse for the kids," Verna said.

Flo swiped sweat from her forehead. "We'll all have a lot of forgetting to do by the time this is over."

Verna smiled at a little girl with darting eyes, clutching a rag doll, then nodded towards them. "Wonder if they're on our ship?"

"Some might be." Annie glanced at those nearest them, "But it looks like it's mainly RAF, British military, and us." She looked up as a Japanese plane screamed overhead.

"We're military." Florence reminded her as she rejoined them after helping a frazzled mother. "Remember we've been part of the Australian Imperial Force since August!"

"I guess so. Doesn't feel any different to the CMF. Do you think they'll ever decide what to call us, you know, get the ranks sorted?" Annie knew they were talking to keep their mind off their guilt, and what lay ahead. Her stomach contracted at the thought of being on the open water again. "I quite fancy being a major."

Verna laughed. "Yeah, I'm sure they'll jump you up the list. Skip lieutenant and captain all together!"

"I reckon we'll all start as lieutenants," Flo said. "Otherwise how will they differentiate between aides, orderlies and nurses?"

Angry shouts behind spun them around. A large group of Australian soldiers jostled and cursed others waiting.

"What the hell are they doing?" Annie asked, looking at the frown on the senior sister's face.

"Do you reckon they're deserters?" Florence asked, her voice low.

"How would you tell?" responded Verna. "And what's the real difference between deserters and evacuees?"

"Orders!" Annie said. She looked around at the nurses who, by comparison, remained calm and collected, training once again coming to the fore as they re-formed after scuttling for shelter from another air raid.

—

The Empire Star loomed ahead. In peacetime, a refrigerated cargo ship with only a handful of cabins, but now hundreds were waiting to board. Whispers heard along the queue had already told Annie, Verna and Florence that the captain did not want women and children aboard. Particularly Australian women, believing them to be troublesome.

"Superstitious sod," Annie muttered. "The anger of the sea gods is nothing compared to the bloody Japs. Or an Aussie nurse!"

Verna stifled a giggle as they shuffled up the bouncing gangway. Captain Capon stood on the upper bridge, stern faced and watched as the women and children hustled down into the hold—that being deemed the safest place. They sank to the floor, trying to carve space for themselves and the few possessions they had managed to bring aboard.

Equipment, trucks, and troops covered every part of the decks. Some men had bandages around their heads, others tin hats. Night had fallen like a stage curtain but still tenders and launches scurried back and forth as the hustle on the wharf continued. As did the shelling.

The senior sister divvied up jobs between the nurses. Florence had drawn deck duty. Once out at sea they would be issued with morphia to have in their pockets in case of attack, for now they had aspirin and a kind voice. Annie, bucket in hand, doled out half a tin mugful of relatively clean water before refilling it for the next person to swig down. "Christ, it's hot!" She murmured as she edged past Verna. "Don't drink too quickly, ducks," Annie said to a gulping toddler, "it'll bounce on your tummy."

"Do you know anything? When we're sailing?" An English woman, a flushed baby tucked under her chin, asked.

"Not a thing, I'm sorry." Annie crouched and stroked the infant's forehead, checking for a temperature. "What's your name? And how old's your little one?"

"Lena Armstrong. Hetty's five months." Tears began to flow. "I begged Richard to let us leave sooner. He kept saying Singapore could never fall."

"We'll be fine." Annie kept her face composed. "We'll be in open waters soon where it'll be cooler."

"Aye, and where we'll be easier to bomb." The grey-haired woman scowled and toed the bucket.

Lena blanched, and Annie moved to block her from the dour Scot. "Are you breast feeding Hetty?" She asked. Lena, bobbed blonde hair stuck to her face, blushed and shook her head.

"What have you got?" Annie asked, her voice gentle.

"Condensed milk."

"Righto. Have you got an extra bottle?"

Lena nodded and rummaged, one handed, in the straw basket at her side, then handed the bottle to Annie.

"I'm going to find the cook or someone with a billy who can boil some water for you."

"A billy?" Lena looked at the Australian in confusion.

"A saucepan," Annie explained. "That way you can dilute the milk, then, if Hetty gets really hot, give her a little water. But only cooled boiled water."

"Thank you, Sister."

"You'll be right, Lena. We all will be." Annie resisted glaring at the Scot.

—

At last, the engines rumbled to life and a sigh trickled through the hold. Annie couldn't decide if it was relief or fear. She felt both. The Scot's words returned to her.

"What's up?" Flo dug her in the ribs. "We're on our way!"

"Not a thing." Annie tried to smile, easing her back against the bulkhead. "Apart from roasting in a tin can. All I need is basting and I could be a chook."

"At least you're not stuffed," said Verna, with a chortle.

"Maybe not stuffed stuffed but I'm stuffed tired!" Flo said.

"And the wit keeps coming." Annie gave a short laugh and got to her feet to check on Lena and her baby. "Come on, we're still on duty." She could feel the throb beneath her feet as they stepped over and around outstretched legs and bags, then the engines stopped. Through the cracked hatch Annie saw a plane streak overhead to drop its load on Singapore. She shivered.

The senior sister told a couple of her nurses, who passed the message on, that the captain had decided to stay in the roads until first light, the risk of sailing into a mine being too great in the dark, even with the Pilot's guidance. They would set sail at first light with a convoy that would include an anti-submarine ship. Annie couldn't decide whether that was a comfort or a risk. She wondered if the Vyner Brooke, with Iris aboard, would be part of their convoy.

Those in the hold settled down for a long night. Sobs accompanied snuffles and moans as the women tried to get comfortable, and laps became pillows for children. Exhausted troops, uniforms caked in sweat and mud, lined the decks, propped against vehicles, against the hulls, each other. There was no space to lie down. Nurses took shifts to tend the injured in the area on deck designated the hospital.

"Thank God, we're off. Again." Verna said as the engines grumbled and dawn could be seen through the slight gap in the hatch, left open to allow some airflow.

Annie wondered if the glow in the sky indicated a glorious day or Singapore still burning. She feared the latter. "Did you count the children on board?" She asked Flo.

"Yup. Thirty-five. And 160 women, including us and the signallers."

"Doubt we'll ever know the number of men on deck." Verna said.

Annie said. "I heard someone say the captain reckoned over two thousand."

Flo dipped her head as the sound of planes could be heard shrieking towards the island they had just left. "I'm not sure how many people are usually carried on a merchant ship but I'd place a bet it's a lot less."

"Let's hope we all make it to wherever we're going?" Annie longed for a cigarette.

"I heard Fremantle. Anywhere is better than where we've just been. Righto," Verna heaved to her feet, "my turn up top."

"Yup, me too."

They reserved their limited water for the injured and the children, and the meagre food supply was, on the whole, shared. About to clear the Durian Strait, south of Singapore, shouts reverberated around the ship. Annie tried to lunge for the hold but felt herself dragged down. Air knocked from her, she twisted to see six dive bombers hurtle towards them.

"Stay down, Sister!" A burly soldier shielded her body draped across his legs.

The Empire Star's usual armament sprang into action, supplemented by RAF machine guns and gunners. One plane burst into flames, leaving a curl of black smoke as the sea swallowed the burning wreck. A cheer went up. Annie wondered about the pilot. The machine guns tipped a wing. Another cheer rang out as the plane broke formation and made for home.

"Thanks, mate," Annie struggled to sit up. She glanced down to ensure the watch pinned to her uniform had not become dislodged. A present from Ma when she'd been accepted into nursing, it had become Annie's talisman.

"Any time." The soldier winked. "You can shout me a drink when this is over!"

"You're on." Annie scrambled into the hold and tumbled over arms and legs to the space she, Verna and Flo had claimed theirs as, over the next few hours, they came under repeated attack. She looked at the pale faces around her and marvelled at the lack of panic. Tears but no screaming. Even from the children.

"Come on, let's sing. Distract the kids," Flo suggested.

"And us," Annie said. "You've got a good voice, Verna. You start."

Verna wet her lips and cleared her throat. "*Once a jolly swagman camped by a billabong, Under the shade of a Coolabah tree …*" she sang, waving at others to join in. Despite the ship's sharp movements, swerving in an attempt to destroy the aim of the pilots and to miss the bombs that fell like a beaded steel curtain, Verna continued. "*… And he sang as he watched and waited till his billy boiled.*"

Annie glanced across at Lena and her baby with a smile, and sang, "*You'll come a Waltzing Matilda with me.*"

After a few rounds, most knew the words to the chorus at least and voices ricocheted around the sweltering cargo hold, to be joined sometimes by the men up top.

"We can't go on singing that." Verna took a breath. "What's next?"

"How about, '*It's a long way to Tipperary*?" Annie ducked instinctively as another plane shrieked overhead. "Everyone knows that."

This time voices roared the lyrics from the deck, as if the Japanese planes could be blown off course by sheer bravado. Other wartime favourites followed, but they kept returning to Waltzing Matilda.

"What's a jumbuck in a tucker bag, Sister?"

Annie looked at the serious little boy sitting next to his mother, his shorts filthy and his shirt ripped at one shoulder. "It's a sheep. The swagman's putting it in his food sack."

"What's a swagman?"

Annie laughed. "A tramp, mate. It's a tramp." She wondered how many others had no idea what the song they had been bellowing out meant. In a break from singing, and as she looked around at the strained faces, she realized her stomach had for the very first time remained neutral. Fear did strange things. Her voice a mutter, she asked Flo, "Do you think we don't scream because we're so terrified we become mute?"

"Oh, my God, Annie, only you would ask an existential question at a time like this."

"I don't even know what that means."

Verna nudged Annie with a tense grin before Flo could reply. "That you're a psycho, that's what!"

"But look at the kids. Even they're not screaming. Crying but not screaming. That's incredible." Then the singing started again as two tin mugs did the rounds, each person taking a sip before passing it on.

A judder vibrated through the ship.

"We're hit!" The yell from the deck curdled Annie's insides.

A few did scream then. Annie and many of the nurses clambered to the deck to help any injured. Along with the RAF doctors aboard, they set up two other hospital areas, trying to keep out of the way of the Chief Officer who supervised the fire crews, diving for cover each time another wave of planes appeared on the horizon.

"Bloody Nips." The words came from the boy's mother, her arms holding him tightly.

"Christ, will it never end?" Another asked.

Annie didn't know if Verna's tears were from fear or exhaustion. She felt close to them too. They must have been dodging bombs for hours as Captain Capon flung his ship from side to side. Ripples from shockwaves slapped the hull as Japanese bombs missed the ship by only ten or twenty feet, but despite the zigzagging, the Empire Star sustained two more direct hits from high-flying twin-engined heavy bombers. An already damaged lifeboat took the brunt of another bomb and became useless.

"There weren't enough for everyone anyway," Flo said to Annie and Verna as she passed on the news.

"Margaret and Veronica were up top during the second attack. That should change the captain's opinion. They threw themselves on wounded lads." Verna shuddered.

"God, I hope Iris and the other girls are safe," Annie said. "The ones on the Vyner Brooke."

"With a bit of luck we'll meet up in Fremantle." Verna said, glaring skywards as another formation flew overhead.

"Don't the bastards ever give up?" asked Flo.

"The captain might not think much of us," Annie said, when it seemed as if they had finally outrun the Japanese planes, "but I think he's bloody marvellous."

"All the crew are," Flo added. "Firefighting, fixing, shooting."

It turned out to be the last attack. Annie noted the time. 1310. Someone counted fifty-seven planes. Three direct hits with fires raging in three places. Annie and Verna spent most of the afternoon and all night taking turns to nurse a soldier whose stomach had been ripped open by machine-gun fire. He died, in agony, at dawn. Fourteen killed, thirty-seven with severe wounds, and numerous others with minor injuries.

Annie leant against the bulwark by one of the hospital areas and closed her eyes. Grey bombs and red streaks of strafing fire filled her vision.

Chapter 5

Batavia and Beyond, February 1942

Splash followed splash as fourteen body bags, weighted and made from sailcloth, slid into the sea to the sound of the captain's prayers, "… We therefore commit his body to the deep … in sure and certain hope of the resurrection of the body, when the sea shall give up her dead …" The plaintive notes of a bugler playing the Last Post drifted over the silent ship to dissolve in the sea air.

Annie, tears trembling on her lashes, clutched Flo's hand. She wondered if anyone had played for Ernest, her brother, one of the many Diggers who had died during the Siege of Tobruk. She scrubbed at her eyes and sniffed.

"You right, lovey?" Flo asked.

"Bloody war!"

"Yeah, it's a whole lot closer now." Verna gave Annie a hug. "Come on, back to work."

Japanese planes continued to fly high overhead as they roared south towards the Dutch East Indies but showed no interest in the Empire Star. Annie, Verna and Flo worried, their voices soft, about Iris and other friends who had been assigned to the Vyner Brooke.

The nurses, their pressure eased by not having to dive for cover every time a plane appeared, continued caring for the sick and injured.

"I'm not sure how we're meant to tell the difference between sheer exhaustion and fear, with beriberi." Annie wiped her hands on her apron. "I mean, I know beriberi is lack of Vitamin B, but the symptoms seem to be the same."

"Skinny as opposed to less skinny," Flo replied. "And some paralysis in the lower limbs. I asked Matron."

"And shot nerves." Added Verna.

"Well, that'll include us too, soon, if the Nips come back." Annie looked skywards.

With the scarce water supply, and the heat and smell in the hold, tempers became frayed and Annie was astonished that more arguments didn't break out.

Captain Capon, who seemed to be everywhere—inspecting damage, talking to the troops, chivvying his sailors, even talking to the nurses—had assured them they would reach Tanjung Priok, near Batavia, the following day. They would moor long enough to make the most pressing repairs before sailing on to Fremantle, in Western Australia.

"Water, Sisters, lots of water," the captain promised them.

"And not all around us, I hope," Annie whispered to the lad whose dressing she needed to change.

He gave a weak grin. "What'd we do without you girls, Sister?"

"You'll be home soon, ducks." Annie tried to distract him as she removed the crusted bandage from around the soldier's thigh. "Where are you from?"

"A property out Wagga way." He gritted his teeth and tried to raise his head, but Annie pressed his shoulders down. "Am I goin' to lose it? Me leg?"

"Not if I can help it, Soldier." Annie swabbed the wound, her touch gentle, then packed it with sulfa powder. With a sigh, she placed a clean lint pack on top and rewound the old bandage, stained side facing outwards. She snapped a syrette of morphia, administered it and said, "Now, have a sip of water, and no dancing."

"Thanks, Sister." He grabbed her hand.

"We'll have you back on a horse in no time, Soldier."

"Me name's Ted."

"Righto, Ted, stay put!" Annie eased her hand from his clutch, "I'll be back to check on you in a while."

Crouching over soldiers and airmen lying on deck, Annie helped another sister administer to a young Digger with a stomach wound as he slipped in and out of consciousness.

"Are you alright, Margaret?" She asked, her voice soft.

"As rain. Why?"

"It can't have been much fun, being on deck during that second attack."

"Not much."

"You could've been killed."

"Ah, Annie, no point worrying about that, we could all be killed."

"Well, I think you deserve a medal."

—

Ships swayed at anchor in the port as the Empire Star crept towards the dock at Batavia. Annie and Verna leant on the steel side and watched. Low shop houses lined the street away from the water, and nothing burned.

After the horror of Singapore's bombed streets littered with bodies, the calm of Batavia soothed the most fractured spirit. Men in white suits cycled, coolies pedalled trishaws, a horse and cart trotted along, and motorcycles swerved around pedestrians sending up plumes of dust. Women in sarongs swayed in syncopated rhythm as they carried fruit and vegetables in baskets suspended from bamboo poles across their shoulders. A flock of white-clad nuns stood at the far end of the wharf. War appeared a long way away, although those aboard now knew Borneo had come under Japanese control, and they'd heard talk that Celebes to the northeast of Java had also fallen.

"You know they won't stop there," Verna said, as they shared one of their last cigarettes.

Annie nodded, savouring the taste of tobacco. "Can I just put in an order for them to hold off until we've left? Selfish, I know, but I'm done with being bombed. For now, at any rate."

"What's the date?"

"We boarded the 11th, sailed the 12th …"

Verna cut Annie off, "Don't you mean bombed on the 12th?"

"That too. We buried the lads at sea the next day. God, was that only yesterday?"

"Yeah. So, today is the 14th. St. Valentine's Day," said Verna.

"We might find a delicious Dutchman to buy us a drink," Annie said, a grin tweaking her tired face. Levity gone, she added, "I heard one of the officers saying Java has oil. That's why the Japs want it. Feed the war machine."

"Please can I have a bath first?"

Billeted aboard a Dutch ship, the nurses and women signallers shared cramped but clean accommodation. Civilian women and the children were given refuge in private houses. Annie, pleased to see Lena and Hetty collected by a rotund woman with a horse and buggy, hoped the young mother would have a day's respite and be able to stock up on milk for her baby. Some of the healthy men stayed aboard, but those injured were stretchered to a local hospital.

"Shouldn't we be going with them?" Flo asked the senior sister.

"No. You girls need a break, too. There's plenty of nursing time ahead. We've still got to get our boys home. I need you rested, even if it's only for a day." She held up her hand as Annie began to speak. "That's an order, Sister. Now, off you go."

Squeals came from the showers.

"Oh, my God, water!"

"Not just water, hot water."

"Don't use it all."

"Hurry up."

"I never thought I'd relish a clean pair of knickers so much," Annie murmured, hanging her freshly washed ones over the end of her bunk.

"Clean uniforms, too." said Verna, "Well, cleanish," she added, smoothing down the creased skirt.

"We're the lucky ones," Flo said. "Some of the women just had what they had on." She buttoned her dress.

"Maybe the people they're staying with can give them some clothes." Verna finger combed her hair.

Annie bent to roll on her stockings, then stopped. "I'm not wearing these."

"Annie, you must. What will Matron say?"

"Don't care. I'll tell her I'm saving them for when we arrive on home soil. Come on, hurry up. We're being wined and dined ashore."

—

Two days of rest did wonders for everyone's spirits and, despite not looking forward to another sea voyage, Annie felt a surge of affection for the Empire Star as they climbed the gangway to shouts of welcome from the troops—most of whom had stayed aboard but with allocated shore leave. The airmen had disembarked to rejoin the squadrons which had fled Singapore.

"Did you see Captain Capon?" Verna asked. "I swear I saw a flicker of a smile."

"He did almost seem pleased to see us," replied Annie. "He looks knackered though."

"Doubt he got much rest." Florence tossed her satchel back in the same spot along the bulkhead, along with her hat. "All right, girls, back to work."

"At least I could stock up on durries!" Annie said, slipping a packet of cigarettes and matches into her pocket.

"The local ones are pretty rough," said Verna.

"Felt like smoking a fruit cake. All that nutmeg and clove."

"Not enough to make you stop though, Annie?" Flo asked.

"Not a chance."

The further south the Empire Star sailed, the lighter the atmosphere became on board and, as the coast of Australia came into view, a cheer erupted on deck. Ships, both naval and Merchant Navy, dotted the horizon as they came and went from the deep-water harbour at Fremantle. One evening, while having a smoko on the back deck, Annie and Verna watched a submarine surface.

"That's a Yank one," the soldier leaning against the rail said.

"I'd hate to be under the water, it's bad enough being on top," said Annie.

"Oh, I dunno," said his mate, "at least you can't see the buggers coming at you."

"I heard the subs are all based in Fremantle." The Digger sounded confident. "'Cos it's too far south for the Nips to fly."

"Darwin's a mess." The other said, blowing on the end of his cigarette.

"How'd you know?" Verna joined the conversation.

"Heard an officer say they'd been bombed."

"I never thought the Japs would reach Australia," said Annie, tossing the butt into the foaming sea below. She sighed. "Come on, ducks, duty calls." Then turned back to ask the soldier, "Have you heard anything about the Vyner Brooke?"

"Not a peep, love." The wind blew his words away.

"It was chaos, Annie," Verna's smile wobbled as they stepped over legs and around soldiers huddled on deck, "forty or so ships leaving Singapore at once. You know Iris has the luck of the Irish with her."

"Yeah, you're right, but I thought we'd hear something whilst in Batavia."

"Perhaps her captain ducked into a bay on another island. You know, to keep out of the way." Verna's voice was uncertain. "I'm sure Iris, all of them, are fine. She'll have stories galore to tell when we meet up."

"So will we," said Annie, smoothing her hair as she went back down into the hold.

Verna, close behind her, asked, "Do you think we'll get leave? I'd like to go home for a few days."

Annie shrugged. "Wonder where next?"

—

Fremantle. Annie knew she'd never forget it.

Rolling up her stockings she giggled. "Told you I'd save them for some sunny day!"

Flo laughed. "Did Matron ever say anything?"

"Not a word," Annie said, with a grin. "Do you know, I think we changed the captain's mind?"

"What do you mean?" Verna tilted her hat to the left.

"About women being on board his ship." Annie looked at Verna, blonde hair neat in a bun, and smiled. "Why do you look so good in a hat?"

"Style, lovey, style! Some of us just have it."

Annie grinned. "Well, mine didn't make it aboard in Singapore."

"Fancy that! A bit like your stockings. Just disappeared."

Laughing, the trio joined the other nurses waiting on deck to disembark.

Captain Capon stood at the gangway, a smile tugging his mouth as he saluted saying, "Sisters, the Empire Star helped in the evacuation of Crete and Greece, but we have never been in such a tight spot as the one we have just survived." His glance took in the rows of nurses then, with tears in his eyes, he added, "I suggest we thank God we are alive, and Sisters, please, never forget the Merchant Navy."

"As if we could, Captain. Thank you," said Annie shaking hands with the doughty man, his uniform crumpled but clean, his balding head brown and glistening in the afternoon sun. Picking up her regulation case, not as pristine as on the voyage out, a tremor trickled down her back, as she stepped onto dry land.

Those who came from Western Australia ran to be embraced by their families, tears etching paths on relieved faces. The press interviewed the Matron, upright and sure in her neat uniform, who named Sisters Margaret Anderson and Veronica Torney as two of her nurses deserving recognition for their selfless behaviour during the bombing raids. "But all," she added, "deserved praise."

The excitement at reaching home soil, of being safe, faded as they left the dockside.

A group of women stood, silent, beyond the gates. Their floral dresses, hats and gloves suggested they might be off to church but as the nurses passed, rather than words of welcome, the middle-aged matrons, their faces stern and unforgiving, held out white feathers.

Chapter 6
Sydney, 1942

Desolation. The barren landscape around Northam where they had been trucked after disembarking at Fremantle mirrored Annie's mood.

"Come on, love." Florence gave Annie's shoulder a nudge. "You can't let a gaggle of stupid women get to you."

"What I don't understand," Verna said, "is where they get their news from. They've probably never left WA, never been bombed. They sure as hell don't know what we've been through."

Flo, ever logical, said, "We don't know that. They could've been in Darwin."

"I doubt that."

Annie saw the filthy look Verna shot Flo, and sighed. "I dunno, but really, white feathers to a bunch of army nurses? Calling us cowards is a bit bloody rich."

"Just remember we know better, so please find the feisty sheila we all love and come back to us. We're not used to you being down in the mouth." Flo gave her a hug.

"And just look at this place. All glamour and glitz!"

Annie's burst of reluctant laughter made them all smile. "You know this place used to be a tuberculosis centre for the troops after the last war. Anzac Farm they called it."

"How is it you always seem to have the inside scoop?" Flo asked.

"An orderly told me," Annie replied.

"Well, now it's a dust bowl, and hot as hell."

"Registered 109° on the mess wall this morning."

"Did you know ..." Florence and Verna groaned. "Did you know," Annie ignored them, "that, as well as being our starting point east on the train, Northam has the most military camps, and depots in Western Australia? And, before you ask, yes, the orderly."

—

"Oh, my God," Annie grabbed Flo's arm as the train bumped the buffer at Central Station in Sydney, "I'm sure I saw Joe! Back there." The window, caked in dust, screeched as she tugged it down then leant out trying to see over the morass of men in khaki. Civilians on trains had become a thing of the past.

Diggers—young recruits—in slouch hats marched towards the converted cattle cars at the rear of the train. Some looked like their faces hadn't yet felt a razor. A cheer went up as the gates opened and men, some in tattered uniforms, stumbled onto the platform. Exhaustion scored filthy faces. Sergeants shouted for lines to be formed and the response, whilst not parade-ground sharp, created some order as soldiers returning from war were replaced by those heading to battle.

"It's him," Annie said, "I know it's him." Her impatience threatened to spill over as she waited for those in front to shuffle along the carriage.

"Here, give me your case," Verna said, "you go ahead. Go on! We'll wait at the entrance."

"Annie," Flo cautioned, "don't get your hopes up."

"Too late! They're already in the trees." Annie grinned. "I know it's him," she repeated. "Sorry, sorry, excuse me." She wriggled her way to the train door then paused a moment to see over the caps and heads before jumping down to start another push.

"Oi, watch it!" A soldier snapped and spun around. "Sorry, Sister." He gave an apologetic grin.

"No, I'm sorry." Annie felt close to tears. "I'm sure I saw my brother along the platform as we pulled in. I just want to find him."

"Oh, well, in that case, come on. Stick close." The soldier, his uniform crisp and new, broad-shouldered a path back through the throng either waiting to board or heading towards the exit, with Annie close behind. "How far along?"

"Near that lamp." Annie pointed and, for once her height an advantage, strained to see Joe's white blond hair. "There," she grabbed the soldier's arm, her eyes not leaving her brother's rangy frame. "He's there. Thank you, so much. And good luck."

"Righto, Sister. You too." He gave a sloppy salute and turned back.

"Joe, Joe!" Her words lost in the hubbub, Annie shouted louder. "Joe!" She saw him turn, puzzled, then shake his head and turn away. "Joe!" Her shriek jerked his head around, a surprised smile deepening the dimples around his mouth.

"Annie? What the hell?" He pulled her into a hug, his chin resting on her head. "You're back. Thank God."

"Didn't you get my letter? I sent it from Fremantle. And one to Dad."

"No, I've been on the move."

"Are you leaving now?" Annie tried to keep her question neutral.

"Yup, 'fraid so." Joe hugged her again, "but I shouldn't be gone long. Are you alright? It hasn't been good news from Singapore."

"I'm fine. Verna, Flo and I got out. A bit hairy."

"Flo?" Joe edged Annie further along the platform, thinning out as troops boarded the train.

"We met on the ship out," Annie paused. "Joe, have you heard any news about ships lost? From Singapore? We're worried about Iris."

He shook his head. "Definitive news is sketchy. I'll see what I can find out. Where are you headed?"

"Three days off, then to Yaralla, you know, the 113th AGH, while we wait for new orders."

"Aren't you going home?"

"Nah. I'm going to Verna's. We're going to lie on the beach and do nothing."

"Fair enough, although Dad'd like to see you."

"I doubt that. He'd just give me grief for not staying to help him."

"Come on, Annie, you've got to give him a chance. With Ernie gone, we're all he's got."

"Then why can't he be nice?"

"It's just not his way, Annie, you know that." Joe glanced along the emptying platform with a frown. "I'm sorry, Annie, I've got to go. I'll call you at the hospital when I get back." He grinned, then with a final hug said, "Be good. Say hi to Verna. Stay out of trouble!"

"I think I should be saying that to you," Annie said, kissing his cheek. "Whatever it is you're doing, be careful." She took a step back and watched as Joe picked up the small case at his feet, then swung onto the train. She watched him ease his way further along the corridor until he came to a window with only one soldier leaning against it. With a smile, he lowered it and leant out to wave as the train gave a hiss, then trundled away.

Annie, her eyes damp, wondered just what her brother's role involved. Perhaps he was right about Ian. The thought of losing Joe to the war as well, was too awful to consider. He'd lost weight, but he seemed even more assured, tired but not cowed, and he hadn't been shoved into one of the cattle cars. She smiled. Two pips on his shoulders—a lieutenant—but doing what?

—

"This is heaven." The sun eased westward, and Annie rolled onto her back, letting the warm water rock her like a cradle.

"It is with the shark nets up," Verna said, swirling her hands to stay afloat. "Although I'd still win a sprint if one was spotted in the bay."

"You'd have to beat me," said Annie, shading her eyes. "Do you know the story of the sun and moon?"

"Can't say I do." Verna splashed Annie. "Go on, tell me."

"Well," Annie paddled her hands, "the Aborigines believe there is a sun-woman—I can't remember her name—and each morning it's her bark torch that provides the dawn light. The clouds at sunrise are created from the ochre powder she uses to cover her body. The same at sunset. Then she takes an underground passage back to the east to start all over again the next day." Annie smiled, "And, not surprisingly, the moon-man is responsible for the night."

"How do you know all this stuff?"

"Ma had help from a woman of the Anaiwan during shearing. You know, each spring, when the shearers rolled up? Lots of extra men to feed." Annie laughed. "Her name was Ani too, but only one 'n' and no 'e'. She thought that funny and while I helped peel veggies or some other chore, she'd tell me stories of the Dreaming."

"The what?"

"The Dreaming." She saw Verna's puzzled look. "The inter-relationship between everything, people and things, for the Aborigines. Their philosophy, I suppose."

"Didn't have anything like that in Sydney."

"Bet you did. You just didn't get exposed to their culture."

"'Spose so."

"Looking back, Ani probably wasn't old," Annie paused. "When she first showed up, she terrified me. Her top front teeth had been knocked out in a fight. I remember Dad not wanting her on the property, but Ma said unless she had help, the shearers would go hungry."

"Your mum sounds a bit of a firecracker."

"Funny, isn't it? I never thought of her as one. It always seemed to be my father laying down the laws, creating tension—with me anyway. But, when I think back, Ma usually got what she wanted. But damn, she worked hard. It killed her, in the end." Annie sighed and, putting her feet down, stood on the sandy bottom before sinking back in the water up to her neck.

"Sorry, Annie with an 'n' and an 'e', didn't mean to make you sad."

"No, that's alright. But that's why it's so peaceful being with you and your family. The house is calm. It's lovely."

"You know you're always welcome. And, just so you know, it's only calm when we're not all at home. When the six of us are here, it's bedlam. That's when Dad disappears to his study at the bottom of the garden."

"Do you know what he told me last night?" Annie laughed then spat as seawater trickled in her mouth. "Ewch." She wiped her face. "He said that when all you girls were little and you wanted a puppy, he would only agree if the dog was male!"

"That sounds about right," Verna said with a chortle. "That would've been Mungo."

"Mungo?"

"Yeah, cos his coat felt like felt."

Annie rolled her eyes. "Oh, of course!"

"Come on, let's go in, I'm turning into a prune. Sally is coming over with the kids for tea, and Emma said she'd try and pop in too."

"My money's on Mr. Davidson disappearing to his study." Annie squeezed sea water from her hair then followed Verna up the beach.

"Nah, he loves those boys. He's making up for not having any himself."

"I'd have loved to live this close to the sea. Not so much this," Annie added, sand blowing back at her as she shook her towel.

"You must've had swimming holes." Verna slipped a dress over her wet cozzie.

"Yeah, we did. Dangar Falls." She shivered, remembering the feel of freezing spray as they'd dive under the cascades. How, from the water, the cliffs seemed to touch the sky. "Rainbows glistened through the waterfall mist like dragonfly wings." Annie smiled. "It amazed me that wattle could cling in the crevices. Turned the whole ravine yellow."

"I'd like to see that." Verna didn't look at her friend as they walked to the house. "Annie, is it because of your dad that you've never asked me to Armidale?"

The sound of a tram heading to the beach from Randwick broke the sudden silence.

"Yeah," Annie replied, "it would've been different if Ma had been alive."

Verna linked her arm through Annie's and hugged her. "Did he ever hurt you, ducks?"

"You mean whacked me? Sure, but no more than he did the boys. And probably deserved. But no, he never laid into me." She sighed. "He just wanted boys and can't see the point of girls." Annie lightened the mood. "Well, apart from the obvious!"

"Makes you wonder how your mum fell for him," Verna said.

"I've often wondered. But one thing I can say about my dad, is that even though he could be brusque, he adored her. And," Annie sighed, "for some reason, she him, even when he was being difficult. And that was often."

—

Annie, Verna and Florence giggled like schoolgirls on seeing their new home. They had not known what to expect when reporting for duty at the 113th Army General Hospital at Yaralla. The Nurses' Home, a gleaming modern building with a balcony running around the upper floors, was a far cry from where they'd trained.

Pushing open the doors to a large vestibule with a glass block wall to one side, Annie bounced on her toes as she said, "Bloody hell, it feels like the floors are rubber."

"I hope the wards are the same." Flo grinned. "No more back ache for us!"

"It'll be a bit different to nursing on a tennis court," Verna added.

After reporting to the home sister's office, and with their shifts and bedrooms assigned, they continued exploring. Nurses, all in uniform, some reading, some chatting, looked up from low chairs as the women entered the sitting room. Smiles greeted the newcomers.

"We wondered when you three would show up," a woman with strawberry blonde hair escaping from under her cap, stood up and gave them each a hug. "A bit grander than the Empire Star, eh?"

"It looks more like a fancy hotel than nurses' quarters," Annie replied.

"Great room for a dance," Verna said, doing a jig on the parquet flooring. "Roll up the red carpets and we'd be off."

"Just a pity Matron's flat is on the other side of the corridor!" Another from the ship joined in. "Come on, I'll show you to your rooms."

Annie, her room on the 6th floor, gasped. A floor to ceiling window covered with a gingham curtain made the room appear larger. A low bed, with an attached bedside table was placed by a radiator, a dressing table and stool completed the furnishings.

"Blimey, it's a bit different to our last billets, or Prince Henry's for that matter, isn't it?"

"It does seem as if grim quarters are a thing of the past," the nurse turned to go.

"At least until we're posted again, eh?" Annie asked.

The nurse nodded as she closed the door, her smile hopeful, "Let's catch up properly over a cuppa later, Annie."

Her door opened the same time as the knock sounded.

"You said you loved the water, as long as you weren't on a ship," Verna said, tugging the curtain aside. "If you lean out far enough you can see the Parramatta River." She looked around the room, "We might still have twelve-hour shifts, but at least we'll be comfy when we're off duty."

"And joy of joys," Flo joined them, "the dunnies and bathrooms are nice too. It really is more like a hotel."

"Come on," Annie shoved her case under the bed to unpack later, "let's go and find the smoking room." She glanced at her watch, pinned, as always, to her left breast, the only possession she'd worried about when they'd evacuated from Singapore. That, and getting out alive. "I'm on nights."

"Wonder how long we'll be here," said Flo as they went downstairs.

"Don't know, but I'm happy not to be shot at, or bombed for a while," Verna said.

"Iris would like this," said Annie, her voice sober. "God, I hope Joe can find out something about her."

"If anyone can, I reckon it's him," Verna agreed.

Annie nodded, "It's the not knowing that's so difficult." That had been the hardest thing as they had waited for news about Ernie. When it had arrived, the details had been sparse, leading to more questions which, Annie now recognized, would probably never be answered.

Verna sighed, "If the Vyner Brook had gone down with no survivors, we'd have heard."

"That's almost worse."

"What do you mean?"

"I can't bear to think of Iris being a POW."

"Then don't, Annie. There's no point. It's something that could happen to any of us."

Annie straightened her cap, saying, "And with that happy thought, I reckon New Guinea's next for us. But who knows when?"

Chapter 7
Moving On

As 1942 progressed, Annie remained convinced they would be sent to New Guinea. In spite of heavy losses on both sides, the Battle of the Coral Sea in May had been hailed a strategic win for the Allies. For the first time, the Japanese advance had been slowed and their fleet recalled to Rabaul, on New Britain. However, the commander of the South Seas Force, General Tomitarō Hirii, remained determined to cross the inhospitable Owen Stanley Range from their bases on the northern coast to take Port Moresby—the obvious stepping stone to Australia.

When Annie and Joe met in Sydney before he disappeared again to where she did not know, he confirmed news that had begun circulating the wards about fierce fighting on the Kokoda Track. After finding a map of New Guinea, Annie traced the path leading to Wairopi on the northern side of the Owen Stanleys. She couldn't imagine the struggle soldiers, on both sides, had to face.

And she worried about Joe. Did he have information because he was involved? Always energetic, although not in the sporty way Ernest had been, Joe, thinner than ever, now seemed to be running on neat adrenaline.

"I'm ding dong, Annie, don't fuss," he'd said, kissing her cheek as they parted.

His back straight, his casual saunter sending a message of not a care in the world, Joe headed back to Central to get his train to Melbourne, where he seemed to be based. But she knew him too well. Was it the underbelly of war, of soldiering, and the renowned indifference Diggers had to authority that kept him flying around Australia, and maybe overseas? They had all heard whispered words from patients about insubordination. If that was Joe's role, Annie hoped he was on the side of the Digger.

Instead of New Guinea, Annie, Verna and Florence were attached to the 11th CCS in Gunnedah, about 260 miles northwest of Yaralla and near, by Australian standards, to her father's property outside Armidale. A closeness Annie could not ignore when given three days leave.

With little prospect of a happy reunion with her father, she hitched a ride in the cab of a troop truck into town, then caught the train on up to Armidale.

"Cooee! Annie!"

Intent on climbing down from the train, Annie had not seen the uniformed woman approach, but glanced up at the familiar voice.

"Good grief! Gracie?" After Ernest's death, letters from Gracie had come regularly but Annie hadn't heard anything for months. They bussed cheeks, then Annie held her away and studied the navy wool suit with the red cross badge. "You're a VAD. When did that happen?" Even in uniform Gracie managed to look dainty.

"I was done sitting at home. Ernie's gone. Time to get on with life!" Gracie rushed on, ignoring Annie's sharp intake of breath. "I'm not clever enough to be a nurse, so my options were either join this lot," she glanced down at her uniform, or become a Land Girl, and I wasn't going to do that. Break too many nails. I'm working in the canteen at the AGH here in town."

Gracie's tinkling laugh drew attention from soldiers around them. Annie wondered, again, how Ernie's girlfriend had ever thought she could be a farmer's wife. She shook her head, her eyes watering. Not an issue now.

"Come on, I've got you a lift out to the property, or to the gates anyway. It's a truck taking a couple of boys back to Glen Innes to convalesce. The driver said he didn't mind making a slight detour."

"How on earth did you manage that?" Annie felt a flash of affection subduing her irritation at Gracie's apparent callousness. She had wondered, with petrol rationing biting hard, how she'd get home.

"I told James. You know he's at the army hospital here now?"

"No, I didn't know."

"So, he mentioned it to another doctor friend of his, and Bob's your uncle!" Gracie drew breath and looked up at Annie. "You know, he misses Ernie dreadfully. They were good mates."

Annie nodded. She didn't ask if Gracie missed him too, but instead asked, "Just out of curiosity, how did you know I'd be coming home?"

"Oh, Annie, you know what I'm like. Got to know what's going on." Her laugh tinkled again as she tucked her arm through Annie's and moved her along the platform. "One of the Land Girls on your dad's place is a friend of mine, and he mentioned it to her, and she to me ... if you follow."

"But I only found out a few days ago." Annie had to laugh. "And I didn't know Dad had girls from the Land Army."

"You would if you came home more often."

Surprised at Gracie's rebuke, Annie stopped short, but before she could respond a truck drew up in a fog of fumes. The driver jumped down and gave Annie a sloppy salute.

"G'day, Sister, you ready?"

"Of course, and thanks." Annie turned to embrace Gracie, "Thanks, this is really nice of you. If you're not working, perhaps we can grab a cup of tea on my way back." She had a sudden thought. "If you're working at the hospital, are you still living at home?"

"God, no. I'm staying in the girl's hostel. Much easier, and much more fun."

Annie sensed the impatience, not from the driver who looked as if he could watch Gracie all day, but the man peering through the window of the truck cab. "Righto, gotta go." She handed her case to the driver. "Thanks, Gracie, and say g'day to James for me."

"Hooroo, don't do anything I wouldn't do!"

"Sister." The man helped Annie into the cab then climbed in after her.

"Thanks," she said, sliding across the bench seat behind the steering wheel. "Afternoon, Major," she nodded to the other occupant. As they bounced along, Annie edged nearer the driver, preferring an occasional elbow from him to the proximity of the forbidding doctor on the other side.

"Righto, Sister, where too?" the driver asked.

"Fifteen minutes along the Bundarra Road would be perfect, thanks." Annie glanced at the stern face to her left. "I can walk from there."

"Nah, we'll see you to the door."

"No need, really." Annie could imagine her father's words if she showed up in an army truck. Something about requisitioning vehicles for personal use, for sure. "I walked it every day as a kid. I can certainly manage it now."

"Wha' d'you say, Doc?" The driver leant forward to ask his other passenger.

"Whatever the Lieutenant wants, Jock." He lapsed into silence, watching the landscape, the weak spring afternoon sun mirrored on his face.

Annie found it difficult to believe James, Gracie's brother, a bloke always up for a laugh or a game of tennis, could be mates with the surly man beside her. The entrance to Gunida, the family property, couldn't come soon enough and that was saying something.

"Just around the next corner would be great, thanks, Jock." At the gates Annie saw a horse and cart, then a girl rising from amongst bales of hay on the flatbed.

"Looks like you've got a welcome committee, Sister," Jock said with a chuckle, "no walking for you today. I bet the party line has been in action."

"So it seems." Annie could just imagine the chat as people in the district listened in to each other's telephone calls, aided by Mrs. Somers on the switchboard.

"Don't you know who it is?" The doctor asked, squinting through the windscreen.

"Not the foggiest. I imagine a Land Army girl. Gracie told me Dad has a couple working here."

"Gracie? The sheila at the station?" Jock asked. "She works at the hospital then?"

Annie nodded.

"Might look her up. She's not taken?" He pulled on the hand brake.

Annie swallowed hard. "No, Jock, she's not taken." She gathered her hat and bag and waited for the doctor to move. "Thanks, again."

—

"G'day, girl. Wondered when you'd show up." He patted her on the back. His awkward touch surprised Annie. Perhaps the thought of losing her, and maybe Joe, had softened his manner. But the flash of affection did not last, and tea had been a silent affair. Ian, as Annie more and more often thought of her father, showed little interest in her life. He ate what she had cooked, pushed his chair back, lit his pipe and read *The Armidale Express* that she had brought him. Next morning Annie had thought to saddle up Bessie and help the Land Girls but her father had told her not to bother them.

"They're doing things the way I want them done. I don't need you going in and interfering."

"Well, shall I cook tea for them? They must be tired when they finish."

"What, and traipse it over to the shearer's quarters?"

"It's across the home paddock, Dad. Or we could have them here," Annie suggested. "A bit of comfort might be a nice change for them."

"Don't be dafter than normal, girl. I don't want them in my house."

"But it's alright for them to work like navvies in your paddocks? You look after the shearer's better than them, Father." Annie could feel her temper flaring, and thought of the empty house that would've been Ernie and Gracie's home. "Couldn't they at least live in the cottage?"

"No! And I pay 'em. Thirty shillings a week."

"Bet it's less than men get."

"Oh, don't go getting on your high horse, Annie. It's a fair wage. And I don't charge them board and lodging."

"You're a regular hero, Dad. It's the minimum wage. And you don't give them any board."

"If your brother hadn't gone off to fight someone else's war I wouldn't have this problem. Or if you came home and did your bit."

"You don't consider nursing our boys as doing my bit?" Annie slammed her mug on the kitchen table, spilling tea, and stormed out to the verandah breathing deeply.

What was the point? He wouldn't change now. Without Ernest or Joe to ease the way it wasn't worth coming home. "Some home!" Annie mumbled, and wiped a tear away before straightening. If Ma had been alive, Annie knew it would have been different. She'd have been proud. But still it hurt. Going into her bedroom she pulled down one of her favourite books, *The Lute-Girl of Rainyvale* by Zora Cross, and lay on the narrow bed. She wondered if love and mystery would transport her to Northern Queensland the way it had as a girl.

—

The two days had dragged and Annie decided to walk to the gate first thing in the morning and hope to hitch a lift with anyone going into Armidale. She had her book in her bag to while away the time.

"I'm going to town early, Father," she said at breakfast, sliding a plate of eggs and bacon in front of him. "I'd like to see Auntie May."

"What for? I haven't seen her since your mother died." He drowned his eggs in mustard.

"I have. Many times. She's a dear."

"Bad-tempered, I'd call her."

"Perhaps because she didn't like the way you made Ma work," Annie said, her voice low.

"That's enough of your lip, girl." He pushed his chair back, picked up his pipe, then stopped at the door. "Will you be back?"

Annie's head shot up, surprised at the wistful tone. Perhaps she should give him some leeway, as Joe kept suggesting. He must be lonely. First Ma, then Ernie. "Don't know, Dad. Depends what happens next." Annie stood to hug him, but he jammed his hat on and moved away. The moment gone.

"Righto, well, I'll be seeing you." The screen door slammed behind him.

"Miserable bastard," she muttered, sloshing the plates in the sink and leaving them to dry on the draining board, but a part of her longed for an embrace. Anything to show he cared.

Back in uniform after two days in comfortably worn civvies, Annie picked up her case, looked around her bedroom and said a silent goodbye to the chair she and Ma used to sit in together when she'd been a little girl. She took a puerile delight in leaving the kitchen as it was and, as she left, doubted she'd be back, unless Joe came too.

"Cooee!"

Annie spun to see Bessie harnessed back into the cart, the reins being held by Helen, the Land Girl who had met her.

"I'm heading to the far paddock, easy detour to the gate. Up you get!"

"Thanks, Helen." Annie swung her case up, then followed.

"Good to see your dad?"

"Not particularly, but duty done."

"Yeah, he's a bit of an old bugger, isn't he? I think he's lonely. But he's not interested in being with us girls."

Annie nodded. "I know. I'm sorry he's difficult."

"We've got used to him. Ignore him most of the time, unless we're getting instructions of course."

Annie gave a sad laugh. "Can't say I blame you. How much longer have you got here?"

"Oh, about five months, but we'll probably sign on to stay. No point having to break in another misery guts." Helen threw her head back and guffawed.

"Don't you miss the city?" Annie knew she came from Sydney.

"I did at first. The country can be strange. Noises I'd never heard. Never seen a kangaroo. And," Helen laughed again, "I didn't know one end of a horse from the other. Tried to bridle the wrong end, didn't I, girl?" Helen leant over to pat Bessie's rump. "But don't think I could go back now. I love it out here. So peaceful. Well, away from your father, that is!"

"He's lucky to have you."

"In fairness, he has taught us a lot." She pulled on the reins. "Righto, here you go. Good to meet you, Annie. Good luck."

"And you. Don't let the old man get to you."

"Nah, we don't. Hope you haven't too long to wait. Be seeing ya!"

Annie watched Bessie head back, veer off the track and through an open gate, then wait patiently as Helen climbed down to close it. The girl waved then disappeared behind a copse of gums.

"And that was home." Annie perched on the large rock, by the sign in need of paint declaring the entrance to Gunida, where she had waited for the bus with the boys when they went to the local school before going to boarding school in Armidale. Glad the wind had died down, she opened her book but didn't read. Instead, she soaked in the solitude of the landscape she loved. Daydreaming, she didn't see a truck until it almost reached the sign. Jumping down, she waved but it had already slowed.

"G'day, Sister. Us again! Need a lift?"

Annie peered around Jock's grinning face to see the doctor, no smile on his face. "How on earth did you know, Jock?"

"You've been away too long. Forgotten the power of the party line. Mrs. Somers, on the switchboard, heard from your friend Gracie that you'd only be here a couple of days. Mrs. S. told my mum in Glen Innes, so here we are."

"Thanks, again. Morning, Major." She got a grunt in reply.

"You'll be on the train together. The doc here is heading to Gunnedah, too."

"Really?"

The driver rattled on. "It's not till later. So you'll have to cool your heels a bit longer." They travelled in silence until reaching the outskirts of town, when he glanced at the grim-faced man next to her. "Where can I drop you, Sister?"

"How about Jessie Street? My aunt lives there."

"Easy!" He chuckled. "You and the doc can meet again on the train. Do you want me to pick you up?"

"No, no, but thanks, you've been great."

"Be careful out there, Sister."

"You too, Soldier." Annie took her case from the driver, waved, and clicked the gate to Auntie May's house.

"G'day, darl."

Annie, pulled into a warm embrace, felt the previous two days slough from her shoulders. "Not an easy time, huh?"

"Not really. But it's lovely to be here."

"Next time don't bother going to see the old bugger, come and stay with me."

"He's still my dad, Auntie May, and I know he's lonely. He just makes it so hard. I miss Ma so much every time I go home."

"I know, darl."

The morning went by in a cosy haze of tea and cake while Auntie May's cat, Pearl, kneaded her lap. At noon, they walked to the station where Annie was again hugged tight.

"I know you don't know where you're off too next, darl, but you be careful."

"None of us know where we are half the time," responded Annie, with a laugh, "there are no bloody signposts anywhere!"

Relief kept Annie relaxed when she saw the major did not get on the train with her and, lulled by the soporific motion, she watched the scenery in a sleepy daze until they reached Tamworth.

"Well, how was it?" Verna asked, a few hours later, as they prepared to go on night shift.

"Lovely to see Auntie May, but as expected with Father."

"You know you've always got a home with us, ducks. Dad thinks the world of you, even though you're another 'female' in the house! And Mother loves that Dad thinks that."

As they welcomed the New Year, the 11th CCS began their move to Kingaroy in Queensland.

Chapter 8
Heading North, 1943

Annie, Verna and Florence itched to get back to the war. With the situation less volatile on the Papuan side of New Guinea, and servicewomen now being permitted to serve in the islands north of Australia from October 1942, rumours swirled around the camp as to when a move would happen.

The stepping stone for their unit—now renamed the 111th CCS—was Queensland.

"I thought Kingaroy was meant to be humid, subtropical. This is bloody freezing," Annie complained, her hands like icicles as she lit a cigarette.

"At least we get sunny days," Verna said, inhaling deeply.

"Funny name for the peanut capital of Australia," said Florence. "Should be something like 'Nutsville'!"

"Very original, ducks." Verna laughed.

"I happen to know why it is called Kingaroy." Annie looked at her friends with affection.

"'Course you do. Another orderly?"

Annie shook her head. "Nope, one of the Yank pilots."

With a grin, Flo said, "The same one, I believe, who gave me some chewing gum."

"Don't let Matron see you with it. She'll have your guts for garters." Annie, pulled up short for having a button missing from her belt, had felt the matron's wrath.

"I spat it out. Disgusting stuff."

"Do you want to know, or what?" Annie asked.

"Go on then," Flo urged, "but hurry up.

"Are you sitting comfortably?"

Verna gave Annie a shove. "Get on with it!"

"Well, apparently it comes from the Wakka Wakka Aboriginal word for 'red ant'."

"Begs the question, why name a place for a biting insect?" Flo watched smoke hang for a moment before drifting off in ever-decreasing swirls.

"Because when they surveyed the land their campsite swarmed with them. Here endeth the lesson. And now," Annie stubbed out her cigarette, "back to work. Bet it's baked beans for tea."

"Another thing to thank the US Army for," said Flo, her smile wry. "Do you think they get the irony—calling their favourite food 'navy' beans."

"Doesn't matter. They've obviously got enough clout if they can demand our government plant them. Another thing to make Kingaroy famous. Peanuts and baked beans."

—

Then, in mid May, all levity vanished.

Annie found Verna sobbing in the sluice room.

"What's happened?"

"Ruth. She's gone."

"What do you mean 'gone'?"

"The Japs torpedoed it. The hospital ship Ruth was on. The Centaur. Yesterday. Before dawn."

"Oh, God, no." Annie put her arms around Verna, an image of her friend's sister laughing around the kitchen table at the house at Coogee flashed before her. "Goddamn the Japs to hell! It must have been marked. Green band, red crosses. Lit up like a Christmas tree. They can't bloody do that." Her tears dropped onto Verna's shoulder.

"Well, the bastards have."

"Verna?" Flo rushed in. "I've just heard. I'm so sorry, lovey."

Verna pushed her fingers onto her eyelids and, through her gasping sobs said, "She was cock-a-hoop to be chosen. One of twelve nurses on board."

Annie held onto a sliver of hope. "Ducky, are you sure? About Ruth, I mean."

Verna eased away, pulling a handkerchief from her pocket, and nodded. "Only one of them survived. And it wasn't her." She scrunched her eyes tight. "It went down northeast of Brissie. On her way to Cairns. Ruth loved it. Oh, God, sharks. About the only thing that terrified her."

"You can't think about that," Flo said, wiping her eyes with the back of her hand.

Fresh tears spilled as Verna hiccupped. "The ship sunk in just a few minutes. No chance." She looked around the room, her eyes vague, "I've got to go home."

"Of course you do," said Annie, "you go and find Matron, we'll cover you here."

In no time posters appeared urging Australians to 'work—save—fight and so avenge the nurses!' The graphics showed the Centaur clearly marked as a hospital ship, with crew jumping from the sides, survivors clinging to debris in oil-slicked water.

None of which helped Verna. Her hatred of the enemy had become personal, and Annie knew from her own anguish at Ernest's death, that it would be a long time, if ever, before the visceral loathing would dissipate. Never leave entirely perhaps, but ease enough to allow compassion to return. She wasn't sure if it had, but it had probably made it easier for her not being anywhere near the Germans, or Italians.

At Kingaroy they got used to the sound of the RAAF planes taking off and landing. Some of the nurses learnt to distinguish the different models, helped by patients either bored or desperate for something to take their minds off their injuries. To Annie all planes sounded the same. Menacing. And at night the lights would sometimes generate a moment of stark fear.

—

"Good afternoon, Lieutenant, very neat."

Annie, bandaging a soldier's sutured wound, did not look up but her brow wrinkled as she tried to place the voice.

"Don't distract her, Doc," the soldier said, "I want her concentration on me."

His laugh made Annie smile and, the wrapping pinned, she patted him on the shoulder and stood to see the looming figure of the grumpy major she'd sat beside in the truck cab during her brief visit home.

"We meet again." An unexpected smile lurked at the corners of his mouth as they moved to the next bed. "How are you, Soldier?" He asked, checking the pupils of the injured man whose head, covered in bandages and strapped around his chin, resembled a medieval knight. "Do you need anything?"

"Not from you, Doc, but maybe from the sister."

"Behave," Annie said, her hand gentle as it brushed his covered cheek.

They continued down the line of beds until, at the end of the ward, the doctor spoke. "A couple of things, Sister, sorry, Lieutenant." He hurried on, his voice low. "I owe you an apology, and an introduction."

"You're right, Major, you do, but I don't have time to talk, so both will have to wait." She nodded, picked up a basin of water and moved back down the aisle, sending a silent prayer of thanks the Matron had not heard her disrespectful words.

The day passed in a blur of dressings, bathing, comforting and sometimes sadness, made poignant by the refusal of most on the ward to feel self-pity no matter what their injuries. Going off duty after a twelve-hour shift, she went to the mess tent. Pouring a cuppa, she took a couple of biccies from the tin and wandered over to an empty trestle table and sat down, her hands clasped around the mug for warmth.

"Good evening, Lieutenant."

She stifled a groan. "I'm sorry, Major, I'm tired, I just want to finish my cup of tea and go to bed." Annie put up her hand to stop the doctor speaking, "Please, I know who you are, so no introduction necessary. And I accept your apology for having been bad-tempered. And," Annie continued, "I don't like that you are making me sound as bad-tempered as you, but I really don't feel like talking. Now, please, go away."

Annie shut her eyes, willing him to leave. Instead she felt the weight of his arms lower the table as he settled on the bench opposite.

"I'll just sit here."

"Oh, God. Fine, Dr. Townsend. Speak away." She glanced around, hoping Florence or Verna would be around to come and save her. Looking back at the man she noticed he, too, looked tired.

"Thanks. I'm William Townsend—Bill, to most. And I owe you an explanation for my behaviour in the truck."

Annie replied, her voice weary, "No, Major, you don't. We all have bad days."

"But I want to explain."

"Righto. Off you go." Annie sipped her black tea.

Subdued, Bill said, "I went up to Glen Innes for my mother's funeral."

"Oh, God, I'm sorry." Instinctively Annie reached across and touched his hand, then remembered where she was. "Now I feel a real heel. It's a dreadful time."

Bill gave a half smile. "Thank you, and yes, it is. Expected but still difficult." He paused, closed his eyes for a second, seeming to make a decision. "I disappeared into a hole for a few weeks. Brought back memories of my wife's death nearly six years ago."

"Oh, hell, Major. I'm sorry again. Christ, you have been through the wringer. Here you need this more than me." She pushed the mug across the slatted table. "Sorry it's nothing stronger."

With a slight smile, Bill stood and taking her mug, Annie watched him refresh it and get one for himself. For a moment she thought of her cot, then shrugged. What was another ten minutes?

"Thanks." Annie took a sip. She had to hand it to the mess staff, tea could always be relied upon. "You know, before the war I wouldn't touch tea without milk. Hardly a sacrifice, I know, but funny how we change." Noticing the major's quizzical look, she took another sip and added, "I have absolutely no idea why I said that."

Their laughter eased the tension.

"So, Sister Cutler, did you have a good trip home?"

"Not particularly."

Bill looked down, "It's difficult to drop in and out of people's lives."

"Sadly, Major, I can't blame the war. I have a prickly relationship with my father."

"No mother?"

"She died a long time ago."

"Big foot in bigger mouth. My turn to apologise, again."

"We're doing a lot of that. It's alright." Annie realized she had relaxed. "Ma kept us all in line, especially Dad. Is your father alive?"

"Yeah, I'm lucky. He's a good man. He's why I'm a doctor."

Annie tilted her head. "Oh, I am dim. Glen Innes. Your father's Tom Townsend. I know of him, from James Sinclair."

"James? How do you know James?"

"He's Gracie's brother. The girl at the railway station, when you collected me." Seeing Bill's confusion, Annie continued. "Never mind. We all grew up together. I remember he worked at your dad's practice one summer. James was my brother's best mate."

"Was?"

"Yup. Ernest died in Libya." Grief rasped her voice, and she swirled the tea, gathering herself. "He and Gracie went steady."

Bill stayed silent a moment. "We seem to be digging deep."

She sighed sadly. "That's alright. It's the war. Makes us talk too much sometimes."

"Yes, I suppose it does. But I'm sorry, Annie. So many families broken."

She looked up. He knew her whole name, too, then. She noticed the major's eyes. Muddy green like the dam at home on a summer's day. And his hair, up close and with no cap, was more grey than blond. "Have you children, Major?"

His eyes snapped shut. Wrong question. Good one Annie. He shook his head.

"My wife died in childbirth." It was his turn to focus on his mug. "As I said, years ago."

There's not a hole deep enough for you, Annie Cutler. "Doesn't make the awfulness go away." Annie stood up. "I think it's time I went to bed, before I say anything else. I really am sorry, Major." She picked up her mug, and nodded to his. "Are you finished?"

He nodded and rose. "I'll walk you back."

"No, you won't." Annie's smile lessened her retort as she took his mug too. "What would Matron say? Good night, Doctor."

A chill had descended with sundown and Annie shivered as she switched on her torch and lengthened her already long stride as she went to the nurse's building. A red flare made her gulp in fear. Stupid. A match, that's all. She took a deep breath.

"Annie? Over here." Verna's voice came from the shadows. "Thought it was you. Want a ciggie?"

"I do, thanks."

"So," she lit Annie's cigarette, "was that the dashing major I saw you talking to? In the mess? In case you can weasel out of an explanation about being on the ward."

Annie, pleased Verna could tease her, replied, "Hardly dashing. And he's old."

"Alright. Was that the ancient and mouldy major you were talking to?" Verna giggled.

A sound Annie hadn't heard her friend make since her return from Ruth's memorial service. "Yeah. He's the doctor I mentioned. You know when I went home. The grump in the truck." Annie groaned. "I really put my foot in it. Again. He went to Glen Innes for his mother's funeral. And his wife died."

"Bloody hell! At the same time?"

"What are you two whispering about?" Flo asked from the door. "Can I join in?"

"I'm just hearing how our friend here has managed to upset the new doctor. Twice in the space of a few minutes."

"That's not fair," said Annie. "How was I to know? And no," she returned to Verna's question. "His wife died a few years ago. Having a baby."

"No wonder he looks so gloomy," said Flo, watching a fine stream of smoke dissolve in the cool air.

"He didn't look too dejected when I saw him talking to Annie."

"Do you have a beau?" Flo hooted.

"Oh, shut up, both of you. You're mad. Right, I'm going to bed. G'night."

Glad the night hid her blush, Annie went inside and splashed cold water on her face, surprised at her reaction. Growing up with two brothers, she had never felt the least bit romantically drawn to any of their friends. Then life had got too busy. Nursing. War. The possibility of losing someone had convinced her not to contemplate falling in love.

For God's sake. You've had one conversation with the man. It's only because he's sad. She comforted herself with the thought as she snuggled under the blanket and into sleep.

Chapter 9
Cambridgeshire, 2003

A tingle trickled down Annie's back. She sat a moment longer, then stood, "Come on, Eartha," she called, "leave the birds alone." Going back to the dining room she gathered up the breakfast detritus and dumped it in the kitchen sink. Eating a banana, she gazed out the window and waited for the kettle to boil, noting the apples needed collecting before they got squished on the drive.

Coffee drunk, Annie took two baskets from under the hall table, one for the marginally bruised fruit, which she would lay out on straw along the shelves in the garage, the other for the battered and pecked apples. Those she'd make into chutney and, if she had the energy, an apple pie. Make a couple and give one to Susie to take home with her tomorrow. Or one each for the twins.

Annie groaned as she straightened for the last time, rubbed a not-too-grubby apple on her trouser leg and smiled around a bite. The fact she still had her own teeth made up for the aching knees. She left one basket by the tree nearest the front door, the other she kick-dragged to the garage. Enjoying the tartness, she leant against the car and watched a cluster of bees humming around a half-eaten core. Time to swap a jar of chutney for a jar of honey from old Mr. Thams at the farm. Wiping a dribble of juice with the back of her hand, Annie chuckled. Who was calling who old? "I hope no one calls me 'old' Annie," she said to the bees.

"Good morning, Annie. Are you going doolally, talking to yourself?" The voice came from the gate.

Annie pushed off the car in surprise. Brough Mallory, a stickler for routine, never walked by this early. He raised his cap as she ambled over. "Morning, Brigadier, and yes, quite probably going mad!" She bent to fondle the almost-cocker spaniel's ears and greying muzzle. "Molly got impatient, did she?"

"No, no, not her. I'm having lunch in Cambridge so have had to bring my day forward." He pushed his glasses back up his nose. "Haven't you got better things to do than note my timetable?"

"Nope!"

The lanky man, regimental tie knotted in a Windsor, laughed and nodded towards the apples. "I hope you're going to be making some chutney, my dear, I'm nearly out. Almost as good as Fiona's used to be."

"High praise indeed," Annie said, thinking of the buxom woman who had collapsed and died eight years earlier whilst deadheading roses. A death that had shocked the village and sent the bamboo-thin man into a foxhole. It had been David, many months later, who had persuaded Brough that a dog from the pound would help ease the loneliness and had gone with him to choose Molly. "And yes, I shall be making chutney. Some for the harvest festival fair too." She tossed the core onto the front lawn—another for the bees—then said, "If you're lucky I might slide a jar your way, gratis."

Their laugh, companionable and easy, prompted Annie to ask, "Would you like to pop in for a whisky this evening? Normal time?" She, David, and Brough had spent many happy evenings playing cribbage over the years and, since David's death, Brough had taken to checking up on her every few days, especially since she'd fainted on one of their walks.

"Thank you, my dear, but not tonight ..."

"Josephine?" Annie sniggered.

Brough frowned. "You do know that phrase has been erroneously quoted, and attributed to the dumpy little Frenchman, don't you?" Before Annie could comment, the Brigadier continued. "The phrase comes from a Vaudeville number sung by Ada Jones and ..." he stopped, "no, can't remember his name. Anyway the song is *Come Josephine, in My Flying Machine*."

"All this because I asked if you wanted a drink this evening," Annie said with a laugh. "Now, if you're going to make it into Cambridge, you'd better get on with Molly's walk."

"Yes, indeed," Brough glanced at his watch. "How about tomorrow evening instead?"

Annie shook her head. "Afraid not. Jake and the family are coming for lunch. Or rather they're taking me to The Swan, so I'll be ready to drop after that."

"Wonderful, do give them my best regards, won't you? Right, must on, on. Goodbye, my dear."

"Bye, Brough." Annie tickled Molly's chin one last time. "Bye, lovely girl. Go and chase a rabbit." She watched them walk down the lane, then turned to see Eartha Kitty eyeing her.

"Silly cat, I love you the most."

The basket of apples by the door reminded Annie of the paddling pool filled with yellow, red, and green balls that the twins had when they had been toddlers, when they had liked nothing better than to wallow in a sea of bobbing colours.

Heaving the basket onto the kitchen table, she began to sort apples again. Ones for now, ones for the freezer. She'd leave the ones in the garage for another day. Apple peel fell in swirls. Annie's chuckle bounced back from the chopping board. How light-hearted she, Flo and Verna had been. And Iris. How they'd giggled when, bored with watching the endless blue of the ocean as they sailed to Singapore, Verna had told stories of growing up in a houseful of girls at Coogee.

"We used to drive Dad mad. When we peeled the spuds, we'd toss the skin and debate whether the shape looked like a letter. If it did, that would give the first letter of the man we'd marry!"

Iris's voice floated in as if yesterday. "And? What letter did you get?"

"Whatever boy I fancied at the time!" Verna replied.

Annie had laughed. "I bet your dad'd disappear to the shed?"

"Always!"

"I used to long for a sister. Someone to be girly with, even though I adored Ernest, and Joe—but he was the baby."

"Well, lovey, you've got us."

Annie blinked, could almost feel Flo's hug. She still missed them. Despite having dear friends in the village, and in London, those wartime friendships had never been replicated. She gave a rueful grin. That Nightingale System, so instilled in nurses when they'd trained together, had certainly worked. Care and comradeship! She poked at the apple peel curling on the board. 'B' jumped out.

Dear Bill. She had never again seen the boorish man from the army truck in Armidale, only the person he really had been—compassionate, dedicated and kind. Annie's fingers went to her lips, remembering. After a long day, they had left the mess tent at Kingaroy and, their shoulders touching, had walked to the edge of the camp. Flat land all around them. Peanut silos in the distance. Bill had tugged her behind a service hut and, RAAF Avro Ansons and Kittyhawks thundering overhead as they took off and landed, had put his arms around her. That tentative, wondering first kiss as warmth that had spread throughout her body had confirmed what her heart had been hinting.

Then David. How lucky she had been to love, and be loved by, two such dear men. Annie tossed another apple peel. "Huh, 'S'." She smiled.

Susie had been a wonderful addition to the family. Annie gave a shudder. Some of Jake's girlfriends had been truly awful. She snickered as she thought of the one even David, kind as he was, had taken exception to. "What was her name? Oh, well, doesn't matter." She wiped her hands on her jumper. The multi-pierced ears had not been a problem but the eyebrow and nose piercing, connected by a chain, had caused much merriment later in the privacy of their bedroom. The girl's entire demeanour had been challenging, and Annie's acceptance of she and Jake sharing a bedroom had seemed to enrage her. Annie had heard Jake explaining that it really was okay because his mother knew they slept together, so why make it an issue. Annie laughed again at the memory of the silly girl's retort, "It's not normal for parents to be like that."

Annie had liked Jake's response. "My parents aren't normal."

Both she and David had been relieved that particular romance did not last much longer. They had comforted themselves that Jake needed a taste of the fringe before finding Susie, although it had taken a few years. Susie was a stunning woman, made more so by her lack of awareness of the impact she made. Annie smiled. How could she not love a woman who adored her son the way Susie did? She had given up her Sloane Square medical practice in London to join Jake, part-time since the boys had been born, in his country surgery, and thrown herself into country living.

Eartha jumped onto the counter to watch the apple peels browning on the chopping board. "Get down!" Annie nudged the cat off, her mind wandering again. If only Hugh could find someone. Hugh, her adventurer. She never quite knew where he was, or what he was up to. A bit like her brother, Joe. One of Annie's proudest moments had been when she and Jake went up to the Palace to see Hugh receive an OBE from the Queen for services to Afghanistan. If only David had been alive to see it. She sighed. Jake had been the one who told her his brother's regiment had orders to prepare for a tour of duty in Iraq.

Something she was glad David wasn't around to witness. Annie rather wished she wasn't. Bad enough when you were in the thick of it. Somehow it seemed harder being on the sidelines. Every time the phone had rung when Hugh had been in Afghanistan a spasm of fear had shot along her spine. When he'd railed at the number of inoculations he'd had to have to go to South Asia, she had waved his grumbling aside. Then had hauled Jake into the discussion, convinced a brother who happened to be a doctor would have more sway than a mother, who hadn't nursed for decades. Between them, they had insisted he sign the consent form and have the anthrax vaccine offered against biological warfare, along with the more common vaccines.

"I suppose it's a good thing Hugh doesn't have a wife to worry about. I wonder if that's why he's coming down tomorrow? To tell me he's off." Annie asked Eartha, back on the counter, as she sliced apples. "You really are a naughty cat." She pushed her off again. This time her mind going to another kitchen, in another time and on the other side of the world.

Chapter 10

Hell is Port Moresby, New Guinea, 1943

The kitchen, more a lean-to propped against the mess tent, often had a nurse or two helping the staff. Not that anyone had much free time, but the tedium of washing weevils from the rice bought from the Chinaman on the edge of town, or peeling yams, helped block out, or at least dull, some of the horrors they saw daily.

Skimming dead weevils from the top of the huge cooking pot of chlorinated water, Annie reconsidered for a moment the benefits and comforts of nursing at Concord—the 113th AGH where she, Verna and Flo had been based on their return from Singapore.

She swirled more water in the pot, dug her hands into the rice and waited for errant weevils with their trident-like heads to float up. She'd be fine with a few. Added protein. But the cook had been appalled and so Annie continued to skim, flicking an occasional weevil from under a fingernail. At least rice added something to the tinned and dehydrated food.

Durand Airfield, named in honour of an MIA pilot, but more commonly known as 17 Mile Camp due to its distance from the capital, Port Moresby, became their new home. Low hills around the camp housed anti-aircraft gun pits made up of 55-gallon drums, with many of the structures being built on gravel from a nearby quarry. Alongside the camp and hospital ran a single runway. Built by the Americans in March, it ended at the crocodile-filled Waigani swamp—a snapping incentive to keep pilots on their wings as they took off and landed.

A bout of dysentery left Annie feeling tired and tetchy. She comforted herself as she jogged down the hill to the latrines, with the thought that at least they weren't under constant bombardment as they had been in Singapore. Or facing wave after wave of Japanese planes bombing and strafing them on board the Empire Star.

"Damn it," Annie muttered, hefting a heavy oxygen cylinder, "will it never stop raining?" She lifted a mud-caked shoe and looked along the tent ward. It didn't take long for the trenches around the wards and mess tents to fill with water, then pool in other low-lying spots.

"I heard they're bringing more gravel, Sister." A patient on the nearest cot, his shattered leg raised on a pulley, his face creased with pain, told her hoarsely.

"Hope you're right, Soldier. Would you like a cuppa?"

He nodded, and Annie lifted the curtain separating the ward from a make-shift kitchenette where a Soyer stove and a kettle, teapot and tin mugs saw constant use. Another constant being the attempt to keep rats at bay.

"I heard that too," Verna said as she joined Annie, "they'll jolly well have to if we need to put stretchers under the beds, again."

Their voices low, Annie said, "I heard from Flo that patient numbers are up. Not quite as bad as during the battle along the Kokoda Trail, but close."

Verna nodded. "If we didn't have so many sick, on top of the injured, it would help."

"Yeah, it's a cocktail of nasties. Scrub typhus, malaria and blackwater fever." Annie tipped boiling water into the teapot and waited for the tea to seep. It had taken all her training not to gag when she'd seen a patient pee black urine as she'd held a urinal for a man with bandaged stumps where his hands had been. The soldier had died later that night and Annie couldn't help feeling relief. For him, for his family, although she doubted they'd feel that way, at first.

She shook her head and shuddered.

"Right," she poured tea into a mug, stirred in sugar, and handed it to Verna, "for the bloke on the other side of the flap, with my compliments."

She watched her friend, still reeling from Ruth's death, prop the soldier up to drink. Ernie, Ruth, Iris, how many more? Although they had heard nothing definitive about their friend, and still harboured hopes that she had been taken prisoner and not killed whilst on board the Vyner Brooke.

Nights, particularly moonlit ones, drew the threat of air raids. Life became a blur of bandages, blood, shattered bones and lives as well as diseases. Days followed days, sometimes relieved by a giggle. Like when the nurses had received their new army attire to replace the grey cotton dress. Or some of it. Now a skirt and safari jacket could be worn, with the practical addition of pockets, lots of pockets. Better still were the baggy drill slacks that could be worn instead of the skirt, with brown boots, and modified puttees. Khaki boiler suits, boots and gaiters were an alternative. Black shoulder tabs showed their rank. Whatever attire chosen, long gaiters had to be worn in the evening as some protection against voracious mosquitoes.

Annie pinned her treasured fob watch to the jungle uniform and twirled. "Pretty classy, eh? Finally someone has listened. No more damn grey dresses and stockings in this mud."

"But only in the evenings." Flo primped her hair and posed like a pin up. "Or veils, anytime!"

Verna wiggled her ankle encased in a tight gaiter. "I defy creepies to get through these."

—

The pincer movement to isolate Rabaul continued. Still under enemy control and the base for a large enemy naval fleet on the northern edge of New Britain, the town gave the Japanese command of shipping in the southwest Pacific, hampering General MacArthur's push to regain the Philippines. It had been in Rabaul that six Australian nurses, along with over 200 civilians, had been interned, some of whom lost their lives as they were being transported to China by the Japanese on the unmarked Montevideo Maru, and were torpedoed by the USS Sturgeon. Forty-five nurses from the mission of Daughters of Mary Immaculate or FMI refused to renounce their faith and were interned at Ramale.

Despite military successes and the Japanese in retreat, the terrain over which the Australians fought was not suitable for Casualty Clearing Stations and so Jungle Field Ambulances ministered to the immediate needs of those injured, before moving them to the hospitals in Port Moresby.

Sitting on cane chairs clustered around the entrance to their tent one afternoon, cigarettes and chatter easing the day's busy-ness, the nurses watched the stray puppies they had adopted frolic in the shade. The natives who assisted with orderly duties around the hospital had endeared themselves to the nurses by planting hibiscus, bougainvillea and bananas around their quarters, offering splashes of colour in the drab confines of camp.

"Did you see that convoy of Fuzzy Wuzzy Angels arrive this morning?" Verna asked. "I don't know how they do it. Carrying stretchers down the mountains, through swamps. Sometimes shot at. They're bloody marvellous."

Flo nodded. "Yeah, I did." She rubbed her eyes. "We had one who wouldn't let us look at a nasty gash on his leg until we'd seen to the bloke he'd carried in."

"What happened?" Annie asked, rubbing her tired calves.

"He got stitched up, slugged a gallon of water and headed back up the trail for the next batch."

"Why don't the locals seem to get malaria as much as our chaps?"

Annie shook her head. "I don't know. Perhaps they've built up an immunity. I wonder if the betel nuts they chew are a natural repellent to the mossies." She frowned. "You know, right now, we've got more medical cases than battle casualties. Mostly malaria."

"Well, I'm sure some bright spark somewhere is trying to figure it out." Verna stretched the kinks out of her neck.

"I could do with a gin and tonic," Annie said, with a sigh. "Purely for the quinine, of course!"

"Considering New Guinea is dry, there's not much chance of that," said Flo.

"Although," Verna said, "one of the lads on the ward told me you can make a home brew from oranges hung over alcohol. Sounds lethal."

"Not to mention the problem of getting oranges." Annie sighed. "Even though the Red Cross are doing a great job with provisions."

Flo petted one of the puppies. "Did you hear about the brew the radiology department have made? One of the AAMWS girls told me."

"I heard they nearly got caught by the CO." Verna cackled. "He was taking some bigwig around. But one of the lads switched on the warning light, then said film was being developed so they couldn't enter."

Idle chit chat lulled them into relaxation until Annie felt Verna kick her shoe. "What?"

"There's someone heading our way."

"Matron?" Annie asked, sitting up straighter.

"Nope. Looks like a bloke."

Flo groaned "Argh, I bet it's an orderly." She started to rise. "No rest for the wicked!"

"Sit down." Laughter trickled around Verna's words. "He's white. It looks remarkably like a doctor you might know, ducks."

Annie spun around, then leapt to her feet, tiredness gone in an instant. Chuckles followed her fast walk.

"G'day, Annie."

They stood inches apart.

"I didn't know." She wanted to throw herself into his arms.

"I didn't either."

"What happened to Darwin?"

"The men in charge decided they needed me here."

"I need you here." Annie blushed. "I mean, I'm glad you're here."

Bill reached for her hand, "I'm glad too." His grip tightened as she tried to pull away. "Matron's in the medical ward." The gap between his front teeth showed in a childish grin. "Are you done for the day?"

Annie nodded.

"Come on, let's go for a walk. I've got …" he glanced at his watch, "… about fifteen minutes."

Their arms touching through the khaki, they moved back along the quarters to a path used by native orderlies that lead to the edge of 17 Mile

Camp. As they disappeared into the bush, Bill took Annie's hand and drew her behind a squat sago palm. His arms tightened as his lips bent to hers.

"I have wanted to do that since you left Kingaroy."

"Our second kiss," Annie spoke to his mouth.

"Here's the third!" Bill's laugh breathed into her. "Oh, Annie, if there's one good thing about this bloody war, it's you."

Annie, her eyes shining and hair unpinned, wanted to melt into him. "You're not so bad yourself, Major." Their soft laughter cocooned them for a moment before Bill sighed. "I threw my kitbag on the floor and came to find you, but I've got to report back now."

"Yup, I know." Annie reached up and kissed him lightly. "Come on." They returned along the path and separated by the far end of the nurse's tents. "Maybe see you tomorrow."

Bill squeezed her hand, "Sleep tight, Annie."

Her heart dancing, Annie watched him go. So this is what love felt like.

"Well, well, Lieutenant Cutler."

Annie, jolted from her daydreams, laughed at Flo peering through the fly screens.

"Bill's back."

"Oh, really? None of us noticed."

"I feel like dancing." Annie did a jig and shimmy.

"Who wants to dance?" Verna's face appeared too.

"Our girl out there! The one with the tawny face?"

Annie couldn't stop smiling. "Like yours isn't yellow as well." She'd given up worrying about her colour, caused by the Atebrin they took every day for malaria. "And he likes me, too."

"Oh, really?" repeated Flo, "we didn't notice that either."

"Shut up, both of you." Delight oozed around her words.

"Come on, Twinkle-toes, tomorrow will be here soon enough."

"Technically, not." Annie heard Verna correct Flo, then a yelp as one of them, she couldn't tell which, had obviously jabbed a rib. Joy gurgled through her as she lay in the cot and thought about Major Bill Townsend before she drifted off, exhaustion trumping love.

—

The boom woke Annie. It didn't sound like the usual crump of a bomb or gunfire from the hillside, or even the growl of planes taking off and landing. It seemed splintered, a series of blasts followed by an acrid smell.

A glow at the far end of the camp indicated dawn, and she checked her watch. Just after four. It wouldn't be sunrise for another couple of hours. Groping for her uniform, Annie nudged Verna in the cot next to her. "Wake up, ducks, I think something's happened. Come on, we might be needed. Don't forget your gas mask."

They met Flo and a couple of the other girls as they hurried to the wards. Jeeps, trucks and men bumped along the dirt tracks, lights flashed, and at the end of the runway an inferno gave a clue as to what had happened. "Is it an air raid?

Annie squinted into the distance then up to the sky. "Don't think so. And no sirens."

"Looks to me like a plane didn't make it," Verna said.

"A Yank Liberator has ploughed onto a convoy of trucks after clipping the trees," a soldier said, as he rushed past.

"Landing or taking off?" called Annie.

"Taking off," he shouted over his shoulder. "All those bloody bombs loaded. Fully fuelled."

"Oh, my God, Verna," Annie shuddered, "burns."

The day evolved into a haze of agonized screams, skin peeling off as they snipped scorched clothes away and, strangely to Annie, the smell of charcoal from burnt flesh. Part of her wished she was back on the medical ward. Word soon filtered through that all eleven American air crew on board had perished, as had sixty men from the Australian 2/33rd Infantry Battalion waiting in trucks for air transfers across the Owen Stanley range in a bid to recapture Lae on the northern coast. Ninety others filled the wards.

"I don't know what hell is like, but this must be close." Annie gulped in humid, sulphurous air as she grabbed a couple of minutes to compose herself. She and Florence shared a cigarette out the back of the ward. Anything to get rid of the stench of burning flesh, which the breeze did little to disperse. She'd seen Bill's back as he disappeared into surgery and could imagine his despair.

"Those poor blokes." Flo's hand shook. "Dead in an instant."

"They probably wouldn't have known anything." Annie nodded to the ward, "It's the ones in there who'll be living with it. Some for the rest of their lives."

The long day ended as Annie, Flo and Verna grabbed a late tea in the mess. Like Chinese whispers, murmurs spread along the trestle tables of exhausted nurses, medics and orderlies.

"What the hell?" Annie asked. "Court-martialled?"

"Only if we speak."

"But, Verna, what about the families? Won't they be told what happened?"

"Doubt it." Flo stirred her tea violently. "A telegram. Killed in action."

"That's not right." Annie saw Bill at the far end of the mess, his face not grey with fatigue, but red with anger. "Shall I ask him?"

For once her friends did not respond with teasing words. Flo nodded, then said, "But, Annie, don't make it difficult for him. He might not be allowed to say anything."

"I know." She glanced around the tent, wondering what Matron would say if she saw her approaching the doctor. She shrugged. After today, and now this edict being thrust on them, she didn't care.

"G'day," she stopped herself from massaging his tense shoulders. "You alright?"

A tired smile tweaked the corners of Bill's mouth but did not reach his eyes. "No, not really, love." His voice low, angry, detracted from the endearment.

"Can you talk?" Annie fussed with the teapot.

"Not really," repeated Bill, his jaw tight. He sighed, and with a light touch to the small of her back he urged her towards a table at the far end of the mess. Cicadas had begun warming up for their evening chorale. Humidity hung in soggy sworls.

"Why?" The word burst from Annie, although she kept her voice quiet.

"General MacArthur doesn't think it will go down well. You know, a US plane killing sixty Aussie boys. Not to mention his own crew. So many injured. More will undoubtedly die from their burns. Christ, I've never seen anything like it." He rubbed the peppery stubble on his chin. "Bad for morale, apparently."

"Not even the families." Annie couldn't keep indignation from her voice. Not knowing kept the pain alive. Ernest flew into her mind. Had his death been a cover-up too?

"Not even." Bill gulped his tea. "Just one more thing to keep hidden."

"What about the survivors?" Annie asked. "I mean the blokes who saw their mates alight? What about them?"

"Oh, Annie, is that any different to seeing them blown to pieces?" He rubbed his eyes. "There are going to be a lot of things buried deep after this bloody war. Not only the scars of battle. But murder. Rape."

Annie's thoughts flew to the nurses in Hong Kong. "So, this is just one more?"

"'Fraid so, love."

"But how can the pilot be blamed? He probably wasn't more than a kid. Night flying. There's been so much rain. Lumbering plane."

"I know, Annie." He paused, then lowered his voice even more. "The question that should be asked is why was a battalion waiting in trucks at the end of the runway?" Bill's fingers brushed her hand as he stood. "Right, I've got to go back to surgery. You get some sleep."

Chapter 11
Tides of War

With the success of the Australian and American forces at Nassau Bay and further along the coast at Salamaua, Operation Postern was launched to retake Lae—the same operation in which the US Liberator had crashed at 17 Mile Camp. Amphibious landing forces east of Lae met little resistance, but Japanese bombers killed over a hundred Allied naval and army personnel. And nature played against them. Lashing rains had swollen the fast-flowing Busu River. Lack of heavy equipment stopped their advance across the wide and raging torrent. That, and, on the opposite side, a bank full of Japanese soldiers hidden in the reeds.

Next, the 503rd American Parachute Regiment, along with gun crews from the Australian 2/4th—mostly soldiers who had only received a crash course in jumping—landed at Nadzab Airfield along with 25-pounder artillery pieces, cut down for transportation. After rebuilding them, and fierce fighting in which more than three hundred Japanese soldiers lost their lives, Allied Forces entered Lae on 15 September 1943.

Annie wondered if they would be sent to Lae next, where the town was being transformed into two bases—Australian and American.

"Nips running, Shista." Annie smiled down at the lad whose words struggled to find air from the wound that had taken half his face. "'Eard." He winced as Annie helped him sit. "From m'mate."

"Best news so far today." She pulled a stool closer to the cot and sat down. "And I've got a snippet for you, Soldier," she watched his one eye blink rapidly. "You're going home. Next hospital ship out."

A tear leaked down his undamaged cheek as he clutched her hand. "No' ready."

Annie held the straw in a mug for him, as he tried to sip the lukewarm tea without dribbling. "Well, not home home, but back to Australia. I'm guessing to Concord for rehab." Annie remembered his name. "Where are you from, Mike?"

She waited for him to move his tongue around the word.

"Bourke."

"That might be a bit far for a family visit, but it's closer than here. You'll be home in no time."

Another tear slid out of his blinking eye as he shook his head and repeated, "No' ready." His good hand flailed at where his eye and cheek had been.

A lump caught in her throat. Razor blades were in short supply and so the healthy side of his face had not been shaved for a few days but even so he looked young. "They can do amazing things, Mike, with plastic surgery."

"Neva get girl." He looked her in the eye. "Like you."

"Think I'm a bit old for you, ducks." Annie tried to make him smile. "I'll let you in on a secret. I'll be thirty soon."

"Bewful to me." He closed his eye and turned his head.

Heavy-hearted, Annie watched him a few moments, then quietly stood and took the mug away. She checked his notes. Nineteen.

—

The news that Allied forces had retaken the Solomon Islands lightened the atmosphere around 17 Mile Camp, although casualties still poured in. The Red Cross arranged dances and days out. Entertainers arrived to lift everyone's spirits, sometimes with joint concerts for both Australian and American troops. The nurses and orderlies held their collective breath, none more than Annie, when word purred along the wards that the Australian star, Gladys Moncrieff, would be singing.

"I bet I'm on duty."

"I'll swap with you, ducks," Verna said.

"You're a darling, but no. Can you imagine what Matron would say?"

"Not even worth the risk for a dance with your dashing doctor?" Flo chimed in.

"Not even," replied Annie with a laugh. "Anyway, he'll probably be on duty too."

"Bet he'd wangle something if it meant dancing with you." Verna sounded wistful.

Annie gave her a hug. "Well, it might be you and me and Flo, dancing together!"

"Yeah. Wonder what it'll be like to be normal again?"

"As opposed to being crazy?" Flo tried to lift Verna's spirits.

"Oh, you know, do normal things. Wearing civvies would be a good start. I'm sick of bloody uniforms."

"Do you realise," Annie said, "Bill has never seen me out of uniform?"

Her friends burst of laughter took her by surprise. "What?" She replayed her words, a giggle escaping. "Oh, yes. Well, that too!"

"God, we'll die virgins." Verna lit a ciggie and watched the smoke drift into the night.

"Speak for yourself!"

"Flo! Really? When?"

"Shhh, and don't you mean who?"

Annie laughed. "That too!"

"Not saying." And with that Flo, with a sashay, sauntered back to the medical ward.

Annie watched her go, then turned to Verna. "It feels good to laugh, ducky. You haven't done much of it since Ruth died." She held up her hand, "No, let me finish." Annie paused. "I've been worried about you. And Flo. Believe me, I know the signs. I wanted to either kick out or curl up and die too, when we heard about Ernest." She put her arm around Verna.

"I was doing fine. Well, not fine, but okay." Verna sniffed. "But I got a letter from Mum the other day. She didn't say anything specific but hinted, you know, between the lines, that Dad isn't doing too well."

"Oh, Verna, is he ill?" Annie thought of the kind, twinkly eyed man retreating to his garden study when the chaos of six daughters got too much to bear.

"No. But the stuffing's gone out of him." Verna wiped her eyes. "As if, Mum said, he hadn't been able to protect his chicks. That's what he used to call us, when we were little."

"It'll take time. I doubt we'll ever, any of us, be the same again but, ducks, we've got to go on."

"Yeah, I know. Most of the time I'm alright. I suppose I'm envious of you. And Bill." Verna hurried on. "Not jealous, Annie, just really pleased for you, both. I want some of it too."

"You'll get it!"

"Hope so." Verna's smile was wan. "Now, come on, we've got to get back."

—

An afternoon haze hovered over the rows of animated soldiers, airmen and medical personnel as they waited for the show to start. Patients on crutches, men bandaged but ambulatory, men with missing limbs all waited for the hangar doors to open.

Annie, on the edge of the crowd, turned around searching for Bill, who had promised to get away, even if only for a few moments, but she tried not to hold her breath. They had laughed the previous evening, in their stolen minutes, that they had never even had a dinner together, much less a dance. Annie, had though, seen Bill throw back his head in rollicking laughter when she relayed her words about him never seeing her out of uniform. She felt a blush creep up her neck at his words about having to do something about that.

"G'day, love. I made it." Bill's hand caressed hers. "But just for a while."

Turning her hand into his, Annie, smiled. "A while will do nicely, thank you, Major."

Cheers and catcalls erupted as the doors opened and without any words, Gladys Moncrieff started singing, as if, Annie thought later, she knew time was limited.

"Do you like opera?"

"Not the heavy stuff," replied Annie, "but this is wonderful."

"From *The Merry Widow.*" Bill turned her to him and, before she could argue, began to waltz on the spot singing quietly into her hair, "*Now or never and forever, I love you.*"

Annie, eyes shining, leant back to look up at him towering over her, "Really?" As he nodded, she relaxed into his arms. Sod Matron. "I do too," she murmured back, feeling his arms tighten.

"Nice one, Doc!"

"Good on yer, Sister."

The comments came fast as the song ended and the enthralled troops saw them. Annie didn't give a toss.

"You'll get me into trouble." She pulled away and patted her hair.

"Matron's over there, smiling away. Not in the least interested in us. But," Bill smiled down, "I do have to go now."

Annie nodded, "I know. Thank you for our first dance."

"But not our last!"

—

And then Christmas arrived, and the mess angels did the hospital proud. Sandwiches and cake on Christmas Eve set the mood, followed by a breakfast treat the next morning with comfort packages from the Red Cross. Later, tables lined the middle of each ward, sagging under mounds of fowl and vegetables, plum pudding and jelly. A celebration that fed patients, doctors, nurses and orderlies alike.

"Sister, I haven't had a real egg since I left Brissie."

Annie grinned at the boy. "You deserve it, ducks." She knew he would be shipping out soon for more surgery and rehab in Australia but marvelled at the difference to the lice-infested soldier who had arrived a week earlier, his tattered uniform barely covering his broken body. He had not wanted to be touched by any of the nurses because of his filth. She looked at the remnants of the feast and said, "Don't know how they do it, but those girls can get their hands on all sorts of things!"

Word trickled in that the tides of the war might be turning. And along with smatterings of news came more rumours. 17 Mile Camp would contract, and nurses would be transferred to Lae to support troops in their push to chase the Japanese off New Guinea once and for all.

Annie's heart sank. The chances of Bill going as well seemed slim. Luck couldn't work twice for them. They grabbed brief moments. And had one glorious day just after Christmas, the threat of separation pushed to the back of their minds, when Bill wangled a Jeep and they drove to Kirra Beach.

The road along which they bounced, little more than a dirt track with abandoned Japanese tanks pushed into the ditches, provided a sharp contrast to lazy waves lapping the long white deserted beach. Annie had heard from one of the AAWMS girls that they had been promised a beach hut sometime, but as everyone knew 'sometime' could mean anytime, or never.

Self-conscious in her spotted and ruched navy and white halter necked cozzie, Annie felt her colour rise when she emerged from behind some scrub to feel Bill's gaze on her. She ran through the shallows and dived under the clear waters to rise and see Bill powering past her. She watched, envying his sure stroke, scanning the horizon for sharks. She wondered if he surfed. She giggled. Not in Glen Innes! Perhaps when he trained in Sydney. So much she didn't know about him. But did it matter? She floated on her back, never out of standing depth, daydreaming.

A splash and hands encircling her waist brought her back.

"Your legs look even longer in the water," Bill said, nuzzling her neck.

After a picnic on the beach, washed down with hot tea from the thermos Annie had borrowed from the mess, they wandered along the shoreline and past the point. Bill pulled the towel from around his neck and dropped it onto the sand, then drew her into his arms, kissing her neck and breasts, as he eased them both to the ground. Annie had never felt so alive.

Walking back, hand in hand, from the far end of the beach, Bill laughed and said, "Well, at least now I've seen you out of uniform!"

—

The euphoria of their day together turned to dismay as the rumours became real. Having been in New Guinea for twelve months, although technically they were on the Papuan side of the island, many of the nurses were to be relieved and sent back to Australia on leave.

Annie tried to keep her tears in check. Her father's words floated up from the basin. The ones he spoke when Ma died. "Stop your crying, girl. Never helps anything." She sniffed and splashed more tepid water on her face.

"You right, ducks?" She felt Verna's hand on her shoulder.

Annie shook her head. "Nope."

"You've got it bad. I've never heard you admit to anything."

"I hate this bloody war."

"Don't we all?" Verna handed her a towel. "Come on, mop up. One more shift. Keep busy. A quick goodbye to the major and then you can cry on the ship."

"Then what?" Annie felt more tears coming. "Home? I don't think so."

"Where's Joe at the moment?"

"Don't know. His last letter arrived months ago, and it was pretty cagey."

"Well, maybe he'll be in Sydney. And, Annie, you do know you can always stay with us at Coogee. Mum and Dad would love it. You know them—the more in the house the better."

"Thanks, Verna, but you need some time to yourselves, although I might well show up on your doorstep." Annie sighed. "I know I have to go home, but just for a night, then I'll stay with Auntie May."

Annie combed her hair, ignoring the sliver of mirror above the basin. She didn't need to see bloodshot, puffy eyes. She gave a lopsided smile to Verna. "If I hadn't fallen in love, I'd be cock-a-hoop."

Chapter 12

Across the Owen Stanleys, January 1944

Time on her father's property outside Armidale had been everything Annie had expected. She wondered when she'd stopped thinking of it as home. Her father's initial pat on the back soon dissolved into a sullen silence. At his insistence, one night had turned into three, although Annie didn't understand why. Surly comments deflected her every word or action. Fed up, Annie, had joined Helen, the Land Girl, who had stayed on to help, and a new recruit, Sally, in their cottage on her last night; Ian finally having allowed them to move from the shearer's sheds. They had talked and laughed long after sunset and, impressed, Annie had admired the girls' ability to shrug off Ian's rude indifference. Too late for her. She hadn't even told him about Bill.

"G'day, darl," Auntie May's greeting never changed. Nor the scent of fresh bread and lavender that clung to her like a warm quilt.

Annie melted into her wide arms.

"Whoa, darl, what's happened?" May lead her into the kitchen which opened onto the back porch overlooking her rose-filled garden, nurtured through the hottest summers with tender care. Putting the kettle on, she asked, "It's not Joe, is it?"

When Annie shook her head, she added, "Or your father, the miserable old sod?" That at least evoked a smile, but she shook her head again.

"It is a man though, isn't it?" She poured water into the pot. "What you need is a cup of tea, and a piece of Victoria sponge, although it's not very spongey—the bloody chooks have stopped laying—so it's made with powdered muck." Auntie May picked up the cake. "You bring the teapot. Cups are out there already." She settled herself on the sofa and patted the space next to her. "Righto, darl, start talking."

The words, jumbled at first, flew out along with tears.

"It's so silly." Annie gulped, "I mean, I hardly know the man." She picked up the cup Auntie May had refilled and blew. "You know what he does? When he finishes a night shift?" Annie didn't wait for an answer. "He puts a hibiscus on my window sill so I see something beautiful every morning." She touched her lips. "Before the sadness and gore of the wards."

May stayed quiet until Annie's sobs subsided and only hiccups remained. "Sounds like he knows you pretty well." She licked her finger and picked up crumbs from the plate. "Darl, I have to ask, are you having a baby?"

Annie blushed. "No, Auntie May, I'm not."

"But you have lain down with him?"

May smiled at Annie's blushing nod. "Alright then. No complications. Baby or a married man. That's good."

"Doesn't feel it." Annie sipped her tea. "I don't know when I'll see him again."

"Good grief, darl, this must be love. I've never seen you so down on a maybe."

"What do you mean maybe?"

"Maybe you'll see him in New Guinea again. Maybe you won't. Maybe he will be sent to Lae. Maybe he won't. Maybe you'll have to wait until the end of the war. Lots of maybes, Annie, but from what you've said there's no question about if you see him again. You love each other. That's all that matters." Auntie May poured another cup of tea.

"I didn't want to love anybody. Not in wartime. Not after Ernie."

"Oh, Annie, it doesn't work like that. Love whacks you around the head like a breaker dumping you in the surf." She hugged Annie. "You come up spluttering, wondering what hit you."

"But war changes everything."

"Of course it does. But you can't time these things, darl." She nudged Annie in the ribs and winked. "It's not like doing your ward rounds on the clock."

Annie gave a watery smile. "What if something happens?"

"What if it doesn't, Annie?" May touched a rose petal. "You can't waste your life on what ifs. You grab every moment of happiness you can. Don't give a hoot about what people say. Just grab life, Annie. It's too damn short for worrying about what ifs."

May stood, tipping Pearl off her lap. "Righto, lecture over. I think it might be time for something stronger."

Annie picked up the tray and followed her aunt into the kitchen, then watched her take down a bottle of whisky and pour two slugs.

"It's cooling down. We'll sit in here. Now," she asked with a grin, "is there anything wrong with this man?"

With a laugh, Annie said, "Not exactly wrong, but he has a dancing eyebrow."

"A what?"

"His left eyebrow has a mind of its own. When he laughs, it does a jig."

"Thank God," she tapped her glass against Annie's, "an imperfection!"

Annie spluttered over her drink. "No, more a quirk! Did I mention he knows James? In a roundabout kind of way, that makes it seem as if he almost knows Ernie." She paused. "That sounds a bit crazy, doesn't it?"

"Not really. Just a woman in love. I'll have to get an unbiased report from Joe, or, better yet, meet him myself."

"You will, Auntie May. As soon as we're in Australia together, you'll be the first." Annie stroked Pearl, now sitting on her lap.

"In all that rush of words you didn't say where Bill is from."

"Glen Innes."

"Well, at least he's sort of local. Not about to whisk you off to the other side of Australia or, God forbid, to Victoria."

Sidetracked for a moment, Annie asked, "What's wrong with Victoria?"

"Snobs!"

"An entire state labelled in a word. You do know you're a bit mad, don't you?"

May nodded with a satisfied grin. "That's why you children love me, and your father doesn't."

"You know, I never understood what Ma saw in him."

"As a young man he was beautiful. Can you call a man beautiful? Dunno! But he was. And you know your Ma was a looker. They made a stunning couple. She tried so hard to be everything. But for some reason that wasn't enough. She nearly always agreed with him."

"Apart from allowing him to walk over us," said Annie.

"She did love him, Annie, but maybe that was the issue. Her time diluted by you kids."

"Then why have any?"

"Well, darl, that isn't always an exact science, is it?"

"Auntie May," Annie paused then blurted, "why didn't you marry? You'd have been a wonderful mother, just like Ma."

"Never met 'my' Bill, darl, but I had some fun looking." Her laugh felt like a hug. "And I wasn't prepared to settle for less."

—

After a week in Sydney with Verna and her family, the girls met up with Flo and reported back to the AGH at Yaralla. The expected month or so evaporated and they, with the rest of the 2/7th, caught the troop train back to Townsville, this time headed to Lae. Their ship, the newly repaired SS Ormiston, had been one of four ships torpedoed by a Japanese submarine off the coast of Coffs Harbour in a six-week period the year before.

With a letter from Joe waiting for Annie at Concord, revealing very little, and no letter from Bill, she clung to Auntie May's words about 'maybes' not 'ifs'.

"For God's sake, Annie," said Flo, "we're in the middle of a bloody war. Mail is unreliable. And, lovey, we've only been gone a few weeks."

"A letter could be following you around for the next year," added Verna, leaning over the rail and watching the Australian coastline slide past. "You feeling alright, apart from Bill, I mean?"

Flo studied Annie. "Yeah, you do look a bit peaky."

"It's because we're not being bombed or strafed," Verna said.

"Why," asked Annie, "am I the only one who only gets seasick in times of calm?"

"'Cos you've got nothing else to think about, ducks," Flo replied with glee. "See, you've even stopped thinking about that doctor fellow, what's his name, Verna?"

"Oh, shut up, both of you! I don't know why I like you!"

Despite the waters between Australia, New Guinea and the Solomon Islands now being free of Japanese vessels, tension heightened as they neared the Huon Gulf on the northern coast where they would disembark onto landing barges. Japan still held Rabaul on New Britain and patrolled the waters along the northwestern part of the New Guinea coastline.

"If I never see a ship again, it will be too soon."

"You might be 'ere a while then, Sister," said a rating, steadying her as she slid onto the barge, then stood, squashed in rows with the others as they surfed towards Lae.

They had little time to get used to their new, rapidly built hospital on the banks of the Busu River before the first sixty patients arrived. Within a couple of weeks, the numbers had risen to over a thousand.

Not only did they nurse Australians and natives in tent wards, they opened one for a group of Sikh POWs who had been abandoned by the Japanese on one of the Admiralty Islands, north of New Guinea.

"There was uproar in the Sikh tent this morning!" Flo fluffed her hair.

"What happened?"

"An orderly tried to shave a chap's leg to clean an infected wound."

"And?" Annie asked, yawning.

"Don't really understand. But we think cutting hair might be taboo. 'Cos they've all got long hair and beards. And," Flo added, "they wear steel bangles."

"It's interesting, isn't it?" Annie searched for the right words. "We're taught all the basics, but we assume all patients are the same. You know, about customs, beliefs about dying, and stuff like that. But I bet each religion is different.

Flo nodded. "I wonder if the padres know them all?"

"Dunno, but that's my brain power totally depleted now. I've got to sleep."

—

Once again, there proved to be little time to think as wards became full to overflowing with predominantly medical patients. The worst cases jolted out to Nadzab Airfield in trucks to be flown to Port Moresby, then down to Australia on hospital ships.

Scrub typhus continued to be the most serious of the medical ailments, and Annie came to loathe seeing soldiers brought in covered in lice and chigger bites, knowing that, even with the arrival of penicillin, complications with organs would mean many could not be saved.

Malaria and dengue played havoc with the troops and nurses. Mosquitoes had free rein in their quarters and the mess, which were native huts with palm leaf rooves that creaked and sawed in any breeze, surrounded by red hibiscus and orange cannas like the parakeets from home.

"Do you know about the only thing that made my father laugh was me looking yellow?" Annie spread her hands out in front of her.

"He's a real charmer, your dad!" Verna said.

"Remind me, when this is all over, never to go to the tropics again." Flo joined in. "I never want to see an Atrebin tablet again."

But taking the drug every day did not guarantee immunity.

"Oh, God, I think I've got dysentery again." Annie lay on her side and clutched her stomach.

"Have you got the trots?" Verna asked, feeling Annie's forehead and glands.

"No." She groaned. "I ache."

"Roll over, ducks." Verna palpated her friend's liver. "I'm betting you've got dengue. You're burning up, too. I'll be back in a minute."

Annie closed her eyes to the pain shooting through her joints. She groaned as she felt the bed sink as Verna sat down to help her. "Up you sit, and drink this." Annie took the tepid tea with a grimace. "You know you've got to keep the liquids up."

"Bucket!" Annie thrust the cup into Verna's hand and bent over the side of bed. "I'm going to upchuck."

Verna held her head, and waited until Annie finished, wiped her face and gave her a sip of water, then said, "I'm going to get Matron."

It took four days of feverish misery, during which tracer fire streaked across her vision like the strafing from Japanese planes aboard the Empire Star. Sapping humidity and cold sweats drenched her, and tears seeped in silence down her hollowed cheeks.

From a distance Annie heard Verna and Flo. A doctor came, and Matron. But distinguishing their voices took too much effort. And her head ached. Her elbows and ankles throbbed.

"You must drink, lovey." Verna's face came into focus, as she held a glass of water for her. "You're vomiting so much, you can't get dehydrated. You know that, Annie."

Tears spilled again. "If I drink, I have to pee, and it hurts to move."

"Don't care, ducks," Flo chimed in. "Come on, drink up."

Another week passed before the joint pain and lassitude eased. Flo had borrowed an Agatha Christie mystery from the Red Cross for her to read, but the words blurred and hurt Annie's eyes, and so her mind roamed. To Bill, mainly. And Ernie and Joe. Her father made an appearance in a dream. As Annie struggled to wakefulness, she felt a warm surge. He had seemed to care.

Flo's face appeared around the door. "Well, you're looking a bit better. Not gorgeous, but getting there!"

Verna pushed in behind her. "You had us worried. Especially with the bruising, and bleeding from your gums. Don't scare us again, alright? We have enough drama without you adding to it." Her words were tempered with a hug. "Bloody hell, Annie," she looked out to the jungle beyond, tears in her eyes, "we thought it might be haemorrhagic dengue."

It took another week before Matron felt she was well enough to return to the wards, but much longer for her appetite both for food and life to return.

The latter was helped by a letter from Bill, whose pages were in fear of crinkling from the constant reading. He too had been sent back to Australia, but expected to return to New Guinea at some stage. He loved her. Annie's world turned rosy.

"Did you hear," she tittered, "what Matron said to the colonel when he told her we had to take our clothes line down because it made the camp look like a brothel?"

"What?" asked Flo, looking up at bras and knickers hanging between the trees at the back of their tent.

"That, not having visited such an establishment, she would take his word for it."

It felt good to laugh

Then the three, along with another six nurses, moved again. This time to Finschhafen.

—

The recapture of Finschhafen on the coast west of Lae in 1943 had severely damaged Japanese supply lines, and allowed the Allies to develop their own strategic naval and aircraft base. From there, American and Australian troops, planes and ships would push the Japanese further along the northern coast and down from the Finisterre Range towards Madang, hoping eventually the town would become a supply depot during the fight for Rabaul.

In the meantime, a Casualty Clearing Station was to be established to accept patients at Finschhafen, which would cut the time for those fighting in the grim, hostile mountains that created the spine of New Guinea. Disease still outnumbered battle casualties, and the wards filled with men writhing in pain from mosquito-borne illnesses, chigger bites, dysentery and exhaustion.

"I don't know how they do it," Annie said during a brief lull. She lit a cigarette, the first since her bout of dengue.

"Who?" asked Verna, sitting on the steps to the mess hut.

"The Fuzzy Wuzzies. Their stoicism and strength is incredible."

"You know some of the natives supported the Japs?"

"Wouldn't you, if they threatened your village, or offered you riches?"

"Yeah, I suppose so." Verna flicked an ant off her leg. "One bloke told me that one of the villages they slithered into had been torched. The locals had heard the Japs approaching and disappeared into the bush. But their homes and crops were still burnt."

"And they haven't got much to start with. What happened?"

"He said they just started rebuilding."

"Like I said, stoic!" Annie smiled at a memory. "One of them came in, a soldier over his shoulder, nothing on but a lap lap and a hibiscus stuck in his hair. It just seemed so incongruous. Most speak a bit of English but I wish I could say more."

"What, more than adding 'em' to every word?" Verna stretched as she stood. "I know what you mean, though."

Annie stubbed out her cigarette. "Righto, work calls. I'll catch you later."

Back on the surgical ward, Annie focused on a soldier whose appendix had ruptured on the trail. His life teetered despite having had immediate surgery on his arrival. Checking his pulse, she failed to see someone approaching.

"G'day, Annie. Up for some tennis?"

Annie looked up, confused. "Oh, my God, James, sorry, I mean, Doctor, Major, whatever you are!" She laid the lad's hand back down by his side and stood, wanting to hug her old friend. "I had no idea you were in New Guinea."

James grinned. "Gracie told me you were up here somewhere, and I wondered if I'd bump into you."

His voice brought back memories of summers spent on the tennis courts, or at picnics they all had together at Dangar Falls. And of Ernest. Even then Gracie had been precious. Not wanting to get her hair wet. Annie shook her head. Dim, but kind. Maybe that's why Ernie had fallen for her. She glanced around then touched James' hand. "It's great to see you."

"You too, Annie May Cutler." James's use of her full name made her laugh. "I'm on my way to the medical ward but someone mentioned your name, so I had to swing by. Let's talk later. At the mess?"

"Righto. It'll be fun to catch up." She watched him stride down the aisle with a smile.

"That your beau?" The voice came from the cot on the other side of the ward. A soldier, bored and itching to go back to the jungle, his wound almost healed. "'E's too short for you!"

Annie laughed and shook her head. "Just a friend from home, Soldier!" Turning back to her patient, Annie felt a pang of guilt. James wasn't the doctor she wanted to see.

Chapter 13
Japanese Retreat, 1944

With American and Australian sappers building the camp, Finschhafen became a busy place, noisy with trucks and planes. Annie enjoyed meeting some of the American army nurses at a tea party one afternoon where, still in uniform, they sat in camp chairs and drank from tin mugs.

"You know what I'm most sick of?" Before Annie could respond, the girl from Texas continued, "Not living in a tent—that's okay. It's washing my underwear in my tin hat!"

After the laughter died down, Verna said, "At least we've got steady power here."

Stories were swapped but, Flo noted later, horrors seen or experienced did not make up any of the talk. "It's as if …" she said, later, "… as if, if we don't talk about horrible things, they didn't really happen."

"That's self-preservation."

"But, Annie, don't you think all those hidden thoughts will fester, and boil up, perhaps years later?"

"I dunno. I suppose we'll find out."

"We should know already. Look at all the men who came back from the First World War. Mum said my Uncle Charlie hardly spoke at all, never married, but before he went to war, he had been the joker of the family."

"I used to wonder if that's why my father is such a sod," Annie said, "but I don't think so. Auntie May thinks it's because he resented sharing Ma with us. Joe is six years younger than me, and even though he's as golden a boy as you could want, nothing is ever enough. And Ernie. He just accepted he'd take over the property. No one ever asked him if that's what he really wanted. Then he was killed." Annie looked at the tip of her glowing cigarette. It had taken months for the family to learn where it had happened, even then details had been sparse. His infantry battalion, the 2/3rd, had been ordered to breach Tobruk, the Italian naval outpost surrounded by concrete walls, an inner anti-tank ditch, barbed wire and booby traps. And they had. The battalion had then advanced west, attacking defence posts along the way. What they didn't know was whether Ernie had fallen that first morning, on 20th January, or later. Perhaps they never would. Annie shook her head, suppressing images she didn't want to imagine: of her brother—broken, dead.

Flo broke the short silence. "You know what I want to do, when this is over?"

"What?" asked Verna, stitching a button back onto her uniform.

Flo looked embarrassed. "Don't laugh."

"'Course not."

"I'd like to retrain, specialize. In psychiatry."

"Wow!" Annie rejoined the conversation and looked at Flo in surprise. "As a nurse?"

"No. I want to go to medical school. Become a doctor."

"Hell's bells, Flo. That's fantastic." Annie hugged her friend.

"You'd be great. Smart, and book smart," said Verna. "But, just to be clear, ducks, I'll never call you Doctor Taylor. I don't care how grand you get."

"Right then," said Annie, "we'd better get on and finish the war." Her light-hearted tone changed. "At least then we might find out what happened to Iris."

—

Japanese troops pulled back to Sattelberg, a sheer-sided mountain, only six miles west of Finschhafen where fierce skirmishes continued. At nearly 5,000 feet, the exhausted troops, wearing battle-torn and filthy uniforms, fought not only the Japanese, but the elements too. Wounded and sick soldiers arrived daily, carried in by native bearers pushing through bush and kunai, the lacerating razor grass.

The bearers barely rested before heading back up the mountains, two blankets cushioning their shoulders or heads, as they carried supplies back to the troops. Paid six pence a day, plus food, clothing and baccy, admiration for their tireless dedication grew.

Disquieted by the discussion with Flo and Verna about the psychiatric needs of patients, doubt nagged Annie. Had she dismissed some of her patients' faltering words and failed to listen to what was not said? Perhaps not deliberately, but in her haste to get to the next stretcher or bed, she might have.

"How are you doing, Soldier? We'll soon have you more comfortable." She started to snip the tattered and blood-stained sleeve to see the extent of his injury. As she lifted his hand, his eyes scrunched up and he began to shake. Annie laid his hand back on the bed, put the scissors down and pulled up a stool. "What is it, ducks?" She began to smooth the shaggy matted hair back from his forehead, but his good hand shot up and, with surprising force, pushed her away. Annie sat back, watching. She felt another nurse approach but before she could speak, gestured for her to leave them. She waited for the shaking to subside and the boy to open his eyes. They stared at her. Vacant at first.

His voice, when he finally spoke, came as a croak. "I found an 'and. Then a foot. Me mate, he saw another foot." Tears trickled down the soldier's dirty stubbled cheeks. He made no move to wipe them. "Hacked off, they were."

Annie swallowed a retch.

"White 'and, it was. Not native."

The boy's eyes opened then, like a log in the torrent of the Busu, his words spewed up in a hoarse rasp. "You know, Sister, we was told about the natives. Used to be cannibals. Some still are maybe. Right up in the high bush. But I reckon it was the Nips. We knew the village was a friendly. A few of their blokes are Fuzzy Wuzzies."

Annie waited.

"I can't unsee it. Them." He closed his eyes again.

She touched his shoulder and he flinched.

"Sister?"

"Yes, ducks. I'm here." Annie leant closer to hear his stuttered words.

"I, I did it."

"What?"

"No, Jesus, no." Tears spilled again. "Not the 'and an' foot. I shot meself. Right in me arm."

Annie checked no one else could hear. "Listen to me, Soldier. I'm going to clean you up, have a look at that arm, then get the doctor to see you. Let's take things one step at a time."

"I shouldn't 'ave left me mates."

"I think you've done enough for this war, ducks. Let's try and get you home."

Training took over and Annie managed to get the lad cleaned. His bullet had made a mess of his upper arm. She doubted it would ever be much use, and wondered what he'd done before the war. She called the doctor, glad to see it was James. She knew he would see the injury was self-inflicted. They had all seen enough gunshot wounds to tell.

"You're going to need surgery on this," James said. "Then, when we can, get you on a flight to Port Moresby," he continued, "from there you're going home."

A shudder ran the length of the boy's body.

Annie, seeing the soldier through to the surgery and promising to be there when he came back, made it to the back of the nurse's tent before she vomited.

One more horror to bury.

—

With the Japanese in retreat, Madang town fell with minimal resistance and allowed Australian landing craft carrying the 8th Infantry Brigade to enter the harbour. From there, the Allies moved on to secure the deepwater harbour at Alexishafen. A hazardous exercise, as the retreating Japanese had planted mines with massive bombs beneath them in wheel tracks along the old German-made road.

On 25th April—Anzac Day—1944, the 35th Infantry Battalion landed near the previously held Japanese Naval Base at Hansa Bay, two hundred miles further along the coast, where they found abandoned supply stores. Another blow to the Japanese Imperial Army.

The Huon Peninsula was now considered to be in Allied hands, and for Annie, Flo and Verna it meant another move. This time to Alexishafen. Annie wondered if she and Bill would meet up again before the war ended. Then another letter had caught her up. Another letter to be treasured.

They surfed in again on landing rafts. Palm trees minus their fronds reached into the sky; bare rafters gave little idea of what the skeletal buildings had once been; pylons from destroyed jetties rose like ghostly fingers from the churned water. And naked men.

"Oh, my," Annie gave a hoot, "what a lot of balls!"

Her comment drew a glare from the senior sister, although Annie saw a swallowed smile. "I imagine they haven't seen much water since the start of their campaign. I think we can allow them some leeway. I suggest we turn the other way."

"Not much use in that, Captain," Flo said. Her eyes on the cavorting soldiers splashing and shouting in the sea. Their noise intensifying as they saw the women.

Most of the buildings had been damaged by either Japanese or Allied bombing. Gazing at the shell of St. Michael's Cathedral, the padre told Annie that it had been the biggest in the Pacific before the war. He added, "I don't know where the Archangel is."

Annie resisted a pithy response.

The old hospital at the Catholic Mission had been cleaned and patched up. The concrete floor gave a firm base for the stretchers laid out eighteen inches apart. Tatty clothes hung from the skeleton of the building, with hessian hanging in strips to give some privacy to the patients in the dressing station.

The women were grateful for their quarters, a few feet off the ground with shutters that allowed airflow, or prevented mosquitoes entering, depending on the time of day, as well as giving some protection from marauding rodents. Again, hibiscus and bougainvillea provided spots of colour in a khaki life.

"Annie," Verna sounded unsure, "can we have a chat?"

"Bloody hell, that sounds serious." They moved outside. "When have we never talked?"

"This is serious. I think." Verna lit a cigarette, then offered one to Annie.

"Go on, what's up?"

"James."

Annie grinned. "Oh, ducks, you must think I'm blind."

"What do you mean?"

"You don't think I haven't noticed him hovering? And it sure as hell isn't for me." She laughed. "I know way too much about him for his comfort. Not to mention Bill. And not to mention James is like another brother." Ernie's face swam into focus, and Annie blinked.

"He's wonderful, Annie. I adore him."

"You goose," she hugged Verna, "I couldn't be happier."

"Flo said you wouldn't mind!"

"Well, now I do. You told her before me!" Annie couldn't hold her pout. "Have you talked weddings?"

Verna blushed and nodded.

"Oh, my God, you'll have Gracie as a sister-in-law. Isn't life odd? I thought she'd be mine. Verna Sinclair. It has a lovely ring."

Verna, her eyes sparkling, laughed and waggled her hand. "Something I haven't got yet."

"You wouldn't be able to wear it anyway."

"We're going to wait. I don't want to give up the AANS. And James doesn't want to marry before the end of the war. Said it might jinx us."

Annie laughed. "He's always been a bit goofy like that. You know he'd never step on the lines of the tennis court when we played doubles in case it cursed the game." Annie hugged Verna again. "You, the soon-to-be Mrs Sinclair, have made my day. And just so you know, even if Gracie is a bit flighty, she and his parents are lovely. No wicked mother-in-law waiting in the wings."

Verna sighed. "A pity we can't celebrate with anything stronger than tea."

"Cooeee," Flo's voice called from inside. "Is the way safe?"

"Idiots, both of you." Annie looked thoughtful, then shook her head as Flo joined them.

"What?"

"The thought flashed that we could probably scrounge up something resembling liquor from the ambulance boys, but that could be the end of us."

"Army nursing for sure, life very possibly," said Flo. "I've boiled water. Tea will have to do."

—

The prolonged time troops spent climbing and sliding around in the mountains behind the coast chasing the enemy, coupled with a poor diet and exhaustion, gave a fertile feeding ground to chiggers. The larvae happily jumped from pigs roaming the villages to the soldiers thrashing through the undergrowth, and the numbers at the Alexishafen Clearing Station grew dramatically. So much so that three extra nurses arrived to help.

Annie had hoped it might mean Bill would also ship in from Lae, where he had arrived just after she left. She couldn't believe the bad luck in their timing, and longed to see him. Watching James and Verna delight in each other in snatched moments made her miss him even more. She found it difficult to see her friend so happy, able to mention Ruth without sliding into sadness. Annie felt relieved she could hide behind busy-ness and sometimes avoid seeing their growing joy. An envy she could not dispel, and not something she liked in herself.

The war might be going the Allies' way on New Guinea but they were now also receiving casualties from the other islands. Days off, never regular and often missed, became a forgotten luxury. A quick swim or wallow in the little bay reserved for the nurses could revive Annie in an instant, as long as a lookout stood guard for crocs of both varieties—soldiers and reptiles.

Sitting on the steps to their hut, drying her hair in the last of the sunshine after a dip, Annie saw one of the Red Cross girls heading her way.

"G'day, Annie, letter for you."

For an instant Annie felt guilty she was glad it wasn't from Joe, then ripped open the envelope. Two pages of looped, scrawled words. She smiled. She'd never met a doctor who could write clearly.

Dearest Annie,

I miss you. I want you. I love you. There, all down in black and white. Considering I've never written love letters before, I think I've taken to it rather well!

Funny thing is, I never wrote anything to Edith. I suppose I didn't have to. I want to tell you about her. Are you right with that? We grew up together and were only apart when I was training. But I never wrote to her. I wonder why? She didn't write to me either. We did love each other, but Annie, what I feel for you is different. I love you to my core. When Edith died, and the baby—a little boy—I thought my world had ended. We'd waited a long time to become parents. Not through choice.

My life had followed a set path. Take over the practice. Don't get me wrong, I didn't become a doctor because Dad was one. But when this bloody war is over, I'd like to go into plastic surgery. Help some of these poor boys. I've done a lot of stitching up since I've been here, and I try my best, but I want to learn more—about skin grafting, rebuilding faces could help to rebuild lives. I want to try new techniques.

I remember you telling me about the boy whose face had been blown away. You felt so helpless. That's how I feel most days. But, Annie, dearest, you, and all the nurses, must know how much you mean to these boys. The kindness of a touch, not shying away from shattered faces and bodies, sometimes does more than stitches. I want you to know how much I admire you. All of you.

More importantly, to me at least, is that I want you to know that you have changed my life. A life I thought would revolve around a country practice. Glen Innes isn't a bad place. But it's not the place for me now. For us. And not just because of old memories.

If it's alright with you, I'd like to make our life in Sydney. For work, and for us. At least the Japs have gone from here, and where you are, thank God.

I'm rambling, aren't I? I wish we could be speaking. I wish I could be holding you. Loving you. Thank you for the day at Kirra Beach. I sound like a lovesick boy. That's because I am. A lovesick boy who's sixteen years older than you. That's a lot, Annie. I'd be an old father, but wouldn't it be wonderful? To have a child. Maybe two, or three. A dozen. I don't care as long as I'm with you, and that you're happy with me.

I never thought I'd write words like that. Who said Australian men can't be sensitive? See what you make me, Annie, love of my life? Love I never knew I could feel. I don't say again, because I've never felt like this before.

It's night. I'm tired, as I'm sure you are. I hold you in my dreams until I can hold you in my arms.

My heart is yours, Annie May Cutler. B

"Annie! What's happened?" Verna stood in front of her.

"He loves me!" Annie smiled through her tears.

"Oh, you galah, you had me worried. Of course he does."

Chapter 14
Cambridgeshire, 2003

"Damn," Annie prodded the butter, "forgot to take it out!" She cut it into chunks to hurry the softening, then switched on the kettle. She'd just have to have another coffee while she waited. Uncomfortable, she shrugged her shoulders, wondering why she'd worn a bra today. Apart from a corset, or suspender belts, it was arguably the most uncomfortable item of clothing ever invented and, Annie remembered reading somewhere, it hadn't even been invented by a man, but by a girl. Certainly not an elderly woman. Annie clutched her breasts with a giggle and jiggled them. At least they weren't down by her knees. But enough was enough. She ducked behind the door and unclasped it, then wriggled the straps down her arms under her blouse. With a swirl of the offending garment, she hung it on the newel post to remind her to take it upstairs later.

Plonking down on the stool at the kitchen counter with her coffee and a chunk of chocolate, she gazed out the window. She hoped Hugh wasn't coming down to tell her he was shipping out. Her mind skipped back to Afghanistan. Iraq probably required the same vaccinations. At least malarial prophylactics didn't turn you a sickly yellow these days. She'd read somewhere that there was now a pre-treatment drug against nerve attacks.

"He'll bloody have that too!" she muttered as she broke off a piece of chocolate. Gone were the days of biting it. David had lost a front crown by biting chocolate. She smiled. He'd had to give a sermon with a gaping hole, and his hand over his mouth. Full of sympathy, she'd offered to make him a Hannibal Lecter mask.

How lucky she'd been.

She still had Bill's letters. Tucked into a dented Quality Street tin, in one of the drawers under her bed. She couldn't remember the last time she'd read them. Decades. Perhaps it was time to get rid of them. It might be a bit of a shock for the boys to find out about her first love. She'd rarely spoken about her war years. About Berlin, but not Singapore or New Guinea. Annie's eyes glistened with unshed tears. She shook her head. Silly old woman. Such a long time ago. Yet she still remembered the joy of Bill's letter professing his love. And the worry.

No, it was better Hugh didn't have a wife, or girlfriend. Selfishly, Annie didn't know if she'd have the energy to support someone else through another war. She had enough trouble keeping herself sane when consumed by worry. "Oh God, why?" she asked the kitchen. Why did she have to have a son intent on the military? "Why couldn't he be an accountant, or a lawyer?" She shook her head. No, not that. That hadn't kept Joe out of the war.

David's words drifted in. She'd asked the same question when Hugh had told them, after he'd got his degree, that he'd been accepted into Sandhurst. Annie had been livid. She hadn't even known he'd applied. Although David had. That had hurt. She'd managed to keep it together until Hugh had left.

It had probably caused her and David's most vitriolic fight. On her side anyway. She hadn't wanted David's calm acceptance. His reassurance. She wanted him to be as furious and against it as she was. "Don't you care?" she'd screamed.

"How dare you?" he'd thundered.

Then to make matters worse, in her eyes, he'd stormed from the vicarage and gone to his church, leaving her irate, and sobbing down the phone to Flo. Annie sighed. Flo, her stalwart; adored by David, and the boys, who she had regaled with stories, usually about their mother putting her foot in it. Dear Flo.

Annie poked the butter. "Soft enough." She got to her feet, added flour and started crumbling it together. She'd have to be positive, and proud of her younger son tomorrow. Today, in the quiet of her kitchen, she could be upset. She was glad the Brigadier wasn't coming over this evening. She didn't have the energy to pretend. A grin creased her face. "Come off it, Annie, you've never been very good at pretending."

She finished making the pastry, put it in a covered bowl then balanced it on the egg carton in the fridge. Hooking her bra over her wrist, Annie made her way up the stairs. In her bedroom, she slid down onto the floor and took out the Quality Street tin. She shuffled back against the bed and sat with it on her lap.

Eventually, she prised open the tin. "Oh, Annie, you floozie." Her laughter brought Eartha upstairs. The cat nudged against Annie's feet, then sat on the letters Annie had scattered. She'd forgotten they weren't just from Bill, but David as well. Two wonderful men. And to think she'd never thought she'd find one. And important letters from Verna, Flo, and Joe.

The letters strewn around her, and under Eartha, provided the link between them, told all their stories, sometimes their fears, and always the joy. Sad really, people were writing fewer and fewer letters these days. Jake had tried to show her how to message on the new mobile phone he'd bought for her. She'd given up. If she had a phone in her hand, why not just call? Anyway, the bloody thing was never where she wanted it. At least the land line didn't keep disappearing down the sofa, or into a pocket!

Annie put the letters back in the tin, unread. "My life in a chocolate box," she told Eartha, as she slid it back into the drawer.

Chapter 15
Alexishafen, 1944

Rumblings circulated around the camp that General MacArthur planned for the Philippine campaign to be an all-American assault. But Prime Minister John Curtin and his generals wanted Australian troops to be involved, a kind of quid quo pro for agreeing to an American general in overall command of Australian troops in the South Pacific. A compromise of sorts was hammered out, but as the continued routing of Japanese forces from the islands north of Australia took a large part of the Australian Military Forces, it meant only two divisions would be available for the Philippine strike.

After nearly a year back in New Guinea, Annie doubted the 111th CCS would be engaged in support to the other islands, and she dreaded the thought that Bill would. It could be months, years in her darker moments, before she'd see him again. Their communication had been relatively easy whilst they both served in New Guinea, but Annie knew that would change if he went on the road to the Philippines, or worse, Japan.

Alexishafen bustled with army, navy and airmen. Australian and American forces fought together and sometimes partied together. Concerts relieved the pain and tedium of recovery for patients and provided moments of light relief for the forces who might be at the camp.

"Have you heard of her?" Flo asked Annie and Verna over tea one evening in the mess as rain beat a tattoo, splatters hitting the shutters.

"James says …" Verna looked indignant at the other's laughter. "What?"

Annie patted her friend's arm, "Do you know how many of your sentences start with 'James says'?"

"They do not!"

"They do. Just remember, ducks, I've known him since we were in nappies."

"Go on then," said Flo, interrupted with a smile, "What does James say?"

"Don't know if I'll tell you now." Verna grinned at their groans. "Fine! James says Frances Langford is known as the GI Nightingale."

"That's it? That's what we've been waiting to hear?" Annie ducked Verna's thrown serviette.

"No. She's often Bob Hope's sparring partner. Funny, apparently."

"And, no doubt," Flo said, rolling her eyes, "a blonde bombshell."

"Well, we've got Vera Lynn." Annie longed for the star's signature song, *We'll Meet Again Some Sunny Day* to ring true for her and Bill. "Anyway, it'll be fun. Whoever she is." Annie looked at the fob pinned to her uniform. "Argh, I promised I'd go back and help tidy the supply room. There are bandages and buckets all over the place. Matron'd have a fit if she saw it." She stretched, her long arms reaching up. "Righto, back I go. Hooroo."

Rain lashed down, again, and Annie jumped puddles and ducked under awnings on her way back to the ward. It struck her that not only did their skin look jaundiced, their clothes had taken on a musty, mossy hue because nothing ever completely dried. Either because of humidity or rain.

She flung off the Mac, stomped mud from her gumboots and, shaking drops from her hair, sat on a stool and began to roll bandages, her head happily in a tomorrow.

"Sister Cutler? Annie?"

Oblivious to the door opening, she started then leapt to her feet, sending the rolled bandage unspooling across the floor. "Sorry, Matron, I didn't hear you." She bent to pick up the crepe but felt a hand on her arm. "Leave it, come and sit down."

Annie frowned. "Is it Joe? My brother?" She hadn't heard from him for months.

Matron bowed her head. "No, Annie … I'm sorry."

"Oh, God, please no …"

"I'm afraid it's Major Townsend."

Annie swayed on the stool as if punched. "I thought Lae was safe. No more Japs. He said so. In his letter last week."

"My dear, I am so sorry. I do know Bill. We served together in Queensland. He was a caring and talented doctor. Always calm."

The supply room closed in on Annie. Rain hammered the tin roof of the ward. She shook her head trying to clear the fog. "I don't understand." Her eyes dry, she asked, "What happened?"

"Dengue."

"Dengue?" Anger overtook surprise. "How could dengue kill him? He's a doctor. He knows." She refused to use the past tense.

"Perhaps because he was a doctor, Annie. He thought he could fight it. But he left it too long. You know how busy we all are. He kept going."

Furious, Annie stood. "Why didn't someone tell me?"

"He only died a few hours ago. It was radioed through. Everyone knew about you." Matron's smile was slight, sad. "Even I knew about you both. There aren't many secrets." She paused. "You know, Lieutenant, how quickly it can turn to haemorrhagic dengue, and that it usually happens after the fever has broken, when we think we're over the worst. That's what Bill thought, I'm sure. But it was too late."

Bile rose and Annie gagged. Images of bleeding gums, Bill's skin bruising and blood pooling under it. Sweat oozing. Thrashing fever. She retched again.

"Here," Matron patted Annie's shoulder as she passed a bucket to her.

Annie pushed it away and stood. "No, I'm alright. Thank you. Thank you, for telling me. I'll go now, if that's alright?"

"Sit down, Sister Cutler. I've sent for Davidson and Taylor." She tried to smile. "You do know you're known as The Triumvirate?"

"No, I didn't—we've been through a lot together."

"I know. And Annie, this is one more thing. You will get through this. Keep busy. That's the key." Matron moved to the door. "Ah, here they are."

"Evening, Matron," Verna and Flo said in unison, their eyes taking in Annie's ashen face.

"Oh no, not another," Verna said as she crouched at her side.

"I'll leave you girls, now. Take Annie to your quarters, please. Hot tea and bed. I expect you on duty tomorrow morning, Lieutenant Cutler." Matron patted Annie's shoulder again, then closed the door behind her.

"Oh, ducks," Verna's arms went around Annie. "Bill?"

Annie nodded.

"Goddamnit," Flo's voice exploded. "When will this bloody end?"

"It wasn't the war," Annie said, "it was dengue."

"Oh, Christ. That's worse somehow. I mean … oh, God, I don't know what I mean." Verna helped Annie up. "Come on. Let's get you to bed."

Flo glanced at the roof. "It's still lashing down. Put your Mac on, lovey."

Not running the way they usually did in the daily downpours, the three huddled together as they stumbled back to their quarters. Annie looked up. She didn't know if it was the rain that made her tears start as they mingled to course down her cheeks, but the rain fell until it seemed the sky could cry no more.

—

Curled in a ball, sleep had finally given Annie a short reprieve from the pain as dawn began to filter through the sago palm fronds still dripping from the night's torrential storm. Timid sunshine nudged her awake, and she whimpered as a wave of desolation crashed through her.

"Good morning, Lieutenant Cutler."

Annie, startled by Matron's appearance at the entrance to the ward, mumbled a reply. Her eyes stung and her head ached.

"You will be in surgery today, please, Sister." Matron's voice penetrated the fog. "There is a busy caseload, and we are expecting more arrivals this afternoon."

"Yes, Matron." Annie's response was automatic. Her body hurt, as if she'd been punched and couldn't catch her breath. Only at the end of the day, exhausted beyond thinking, did it occur to her that the unusual reassignment had been deliberate.

"How are you doing, ducks?" asked Verna, as she sat down opposite Annie in the Mess. "Have you eaten anything today?"

"Not hungry." Annie's hands clutched a mug of tea.

Verna stood and Annie watched listlessly as she went to the canteen. She returned with two plates of Bully Beef and an Anzac wafer that she plopped down on the table. "This is the best cuisine the chef can offer. Pavlova to follow!"

A tight smile cracked the sadness. "Now wouldn't that be a wonderful surprise." She played with the tinned meat in front of her. "You know you could use one of these," she stabbed her fork at the wafer, "to hammer a nail into wood?" She took a tentative bite.

"Or as traction under a bogged down Jeep." Verna looked up as Flo joined them.

"How about as a doorstop?" Flo lifted Annie's chin with a gentle hand, "Are you right?"

Annie shook her head, her eyes brimming, "Not really."

"Oh, lovey, day one, two, three and many more will be hell, but eventually you'll find the pain eases, just a little."

"I'm so angry with him." Annie rubbed her gritty eyes. "I mean, how could he be so stupid? Arrogant."

"That's a bit hard," said Verna. "Bill was doing what he always did. Putting others before himself. You know that."

Flo sighed. "Being livid won't help, Annie."

Her head down, Annie mumbled, "I know. I know. But I am. I can't help it. We had so many plans. Dreams. Children. If it had been a bomb or a bullet it would be easier. That's war. But, for God's sake, dengue!"

"Not going to argue, Annie." Flo paused, "But, honestly, I don't think any way his death happened would make it easier."

"I thought you weren't going to argue." Verna picked up the empty mugs. "It's bloody silly New Guinea is dry. We could all do with some booze. We'll have to toast Bill in sodding tea."

Days merged into a morass of pain. Both hers and the patients. Flo and Verna kept a close eye on her, and Matron seemed to appear on the ward more than usual. Annie focused on each action, each medication given, each word said. Anything to stop her thoughts going into a spin. A small box came from Lae, hand delivered to Annie by a doctor sent to join their clearing station in Alexishafen. It held Bill's cigarette lighter.

And then, ten days later, a letter arrived. Annie didn't understand the delay, didn't know whether to rip the envelope open or keep it until she felt stronger. She ripped it open.

Dearest Annie,

I miss you. I want you. I love you. This is my new mantra.

Just a quick note this time. I've had a touch of dengue, back at work now. All fine, but I'm dog tired. Where did that expression come from, I wonder? Anyway, I am. I've taken myself off to bed early. Been a hectic day in surgery. Patients shipping in from New Britain.

I had one chap, from the Papuan Infantry, nasty wound that he ignored. They're tough blokes. Sepsis had set in and he didn't make it. I loathe those ones. Operating but knowing it's useless. He's from one of the villages on the other side of the Owen Stanleys, near Moresby, I think, but I doubt his body will make it back. I've learnt that here in New Guinea there is a sense of perpetual community with the dead, at least for a few generations. Although I think each tribe probably has a slightly different take on death rituals. I can't help wondering how that will affect his relationship with his village. Not having a body to venerate. Perhaps his spirit, his tambaran, that's a good word, isn't it, will waft over the mountains—I'd like to think that. These Papuans, and the New Guineans have given such a lot. I admire them. I wish I could speak better Pidgin. I know the bearers and native troops have to speak some English, but you can never know a people unless you know at least some of their language.

I wish we could talk, Annie. There's so much I want to know about you. You often mention your mother, and Ernest and Joe, but never your father. Will you tell me one day?

And with that question I say goodnight. I'm tired and still have a bit of headache. All will be well in the morning.

You have my heart, Annie May Cutler. B

The letter, soggy from her tears, lay on her lap. Annie kicked off her boots, then lay down, still in her boiler suit and clutched the letter. "But all wasn't well in the morning, was it, my darling?"

Her whispered words merged with the sounds of evening. Crickets, cicadas, the generator grumbling, a plane landing or taking off, a dog barking, rats rustlings under the hut. She heard Verna come in and pretended to be asleep. She doubted she fooled her friend, but she couldn't talk.

Sleep came through exhaustion, but with each day, as Flo had said, the physical pain eased. Her anger still reared up, out of nowhere. Almost as if that way she could hold Bill close. But mostly she felt empty. Barren.

Chapter 16
Going Home, 1945

With news of the successful Normandy landings in June the previous year, the failure of the Nazi offensive in the Ardennes in the winter, and the Red Army advancing toward Berlin from the east, spirits rose in Alexishafen that the Pacific war would follow suit. That Japan would recognise the futility of continuing the battle.

"They won't you know," Verna said, "no one wants to give up first."

Flo looked up from her papaya and tea breakfast. "Well, you're cheerful this morning."

"They signed a non-surrender pact. Germany and Japan." Verna's mug clunked down on the mess table. "I'm done with this. I just want to go home and get married."

Annie gasped, and Verna slapped a hand over her mouth. "Ducks, I'm sorry."

"Oh, we know, that's all we ever hear about." Annie stood, her face blotched and angry.

Flo thumped the table. "Enough!" She pulled Annie's arm. "Sit down, that was unfair."

"No, it's my fault. I know I talk too much," Verna said, tears in her eyes. "I'm so sorry, Annie."

Annie tugged Bill's lighter from her boiler-suit pocket, and lit a cigarette. "It's fine, Verna. I'm sorry I snapped. Don't seem to have much control over my temper these days."

"We're all done with this war," Flo, her face concerned, looked between the friends, "but we have got to get through it together. Then you can both have a right royal ding dong. Till then, we nurse. Righto?" She held her hands out to them both. "And, Annie, for God's sake, don't let Matron hear you snap at anyone. She won't give a tuppence about your captain's pip. She'll have you emptying bedpans for a month.

It really did seem as if the war might end after VE Day on May 8th, seven days after Hitler's suicide, and hopes surged around the casualty clearing station about the Pacific theatre.

—

The regulation leather suitcase lay open on her cot, no longer brown but tinged a muddy sage green where mildew stubbornly refused to be brushed off. Annie packed her underwear, a sludgy grey from too many washes and not enough soap. A smile tugged as her mind wandered to their early days in Alexishafen, when the CO had complained about the nurses hanging their knickers on a line behind their quarters. Next, Annie tucked the bilum, the string bag one of the bearers had given her, under her second uniform. Her eyes watered as she stuffed her blue and white cozzie into a corner of the case. She took it out and bundled it, and the hated gumboots, into a satchel to be left behind. Too many memories tied up in it. And anyway, it was baggy now, the cups no longer filled. They had all lost weight.

"No more uniforms for me soon," Verna sang from the other side of their room. "Oh, God, Annie, I can't wait. I know James will stay in the army until this sodding war is over but at least we'll be in Australia. He can't wait to get to Yaralla. And I can't wait to introduce him to the ps." Annie saw a moment of uncertainty mar her friend's delight. "They will love him, won't they?" Verna stopped talking. "I'm sorry, ducks." She crossed over and hugged Annie. "I'm wittering on again. Selfish."

"Don't be silly, Verna. I'm happy, no, more than happy—what's more than happy? I know, I'm ecstatic for you both."

"Who's in ecstasy?" Flo's voice came through the flimsy wall.

Annie called back, "Our friend." She snapped the clasps on the case and pulled it off the bed, then glanced around the room. "Mad as it sounds, I'm going to miss the Primrose Hut. Geckos and all!"

Verna slapped her thigh. "I won't miss the damn mozzies. I swear my boiler suit has a million holes where they've penetrated."

Boarding SS Ormiston, again, the triumvirate watched as ropes were hauled, and anchors cranked and groaned their way aboard so they could begin their voyage back to Townsville, stopping in at Lae and Port Moresby. Their war over.

"It is a beautiful country," said Annie as she gazed at the shoreline. Palm trees lined golden arcs that sifted into the clear sea as they passed inlets and bays. Sometimes a child, naked, or with an arse grass tucked under a protruding belly, would wave. "I wonder what they think of it all? Strangers—Japs and us—trampling crops, taking their men away, dropping bombs."

"I'd like to think," Verna linked her arm through Annie's, "they're glad it's the Aussies and not the Japs who won. Here anyway."

"Do you think the villagers who helped the enemy will be, I dunno, ostracised by others?" Flo stood on the other side of Annie.

"I doubt it. They'll probably go back to the way it was before the war. Arrows across the valleys."

"'Spose so. I never knew one country could have so many different people. Languages. Customs. Bill," Annie took a deep breath, she had to get used to saying his name and not dissolve into a puddle of misery, "Bill loved learning the culture. You know he even started to learn Pidgin."

"He was that kind of man, lovey," Flo said.

"Do you know what cattle are called here?" Annie gave a sad laugh. "Bulmacow!"

"It's actually kind of lyrical sometimes. Not to mention descriptive." Verna giggled.

Annie laughed, properly. "My favourite will always be 'im bugger im up pinis'."

"Can you imagine saying that to Matron when you've finished cleaning the sluice room at Yaralla?" Annie chortled. "That'd be worth staying on for, Verna!"

"Won't you miss it? The nursing?" asked Flo.

Verna was quiet for a moment. "You know what, I don't think I will. I've had enough."

"She'll be busy making curtains and babies, won't you?" Annie looked fondly at their friend.

"Won't be doing that for a while. We're going to live with the ps until we can get our own place." She paused. "I suppose it will depend on when James leaves the army. And that depends on the war."

Annie knew he and Bill had exchanged letters about the possibility of working together, to help men disfigured by burns and bullets. Each sharing what they had learnt under the scrutiny of not just nurses but natives peering in the open-air operating room windows. Until Bill died. "If he wants to work in plastic surgery wouldn't it be better to stay in?"

"James says not. And we don't want to be moved around. Either of us."

They lapsed into silence until Annie said, "God, would you look at those mountains? The tops are shrouded in mist most of the time. I can't imagine walking the trails along the ridges, let alone fighting on them. Gutsy bunch, our boys. And their ghosts."

Flo nodded, then lifted her hands from the rail and spread her fingers. "You know what I won't miss? Atebrin. I'm tired of being yellow!"

—

SS Ormiston picked up patients in Lae and Port Moresby. Annie had dreaded going ashore in Lae, the thought of walking around the hospital too raw. It seemed Matron had thought of everything and had set her to readying nursing bays on board. She wouldn't have to go anywhere near 17 Mile Camp, so she did go in to Moresby, where there were no ghosts.

Next, they crossed the Coral Sea, and the nurses returning to Australia kept busy with injured and sick men. After the rugged mountains of New Guinea, then the mangrove swamps around Milne Bay in Papua, a cheer went up from those on deck as the flat wilderness of Cape York Peninsula, the tip of Australia, came into view.

"I don't care if I never leave Australia again!" The soldier flicked his cigarette butt into the water and grinned at Annie.

Trying to stop hair whipping her eyes, Annie turned to face the gnarled and greying man, deep lines around his eyes showing his exhaustion. "Ever?" she asked.

"Ever! I'm goin' home. To me cattle, me dogs, me missus. She's been bonza. Holding down the place."

"Where is it?" A fleeting thought wondered at his order of importance.

"Out by Cunnamulla. I don't care if I never see another bloody mountain or desert. Or another war. Two's my limit." He spat over the side. "Where you headed, Captain?"

"Sydney, I suppose. The rehab hospital at Yaralla."

"Don't know how you girls do it." He grimaced. "Me mate got shot up pretty bad, but said it was worth it to 'ave one of your lot stroke his 'ead." He put his hand out. "Thanks, Sister, from me and all me mates. Dead and alive."

Annie, tears never far from the surface, shook his hand, smiled, and turned away.

Pandemonium, and a wait for a train south met them in Townsville. Even though the fighting had eased in New Guinea, troops and supplies still had to be transported to and from there, and New Britain. Troop trains, often converted cattle cars daubed with painted threats to both the German and Japanese, clogged the railways. Tanks and armoured vehicles lay like silent silhouettes on flatbeds as they shuffled back and forth across Australia.

"I do not understand why each state has a different gauge for the railways," said Flo as they watched another train chug through the town to the station on Flinders Street. "I mean we're one country, for God's sake."

"Money!" Annie said, looking at the red brick building with imposing balustraded verandas below a gabled and hipped roof. "It's always money and pride, oh yeah, and men. My balls are bigger than yours sort of thing."

"And Hitler only had one of them." Flo sang with a chortle. "When did we become so crude?"

"We'll have to learn how to behave in polite society again. You know what I'm tired of? Sleeping in tents," Verna stretched her back, "I can't wait for my bed at home."

"With James in it," Flo dug her in the ribs.

"Well, maybe that too."

"I don't want to ever eat another herring in tomato sauce." Annie screwed up her face. "I never liked them in the first place."

Flo, all humour gone, asked, "You know what I wonder?"

"What, oh, wise one?"

She ignored Annie's teasing. "I wonder how all the women, the ones keeping everything going at home—not just here—but everywhere, all sides, are going to feel once the men come home. The ones who do." She took a deep breath. "I mean, the women have done everything. Run cattle stations. Shorn sheep. Made munitions. Everything."

Annie picked lint off her uniform. The Land Girls on her father's property sprang to mind. "Yeah, it's different for us, I 'spose. We'll just go on nursing."

"Not me," Verna said. "But, yeah, it will be strange for lots. I mean, we've been away with their men."

"I reckon that's going to be a problem, too," said Flo.

"What do you mean?" Annie looked at her friend.

"Well, we might not have been shot at, or bombed all the time, but we've seen our share of bad stuff. Will the boys want to be with someone who knows what it's like? Won't they want young things who have no real idea of what went on."

"Dunno," Annie said.

"Another thing to tuck away, I suppose. You're lucky, Verna. James and you, you both know what to expect from the other. Many won't have that understanding."

"I never thought of it like that, but you're right. Anyway, I guess you'll both find out."

Annie shrugged. "Nah, I'm done with love. It hurts too much."

—

The day before their enforced wait in Townsville for a train south ended, mail caught up with them.

"Oh no! No, no!"

"What is it?" Annie moved closer to Verna.

"James?" Flo asked, her hands reaching across the mess table to retrieve the fallen letter.

Annie, her arm around Verna's shoulder, asked, "Who's it from, ducky?"

Tears fell in a quickening stream as Verna answered. "Mum."

"Your dad?" Annie could picture Mr. Davidson, head bent, pipe in his mouth, heading to the garden shed. "For Christ's sake, Verna, what's happened?"

"Iris. You read it, Flo, I can't."

Flo scanned the tightly written words, then began, her voice shaking. "Mrs. Davidson popped in to see Iris's mum, remember, she'd moved to Sydney from Armidale. She'd just had confirmation."

"Of what?"

Annie lurched over to grab the letter but Flo held on and read. "*'I'm sorry to tell you, love, but I know you girls would want to know. Iris died on the way back from Singapore. I can't remember the name of the ship.'*"

"Vyner Brooke," Annie murmured. "How? We know it sank, but there were survivors."

Flo read on. "*'Word has finally come through about POWs, but Iris wasn't on the list.'*"

"She drowned?" Annie's voice was hoarse through her tears.

Flo shook her head and continued. "*'Iris made it to land, after a night clinging to a piece of the ship. Her mum was just told she died on the beach.'*"

"That's it? No more details."

Flo shook her head, tears on her lashes.

Angry, Annie stood. "I don't believe that."

"What do you mean?" Verna asked, her face streaked with tears.

"It's too glib. There's more to it."

"Oh God," Flo sighed. "Another cover up. Like the plane at 17 Mile."

—

The radio in the nurses' Common Room at Concorde, switched on morning and evening for the news, reported that Japanese installations continued to be destroyed as the Americans continued their island hop ever closer to Japan, whose cities were being firebombed.

Then came the news, on August 6th, that an atomic bomb had been dropped on Hiroshima, and three days later, another on Nagasaki. The same day the Soviets declared war on Manchukuo, the puppet state claimed from China by Japan in 1931. It took another five days, as images of the horror appeared on the front pages of newspapers around the world, for Japan to surrender and for the Pacific war to end.

—

Annie waved flags with Flo when they joined crowds thronging down to the harbour. She laughed and danced with strangers on George Street at the Victory Day parade but knew, when the euphoria passed, the empty chairs and missing limbs, the broken souls and hearts, the nightmares, would remain for so many. Those vanquished returned home subdued, to devastation of countries, governments, ways of life.

She swayed between relief that the war was over, and outrage at the barbarity of the bombs. Flo, as always, proved a measured sounding board.

"Terrible things happened, on all fronts, ducks," Flo said, as they walked back up the hill on their day off.

"How much more terrible can it get than those two bombs?"

"That's blacking and whiting things, Annie. You can't do that. Anytime, but especially in war."

Annie bent to tie a shoelace. "It's the sheer numbers. Mainly civilians."

"Those bombs ended the war, Annie. For that we should be grateful."

"Yeah, I know." Annie linked arms with Flo with a sigh. "What would I do without you?"

"You'd find some other sucker to listen to you. Now come on, or we'll be late."

—

The wards at Concord Repatriation Hospital remained full, and Annie buried herself in busy-ness. Flo transferred to a psychiatric ward in her bid to retrain, and Verna floated around Coogee in a fog of delight as she prepared for the birth of her and James's baby.

Joe, still more out of uniform than in it, continued to flit in and out of her life. Sitting with him on a bench in the Botanical Gardens, they talked about Ernie. Sadness tinged their memories, but it felt good to laugh about him too. Then Annie had wept the tears she had fought hard to stop as she talked about Bill. The lost dreams. The emptiness. A colourless horizon.

It had been Joe who'd persuaded her to go home. Even for a few days. If only to close the book. She felt she'd already done so, but she went anyway.

Annie looked around the familiar kitchen. Tidy, dishes stacked where they'd always been, although now everything appeared shabby, tired. A bit how she felt. Home. Home would have been Bill. Not the cold kitchen that reeked of pipe smoke and swirled with angry words. She couldn't help but glance at Ma's chair. Could almost hear her voice telling her to, "Buck up, Annie May, it's a good life."

It didn't much feel like one. Annie shivered in bed recalling her father's dismissive greeting. But could she really blame him? It had been over a year and she made no effort to go back to Armidale. She'd only called a couple of times. Helen, the Land Girl, had stayed on and, somehow managed to handle Ian's outbursts. She'd made the cottage across from the homestead a haven of soft greens and ochres, almost, Annie told her, as if she'd brought the outside inside.

"Morning, Annie."

She spun from the sink at Joe's voice. "G'day. I didn't hear you." She noted his tired eyes. "Didn't sleep?"

"Not much. Ghosts trampling my dreams."

Annie nodded. "We've got a few around here. Tea's on. Dad's out already. I heard the screen door slam." Annie pushed his mug across the table. "Here you go." She waited for him to spoon sugar into his tea, then asked, "So what's the story?"

"What d'you mean?"

"Well," Annie leant against the stained porcelain sink, "I talked at you in Sydney, for which, by the way, I'm sorry." She ignored his attempt to interrupt. "I'm assuming you can't talk about a lot of what you've done but what about the future?"

The gap between his teeth, which always reminded her of Bill, showed in a tight smile. "I'll be tied up for a while yet. I know you think I've been cloak and dagger, Annie, but I haven't. I've been a fountain-pen fusilier!" His laugh rueful, he continued. "I'm assuming you know the term?"

"I doubt you'd be surprised at some of the terms I've heard," Annie agreed. "I quite like the 'shiny arse' one—just about says it all about a pen-pusher. We Aussies are descriptive if nothing else. But," she looked at her brother, "somehow I don't think you spent the war counting paperclips."

"No. A lot of moving around. Still more to come. That, Annie, is why I wanted you to come home with me. Last time I'll be here for a while." A grin spilled across his face. "I'm going to London."

"Never!" Annie ran around the table to hug her brother's thin shoulders, then pulled out the chair next to him. "Go on." She didn't think she'd ever seen Joe look bashful.

"Someone had a word with someone, and as I'd only a few months left to go and my marks had been okay, that, combined with the work I did during the war, convinced the Chancellor to award my degree."

"Oh, Joe, that's terrific. Congratulations." Annie looked to her mother's chair, again. "Ma would be so proud. Have you told Dad?"

"Nah, not yet."

Annie watched Joe gather his thoughts.

"Anyway, one of the missions is to help document the industrial progress in Germany which the Nazis made during the war. It's got a fancy name. The Australian Scientific and Technical Mission, and I've been put forward as part of the team."

Annie, her brow creased, said, "But, Joe, you're not a scientist. I don't understand."

"No, no, I'd go to dot the proverbial 'i's. Make sure everything is above board throughout the transfer of their science and technology to us. It's part of Australia's foreign policy." He paused. "It'll be under the umbrella of British Intelligence at the start. Then we'll see."

"I knew it, I knew you were a spy." Annie punched his arm, as if they were children roughhousing again. An image of Ernie floated in. He'd have punched Joe's other arm.

"Idiot! I most definitely was not."

"How long will you be gone?"

"Dunno. Everything's a mess over there. Sorting out Germany with the Russians is going to be touchy."

"I'm not sure how I'd feel, working with the Germans. I mean after, Ernie."

"Oh, Annie, you can't think like that. It could've been an Italian who fired the shot. If we're ever going to get this world sorted, we have to show compassion for those who lost."

"I know. That's just what Flo said. Slightly different words, same gist."

"Thank goodness there'll be someone to keep you in line while I'm away!"

"Ha, ha! But really, Joe, I'm so chuffed for you." She punched him again. "That's why you wanted me to come here with you. To tell Dad. Oh, that's low."

"I know." Joe hugged her tight. "Good thing you love me, eh?" His face tightened. "He's a miserable bugger, and he's got worse since Ernie, but he is our father. Thank God for Helen, but we've still got to get some things in place for him. This can't all fall to you."

"Thanks, mate! Perhaps I'll go to London too."

Chapter 17
London, 1947

Ribbons streamed down from the decks of the ship. Some landed on the wharf, some draped the gangplank and some, like a tenuous thread, were grabbed by well-wishers not ready to say goodbye, as if by holding on they could retain a tangible link. Even if those onboard were not heading off to war, who knew when families and friends would meet again.

"Annie!" Joe's voice found her through the shouts. "Up here!"

"Idiot," Annie mouthed. "Where else would you be?" She shouted and tried to smile, but her eyes brimmed with unshed tears. More to bottle.

She felt a shove, then an arm over her shoulders. "G'day! I made it. Balls up at the hospital." James, his hair dishevelled, asked, "Where is the bugger?"

"Up there." Annie pointed and saw Joe's smile widen as he spotted their childhood friend.

"Damn, I hoped I wouldn't miss him."

"You can wave." Annie looked over James' shoulder. "No Verna?"

"Your goddaughter kept her up most of the night. Teeth, I think. So you'll just have to put up with me." James gave her a hug. "You right?"

"Yup. As long as I don't think too much. I'm going to miss Joe. I liked having him around."

"Well, you'll just have to manage with us."

The long, mournful wail of the ship's horn sounded, and voices called farewells as a cheer rose from the wharf and the vessel eased away, pulling streamers taut until they broke and trailed in the water. Annie and James waved until Joe disappeared in a blur of faces.

"Come on, I'll shout you a drink at The Australia."

"What would my father say?" Annie asked, taking comfort from James knowing the family history.

"Sod the old sod!"

—

Each time a blue onionskin letter arrived from Joe, Annie would savour his stories of life in post-war London. She had been shocked to hear how severe rationing remained in England, and how desperate many felt with austerity gripping the country. Industries instrumental to the war effort, such as aircraft manufacture, now being merged. They had drawn funding from the railways and coal mines, and, with little to export, ways to pay for imports were scarce. Jobs taken on by women during the war, which Annie and Flo had discussed, returned to men. Girls and women once again relegated to the home, often unwillingly.

Dear Annie,

It's a drizzly, miserable day. After the freezing winter, rain and floods in some parts add to the misery. People walk with their heads down, tucked under black umbrellas. Postwar London is a monochrome city. And yet, despite the greyness of both the weather and general despair in certain quarters, there is a sense of hope, a sense of exciting things to come. A bit like spring, Annie, which I'm told is just around the corner. I hope so. I'll never complain about Armidale weather again.

I don't think any of us at home realised just how much damage the Luftwaffe did during the Blitz. Whole streets are still rubble. I can't remember whether I mentioned that I had a fleeting visit to Darwin just after the Japs attacked. Probably not. Decimated. So many of those buildings were wood and they splintered like stripped bamboo, but London was built with sterner stuff. Grand old stone buildings reduced to dust and gaping caverns. Rebuilding has begun, but lack of materials is really hampering the effort. As is the lack of housing in general. I read somewhere that the government estimated the need for 750,000 new homes. They've started building what they call 'prefabs'—bungalows built in factories which go up in about a week.

I've moved into a flat on Cork Street, behind Piccadilly. I justify having three bedrooms, although one's more like a box room, by putting up visiting Aussies.

The destruction is remarkable, Annie. To the left of my building, three places along, is a hole in the ground where a bomb blew it to hell. On the other side everything looks like a typical London street.

My landlady—gentility without the means—occupies the ground two floors, and I've got the top two. Her husband and two sons are dead. All naval officers. What a waste. Anyway, she's pleasant, and I think appreciates someone handy with an axe who can chop logs. You see, Annie, a country-upbringing has its advantages.

I'm off to Berlin again for a few days. Now that is a city in total despair. And I don't trust the Russkies one little bit, but everyone is playing nice at the moment, on the surface anyway.

Righto, that's it for now. I wrote to Father, but he hasn't responded. No surprise I suppose. Have you been home again? Somehow, I doubt it. Hope Concord isn't getting you down too much. You can't blame some of the chaps for maybe bludging a bit, Annie, they just want to get out of uniform and back on their land.

Oh, by the way, have you met any of the Ten Pound Poms yet? Brits flocking to Australia on the promise of jobs, houses, and a sunny new life.

Remember to smile, Annie, Bill would not have wanted you to forget how!

Love,

Joe

P.S. Babies are booming—never seen so many prams!

The Parramatta River glinted through the trees beyond the nurses' quarters. Annie stood at her window, holding Joe's letter. She missed him. She half smiled. He knew her well. Of course she hadn't been home. She called every few weeks to check in but rarely got more than a grunt, or a demand for her to return. Helen was the one who kept her informed, and Annie marvelled at her patience. From odd comments, she knew Helen pretty much ran the property now.

'Ten Pound Poms' hadn't crossed her path yet, but she'd heard about the scheme started to help increase Australia's population and provide manpower for the burgeoning industrial sector. Browbeaten by war, the scheme offered assisted migration, charging ten pounds per adult, with children travelling free, which must have seemed a lifeline for many Brits. The only proviso being that they stay two years.

Seemed funny that Joe would be going into spring as she headed into autumn, though Sydney probably wasn't as bleak as London in the cold. Annie glanced at the watch pinned to her uniform. Half an hour until night duty called. Time for a cuppa. She wondered how Flo had got on with her interview with the medical board. It would be a big leap from nursing to studying again, and psychiatry at that.

Later, in the soft glow of the lamp on the desk at the end of the ward, Annie looked along the row of beds. She liked working nights here. The silence soothed her. Although sometimes it would be broken by a scream as a nightmare shook a patient awake, trembling at re-lived horrors. She'd sit at their bedside listening, as words held back in daylight hours, became freed in the smudge of night when tears rolling down worn cheeks could not be seen. Sometimes a cup of tea would calm them, or sometimes Annie would just sit, holding their hands—the warmth of human touch better than any words.

Tonight was quiet. She pulled Joe's letter out of her pocket and reread it. A kernel cracked as she remembered her tossed away line to him before he left Sydney, the memory floating in with the dawn.

—

"So, what do you think?" Annie tugged her jacket tighter under her chin as the chill of the breeze coming off the sea ruffled her hair. She kicked sand as she waited for Verna or Flo to say something.

Verna took her hand. "I think it's a wonderful idea. I'll miss you, but I'll forgive you for missing out on your goddaughter's toddlerhood. And you won't be gone forever." She called Flo, who had walked a few paces ahead. "What do you think, ducks?"

"I think," Flo spun around, "I think I'm coming too."

"What?" Annie's laugh whipped away in the wind. She laughed again at Verna's open mouth.

"Why stay here, apart from you, Verna? And you've got James and Ruthie—I love that you called her that, by the way. I don't think I ever said."

"Yeah, you did, at her christening. When I got all weepy over Ruth not being there with us."

"Well then, I'm saying it again! Now," Flo looked out to sea for a moment, "back to the matter in hand. Those pompous old buggers turned down my application, so what's the point in staying?" She grinned. "Who knows, I might have better luck in London. Maybe they're not so stuck on women staying in their prescribed place in England. Anyway, it can't be any worse that the drongos who interviewed me here."

"You really mean it?" Annie searched Flo's face.

Verna's smile trembled and she looked close to tears. "Oh, great, you're both going to desert me." She pushed between the two women and swung their hands. "So, we'll just have to cram as much time together before you disappear. I want Ruthie to know her godmothers."

"It could take ages to demob. We are still serving army nurses."

"It didn't take me long, Flo," said Verna.

Annie frowned. "I wonder if the AANS will give us references?"

Verna laughed. "If they don't, James will." She paused. "Are you really sure, both of you? I mean, from what you said Joe wrote, it doesn't sound like all roses over there."

"No, I know. But, apart from you, Verna, there isn't anything holding me here. I need a kick up the jacksie—a new adventure."

Flo, her laugh creating arcs at the sides of her mouth, asked, "And we couldn't let her go alone, could we, lovey?"

"Yeah, we could. She'd have Joe to look out for her." Verna sounded dejected.

"Excuse me, I am still here." Annie picked up a flat stone to skim out to sea. "And, anyway, it sounds as if he's travelling around." She watched the pebble skip three times before being swallowed by a wavelet. "I wonder if we could stay with him. You know, until we can find our own place."

"We might cramp his style!"

"Nah, he's got no style."

"Spoken like a true sister. And, Annie, that's not fair. Joe's a lovely bloke."

"I know he is, Verna. But I've never seen him with any women who aren't just friends."

"Lots of blokes like that during the war. Worried about getting hitched, then killed." Flo clamped her hand over her mouth. "Oh, damn it, Annie. I'm sorry. Both feet in mouth."

"That's alright, ducks. I'm not that fragile."

Verna hugged her. "You have been, you know." She glanced at her watch. "Come on, I promised Mum I wouldn't be too long. Ruthie'll be getting tired and cranky." As they turned to walk back along Coogee beach, Verna took Annie's hand. "Honestly, Annie, I do think it's a good idea. It's just that I'll miss you both. Who else will understand I'm not really moaning about James when I moan about him?"

"Well, it's early days. Plans change."

Flo scowled. "Not if those sods at the medical board have anything to do with anything."

The tea-pot under a crocheted cosy, and the milk jug and mugs of tea clumped in the middle of the kitchen table looked like a still life, but served a more practical purpose, that being away from Ruthie's probing reach. The toddler bounced from lap to lap as conversation, interspersed by comments from Mrs. Davidson, washed around them like a warm bath.

"I'd have liked to travel." Mrs. Davidson folded a tea towel over the Aga rail.

"Really?" Verna looked up from Ruthie's tangled curls.

Annie asked, "Why didn't you, Mrs. D.?

She laughed. "Fell for a bloke. Had six daughters. How's that for starters?"

—

Chatter curled around the nurse's common room. Rain pelted the windows and had tempted few out on their day off. Annie, about to move into the smoking room, heard her name and looked towards the door.

"Call for you, Annie."

"Me?"

"You're the only Annie in here. Course it's you."

"Oh, righto." She moved to the telephone tucked into a nook in the hallway, shielded a little from passing interest and with a low chair next to it. "Hello?"

"Is that you, girl?"

"Dad?" Annie blinked. In all the years since she'd left home, Ian had not once rung her. She swallowed hard. Well, he obviously wasn't dead. "What's happened?"

"Your mother's sister died last night. Just like that. Got a call this morning."

"Auntie May?"

"Who else would it be?"

Tears trickled down her cheeks and she clutched the phone, pressing it into her ear.

"You still there?"

Annie gulped. "Yes, Dad."

"You'll need to come home. Sort things out. I can't do that. I didn't even like her."

Annie heard an intake of breath across the party line. Mrs. Somers. Their conversation would be relayed around the district by the woman on the switchboard. Annie's grip tightened on the phone and, tears now streaming, she wiped her nose and replied. "She didn't like you either, Dad. So that's alright."

"Right then. Helen can meet your train."

"Don't bother. I'll stay at Auntie May's. Who found her?"

"Her nosy neighbour. Called the doctor, who called me. Dunno why. I haven't spoken to her since your mother died."

Anger bubbled with her tears. "Mrs. Elliot. She's a lovely woman. I've got her number. Thanks for letting me know. Bye."

"I'll be seeing you."

"I doubt it, Dad." Annie put the receiver back and leant against the wall. She reached for Bill's lighter in her pocket. The only thing she had of his. She'd have a cigarette then call James. Perhaps he'd go with her to Armidale for the funeral. It would be nice to have him, and Gracie with her, especially as Joe wouldn't be there. And they'd both known and loved Auntie May.

—

The heart of the house on Jessie Street had gone, buried with her aunt. The emptiness reminded Annie of when Ma had died. The homestead had become a shell. Perhaps that was why she never felt like going home.

Pearl, Auntie May's cat, had migrated next door to Mrs. Elliot with barely a twitched whisker and, as Annie wandered through the rooms, the fanciful notion that she would perhaps keep the house, dissipated. God knows where Joe would end up. Gracie, while on the edges of Annie's childhood, had never been a close friend and, with James, Verna and Ruthie ensconced in Sydney, it would be no surprise if she joined them in the city. No, it was time to say goodbye.

Heading back to the kitchen, Annie opened the cupboard in which Auntie May had kept the whisky. She took a cut-glass tumbler from the cabinet and poured a hefty measure, then settled on the steps leading down to the back garden. She brushed her hand across a tub filled with lavender from which her aunt had filled sachets for her clothes drawers. Roses tumbled down the trellis in a cascade of soft pinks and creamy yellows. Annie couldn't remember their names, but the scent cocooned her in a gentle fragrance.

Auntie May's words drifted in. "What you need, darl, is a new adventure."

Taking the glass of whisky Annie went back through the house. She would keep a couple of the paintings—watercolours of outback scenes, a box of jumbled photographs that she'd go through later, the silver cutlery that had been her grandmothers, and a few other bits and pieces, including the Paisley shawl given to Auntie May by a Turkish pasha. The story had always seemed so fanciful. Meeting a man on the deck of a steamer chugging down the Nile between the wars. A story on which her aunt would never expand.

With a sigh, Annie drained and washed the glass. With the money her aunt had left her, the sale of the house, and the contents, she would not need to panic about finding a job the moment she arrived in England. Maybe take a break from nursing. She dried the glass and put it back in the cabinet.

Looking around the kitchen, she smiled. "Thanks, Auntie May, for everything!"

Chapter 18
Cambridgeshire, 2003

Annie pummelled the pastry before rolling it out for the apple pies with unnecessary force. It had been David who had helped her with the demons. Had shown her how life could be good. He was a wonderful father to their boys. She had never really understood how he had been able to reconcile the horrors he'd witnessed during the war with his staunch faith.

The jangling phone pushed images of Gunida and her father away and brought Annie back to Cambridgeshire. Wiping floury hands across her pinny, she hurried to the hall.

"Hello, the Old Vicarage," she puffed.

"Hello, Mum, how are you?" asked Hugh, subject of her recent thoughts.

"Oh, darling, what a lovely surprise. Both my boys in one day."

"Hardly boys, Mum, but both certainly yours. I just tried to call Jake but he was on a house call. He and Susie must be the only doctors left in England to do them."

"Good for them," Annie replied. "What are you up to? Where are you, or can't I ask?"

"Been in London, at the FCO all week. But I've a couple of days free so thought I might pop down and see the country bumpkins."

"Oh, did you indeed? We might all be otherwise engaged." Annie pushed hair off her face, then wondered if she now had a flour streak. She shrugged. No one to see it.

"Good thing I spoke to the sainted Susie first, then." Hugh's warm laugh came down the wire. "She's invited me to stay. I'll head up the M11 when

I've finished here and will hopefully be in time for a noisy supper with my nephews, and an early drink with my brother before they go off for some fancy dinner. I'm the babysitter."

Annie laughed again. "I wonder if they know what they're doing?"

"Thanks, Mum! Responsible is my middle name."

"I'm not worried about the boys. I just wonder if you're up to it. Commanding a company is not the same as taming ten-year-old twins."

Hugh groaned. "Another vote of confidence. Good thing my colonel can't hear you."

"Are you coming for lunch tomorrow, too?" Annie asked.

"I thought I might," Hugh laughed again, "unless you'd rather have the favoured number one son to yourself."

"You are an idiot. But yes, it will be difficult dividing my time between my equally favoured sons!"

"It's okay, Mum. Jake and I know neither of us stand a chance with your grandsons around."

Annie smiled. She and David had done something right. Their boys had turned into good men. "True, darling. So glad you recognize your lowered status. Now, you can tell me all your news tomorrow. I'm in the middle of pie making."

"Alright, Mum, see you tomorrow."

"Bye, darling."

"Mum," Hugh's voice caught her as she lowered the receiver, "you do know I love you, don't you?"

"Of course I do, ducks. What brought that on?"

"No idea. Just needs to be said every now and then."

"Well, then, I love you too, darling. Now, gotta go. Bye."

"Bye."

Annie put down the phone and frowned. Jake had always been the more demonstrative of their boys. She ambled back into the kitchen, swooshed her hands under the tap then began to work the pastry to form her grandsons' names—John and Henry. One name on each pie. Equally as precious. The telephone rang again.

"Now what?" she asked Eartha. She let it ring as she slid the pies into the oven. "It can go days without ringing and today it hasn't stopped." She swatted the cat off the chair and plonked down. "Hello, the Old Vicarage."

"Morning, Mrs. Rowland. It's Kathy, at the pharmacy, just to let you know your new prescription's ready."

"Thank you, ducky. How are you today? Has your cold gone?"

"Almost. Why is it that summer colds hang around forever?" Kathy replied with a sniff.

"Don't know. I'll nip down later and collect the pills. What time do you close? I can never remember."

"Five o'clock."

"Righto, I'll see you before then."

"Okay, bye, Mrs. Rowland."

Annie leant back into the chair and hauled Eartha onto her lap, stroking the soft fur, her mind on the local doctor. Young—well, Hugh's age she guessed, but he didn't treat her like a doddery fool. When she'd told him she needed stronger tablets, he'd checked her blood tests and agreed.

Doctors had been like that during the war. Listening to the nurses. Allowing them latitude to know their patients' needs. When an extra dose of morphine might relieve both the pain of body and spirit, even for a moment. Or, just sometimes, to ease them into death. Penicillin. Now that had been a game changer. No more sulfa powder. Annie shuddered. An image of a soldier in a jungle-ripped uniform, lying on a stretcher that sank into the mud of the ward floor the moment the Fuzzy Wuzzy Angels laid it down, invaded her thoughts. The slash from his groin to his thigh had been held together with safety pins because the field medic had run out of sutures.

The pinger on the oven shook Annie from her reverie. She wondered if she'd dozed. The memory had been so strong. "Old stories, Eartha," she said as she ditched the cat and took the pies out of the oven. She could smell them now.

The boys' names stood out a deeper gold than the crusts. They'd be pleased. Still young enough to get pleasure from the simple things in life. And it didn't get much simpler than a pie with your name crafted across it.

She knew. Another memory slid in. Her birthday. At 17 Mile Camp, not long after Bill arrived. Flo, Verna and her sitting in the Mess tent celebrating with tepid tea and tinned ham. Annie had felt his hands over her eyes and had giggled like a schoolgirl.

"Close your eyes."

She sensed people gathering, then heard a match strike. She tensed, the image of sulphur flaring reminding her of Japanese strafe fire on the Empire Star. She shivered, then relaxed back into Bill's bulk.

"Righto, you can open them now."

Verna, Flo and the Mess staff sang Happy Birthday and toasted her with tea, but the best part was a tart with her name patterned across the mango filling. A lone candle stood in for the dot on the 'i'. The cook had made a handful of tarts with precious powdered eggs, and most in the Mess got a slither.

"Many happy returns, Lieutenant." Matron's voice came from the door.

It still sounded strange being addressed by rank and not as sister, although Matron always seemed to be Matron. They had leapt to their feet, licking sticky mango from their lips.

Matron glanced around the Mess. "There's a convoy coming in. I need five of you to report back to your wards. The rest get some sleep. You'll be needed soon enough."

Annie had seen her glance go to Bill with a slight smile, then Matron nodded at him. "Doctor, I believe you're required in surgery."

"Right away, Matron. Thanks."

"Lieutenant Cutler, a moment, please."

Annie had watched Verna, Flo and the others disappear, and wished she could go too.

"I am well aware of the romance between you and Major Townsend, Sister. I also know neither of you are impulsive. I just ask that you do not forget you are an army nurse, first and foremost."

"No, Matron. Of course not."

"Good. Now back to the ward, please."

—

The clock in the dining room dinged midday. Where had the morning gone? Annie poured milk into the pan, eschewing the hated microwave, and as it started to bubble, added coffee and a teaspoon of sugar. She slathered mustard on a sliced croissant, added ham and cheese, put it and the frothy coffee on a tray and, with her unsettling memories, took it out to the garden.

She loved days like this. The sun at its zenith. Bright skies that reminded her of spring on the New England Tablelands. Here she was grateful for a few more weeks of warmth before autumn began to bite. A contrail provided a streak of white in the cornflower sky.

"Move over, cat."

Eartha Kitty, languid on the low bench dappled with the sun shining through the gum leaves, watched Annie's approach. Annie leant her head back, enjoying the September warmth. Plenty of time before she had to pick up her prescription.

Roses climbed the trellis to create a bower around the tree and bench. The boldness and layers of yellow petals made Annie smile as she breathed in the subtle scent of tea tinged with a hint of spicy myrrh. David had planted them after seeing a display at a flower show, saying that no other plant deserved to be in a vicar's garden more than the Pilgrim Rose, added to which, his love of the *Canterbury Tales.*

Gardening had crept up on Annie and had become just as much her passion as David's. It had, on occasion, been the cause of their few differences. She couldn't put a date on the realisation that she actually liked grubbing around in the beds tugging weeds or digging in new plants. She chuckled, David's words floating down from where she presumed he now resided.

"Well, I suppose I should at least be grateful you're on your knees somewhere," he'd said, coming across her one afternoon, stooping to kiss her head. "Even if it isn't in Church!"

"Hah!"

Annie sighed. She missed him. Still. "That's not going to change now is it, Eartha?" She asked the disinterested cat. Three years. The ache never quite went away, although at least its stab didn't leave her breathless anymore. Just melancholic.

Her legs stretched out, Annie picked at the ragged hole in her jeans. David really would've hated them. Perhaps it was time to toss them, but they felt so soft and comfy, why take the trouble to break in a new pair. A faint ping might have been the doorbell, but she ignored it. What was the point of going ever-so-slightly deaf if one couldn't disregard certain things?

In their early days at the Vicarage there had been easy access to the back garden along a narrow path. After a particularly persistent parishioner had sauntered in unannounced one afternoon, Annie had insisted on having a gate installed. With Jake having a nap upstairs, David and Annie had made love on a rug on the lawn—the afternoon, she remained convinced, Hugh had been conceived. To save any more of David's blushes, he had agreed. She chuckled. Something fluttered and she turned to see what had caught her attention. A downy white feather. Annie picked it up, running the softness across her cheek as she sat back down.

It had taken many late nights of talking with the others for her to forgive, though not forget, the unkindness and ignorance of those women in their church finery waiting for the nurses at the gates of Fremantle docks.

Verna's words swooped in as if it were yesterday. "What the hell?"

Annie, her hand crushing the white feather she too had been handed, had grabbed Verna's arm and propelled her towards the army truck waiting for them. She turned in time to see Florence and many of the others being presented with the same symbol.

"Who the hell do they think they are?" Asked Frances, a nurse who had been in Singapore since the first bombs had fallen. "Safe at home."

"We don't know they've been safe," Flo said. "Perhaps they're from Darwin."

"I don't care where they're from," said Annie. "How dare they call us cowards?" Fuming, she turned to address the women, but was pulled back to the truck by Verna.

"You wouldn't let me say anything. What makes you think I'll let you?"

"Get in, Annie," said Flo, pushing her up on the hitch step. She handed her both their cases before clambering in herself. "It is not worth getting a rocket from anyone."

"But how could they?" Frances looked pale. "They don't know what we've been through."

"We could have nursed one of their boys, for all they know." Annie added, tears of anger threatening to spill.

"Pain makes us do stupid things," Flo said.

"Why haven't they been told to move on? To go away." Annie asked, watching the women disappear from view as the truck lurched off. "Isn't that why there are MPs? To keep the peace?"

"They're there to stop anyone going AWOL, or getting drunk and brawling."

The feather brushing her face, and a voice from the other side of the gate broke Annie's trance.

"Hellooo? Granny Annie? I know you're there."

"No, I'm not!" Annie's lips twitched.

"Can you let me in, please?"

"No, I bloody can't."

"You're mean! Fine."

Annie moved closer and watched the ivy-covered gate wobble, her smile widening as first one hand, then the other, followed swiftly by a face sprinkled with light freckles came into view. Violet eyes met Annie's hazel crinkled ones.

"You're mean!" Gemma heaved herself over the fence and jumped down.

"Yup. And now I've proved who keeps moving, and dressing, my statues. You, and probably that other ruffian, Paul."

Gemma laughed. "I thought the floral toga the best yet. That was my idea. Paul made the wreath."

"Picked from my ivy, I suspect." Annie gave the girl a hug. "G'day, ducks! Would you like some lemonade? I made some yesterday."

"Yes, please. Shall I get you one too?"

"Yes, why not? Put a splash of gin in too, please. But not in yours. I will check."

"I don't like the taste."

"Good, though I doubt very much that your mother would approve of you having tried it already. Or your father, come to that." The lithe twelve-year old disappeared into the house and Annie went back to the bench with a smile. She'd watched Gemma grow from a bubbly baby to a charming child, through the self-conscious tween years to emerge a delightful and funny almost-teenager. And she'd known her mother from about the same age. She, Jake and Hugh had been firm friends, although strangely, the parents had never really clicked. And now Jake's boys loved Gemma, as he had loved her mother.

Annie bent and picked up the feather from where it had blown off the bench.

"Here you go, Granny Annie."

Annie took a sip. "Delicious, the perfect amount of zip added, thank you, ducky." She watched Gemma throw herself on the grass, then reach across and tickle Eartha. "So, what's up?"

"Nothing. I got bored on my own."

"Where is everyone?"

"Mum's shopping, and Dad and Ivan are at the cricket."

"I thought you liked cricket."

"I do. But not today." Gemma looked at Annie's hand. "Why are you holding a feather?"

"Oh, just remembering things. That's what ancients like me do."

"You look sad. And you're not as old as my Granny."

Annie sipped her gin and lemonade. "No, that's right. She's at least a month older."

"So, why are you sad?" Gemma's eyes sharpened. "It's the feather, isn't it?"

"Do you know what a white feather symbolises?""

"An angel?"

Annie laughed. "No, well not when we were given them, although when I think about it, lots of our boys called us angels." She ran the feather across her palm. "Some of us were handed these when we got back to Australia from Singapore during the war."

"Why?"

"Because some people, women, thought we were cowards who had run away."

"But why?"

"I don't really know. We were nurses. You know that. So many people left Singapore those last few days before the Japanese took over the island. Men and women. Soldiers, nurses and civilians." The image of Iris in the hall at St. Patrick's made Annie stifle a gasp.

"What happened to the ones who didn't get away? Or the people from there?"

"All the Europeans and many others became prisoners of war. You've heard of Changi and the Burma Railway, haven't you?" Gemma nodded. "So you know lots of them died. And so did lots of Malays, Chinese, and Indians who helped the foreigners."

"But I don't see why you were given white feathers?" Gemma's voice rose in indignation. "And who started it anyway?"

"It started in the First World War, when young men not in uniform were considered cowards."

"That's cruel. They could have been sick. Or doing something secret. Or something."

"War can make people behave badly, Gemma." Annie rubbed her face.

"You okay, Granny Annie? You look all bleary."

"Just remembering. It's been one of those days." Annie leant forward and tucked a strand of loose hair behind her young visitor's ear. "Oh, my, is that a pierced ear I see? Mum finally agreed, did she?"

"Not exactly." Gemma twiddled the earring.

Annie gave a snort. "You didn't!" Then laughed out loud. "How? I thought you had to have a letter from her giving permission."

"I did."

"You forged her signature! Oh, Gemma. Is she livid?"

"Pretty much."

Trying to stifle another chuckle, Annie said, "That is the reason I am very glad I didn't have daughters! You don't get that subterfuge with boys!"

Gemma rubbed her face along Eartha's warm fur. "Not sure what that means, but I'm guessing not good."

"It means deviousness. You only had a couple of months to wait till your birthday. Why'd you rock the boat?"

"Dunno, really. Joanna got hers done too. It hurt."

"Serves you right!"

They sipped their lemonade accompanied by summer sounds. A lawn mower down the street. Annie could hear a woodpecker somewhere close by. She watched bees dance and dive around the purple blossoms on the phacelia.

Gemma, concentrating on making a chain from the daisies sprinkling the lawn, broke their companionable silence. "Don't you get bored, or lonely, Granny Annie?"

"Have you heard of the philosopher, Friedrick Nietzsche?"

"Nope." Gemma looked up. "Actually, I'm not quite sure what a philosopher is."

"Someone who spends hours and hours thinking."

"Now that sounds boring!"

"In a way, I'm inclined to agree with you. I always much preferred doing to thinking. But not so much now." Annie looked down at Gemma, still stringing daisies. "I'll tell you what Mr. Nietzsche said, although I might not get the words absolutely right. You can impress your father." She laughed, and didn't wait for a response. "Nietzsche said, 'Is life not a thousand times too short for us to bore ourselves?' I must admit though, it's only now that I'm old that I rather agree with him."

"Yes, but do you? Do you get bored, or lonely? And you look sad sometimes. Like just now. When you held that feather."

"To use your word, Gemma, nope!"

"But you sit out here and don't do anything. You don't even read, like you used to."

Annie toed Gemma's bare leg. "I'll have you know I've been busy making apple pies today!"

"Don't do that, Granny Annie. I'm not a baby. I really want to know."

"I'm sorry, ducky. I know you're not. But old women, and men … and actually I think men more than women, but don't tell your father that, sometimes wiffle-waffle on, and then they become the bores. I'd hate to do that."

Gemma's violet eyes gazed up. "But you don't."

Annie sipped her gin and lemonade. "Righto, I'll let you in on a secret." She paused. "I don't get bored because when I'm sitting, doing nothing, I'm scrolling through my memories. It's like a film. A bit of a wobbly film, like it's coming off a reel, because it jumps around a lot."

"But that makes you sad."

"No, it doesn't. Well," Annie paused again, "I suppose it does sometimes. Only when it's something that's happened to someone I cared about. Although that doesn't mean I wish I hadn't loved them. But, Gemma, I don't regret anything I've done." She smiled. "Actually, that's not true. I should never have started smoking. Don't you dare start?"

"I've never seen you smoke."

"I didn't for years. But now, since David died, I allow myself one a night. And a cube of chocolate! If I'm entirely honest, I have chocolate whenever I feel like it."

"Did your kids smoke?"

"No, thank God. Well, I don't think so. I suppose they might have tried it."

"It stinks."

"It certainly does. And it makes you wrinkly?"

"I think Mum smokes sometimes."

"Really?"

"She says I drive her to drink, and I'm pretty sure I've seen her in the garden at night having a cigarette."

"You know she's teasing, don't you?"

"Yeah, I guess."

"And, it should be remembered, Miss Gemma, you did get your ears pierced against her wishes. Now, enough of the deep talk. I've got to drive into town and get a prescription. Off you go, and if I find my statues in a tutu I'll have your, and Paul's, guts for garters! I'm going to put a row of spikes along the top of the fence."

Gemma stood, then bent to kiss Annie's cheek. "No, you won't. Because we make you laugh!"

With a cheeky wave the girl sauntered off, this time through the house. Annie picked up the feather again and, left with her memories sighed as instead of flares shooting down, Iris clouded her vision.

The hospital hall in Singapore had been the last time she, Verna and Flo had seen her. God, the three of them had been so lucky. Iris's ship, the Vyner Brooke, had been bombed not long after leaving Singapore and had sunk off Bangka Island. Annie remembered the hope they'd held on to, that Iris had been interned in Batavia, then the sadness at learning she had died on Radji Beach. It had only been at the end of the war that they learnt the truth, and it had sent Annie into a tailspin, sadness underpinned by guilt and regret.

"Half the truth." Annie's words whispered through the feather held to her mouth. Nurses who had made it through a night clinging to planks, exhausted and terrified, some defiant, had been forced back into the sea at bayonet point by Japanese soldiers, then shot.

Chapter 19
London, 1948

Flo, bundled in a navy coat buttoned to her neck, glared at Annie and said, "Do not say, 'I'm never going on a ship again.'"

"Well, I'm not." Wind whipped Annie's hair out of its combs. "I did pretty well until the Bay of Biscay. You've got to admit that was rough." She peered over the railing to watch gangplanks being tied off.

"I've lost count of how many times I've heard you say that. At least four countries."

"I know. Next time, we'll fly!" Annie hugged Flo. "Come on. We made it."

"Bloody hell, it's cold." Flo shivered. "Wonder how long it'll take to get our luggage?"

"Joe said the trunks will be sent on later. We just take our suitcases now."

"God, can you believe it, Annie? We're in England."

Annie watched the bustle on the quay. "There's something visceral about docks, isn't there? Weird and wonderful smells. Posh and poor, jumbled up together."

"A box of Liquorice Allsorts!"

Annie hugged Flo. "Trust you to think of sweets." She waved her arm, "Isn't this exciting?"

"Says the girl who doesn't have to worry about finding a job tomorrow."

"Oh, ducky, you don't have to, either. We've got enough to let us find our feet without panicking. And you know Joe said we can stay as long as we like. He's hardly ever there, it seems."

"Thanks, Annie." Flo hunched deeper in her coat. "But just to be clear, I'm not bludging from you."

"I know that, Flo. I'm just saying you don't need to grab the first thing offered."

"We might not be offered anything!"

"What's the matter?" Annie turned to face her friend. "What's going on?"

"Cold feet!" Flo stamped her feet on the deck. "Literally. I dunno. Colly-wobbles, I suppose. We always had the army behind us before. Now we're on our own."

Annie swung Flo's hand. "Look at it this way. We don't have to follow orders. Which, you have to admit, has been fun on board."

Flo smiled. "Yeah. Nice to be allowed to talk to a bloke without Matron glaring. But don't think I didn't notice you disappearing for solitary walks on deck." She paused. "My turn for a pep talk. You're allowed to laugh, Annie."

"I do!"

"Sometimes. But then you scurry back, as if you shouldn't. Bill would hate that."

—

After snaking their way through immigration, Annie and Flo boarded the train at Tilbury and, stowing their suitcases, grinned at each other. A weak sun peeped from behind a bank of low-lying clouds, lessening the grime of the port. Annie watched the passing buildings, taking in the streets with gaping holes, like toothless crones where the Luftwaffe had dropped their bombs during the Blitz.

"Can you imagine how terrifying it would've been?" she asked. "Night after night."

"Yeah, we didn't do too badly, did we?"

A steady drizzle sent rivulets down the window as the train chugged into Fenchurch Street Station. Annie pulled out Joe's last letter with instructions on how to get to Cork Street by bus, just in case he couldn't meet them. Looking at the number of changes, she wondered if they shouldn't splurge on a taxi. Besides she rather liked the idea of starting her London life in a hackney cab.

"Why didn't I pack the Vegemite in my trunk?" Flo groaned as they lugged their suitcases to the entrance of the station.

Annie, struggling with her bulging case as well, and a hat that would not stay in place, nodded, "Righto, that decides it. It's raining. These are heavy. And, despite Joe's best intentions, I can't make much sense of his instructions. We're taking a cab. I don't care how much it costs. We're going to arrive in style."

Flo gave a snort of laughter. "You did say Joe's landlady was living in impoverished gentility. She might approve. What's her name again?"

"Mrs. Ida Bellows."

Hailing a cab, the women clambered in and watched with interest as the driver loaded their luggage into the separate compartment next to his seat.

"So, ladies, where to?"

"Cork Street, please? I think it's behind Piccadilly, somewhere." Annie ended lamely.

"That's alright, luv, I know where it is. Got The Knowledge."

"What's that?"

He touched his cap to a passing taxi. "Gotta know all the streets of London before you get your licence. Takes a bit a learnin' that does."

"I'll bet!" Flo stifled a giggle and lowered her voice. "His ears wiggle when he talks."

"Shhh!"

"Aussies?" he asked.

"Yes," Flo replied.

"Watcha doin' over 'ere?"

"My brother's here."

"Dunno why you'd want to be 'ere. We've still got rationin'!" He swerved around a London bus. "I got a mate 'ho's just gone out there. A Ten Pound Pom you lot call 'em!"

"Where's he gone?"

"Synney." He waited for a light to change. "I told 'im I might join 'im, but me missus ain't too keen. I dunno. Get away from the bleedin' rain'd be a good start. What d' you think?"

"It rains in Sydney, too."

"Not all the bleedin' time. Like 'ere." He lapsed into silence as he negotiated traffic and craters still present in some areas, pulling up outside a row of soot-streaked houses. "Right, ladies, 'ere we are then."

Standing on the pavement as the driver unloaded their cases, another cab pulled up.

"G'day, Annie! Flo!" Joe's voice came from the open window. "Sorry I missed you. Got held up."

As he climbed out, Annie flung herself in his arms, half laughing, half crying. "We made it, we made it!"

"I can see that. Has she been like this all the way over?" Joe asked Flo as he hugged her too.

"No, thank God."

Joe paid the cab driver and, as he bent to lift their cases, the front door opened. "Good afternoon, Mrs. Bellows," he said, tipping his hat. "May I introduce my sister, Annie, and her friend, Florence Taylor."

"Yes, yes, Joe, but not on the doorstep. Come in, ladies. Good afternoon. The kettle is on, and Mrs. Clarke's baked a cake. Sadly, with powdered egg, and not much sugar, but," Mrs. Bellows gave a slight smile, "we manage."

"That's very kind of you, but really we couldn't intrude," said Annie, glancing at Joe for help.

"Of course you can, my dear. Mrs. Clarke would be most upset if her efforts went to waste."

Joe chimed in, his eyes dancing, "And, Annie, Mrs. Bellows wants to judge for herself what kind of ladies you are!"

Their landlady flushed, touched her permed hair, and smiling, said, "Really, Joe, what nonsense!"

—

Next morning, Joe kissed Annie on the cheek, picked up his hat and a small suitcase and headed for the door. "See you in a few days. Make yourselves at home and don't let her get into any trouble, Flo."

"Bloody cheek!" Annie tossed a tea towel at his retreating back. "Righto, ducks, a cuppa, then what?"

"Let's just wander today, get our bearings." Flo peered out of the window. "At least it's not tipping it down. Yet." She flicked through to the earmarked page of the A to Z book of maps that Joe had left on the kitchen table. "I think we're in a posh part of town."

"We're near Burlington Arcade, but I read somewhere it had been bombed." Annie chuckled. "I remember, when we were little, Auntie May strutting around her kitchen in a top hat and twirling a wooden spoon for a walking stick, singing that old music hall song, *I'm Burlington Bertie from Bow.*" She laughed. "No wonder Father didn't like her. She was great fun. And Ma, well, she was lighter somehow whenever she and her sister got together."

"Let's stroll down the Strand with our gloves in our hand." Flo finished her tea, "But only after I've figured out that gurgling bath. Do you think it rumbles all the way down through Mrs. B's flat?"

"Dunno. But hurry up, I want to see London."

Annie settled at the table and pulled yesterday's paper towards her. Joe had also bought her the latest edition of *The Lady*, explaining the magazine was well-respected for its classified advertisements, and positions, particularly for domestic service and childcare. Before she got to that section, she spotted an article by someone called Alison Settle that made her smile. "THE coat you buy must have both fashion value and thrift value." With a grin, she glanced across at her coat hanging on the back of the door. If it had ever had any fashion value, it had been lost years ago.

Next, Annie flicked to the classifieds. She and Flo knew, with the soon-to-be National Health Service offering free medical care, there was a nursing shortage in England. It had been one of the main factors in leaving Australia. But, as her finger trailed down the columns of jobs for nannies, private nurses and housekeepers, Annie decided she might not jump into public nursing just yet. She could do with a change. And it wasn't as if she and Flo would be together anyway. Annie had no desire to nurse on psychiatric wards, even though that was where the biggest need seemed to be. And being a private nurse didn't appeal—at the behest of some irascible old codger. She thought of Ruthie and how much she enjoyed her godchild. Annie put the magazine down, her thoughts dancing. Perhaps she'd try nannying? But today, London.

"Ready!" Flo appeared, a woollen scarf slung around her neck. "Come on, let's go and explore. And we must have tea at Lyons Corner House on the Strand."

Stubbing out a cigarette, Annie shrugged into her coat and said, "We don't have to do all of London in a day." She picked up the spare set of keys, "We should probably find a locksmith so we can each have a set."

"Do you think we should check with Mrs. Bellows? I mean it is her house."

"Nah. I reckon we passed the test yesterday. We'll be right. Beg forgiveness, if necessary."

"That should be your epitaph!"

Annie pushed Flo out the door. "Charming."

—

Annie reached across the narrow gap between the beds and squeezed Flo's hand lying on top of the covers. "That was a good day. I'm exhausted from all the walking. But worth every minute."

"Yeah, it was."

"You know something?" Annie didn't wait for a reply, "I didn't think of Bill once today. And, I think for the first time, I don't feel guilty about it. Is that terrible?"

Flo, all sleep driven from her voice, swung out from under the blankets, woolly bed socks a yellow statement at the end of her pyjama-clad legs. She flung her dressing gown over her shoulders and sat on the edge of Annie's bed. "No, lovey, that's healthy. It's been four years."

Annie looked up at her friend's face, eerie in the dim-out lamplight filtering through the thin curtains. "Yeah. I know."

"You'll never forget him, Annie. He was your first, but hopefully not your last love. And," Flo added, "he would hate it if you didn't find someone else." She put her hand up to stop Annie's response. "Just remember, ducks, he found you after his wife died."

"I know," Annie repeated, "but at thirty-four, I think my chances are slim." She poked a finger in Flo's waist, "So are yours!"

"Speak for yourself. I shall be a ground-breaking pioneer in the treatment of trauma patients. Doctors and scientists from around the world will be falling over themselves to hear me speak. To touch the lustre of my brilliance." Flo sighed. "First, of course, is getting a foot in the bloody door. That's tomorrow's task."

"You've got your letter of invitation for an interview at the Maudsley Hospital School, Flo. They'd be idiots not to grab you."

"Yeah, but I wasn't actually honest, was I? I mean, I didn't exactly mention I wanted to become a psychiatric doctor."

"Florence Taylor, you will become a doctor. You will be world famous. You will be so sought after, you won't have time for a lowly midwife like me."

"Never! Now shut up. I'm an ice block from sitting here, and I need sleep. Good night, lovey."

"Night." Annie snaked a hand out from under the blankets and reached for Bill's lighter sitting on top of a pack of cigarettes on the bedside table. She lay awake a long time, turning the lighter over and over until, with a sigh, she replaced it. When Flo went to Maudsley, she'd start looking for a nannying job.

Chapter 20
A Tale of Three Cities, 1948

The freezing damp misery of their first couple of weeks in England gave way to fog as February trickled into March. Annie, almost at the point of splurging on a new coat, as advised by *The Lady*, was glad she didn't because in what seemed like a blink the days turned warm and all thoughts of hats, scarves and coats were gone. White gloves replaced black ones.

Buds began to burst out in soft greens, dressing skeletal trees in spring finery, topped with blossom that floated like snow to lay in white and pink mounds of spun candy floss. People no longer scurried to their destination, but ambled through the awakening parks. And they smiled.

Annie checked the number of the house as she turned off Holland Park Avenue and found Queensdale Road. Number 10. She stopped outside and looked up at the Victorian mid-terrace house, French doors on the first floor looking out over what she presumed was a private garden on the other side of the road. Even a room in the garrets would do very nicely.

Never keen on hats, Annie had decided against wearing one to her interview. Now she regretted her decision—it seemed a hat sort of house. Oh well, too late now. She shrugged and rang the bell.

A scamper of feet skidded to halt with a bump on the other side of the front door, followed by a woman's voice calling for, Annie presumed, the owner of the feet, to slow down and wait. She smiled. The voice sounded amused.

"Hello, I'm Peter." Curious brown eyes stared up at Annie as the door opened.

"Good morning, you must be …" the blonde woman glanced at a list in her hand, "sorry, Miss Cutler. Do come in. I'm Patricia Goodwin."

"Good morning, Mrs. Goodwin, and thank you."

"You sound funny!"

"Hush, Peter. Don't be rude."

"That's alright," Annie crouched down. "I'm Australian, and we do sound a bit different, don't we? Do you know where Australia is?"

"No." He turned a toy car over in his hand.

"It's a country right on the other side of the world."

"I'm five. Are you going to be our new nanny? Janet doesn't want one. She's seven. And Molly's a baby."

"Can we please allow Miss Cutler in, Peter? Go on, off you go. Why don't you ask Mrs. Robbins for a biscuit and a glass of milk?" The woman turned back to Annie, "Please, come in. Let's go into the morning room. It's a bit chaotic."

"That's alright," Annie repeated and followed Mrs. Goodwin into a room overlooking the street. A coffee pot shared space with a baby bottle on the polished table.

"Do sit down, Miss Cutler."

Annie snuck a glance at the list of names on the paper. It appeared that a number had already been interviewed and struck off. One name had a question mark. Three more followed Annie. She waited.

"So, Miss Cutler, it seems you've had a busy war. Why do you want to leave nursing?"

"Because of that."

"I see. But," Mrs. Goodwin looked at Annie's letter, "you've no actual experience as a nanny. Although I see here you are a midwife." She smiled. "I could've done with you three months ago."

"A difficult birth?" Annie asked.

"Not really, just early. Molly was a month premature. But all is well."

"Good."

"Now, Miss Cutler, I'm afraid there has been a change since we communicated. My husband has been asked to go to Berlin," Mrs. Goodwin paused, "and would like us to accompany him."

Annie watched the woman, her skirt a little tight at the waist, turn away and wipe a tear as she gathered herself. "How do you feel about that, Mrs. Goodwin?"

"Heavens! No one has actually asked me."

"Why not?" Indignation made Annie's voice rise. "You're the one who will have to cope with a household in flux, and a new baby."

The woman sighed. "Of course, I have to go. It's expected. There will be an element of entertainment. Rupert, my husband, did suggest we leave the children, but I can't do that."

"Good for you." Aware she had probably overstepped the bounds, Annie, for once, chose her words carefully. "Sometimes, when we feel overwhelmed about a decision not of our making, the fear of the unknown is worse than the actuality. I'm sure you'll be fine."

Mrs. Goodwin drummed the table. A gentle tattoo that sent shafts of shimmering light across the oak table from the brilliant oval ruby and diamond ring on her finger. "How would you feel about Berlin?"

Annie looked out of the window gathering her thoughts. Both Joe and Flo's words nudged in. How could she blame an entire nation for Ernie's death? And from what Joe said, Germany was reeling. She squared her shoulders.

"I've just come from Australia, Mrs. Goodwin, Berlin is as good as London for me."

Annie hoped that would be the case. "Don't you want to ask me anything about children?"

"Not really. You seemed good with Peter. Janet is at the park with one of the maids. As Peter said, she does not believe she needs a nanny. Margaret, Molly—no, actually, me—I need a nanny." Mrs. Goodwin smiled for the first time. "I have a couple more people to interview but just so I know, would you be prepared to move in straight away? I'm pretty desperate."

Annie's thoughts flew to Flo. She couldn't abandon her until Joe returned. How would he feel about having a woman to stay without Annie there? How would Flo feel? "No, I'm sorry, Mrs. Goodwin. I could start working straight away but I can't move in until at least next week. I'd stay until the children were in bed, but then I'd have to leave."

The woman's shoulders slumped. "I understand. There is a Norland Nanny coming to be interviewed. Someone my husband likes, on paper." Mrs Goodwin trailed her finger down the list. "She is very experienced."

"Well, then, she'd probably be ideal." Annie wanted to pat the woman on her shoulder, offer some kind of comfort.

"She, the Norland Nanny, just seems, well, a bit old. I'd like someone I can talk to." Her eyes watered again. "Oh God, this is all so difficult. Perhaps she wouldn't want to go to Germany."

"Like I said, Mrs. Goodwin, things usually work out." Annie stood, "Thanks for the interview, I can show myself out. You sit here a moment, in the quiet, before the next applicant."

"Miss Cutler, Annie, I'll let you know. Perhaps you wouldn't mind coming back and meeting my husband?"

"Of course." Annie pulled the door shut behind her. "Oh, hello again." She stooped down to the little boy, his mouth ringed with milk. "You escaped from the kitchen. Where's your car?"

He pulled the toy from his shorts' pocket and offered it for inspection. "Are you going to be our nanny?" He asked again.

"I don't think so, ducks. I'm more a nurse than a nanny, but whoever your mummy chooses will be wonderful, I'm sure."

"Janet and me didn't like the last one. She was mean."

—

Crowded with lunchtime workers, Annie watched a table being wiped down by a bean-thin woman with hair scraped across her scalp into a severe bun. Then, with a smile that sent lines radiating across her face, she offered the table to Annie. "Here you are, love. Do you need two chairs? Only we're awful busy if you don't."

"Thank you, I do." She tapped the bottom of her cigarette packet. "My friend's meeting me here, any moment."

"Right you are." The waitress gave an extra flick of her rag, "What'll you have?"

"A pot of tea, please. And what have you got to nibble on?"

"Bakewell tart, without the almonds. We make it with lemon instead. And war cake without an egg, made with carrot and not much sugar."

"That sounds good, thanks."

"Not really, but the carrot gives it a bit of sweetness at least. One day we'll be back to normal." The smile, so at odds with her stern face, flashed again.

"G'day." Flo bounced down on the chair. "I'll have whatever she's having, please."

"Right you are."

"So," Annie studied Flo, "what are you looking so pleased about?"

Flo looked bashful, then untucked a letter from her handbag. "I got a response."

Annie raised an eyebrow. "To what? From whom?"

"A—no—the bigwig at the University of Glasgow."

"Glasgow?" Annie shook her head. "As in Scotland?" She leant back and waited until the waitress had set out the teapot and milk jug, along with cups and saucers, and two slices of sludgy brown war cake. "You need to start from the beginning, ducks."

"I decided to spread the net, not just bank on the Maudsley, so last week I wrote to a psychiatrist called Jonathon Callwood. He did a lot during the war, you know, with trauma and shell-shocked cases. And he replied. Wanted to know more." Flo grinned.

"What sort of stuff?"

"About me. And actual patients. The ones who couldn't, or wouldn't speak at all. That sort of thing. I told him about the bloke you mentioned. The one who shot himself." Flo rushed on. "I didn't pretend he was my patient, Annie, in case you wondered."

"'Course not, ducks. Doesn't matter anyway."

"So, Dr. Callwood believes in a balanced approach. Not just drugs." Flo's eyes glowed. "A physical, psychological and social method." She paused. "Like having patients work in the hospital gardens."

Annie jumped in. "You always said they should get outside and do something."

"I know!"

"Anyway, I met him at the end of last week."

"Where? Why didn't you tell me?"

"Didn't want to jump any guns. In case I had to lick my wounds. He was in London for a meeting."

"Oh, Flo." Annie reached for her hand. "After everything you've seen me through. Really?"

"That's different."

"Rubbish. But we'll leave that, for now." Annie poured tea. "What was he like?"

"Nice. Not prissy, like the drongos who interviewed me at home. Nothing formal. I met him in a café, and we just talked. He asked lots of questions about New Guinea. Whether I'd nursed any Japs."

"Huh. Why'd he want to know that?"

"He's interested in how different countries, I think he said cultures, treat psychiatry."

"Did you mention the Sikh POWs we nursed in Lae? The ones the Japs left to rot?"

"Yeah, I did."

"So," Annie eyed Flo over the rim of her cup, "I'm guessing you've heard."

Flo nodded, and with a grin, unfolded the letter and read aloud.

Dear Miss Taylor, "that's me!"

"Flo," Annie warned with a laugh, "get on with it. And your accent is really crook. Is that meant to sound Scottish?"

Thank you for your long letter, expanding on your wartime experiences. Some of them unique. Flo giggled. "It was long but I thought what the hell? My first one wasn't, that was crisp. I might have rambled a little in the second."

Annie groaned. "Read!"

Flo continued.

I admire your aspirations and, dare I say, your determination as a woman to enter this field at a time when, I believe, we are on the cusp of changing how mental health is managed. It is not an area of nursing for the faint hearted.

Indignant, Annie interrupted. "He sounds like the others. I thought you wanted to retrain."

"I do. But this is a stepping stone. Just listen."

Your experience both in the field during the war and afterwards at Concord Hospital speak to your dedication. As I explained, our department is in the throes of formation and there is still uncertainty about its entire structure.

However, I would like to suggest you come to Glasgow, initially as a nurse.

Flo held up her hand to Annie's indignant snort.

As funding becomes more available, and the department is given more leeway, I believe there will be opportunities for people, such as yourself, to be a part of the new and exciting developments coming in the field of psychiatry.

Should this way forward be of interest, perhaps you would let me know. If indeed you decide to come to Glasgow, my wife, Sarah, who was a QA during the war, would be happy to put you in touch with a woman she knows who runs a suitable hostel.

Rest assured, Miss Taylor, I will support any applications you might make, both now and in the future.

Flo sat back, beaming. "What do you think?"

"I think you are amazing. That's what!" Annie took Flo's hand, "I'm so pleased for you, ducky. And proud. I really am. A toast to my already brilliant friend."

"You don't mind that I'm leaving you in the lurch in London?"

"No, ducks, because I've been a bit underhand too. I didn't mention it because there was no point until I knew if I'd get the job. Remember the interview I told you about, the one in the fancy house with two children and a baby?"

Flo nodded.

"Well, Mrs. Goodwin asked me back to meet her husband, who, she told me, wanted to hire a formal nanny—one with training. But she, Mrs. G., didn't like her." Annie paused, her lips pursed, "I don't actually think Mr. Goodwin cares that much about who looks after the children as long as she looks the part. You know uniform, rules and all that. She wants a more relaxed approach."

"You can do relaxed." Flo gave a laugh, "And you're not very good at rules!"

"I can be!" Annie defended herself. "Sometimes."

"Go on, then, did you get the job?"

"Yup." Annie took out her own letter.

Dear Miss Cutler,

Thank you for coming to meet my husband.

I am delighted to offer you employment as a nanny to Janet, Peter and Molly, starting as soon as you are able to arrange your affairs.

Your salary would be £5 a week, with room and board. This reflects our gratitude for your agreement to accompany the family to Germany.

"Germany?" Flo's exclamation turned heads.

Annie, her eyes shining, laughed. "Well, I said I wanted an adventure!"

"Yes, Annie, but Germany." Flo frowned. "Are you sure?" To Annie's nod, she asked, "Where in Germany?"

"Berlin."

"For God's sake, Annie. You've heard Joe. He says it's hellish there. And the Russkies are not playing nice."

"I know. I'm not an idiot, Flo. But it can't be too bad if Mr. Goodwin is prepared to take his family. And me."

"What's he like?"

Annie took a moment to answer. "I'm not sure I like him. He's cold. I don't think he likes the way I sound or speak."

"Bloody cheek!"

"'Tis a bit, he sounds as if he's got a billiard ball in his gullet." Annie giggled. "I'll teach the kids every Aussie word I can!" She took a bite of war cake. "And, unlike Mrs. Goodwin, he grilled me on my childcare experience, asked why I didn't have references for that."

Flo snickered into her cup. "What did you say? You haven't any."

"I might have fudged a little. Blamed the war. Might have appropriated some of Verna's sisters."

"You lied!"

"Fudged."

"What if you get found out?"

Annie could see Flo trying not to laugh. "How?"

"Oh, Annie. Are you sure about this?"

Annie nodded. "Yeah, I am. Mrs. Goodwin is charming, and I think when he's not around, likes to laugh. The children are nice. Well," Annie corrected herself, "Janet might be a bit of a trial. She doesn't need a nanny, she told me, as did Peter, who really is a sweetie. And the baby, well, she's a baby. Not much character yet. Eat, sleep, change. Repeat."

Flo looked hard at her friend. "But Germany, Annie?"

Annie raised her cup of tea. "Look at us, Flo! London, Glasgow, Berlin—all in six weeks!"

Chapter 21
Berlin Bound, 1948

Dust covers fluttered over easy chairs in the drawing room, silver disappeared into felt bags, which were locked in cabinets, and a general air of finality hovered over the house on Queensdale Road. Annie felt perhaps some of the closing up rigamarole could have waited until after their departure, but Mrs. Goodwin had been determined to oversee the proceedings.

The two older children swayed between excitement and petulance as Annie tried to keep them out of the way.

"I don't like eggs like that."

Her back to the kitchen table, Annie warmed milk for custard at the stove and counted to ten, then counted again, as Janet continued to tap her fork on a plate with rhythmic precision.

"Then don't eat it." The words grated out, as each ting sent a quiver down Annie's back. "Eat the toast."

"I don't like toast."

Peter answered around a forkful of powdered scrambled egg. "Yes, you do."

"Don't!"

"Can I eat hers?" Peter reached for his sister's plate.

"Righto. Eat away."

"That's not fair. What can I have?"

"On the menu tonight, Janet, is scrambled eggs and toast. That's it."

"What's for afters?"

"Not an after in sight, unless you have some toast first." Annie turned in time to see Janet's tongue dart back in! "Which is a pity, because I found a tin of peaches in the larder, which would be a real treat, with custard." She smiled at Peter, "Would you like some, ducks?"

"I hate you!"

Peter glared at his sulky sister. "You're not allowed to say that. Or afters. Mummy says you should say pudding."

Annie tried not to smile. "How about one piece of toast, with some of my special spread, all the way from Australia?"

"I don't like Marmite."

Reaching for the jar, Annie said, "This, I will have you know, Miss Goodwin, is Vegemite. Far superior to Marmite. Would you like to try some?"

"I want some too." Peter held out half a slice of toast.

Janet, her voice superior, said, "I want doesn't get. That's what Mummy says."

"And she's right. But, this time, you can both have some. But only a smidge. You can't get it in England, so this will have to last until I go home."

Peter, his cocked to one side, asked, "What if you never go back?"

"Then I'll never have Vegemite again, and that would be terrible, wouldn't it? So eat up, then it's peaches and custard for pudding."

Tidying the nursery, Annie listened to the children's murmurs in the bedroom next door, then silence as Peter went to sleep, and sighed with relief. Time for a cigarette. Looking after three children was proving to be just as exhausting as a ward full of patients. Verna's mum popped into her head. How had she managed with six girls? One was enough.

Thank heavens Molly continued to feed and sleep with complacent and pleasing regularity. At five months she had become more interesting to her siblings, which made life easier for Annie.

As had Mr. Goodwin's departure two weeks earlier. He had been transported by military aircraft to Berlin, ostensibly to get work started and accommodation sorted, but Annie felt sure it suited him not to be around for the family's final days in London, and subsequent journey.

"Are the children asleep?" Mrs. Goodwin asked, as Annie closed the nursery door.

"Peter and Molly are. Janet is reading. I said another ten minutes, but I usually give her fifteen, then she feels she's put one over on me!"

"You're very good with them, Annie."

"They're lovely children. Now that she and Peter understand there are different rules for each of them, harmony mostly reigns. Peter, despite his determination to stay awake as long as Janet, is invariably asleep moments after he clutches Mr. Tinker. And Janet has realised I am not going to baby her." Annie smiled. "That works sometimes, for both of us. We do have a few stand offs!" She looked at her employer, noting the drawn eyes, and fine lines deepening around her mouth. "Forgive me for asking, but are you alright, Mrs. Goodwin?"

"Yes, yes, just a little weary." She turned to go downstairs, then stopped, her hand on the balustrade. "Would you like to join me for a glass of sherry? I'd like one, and don't really want to drink alone." With a slight laugh, Mrs. Goodwin looked down, embarrassed. "I'm sorry, Annie. That sounded most ungracious. Do, please, come and have a drink with me."

"That would be lovely, thank you." Annie glanced at the watch pinned to her blouse. "Just let me get Janet settled and I'll be down."

Fifteen minutes later, Annie, cigarettes and Bill's lighter in her skirt pocket, went into the morning room. The only reception room not shrouded by sheets. "Thank you," she took the glass, "do you mind if I have a cigarette? I usually have one when the children go to bed."

"Of course not, I'll have one too. I try not to smoke in front of the children."

Annie smiled. "If I ever feel like one when I'm with them, I imagine my old Matron's face!"

Mrs. Goodwin laughed. "I should cut down. I do know I feel better if I only have one or two a day, but it does ease the tension somewhat."

"I know. I think we all probably smoked far too much during the war." Annie leant in to light her employer's cigarette.

"Thank you, and cheers, Annie." Mrs. Goodwin clinked Annie's glass. "I can't tell you how relieved I am that you're coming with me. With us."

—

Boats and ships' horns sounded forlorn, train whistles blasted and the usual clamour of the docks added to the cacophony of sounds. Peter darted around their trunks and cases in a blather of excitement. Janet looked flushed and a little anxious. Molly, unused to the commotion, stuck her thumb in her mouth and stared, wide-eyed, from a propped position in her Silver Cross pram. Mrs. Goodwin sat on a trunk clutching her handbag, and Annie wondered what the hell she'd signed up for as they waited for the man from "the office" to reappear with their passes.

"I'm thirsty," Peter announced.

"Me too." Janet agreed.

"Me three," Annie said, as she unscrewed the lid off the thermos. "Just a sip though, otherwise we'll all be wanting the loo. And I," she said nodding along the wharf, "don't want to miss the boat."

"It's a ship. Father told me." Peter looked pleased with himself.

"Indeed it is." Annie had a fleeting image of her and Flo arriving at Tilbury Docks three months earlier. Her words, about never going on a watercraft of any kind ever again, bounced back at her. She shrugged. She'd be too busy to get seasick. She hoped.

The crossing from Harwich to the Hook of Holland had only opened up to civilians a couple of days earlier, on May 31st, although Annie felt sure that with Mr. Goodwin's connections they would have been able to travel anytime.

So much for her words the evening before about only having a couple of cigarettes a day, and never in front of the children. She'd love a smoko right now and, from the looks of Mrs. Goodwin, so would she. At least they had not had to get the train from Liverpool Street, instead being driven up by Bailey, the chauffeur. Annie rather wished he would be travelling with them all the way. His calm manner and patience with Peter's never-ending questions would certainly ease the trip.

"Fine. All sorted." The man from the office looked pleased with himself as he handed Mrs. Goodwin their passes and passports. "I'll help you aboard and then you're on your own, I'm afraid. Until Berlin that is. But it should all be plain sailing, and your husband will be there to meet you."

Annie had her doubts. After God knows how many hours they'd be on the train from the Hook, she had a feeling Mr. Goodwin would unfortunately be detained by some very important business. She had realised early on that her employer did not care to spend much time with his family.

"Come on, ducklings," Annie said, herding the children onto the ferry, with Molly in her arms.

Janet scowled. "Why are we ducklings?"

"Because you're sweet, mostly, and I call people I am particularly fond of 'ducks', and as you are not quite grown you will have to get used to being ducklings. Now, on you go!"

As the ship's siren blasted one long sound, Annie allowed the children to watch the English shore disappear before shepherding them to their cabin to freshen up. Mrs Goodwin and Molly had disappeared to their cabin and Annie doubted she would see them before arriving in Holland. She had decided it would be better to allow Peter and Janet free rein on board before they had to be cooped up on a train for goodness knows how long.

After exploring all the public areas of the ferry, Janet and Peter clambered into their bunks exhausted from the thrills of an unusual day, vowing to stay awake all night so they could watch their arrival at the Hook. Annie promised that, should they happen to doze off, she would wake them in time to see the Continent appear with the dawn. With the cabin light dimmed for just enough to read by, she knew they'd drop off within moments. Words jumbled on the page and when she realised she'd read the same paragraph twice, she gave up. A pad of onionskin paper poked out of her carpet bag. That's what she'd do.

My dear Verna, James, and most importantly, Ruthie,

Sorry I haven't written since our arrival in London, and I'm not sure if Flo has been any better a correspondent, so I'm going to write as if she hasn't!

But first, how is that gorgeous chubbly of yours? I miss her snuggles. I'd like to think she is running her mother around in a delightful whirl of chaos.

Life for both of us has been helter-skelter and we have not been languishing on our laurels—can one do that, I wonder? Anyway, it's been too damn cold to languish anywhere. I am so proud of our girl Flo! She is now ensconced in a basement flat in Glasgow, having decided she had no desire to live in a hostel or nurses' home ever again. Her words, "I'm too bloody old to have to listen to giggling girls worrying about what to wear on a night out!" But I do understand. We must seem positively ancient to the younger nurses who didn't serve.

James, you might know of the psychiatrist she's working for—Jonathan Callwood—well-respected and determined to treat patients in a more compassionate way. Flo and I had a quick telephone call before I left, early days but she seems delighted with him, and how she is being nurtured. Again, her word, not mine. But Glasgow is apparently grim and grimey as industry, particularly ship building, has declined. And cold.

Now, you'll be wondering. What does she mean? Before I left.

Well, as I write, I am in the company of Janet, age 8, and Peter, age 5. Their mother and her baby, Molly, 5 months, are in the cabin next door. Cabin, you ask? Yup. I'm on another bloody ship. Can you believe it? Fortunately, only for about seven hours. And where am I going? Berlin! Not by ship all the way, of course. Train from the Hook of Holland.

I know, I know. Not nursing but nannying. The Goodwins (terribly grand) are delightful. Well, apart from Rupert, the father, who naturally I wouldn't dare call Rupert. He is something in the Foreign Office—I haven't quite got to grips as to what. He uses big words, like 'indubitably' which he thinks makes him sound clever. In my book, pompous would be a better description. He wanted to employ a Norland Nanny—trained, uniformed—he's that kind of bloke. Anyway, as you will have gathered, he's a bit of a drongo. Mrs. Goodwin is lovely, if overwhelmed. I cannot see what attracted her to R in the first place.

It's an odd position. Not quite a servant, but not a friend. Honestly, I didn't think Mr. G. would agree to employ me—although, can you believe someone would be totally immune to my charms—even though Mrs. G. was keen. And I'm not blowing my own trumpet, she told me. So, shame on me, I dropped Joe's name and his position with the Australian administration here, casually of course, into my second interview, and suddenly I'm more employable. That tells you all you need to know about the husband.

Sleepy now, and the children will be awake at the first sign of the ship slowing. Will finish this later.

Wind blew in gusts as Annie and the children, breathing in the briny air, stood on deck to watch the Dutch coastline become more defined, the beaches turning from ochre to gold as the sky lightened. Bunkers and reinforcements desolate reminders of Hitler's Atlantic Wall. Annie listened to Janet and Peter's excited chatter, a stark difference, she imagined, to the faces of the thousands of mainly Jewish children transported to Britain via the Hook of Holland from Germany, Poland and Czechoslovakia prior to the outbreak of war.

"Good morning, Annie. Hello, children."

She turned to find Mrs. Goodwin, Molly in her arms, moving towards them.

"G'day, Mrs. Goodwin."

"My goodness, I slept like a log, and so did this little treasure. Everything all right with you?" She mussed Peter's hair as Molly's legs jiggled with delight to see her siblings.

"We slept in bunkbeds, Mummy," Janet said, planting a kiss on Molly's waving hand.

Peter jumped in. "Annie said we wouldn't fall out even if the sea got rough because of the rails. And we didn't. My bunk had a porthole."

The train idled meters from the ferry terminal and it didn't take long for them to be ensconced in their compartment. Annie set out the tinned ham and pickle sandwiches she'd packed, and watched the children devour them. She'd made herself one with the last of the Vegemite and wondered when she'd taste her favourite condiment again. Joe had warned her to be prepared for delays and possible hold-ups at the border between the British and Russian sectors of Germany, but she hoped they wouldn't be long enough for the picnic basket to be emptied.

As they finished their meal, Annie delved into her carpet bag and, like a magician, pulled out Snakes and Ladders. She also had dominoes, a pack of cards, and pick-up sticks, but doubted that would work on the train, along with a supply of paper and two boxes of crayons. A worthwhile investment, she had told Mrs. Goodwin. Throwing the dice, Annie wondered how many games would be played between now and their arrival in Berlin.

—

8th June 1948 - Well here I am in Berlin. If I thought London austere then this city is unrelenting in its harshness, although I'm told it's better than it was in 1945. In a strange way, Verna, the awfulness of the place has sent any anti-German feelings I had packing. Of course, I know not every German was a Nazi, but it's easier to lump everyone together. Like all Japs are bastards. Wonder if I'd feel the same if I were in Japan. I mean, that was our war, not Germany or Italy. Apart from Ernie, of course. But it's grim. People still living in bombed basements. Little water. Food a real problem.

I can't help feeling guilty, and I know Mrs. G. does too. Our house is pleasant with a walled garden on the edge of a park called the Tiergarten. Well, it used to be a park. Now it's mainly vegetable gardens where Berliners grow what they can to supplement their supplies. The house has comfortable furnishings, and I have learnt from the cook it was requisitioned from an elderly German couple, who have moved into accommodation above the garage. I suppose where their driver used to live. How awful it must be for them.

We've hardly seen Mr. G. (of course he wasn't at the train to meet us) and, honestly, I'm surprised he brought the family over. He is definitely of the school that children should be seen and not heard. I have a sneaky suspicion we're all here because it makes him look good. Cynicism is alive and well in my soul! He puts your father running off to the garden shed occasionally to get away from all you girls, Verna, seem positively saintly!

Berlin is a strange place. I've only had one day off so, of course, don't know much. I wandered around, and it just feels as if something is bubbling. Mrs. G. hasn't said anything—if she knows anything. But the house is tense, and it's not because of her husband. Military blokes, men in dark suits—German, American and Brits, but haven't heard any French yet—come and disappear into the study with the curtains pulled tight. I hadn't realized Mr. G. is a linguist, speaks Russian, German and French. Bit like Joe. No wonder blokes like that are wanted in Berlin.

Oh, I didn't tell you about the train. All fine until we reached the Soviet border at Helmstedt. Grumpy Russian soldiers locked the doors, and we had to draw down the blinds in the compartments. Our passports and papers disappeared—I didn't like that one little bit—but we got them back before the train moved on again.

I slipped out of our compartment for a surreptitious smoko and chatted with a Pom, nice bloke, who is usually driven through the Soviet part of Germany. He told me there are two sanctioned routes. Both lifeless because no one is allowed to approach the roads. They apparently have arrows advising every 25 miles where the next 'safe' spot is. Called, I think he said, Allied Autobahn Aid Stations, but also where there are known to be unexpected bombs. I rather wish he hadn't told me that. Anyway, it didn't sound particularly safe as stations are surrounded by lights and barbed wire.

We, the children and the baby and I, spend our days playing in the garden—thank goodness it's warmer now. I seem also to be a tutor, mainly for Janet, who is a prodigious reader. Can do the basics but hope they find someone more qualified than me. She and I are learning German from the cook, Bertha. I don't know how old she is but I have a feeling a lot younger than she looks. Lost all her family. She's jolly, then dives into some dark places and won't say a word. She likes Janet, and I wonder whether she had a daughter. So many tragedies.

I'm done in. Too much excitement for this sheila, so will end here.

Love and hugs to you all, even you James,

Annie

Later

P.S. I know we've only been here a week but there is an air of distrust. Not just between the Russian and the Allied sectors, but between Germans themselves, or that's what Bertha told me. Who was a Nazi? Who collaborated? Who didn't? Who has been released from a Russian gaol in exchange for information? She also explained that the black market is a thriving business —with ciggies still being valued currency. I'm rich!

Hooroo, X A

Chapter 22
The Blockade

Clad in her dressing gown, Annie checked the children before going to bed, then, as she slipped along the corridor to her bedroom, heard the front door opening. Curious, she peered over the gallery to see men arriving for another, presumably secret, or at least, private meeting, and wondered what was going on.

She knew from Bertha's assiduous reading of *Die Neue Zeitung*, the Western sector newspaper, that the hobnobbing and quiet diplomacy between the four sector leaders had begun to falter, and that the American Military Governor, General Lucius Clay, had started to recognise his rapprochement policy with Marshal Sokolovovsky might not be as strong as he had hoped.

Next morning she quizzed Bertha.

"Bah," the cook spat the word, then continued in broken English. "The Soviets always want more. Ever since 1945, General Howley, the Commandant of US sector, has said they must not be trusted."

As Annie settled Molly for a nap in her pram positioned in the shade of the garden wall, then gave Janet and Peter some paper and suggested they draw as many different kinds of leaves as they could find in the garden, she wondered whether Bertha had suffered at the hands of the Red Army.

"Morning, Annie," Mrs. Goodwin looked up from her coffee.

"G'day, Mrs. G. Do you mind if I ask you a something?" Annie went to the window so she could keep an eye on the children.

"No, might not be able to answer, but fire away."

"Those men, last night. Is everything alright?"

Mrs. Goodwin sighed, her eyes downcast. "Oh, Annie, honestly, I don't know. Rupert doesn't say much." She turned the cup in her hand, her voice taut. "I do know the Soviets are refusing to accept Ernst Reuter as Mayor of Berlin. Refusing to accept the election was democratic."

Annie moved to the door. "Bertha says she heard on RIAS, you know the radio station from the US sector, that the Soviets are offering incentives to Berliners to move to their sector." She shook her head. "She said she knows some, who'd been raped and beaten by the Red Army after the war, have even gone across." Annie shuddered.

"If you're hungry you'll do what you have to. Especially if you've got children."

"I know, Mrs. Goodwin. I'm not judging. Just want to know what's going on."

"Just be careful who you speak to, Annie."

With the warning swirling in her head, Annie went outside to join the children.

—

One evening, closing the door to the nursery and children's bedroom after putting them all to bed—still promising Janet an extra ten, that turned into fifteen, minutes reading time—Annie saw Mrs. Goodwin, dressed for a cocktail party, climb the stairs.

"Annie, dear, would you like to join us?" She glanced at her watch. "They'll start arriving in about half an hour. And dinner afterwards, of course. There'll only be ten for dinner, including you."

"Thanks, Mrs. G., but I'll just nip down the backstairs to the kitchen and bring a sango, a sandwich, up to my room."

"Actually, Annie, that was more an order disguised as an invitation!" She gave a slight laugh. "Rupert has suggested you come down."

Puzzled, Annie asked, "Why?"

"Do you honestly believe Rupert tells me anything?" Patricia Goodwin frowned. "We'll be short of women, and frankly, I could do with some back up. General Herbert, you know, the new British commandant, and his sidekick, Brigadier Benson will be coming, and God knows who else. I can't keep track of all the names, or ranks." Her smile was sad. "I don't think Rupert thinks I'm up to the task." She paused. "I know I ask a lot of you, Annie, but please?"

"Righto, then." Annie glanced down at the tapered trousers she favoured, "I'll get changed, but I haven't anything very smart for evening wear."

"You're lovely, Annie. You don't need glamour."

After a wash and a rummage through her wardrobe, Annie stood back from the mirror and eyed her reflection. She'd washed her hair the day before, so it didn't look too wild and curly. The emerald green silk dress with a sweetheart neckline that she'd had made for Verna's and James' wedding fitted her well. Her one pair of heels had needed some spit and polish but at least the laces hadn't disintegrated. The clasp of her pearl necklace finally caught, and Annie thought of her mother with a smile. She filled in her eyebrows with a pencil, then swiped Vaseline across them, and her eyelashes, enough to make her hazel eyes deepen. Next the victory red lipstick, a variation of the colour worn by just about every woman in England and Australia, and another dab of Vaseline. A spritz of L'Air du Temps from the bottle Joe had brought back from Paris provided the final touch.

"That'll have to do." Annie checked her watch, usually pinned to her chest but now lying on the chest of drawers that served as a dressing table. Not bad. Just over half an hour. "Show time, Miss Cutler!" First, she tiptoed into Janet's room and slid the book off the eiderdown and turned out the lamp.

"Ahh, good evening, Annie." Rupert saw her enter the reception room. "Thank you for joining us."

"A pleasure, Mr. Goodwin." She took a glass of champagne from the waiter circulating.

"May I introduce General Smythe? He's with the Americans."

"The uniform did rather give that away." Annie's tart tone caused both Mr. Goodwin and the general to raise their eyebrows. "I have seen a lot of uniforms over the years."

"Yes, of course. My apologies, Annie."

The general smiled and asked, "What brings you to Berlin, Miss Cutler?"

"I'm the nanny."

"Aah."

Before he could say more, Mrs. Goodwin appeared at Annie's side. "Thank you so much for joining us this evening, Annie. This woman is so much more than our nanny. She helps keep the household running, and healthy. She is a nurse."

"You served?"

"I did." Annie felt the general's reappraisal and had an urge to grind her heel, albeit not very sharp, into his condescending instep. "Probably longer than most Americans!" Annie heard Mrs. G.'s gasp and wanted to swallow her words. Where was Flo's steadying influence when she needed it?

"Touché, my dear," General Smythe said with a slight bow. "My apologies. In the Middle East?"

"Singapore and New Guinea. With some of your boys."

"Then I thank you."

Feeling Patricia's Goodwin's hand in the small of her back, Annie nodded and moved away with her hostess. "I'm so sorry, Mrs. Goodwin. My mouth runs away with me sometimes."

"Oh, my God, Annie, you should have seen Rupert's face."

Annie groaned. "I didn't dare look."

"Priceless. You are henceforth required to add cocktail and dinner parties to your many other duties." She hid a giggle behind her glass. "I almost choked on my champagne."

"I don't think your husband would agree, Mrs. Goodwin."

"Oh, don't worry about him. And Annie, for heaven's sake, please stop calling me that. I'm Trisha to those I care about. Patricia to most!" She opened the silver cigarette box resting on the grand piano. "Time for our daily ration."

They moved towards the open French windows and chatted, then were joined by a woman from the French sector. Annie struggled to remember her schoolgirl French, and wished she had her brother's facility with languages. The reception filled then, and through the babel of tongues, she heard the more drawn out and nasal tones of the Australian accent. She turned, always happy to hear of home.

Her gasp stopped the other two women talking.

"Good grief, there's Joe!" She handed Trisha her glass and pushed her way through the growing crowd. "Joe!"

"Bloody hell." He pulled her into a bear hug with a laugh. "Can't I get away from you?"

"I gather you know each other?" An Australian, a lock of blond hair falling across his forehead, smiled down at Annie.

"Yeah, you could say that. This, Ed, is Annie, my sister!" Joe, still with his arm around Annie, explained. "This is my boss, Edmund Armstrong. Only arrived an hour or so ago and had no idea who our hosts were tonight. Of course, this buffoon didn't tell me."

"I don't recall you asking." The broad-shouldered man joined in their laughter. "You will note, Annie, how little respect your brother bestows on me."

"Runs in the family, I'm afraid, Edmund. I've just nettled an American general."

"Good evening," Trisha Goodwin joined them. "I didn't know you knew anyone in Berlin, Annie," she said, smiling at them.

"This is Joe, my brother, and his boss, Edmund Armstrong," said Annie. "Joe, meet my boss, your hostess, Patricia Goodwin."

"Oh, how wonderful! I remember you telling me, when we first met, that he came and went to Germany. You must both stay for dinner. I absolutely insist." Trisha laughed with delight. "A very dreary evening just got rather better. Now, excuse me a moment and I'll let Bertha know."

"Did we agree?" Joe asked Edmund and Annie.

Annie watched Trisha hurry towards the kitchen. "Nope. But that's about the first time I've seen her do anything without first consulting her husband."

—

Dearest All,

You'll never believe who I bumped into a couple of weeks ago, Verna, at a rather swanky cocktail party. Your dungaree-clad nursing friend is rising in the world! Joe! I suppose it's not really surprising, given he does seem to pop in and out of Germany with increasing regularity, but somehow, I didn't really expect it. Anyway, Mrs. G, now known as Trisha, insisted he and his boss, a bloke called Edmund Armstrong, stay for dinner as well. Mr. G. glowered at not being informed but mellowed as the wine flowed. He really is a pretentious prig.

I'm so glad I got to see him, as the chances of him returning whilst this bloody blockade is in place would seem to be pretty slim. I think I mentioned in my last letter that Berlin is riven with intrigue—certainly from the Russkies end of things—and now of course we're all up the creek without a paddle. Or rather without supplies. The Berliners, poor sods. Each time they must feel as if the hell is ending, another starts.

I'm pretty sure Mr. G. has been involved in financial shenanigans. What a mess. In response to the Soviets announcing their new currency would be the only legal tender in Berlin, the Allies flew in their own dosh—250 million new Deutschmarks. When the West said they'd be agreeable to both currencies being circulated at an equal value, Walter Ulbricht, the German communist and puppet of the Soviets, said nein, or maybe, nyet. Our lot wouldn't be bullied, so here we are. The Russkies decided, on the 24th, to starve an entire city and literally pulled the plug. No coal. Lights out. No power. Sewage is going to be a problem. Remember the latrines at 7 Mile Camp, Verna? Argh. Here I go again! We are now an island within about a 100 miles of Russian waters. I don't think I have a particularly good record with islands, so let's see how this plays out.

At the back of a lot of minds, certainly mine, is that there could be another war. The Red Army literally surrounds us and could, I reckon, pop up from the U-Bahn—that's like the Tube in London—to surprise us and swarm over all Berlin. Not a cheerful thought. Sorry. A bit on edge.

More later. I can hear Molly waking up, which means my day has officially started. Good thing the children are lovely! This is not a lovely time.

Annie mushed up a Farley's Rusk with some Cow and Gate powdered milk for Molly's breakfast. Janet and Peter munched on toast and jam, oblivious to the dramas unfolding in Berlin. As Annie spooned the mush into Molly's eager mouth, she wondered whether Trisha would decide that now was the time to return to the certainty of Queensdale Road.

It was all very well standing firm to Russian needling, but now they faced blatant aggression. Bertha, the cook, had told Annie through tight lips that an ex-Nazi Panzer captain, Paul Markgraf, controlled the police, supported by the Soviets. It did not augur well for safety in the Allied sectors.

Molly, now cleaned up, crawled around under the kitchen table. The yellow wooden building brick she liked as a teething tool, clutched in her hand, clumped across the stone floor. The others had dashed upstairs to brush their teeth with a splash of water before starting a game of Snakes and Ladders, whilst Annie tidied the breakfast things. Washing up could only be done once a day. Lavish entertaining was already a thing of the past.

"Annie, have we enough water for a cup of tea?" Trisha's voice came from the door.

"I made a flask when the power was on."

"Where's Bertha?"

"Out on the hunt for vegetables."

"All right." Trisha hauled Molly out from under the table and sat the squirming baby on her lap before releasing her again. She sighed. "Do you think the children will remember any of this?"

"Janet probably. Peter some of it, but I shouldn't think Molly will. Why?"

"Because," tears sprang into Trisha's eyes, "it seems we are staying for the duration."

"I see. I did wonder, but I imagine getting diplomatic families out is almost impossible now."

"And, so Rupert says, would send the wrong signals to Berliners."

"Yeah, I get that. But I 'spose the other side is that evacuating dependents means needing fewer supplies."

"I said that." Her tears now flowed. "We should never have come. When will I learn to stand up to him?"

Annie reached across the table to take Trisha's hand. "You did what you thought was the right thing."

"No, Annie, I did what was easiest. Arguing is exhausting and just riles him. Now the children will suffer."

"They're remarkably resilient. As long as they know they're loved, they can handle most things." Annie paused. "I had a chat with Frau Müller about digging up some of the flower beds she has replanted since the war and turning them back into vegetable patches. I thought I could get the children involved. Peter loves to get dirty, and it will keep him occupied, and Janet can learn about different plants. What do you think?"

"I think you're a marvel. Thank God for you, Annie."

"Don't be daft." Annie looked at her employer, now more a friend, "You know what, Trisha, you won't be entertaining much, certainly not on the same lavish scale. Why don't you help us?" She sipped her now tepid tea. "Can I ask you something? I promise anything you say won't be repeated."

Trisha blew her nose, then nodded.

"Have you heard anything about breaking the siege by force?" Annie bent down to Molly, giving Trisha time to think.

"Not really. Rupert did say the other night, after a few snifters, that General Clay had mentioned sending in the armies, but backed down when others warned it could lead to war. God, what a mess."

"Yeah, it is. But, Trisha, the world can't be badgered by bullies." Annie twirled Molly's curls, "It's a funny thing, the Americans didn't want to join the war, then did. Now they're the ones wanting to fight."

"Ironic, isn't it?" Trisha gave a watery smile. "At least it seems all the Allies think the same now. We must stand behind Berlin. With Berlin. And if the Brits can say that, when we still have rationing, and no industry, then the Yanks couldn't lose face, could they?"

The door burst open, and the children bundled in. "Can we play now?" Janet asked.

"Will you play too, Mummy?" Peter looked at his mother hopefully.

"Only if you let me win!"

"Righto, I'm going to get this little miss changed and put her down for a nap." Annie picked up the wriggling baby. "Come on, you."

Chapter 23
The Airlift, 1948

Planes, mainly C-47 Dakotas, had roared overhead before the blockade, supplying the western sectors of Berlin with over 13,000 tons of essentials. Most of them battered remnants of the war, so Edmund Armstrong had told Annie. Joe's boss, based in Berlin, had become a regular visitor and carrier of letters from Verna, and Joe, still in the flat on Cork Street. Free of pretension, Ed was quite happy to sit in the kitchen with the children and have a cup of tea. His logistical knowledge meant his role had changed and he would tell Annie and Trisha far more than Rupert, who regarded every ounce of information as classified, and to be hoarded.

"What's going to happen, Ed?" He and Annie smoked a cigarette and watched the children digging up the flowers. "How can those ropey old Gooney birds supply Berlin now?"

"Don't knock 'em."

"I'm not," Annie insisted. "But I've seen them flying over. They're held together with tape and prayers."

"You know why they're called that—Gooney Birds?"

"I heard it somewhere but can't remember."

"Same as an albatross. Can fly huge distances and are tough as old boots."

"But still, Ed, surely we need more now."

"Yup. I'm more concerned about what will happen when the weather changes. Tempelhof is notorious for fog."

"You think this blockade is going to last that long?"

"Yes, Annie, I do." Edmund exhaled and watched the smoke curl and catch on the breeze, "No one is going to give way." He turned as Trisha approached them with Molly. "G'day, Trisha. How's it going?"

"Fine, thanks, Ed. What brings you here?"

"Look, Mummy, we're digging!" Peter broke into the conversation.

"I can see that. Thank goodness we'll have a gardener in the family."

Edmund waited, then replied. "The promise of tea and a familiar voice. I'm surrounded by Yanks!"

"Any news?"

Annie looked at Trisha's expectant face. Her question not one she would ever ask her husband.

"Not really." Ed paused to draw deeply on his cigarette. "But there is a new bloke in town. Bill Tunner, known to all as Tonnage Tunner. Extraordinary man. A US pilot. Pulled off the airlift of supplies to China when Chiang Kai-shek fought the Japs. He's now in charge."

"I thought Commodore Waite had come up with a plan."

Trisha's comment surprised Annie. She knew far more than she often let on. A true diplomat's wife.

"He did. It was a good one in theory. Hell, getting any number of planes into Berlin is a feat. But Tunner has expanded it. He has two rules. All planes must fly the same route, no change of flight pattern and must rely solely on instrumentation."

"Isn't that dodgy?" Annie asked. "I mean instruments can fail."

"If that happens, or if a pilot can't land on the first pass, they have to return to base. That's rule two. No stacking. Tempelhof is the main airfield and they'll use Gatow in the British sector, too."

"Is it just pure luck the skies are free?" Trisha asked.

"I don't think anyone expected the duplicity from the Soviets, so I guess the answer is yes, luck!"

—

Thanks for the letter, Verna. Ed Armstrong, Joe's old boss delivered it this arvo. It is handy having my own courier. I'm so glad everything is going well, ducks. And congratulations. Another chubbly on the way. Ruthie will be a wonderful big sister! The photo of her is lovely.

And I do feel guilty for not finishing a letter I started over a month ago. I've reread what I wrote. Most of it is old news now but I'll just carry on as if you're on the moon and don't hear what's happening in this little area.

The Russian bear paws have us in their grip. It's not a lot of fun. But even worse for the Berliners. At least we get some goodies. Even Janet has stopped being a fussy eater! Or perhaps she was testing me. Either way, she's easier to handle.

Dear little Peter is more interested in the planes and can identify them as they fly over—which is all the time. We live under their constant roar as they land at Tempelhof, which has been upgraded to all-weather. And fuel supplies are flown into the French sector. It's incredible, Verna. An army of Berliners are employed to carry rubble for hardcore, and bricks from the streets to the site. The bricks are used instead of tarmac.

This all sounds very detailed but believe me, ducks, we all rely on these planes so it becomes more than just a cursory interest to us. It is staggering, literally. Planes fly at five different altitudes—you didn't know I knew so much about aircraft, did you? Anyway, they do. And, even more incredibly, they are at 500 feet intervals with planes landing and taking off at 90 second intervals.

Bertha, the cook, has a friend whose daughter is one of the girls taking snacks to the pilots as they wait for the planes to be unloaded. Here's a statistic for you, James. About 65,000 are employed to unload the planes.

Fuel, or lack of it, is a real problem. I'm dreading winter. You know how much I hate being cold. The kitchen is our favourite place but it has a stone floor. Send woolly socks! I'm joking. Bertha and Janet have a lovely rapport, and she enjoys pottering with her, which gives me time to spend with Peter and Molly. He's quite happy to build towers for her to knock down. She's at the cruising stage and needs watching all the time, but she's a hardy little poppet.

I am coming to love these children. My heart breaks at Rupert's total disregard for them. Peter tries so damn hard to please his father. Shades of mine, eh? He, R. is out of the house most of the time, which is probably a good thing. Tensions are not only high in Berlin, but in our tiny enclave too.

Along with socks, please send onions! Yeah, you read that right. Onions are beyond scarce. We have planted some of our own—we're lucky to have a walled garden. Not a flower in sight anymore. Frau Müller, the owner of the house, is lovely and mucks in with us. Oh, I didn't tell you, her husband died a month ago. She came for me in the middle of the night, but I think he just gave up. In a way, she seems lighter. As if she doesn't have to worry about him anymore. I'll have to check that theory with Flo. She, Frau M, often comes into the kitchen now and has a cup of tea. We are so fortunate to have a bit more fuel than most.

Righto, if I don't finish this now, I never will. Joe is not coming any longer. Only essential people fly into Berlin now. I know, from Ed, that he is in Germany quite a lot though. Ed is becoming a dear friend. No, stop grinning, Verna. Just a friend. No one comes near Bill.

Look after that bump, and give Ruthie a big sloppy kiss from her godmamma.

Love to you all, Annie

—

"Trisha, would you mind if I took tomorrow off, instead of Sunday?"

"Don't be silly, Annie. Of course not." Trisha paused. "Hang on, you're not thinking of going to the demonstration, are you?"

Annie nodded.

"Oh, Annie, really? I mean, should you? It could get violent."

"I'll stay well back. I'd just like to be part of something bigger." She sighed. "These Berliners have put up with so much. Now they're calling out communism for the rest of us."

"I know. But Rupert said it's going to be close to the Russian War Memorial. Isn't that a red rag?"

Annie gave a snort. "Red is the right word."

"It's not funny."

"No, I know. But I'd really like to hear Herr Reuter speak. He looks such an insignificant man and yet he has rallied the city against the Soviets. It's history being made, Trisha. I'll be fine."

Dressed in slacks, a blouse and light jacket, and flat shoes, Annie joined the throngs converging on the Platz der Republik. She tried to stay towards the back but found herself carried along by the determined mass. Her lessons with Bertha were paying off, and she understood much of what was being said around her. The air vibrated with cheers as Ernst Reuter appeared and in booming words, ignited the crowd as he told them Berlin was not for sale.

A dishevelled man propped up by a crutch lurched into her.

"You right?" she asked, grabbing his arm.

He nodded. "American? You understand?"

"Australian. Some."

"World must help. No surrender to Soviets." He spoke slowly then got swallowed in the next wave of people. Annie felt proud to be there. Until, her heart pounding, she felt a shift in mood. Anger fizzed as people began shouting, 'Ivan Raus' at a Russian police truck trying to break through. She ducked as a stone whizzed past. In front she could see people pelting the truck with bricks and stones. She turned and looked back. No chance in hell of getting out. The cry 'Russians out' changed to 'Raus mit Kotikov' as the new chant screamed for the ouster of General Alexander Kotikov', the loathed commandant. Only a few months earlier he had been considered to be a jovial host as he charmed guests and, in turn, was charming to his hosts at cocktail parties. But that was before his true intent, Russian domination, became understood. Annie staggered as shots rang out from where the Soviets monitored the demonstration. She squeezed her eyes shut. "Idiot!" Her mutter lost amidst the screams which replaced cheers as the bullets flew overheard. They changed back to cheers as a lad clambered up the Brandenburg Gate and tore down the Red Flag.

Cheers became enraged shouts as word sprang back from mouth to mouth that Red Army soldiers had begun to advance. Not shooting, yet. Panic grabbed Annie's throat as she felt herself being carried along on the swell. Then silence, almost more terrifying, swept the mob.

"What's happening? Was ist passiert?" She asked.

"Ich weiss es nicht," came the answer, as people shrugged and strained to see what had caused the silence.

"We do not know," replied a young woman, her face dirt streaked, her clothes tatty. "You are British?"

"No. Australian."

"You are here why?"

"I work here."

"Journalist?"

"No. A nanny."

"Maybe you should not be here."

"Maybe."

The woman pushed forward to see what was happening, and Annie continued trying to back out. Again, the mood changed as renewed cheers, this time mingled with laughter, filled the square and with it, the heaving mass began to disperse. Slowly. Finally breaking free, Annie rotated her shoulders, relieving the tension as she slipped down an empty side road that she hoped would get her back to the Müller house fast.

Her stride long, her head down, she stumbled when a shout rang out. "Halt!"

Sweat sprung out on her brow and she swallowed. "Guten Tag," she managed through dry lips as she saw the star on their caps as they encircled her. A soldier grabbed her hand, half-way to her pocket for her papers, and she cried out, every horror story of the Red Army flashing before her. "Australian. Australian."

His grip released, as another indicated for her papers. Her hand trembled as, handing over her ID, she repeated, "Australian."

Rapid fire Russian bounced off the bombed walls around her as they looked at her papers. Annie wondered if they could read. She held her breath and her tongue, and waited, her head now high.

"Gehen! Go, now!" One of the soldiers nodded, as they slouched past her.

She willed her legs to move, but stumbled again. "Idiot!" The word exploded as she picked up pace. "When will you learn?" As the Tiergarten appeared, so did tears of relief.

Entering through the kitchen, she collapsed against the back door, wiped her eyes, closed them and took a deep breath, her heart still racing. A hand clutched her arm, and she cried out, as her eyes shot open, "Bertha, oh my God, don't do that. What?"

"Herr Goodwin, he is angry."

"What's the matter?"

"You see him, now."

"Where are the children?"

Bertha nodded towards the walled garden. "With Frau Müller."

"Molly?"

"She sleep."

"He want to see you."

"Righto." Annie patted Bertha's arm. "It's alright. Don't worry."

Annie knocked on the study door, her face set at the curt response. "Enter."

"You wanted to see me, Mr. Goodwin?" Annie saw Trisha, tear-stained, on a chair by the window, and smiled, pushing aside her recent panic.

"Where the hell do you think you've been?"

"At the demonstration."

"I am well aware of that. My wife informed me. It was a rhetorical question."

"In that case, why ask?" Annie watched Rupert's face mottle through red and purple.

"I think your friendship with my wife has given you to believe you may do as you please."

Annie heard Trisha gasp but gave her no time to speak. "Not at all. But I am not a prisoner in this house, and today is my day off. How I chose to spend it has no bearing on my relationship to your wife, or my position."

"You are here under my aegis. My protection."

"I am aware of what aegis means, Mr. Goodwin." Any regret, or fear, Annie may have felt evaporated. Who the hell did he thing he was? "I am back in time to give the children their supper and put them to bed. Not because I have to, on my day off, but because I enjoy their company." Seething, in part because she knew she'd been foolish to join the demonstration, Annie took care not to slam the door as she stalked out to the garden through the front door. She couldn't face Bertha's questions just yet.

—

"G'day, Annie."

She looked up from the castle she had built for Molly to knock down.

"Hello, what are you doing here?"

Edmund crouched down by the baby, holding out a block for her. "Trisha told me what happened. Yesterday."

"Already. Word does get around. I haven't seen her this morning. Are you going to tear a strip off me, too?"

"Nah. Don't think it would make much difference."

"Too right." She sighed. "I know it probably was a bit silly, but nothing happened." She blinked hard. Best to keep the terrifying walk home to herself.

"Let's add risky, Annie!"

"I thought you weren't going to rip into me!"

"I'm not and, just so you know, you'd know if I was!" Ed gave a resigned sigh.

"I just wanted to feel a part of it, not be on the sidelines, while Berlin is being squeezed."

"And?"

Annie looked the Australian straight in the eyes. "It was scary. And I am sorry I caused Trisha trouble. She doesn't need me complicating things."

Ed grunted. "You know he wants to sack you?"

"Major loss of face for my esteemed employer. Admission he'd employed the wrong person to look after his children, and anyway, even he couldn't get me on a plane out of here!"

"Won't make for easy living."

"It won't make any difference. We hardly ever see him." Annie watched Ed rub his hand over his face, then smile down at Molly sucking on a brick.

"A challenging household."

"Only when he's around." Annie scooped up Molly. "Come on, duckling, time for lunch. Would you care to join us?" she asked from the hall.

"No, I just nipped by to make sure you're alright."

"Hunky dory, thanks, Ed." She saw him glance up the stairs. "Oh, just one thing, what happened? At the demo. I managed to leave when I heard the Soviets had sent in the heavies."

Edmund smiled, properly, for the first time. "Incredible. These Poms have guts. An MP, name of Frank Stokes, wandered up to the jokers and whacked their gun barrels with his swagger stick. Surprised doesn't begin to describe their reaction. They buggered off with their tails down." He laughed. "Never again will I mock the swagger stick. Bloody marvellous!"

"Not like the joker in this house." Annie spoke quietly.

"No. It would seem not. Be careful, alright, Annie." Edmund kissed her cheek. "Bye, toots," he waved to Molly.

Annie peeled and chopped half a potato and a slither of swede for Molly and watched it boil while the baby sat on the floor turning the pages of a cloth book, gurgling to herself. Why, Annie wondered, would Trisha send Edmund a note?

—

And then late October and early November sent all petty aggravations to the back burner. A freezing fog shrouded most of Europe. Berliners, used to hardship, now suffered even more. The sky above the city no longer thrummed with the rumble of fifteen hundred planes landing and taking off at the three airstrips in every 24-hour period. Although they tried. Three crashes, one a US Dakota Skymaster, missed the runway at Tempelhof, with the crew walking away with only minor burns; another, a British Dakota, dived into the Russian sector and killed all five on board; and the final one, a British Lancaster returning from Berlin, plummeted to the ground in Wiltshire, again killing the crew.

Berlin needed 5,000 tons of food a day to stay alive. On the worst day, the city received only 10 tons. Salt, delivered first by Sunderland flying boats on the River Havel, then by adapted Halifax bombers, could not land. There was no coal. No water. No food. No nothing. Annie hadn't appreciated how much she looked forward to letters from Verna, Flo, and Joe.

The Soviets watched and waited, wanting the fog to settle over the city indefinitely. It didn't. So they played a propaganda game, and again tried bribery, promising essentials to anyone who moved to their sector.

A short lull in the crippling fog did allow the British to arrange an emergency evacuation of 17,000 hungry children to the western zones of Germany. Annie looked at her three charges, wondering again how mothers had borne the pain of sending their children away. But they had. Anything was better than seeing them starve.

Bertha burst into the kitchen one afternoon after the fog had lifted. Her face, so often pensive, gleamed with delight. "The sky rained chocolate!"

Annie shook her head. "What?" German had deserted her.

"Chocolate. It came from a plane." She grinned. "My friend, her son got some. And others."

It wasn't until she was having a cigarette after the children had gone to bed that Trisha could tell Annie the whole story, one she had learnt from the wife of an American diplomat.

"Apparently, Lieutenant Gail Halvorsen—strange name—gave some candy to children watching the planes from the perimeter fence at Tempelhof and was so impressed that even though they looked emaciated, they shared what he gave them, he promised he'd get more." Trisha smiled. "He's a Mormon, though I'm not sure what bearing that has. Anyway he and his fellow pilots have begun to drop sweets on their flights in. Apparently, he is known now as 'der Schokoladen Flieger.' And the administrations are all behind it. Isn't that a great name—the Chocolate Pilot?"

"How's that for a coup against the Russkies?"

"They'll probably retaliate somehow. They always do." Trisha looked glum.

"Everything all right?"

"Not really. But nothing to be done, so best get on with it." Her smile wan, Trisha turned and went into the sitting room. Annie picked up a flask of tea and went upstairs to her room with a candle. She shivered and pulled on another pair of socks. As if it wasn't cold enough already. She tiptoed in to check the children remained cuddled under layers of blankets. She eased Molly's thumb out of her mouth and tucked her hand under for warmth.

—

Dearest Flo,

This is a moany letter. That I probably can't even send, but I need a whinge. I'm done. Sick and tired of bloody Berlin, of bloody Rupert Goodwin, of the bloody Soviets. There. Better already.

It's alright. It's not as bad as all that. Well, Rupert and the Russians are. I think I told you about 'the chocolate pilot' in my last letter. Thanks for yours, by the way. Arrived in a brief lull in the fog! Can't tell you how happy I am for you. And proud, ducky. My friend, on the way to being a doctor. While I think of it, got a lovely chirpy letter from our Sydney friend. You probably have too. I'm so happy she's blooming. It will be wonderful for her mum to have another baby to dote on. Give her something to look forward to. I can't imagine the house at Coogee without Mr Sinclair skulking off to the shed!

Where was I? Oh yes, well the chocolate drops have well and truly upset the Russkies. The boundary between their sector and the rest of us is now manned. Amazingly, the black market continues to flourish, and food smuggling is everywhere. Spuds are still getting through from the east but the poor sods over there are in a terrible way too.

I don't know how much of what's happening gets through to the rest of the world, so here's a quick run down about the place your chum now calls home. I think I mentioned (it is quite handy being part of a diplomatic household, even if Rupert rarely speaks directly to me) but in the early days of this new hell, the blockade, the Soviets still got reparations from western-occupied Germany as agreed at the Potsdam conference in '45. But Frank Howley, remember him—the US Commandant—reneged on the deal. Good for him, say I! Anyway, that meant almost a counter blockade. No iron, no steel, or rubber, can't remember what else. Which, in turn, meant their industry ground to a halt. Serves the buggers right.

We heard rumblings of military movements on the Russian side, but Ed Armstrong thinks it's all posturing. He says the troops are so demoralized, the Soviets wouldn't risk putting them anywhere near the border in case they all defect.

So that's good news, at least. The airlift is remarkable. Talk about precision flying and timing. Honestly, ducks, when the thrum of aircraft stops, in Berlin it feels like the world has come to an end. Actually, we thought it had during the fog episode. Now about 8,000 tons of supplies a day gets through, minimum, I'm reliably told. Berlin is eating well. Comparably well. Not well well, but you know what I mean. Rations have been increased. Ed reckons the Russians are cracking. We'll see.

Onto the domestic front, life is not bliss. Children are so perceptive. Whenever R is in the house, we all tiptoe around like bloody mice. Even darling Molly sticks her thumb in her mouth, which infuriates her father, and won't make a peep, when normally she's a chatty little thing. Trisha has moved out of the marital bed. All rather awkward, and I'd much rather not be a part of any of it. I rather think Ed has something to do with it, although nothing has been said.

Anyway, we're all stuck here for the time being.

Not a long letter this time.

Sending love,

Annie

P.S. Can't believe it's five years since Bill died. I still miss him, but it's more an ache now.

"Look!" Trisha pulled Annie into the larder and closed the door.

Annie peered into a brown paper bag to see a couple of handfuls of chocolate eggs nestled in the bottom. "Where on earth did you get those?"

"Edmund."

"Oh!" Annie took a deep breath. "Does Rupert know?"

"No." Trisha looked defiant. "And I don't care. We can hide them around the garden and the children can have a proper Easter. They deserve it."

"Alright."

"And," Trisha's eyes glinted, "I also heard that Tonnage Tunner is planning a real thumb-your-nose at the Soviets by flying in even more supplies in a single twenty-four period. It's being called 'one big gung-ho day'!"

Annie laughed. "I hope that man gets as many medals as can fit across his chest." She paused. "It must've been planned for months. I mean you can't just magic supplies from across the world in a day."

12th May, 1949

Dear Verna, James and Ruthie,

It's over! Berlin survived! The bloody Russkies have their tails between their legs. But I'm sure they've something else up their sleeves—if that isn't mixing metaphors, or something! Trisha and I stayed up, smoking in the dark, just to wait for the lights to come on at 0001 so we could turn them off. How's that for nuts?

Bertha was outside on the street with Frau Müller, and they both came in with tears streaming. What a lot those women have had to deal with.

Apparently the first trains arrived at dawn. Another thing that seems nuts is that we, Trisha, the children and I, managed to stay sane throughout the blockade—323 days of it—and now we're leaving. As soon as we can, anyway. Their marriage is over. Pretty brave of Trisha. But she's a lot tougher than I first thought. She's never mentioned anything with Ed Armstrong, but maybe she just needs to get away from R before anything is said, or done.

I'll stay with her and the children at Queensdale Road until she's settled, one way or another. Then I'm going to look for a nursing job, even though I wouldn't have missed the last year. I suppose in a way it helped clear my mind of the war. Even though we've had some grim times in Berlin.

I'll miss my ducklings—they are dear children—and we've had some fun. It does make me sad that I won't have my own. Bill would've been a wonderful father. But I've learnt I don't want to be part of a household, particularly a waspy one. And I can't help feeling most employers in England would not accept me as a friend, the way Trisha has.

I'm ready to go back on the wards. Who knows where?

This is just a quick note for Ed to put in the pouch. Still not entirely sure what he does for the Foreign Office, or why, as he is most definitely Australian, but he certainly isn't cowed by R. Will be wonderful to see Joe again. More when I get back to London,

Love,

Annie

Chapter 24
London, 1950

Joe snapped the last of the clasps on his trunk, then turned to Annie. "Feels strange to be leaving you here. At least I know you'll be safe with Mrs. Bellows."

"You do realize I am quite capable of looking after myself and, might I remind you, I am the older sister. Actually," Annie stopped and grimaced, "at thirty-six, I'm positively ancient."

"But still turning heads."

"Hardly. I'm going to miss you, Joe. Thank you, all the same, for everything. This place for one."

"Well, I'm glad you've got Betty coming in to share the cost with you. And it's company. She's become a real pal."

"Yeah, she has. I'm glad Mrs. B. approves. She likes having nurses upstairs—her just-in-case-policy, she calls us. But we'll probably not see much of each other. Different wards, different shifts. And when did 'pal' become a word we all throw around?"

"Blame the Yanks!"

"Poor old Americans. We blame them for a lot, but they were bloody marvellous in Berlin."

"I know." He put his case down at the door. "Righto, got to go, Annie. Don't want to miss my flight."

"Rub it in. In Sydney in about sixty hours. Incredible! I'd love to fly on Qantas. It's a great name isn't it—the Kangaroo Route?"

"Yup. And the seats recline. And I'm not paying for it.

Annie laughed. "I suppose someone somewhere thinks you're worth it. Say hello to Singapore for me." Tears trembled on her lashes as she hugged Joe tight. "And Dad."

"Will do. Hooroo, Annie. Be good!"

—

Daffodils danced like a corps de ballet in the spring sunshine, taking away the dreary thought of working on Good Friday. Not that Annie had any intention of going to Church, but she longed to sit on one of the deck chairs lining the Broadwalk in Green Park and read a book. Or do nothing. The capriciousness of British weather had taught her to luxuriate in any warmth whenever possible. She sometimes wondered if she'd ever warmed up properly after the winter in Berlin with little coal. With her luck the weather for the rest of the Easter break, which she did have off, would be lousy.

Her mind wandering, she silently thanked Joe for her flat. Living on Cork Street meant she could enjoy the Royal park in all its seasons, as she walked through it either on her way to or from work on the general wards at St. George's Hospital on Hyde Park Corner, depending on her shift. She and Betty rarely shared off-duty time. The arrangement suited them, and they enjoyed the occasional evening at the cinema or a drink in The Goat Tavern, around the corner on Stafford Street. Most evenings Annie felt happy to curl up with a book, or the radio, and a cup of tea.

The mantel clock struck nine as Annie opened the door to the flat. She'd been cornered by Mrs. B. for a chat at the foot of the stairs, when all she really wanted to do was take her shoes off. She had learnt over the last year that to accept tea from her landlady meant at least an hour of talk at her kitchen table.

True to form, the rest of the Easter weekend drizzled then turned cold and stormy. Annie clutched an umbrella and, head down, hurried toward the house on Queensdale Road to see Trisha and the children. She had stayed on as their nanny for three months after they returned from Berlin in July and, in that time, without Rupert's glowering presence, she and Trisha had become firm friends.

"G'day, ducklings," Annie said as Janet opened the door, with Peter and Molly fast behind her. She bent to hug the older children, then picked up Molly, now just over two.

"G'day, Annie!" Janet and Peter said in unison, then chortled.

"Well, I'm glad you remembered something I taught you. At least you can now greet people properly. Where's mum?"

"Here I am! How lovely." They bussed cheeks. "So, so glad you could come over. Not quite the same as Easter last year, is it?"

Peter piped in. "I remember hunting for chocolate eggs in the garden. With Bertha."

"Yes, weren't we lucky the Easter bunny found us?" Trisha asked with a laugh. "And Ed helped, didn't he?"

Janet fixed Annie with her serious eyes. "Annie, did you know Ed is going to be our new daddy one day?"

"We'll still have Daddy as daddy, but now we'll have two," explained Peter.

"I did know, and I am thrilled for you all." Annie glanced at Trisha with a smile. She had never seen her looking so relaxed and happy. "When does he get back?"

"End of the month." Trisha shooed the children back down to the kitchen. "Could you please tell Mrs. Robbins we'll have lunch in half-an-hour, which means you have that much time of freedom until you're chained to the dining room chairs. You too, Molly, off you go. Annie and I have lots to catch up on."

They moved into the morning room and Annie gave a laugh. "It seems longer than two years ago that you interviewed me in here."

"My lucky day, Annie." Trisha poured sherry.

"And mine. Thanks." She took a sip, then lit a cigarette. "So, tell me all."

"I have never been so happy. That's all there is to it, really."

"Has Rupert agreed?"

Trisha nodded. "It's all being done through lawyers. This sounds ridiculous, but I even felt a bit miffed that he agreed so readily. Was I that bad a wife?"

"Don't be dopey. What did he say about the children?"

"Not much. That he will pay for their education, and of course wants to see them whenever he is in England. He wants them to go up to Scotland, to see his parents, every summer."

"With you?"

"Unless he's around." Trisha paused. "I like them. Just not that his mother made Rupert believe he is the best chap the world has ever known."

Annie laughed. "What about your parents? Have they come around?"

"Getting there. They like Edmund, but are not so keen on the idea of their daughter being a divorcée. They don't believe a marriage can break down irretrievably and, even more, hate the idea of fault having to be proven."

"I guess that's the downside of coming from a happy family." Annie felt Trisha's eyes on her.

"You've never talked about your childhood. I suppose I assumed it was happy."

"Not really. Ma was wonderful and held us all together. Father was not. He didn't think much of me. And was hard on the boys, too. I haven't heard from him since I left Australia." Annie's eyes glazed. "I'm at fault too. I've only written a couple of times. I know he's alright because one of the Land Girls, Helen, stayed on after the war and keeps me informed."

"Does Joe see him?"

"Occasionally. He's better able to manage him. Dad's always been a morose man, even before Ma and Ernie died." Annie shrugged. "Enough of that. Happy things today."

"In a minute." Trisha looked down, "One last question. What about Bill?"

"What about him?"

"Don't brush me off. Annie, you're such a lovely woman, don't close the door on finding someone. Good grief, if I can, with three children in tow, so can you."

"Trisha, I'm thirty-six, seen too much, and done too much to want to settle for anything less than Bill. I count myself lucky I had him. Even if it was for such a short time." She laughed. "And anyway, who would want an old maid?"

"Hardly! You have legs that go on forever." Trisha firmed her dress over her hips. "It seems the happier I am, the more the pounds settle."

"I don't hear Ed complaining!"

"He is a darling. I thank Berlin for him."

"Can I ask what Rupert is up to?"

"Still there. He's angling for a posting to the Middle East. Now the legal stuff, you know, the decisions, are out of the way, we actually get on reasonably well. And I thank Granny for leaving me this place, and Rupert for having had the decency to have left it in my name. Having my own home has made the whole process much easier."

"I wonder if he'll remarry."

"Probably. He can be charming. What he needs is a woman who won't rock the boat. A bit like I used to be. Until I got tired of being a show pony who had the right social graces."

Laughter accompanied the lamb chop lunch, with Janet and Peter telling Annie all about school, and promising her the new nanny wasn't nearly as much fun as she had been.

"That probably means she doesn't let you get away with as much as I did."

"You can be strict," Janet assured her. "No, Mary, doesn't get on the floor and play silly games with us, like you did." She looked serious. "Although, of course, I'm getting too old for that sort of thing now."

"Yes, of course." Annie winked at Trisha. "So, you won't want to hunt for Easter eggs? Because I heard from a most reliable source that, because of the rain, the Easter bunny managed to hide them inside this year."

"I didn't say that."

"Oh, that's all right then."

—

After her two days off, Annie went back to St. George's for a fourteen-night shift. She didn't really mind. Five nights on, two off, then four on and three off for twelve weeks. At least she'd get a chance to see some sun through the summer months.

Sitting at the ward desk, lamp dimmed and pointing down to the patient ledger, she loosened her starched veil and glanced along the ward to the bed at the end. No bell had been rung but something drew her to the patient.

Annie had trembled when she'd read his case notes. A man of thirty-one who had been imprisoned in Changi on Singapore by the Japanese in 1942, then spent two years on the notorious Burma Railway before being returned to Changi. With a severely suppressed immune system because of near starvation and cruelty, he had been in an out of hospital since his return to England in 1945, all because of a worm. Strongyloides stercoralis had invaded his lungs. Picked up through bare feet in the jungle as whips and rifle butts ensured the labour of the prisoners-of-war, as well as the thousands of Southeast Asians who had been press ganged into laying the rail tracks.

"Hello, ducks, do you need anything?"

The gaunt man's eyes fluttered at the feel of Annie's fingers on his pulse. She checked the watch pinned to her uniform and noted the skin around his lips and earlobes looked grey. His head rolled on the pillow.

"Would you like me to stay with you awhile? The nights can be long."

A tear leaked down his cheek. Annie hooked a stool over with her foot, then holding the man's hand, she sat down. "I was in Singapore."

His eyes shot open. "When?" His voice was a croak.

"With the Australian Army Nursing Service. Got out on February 13th, just before it fell."

"Knew some Aussies. On the Railway. Lots died."

Annie nodded. "Who were you with?"

He flashed a tired grin. "The Holy Boys."

"The who?"

"4th Battalion Royal Norfolk Regiment." His wheezed words turned to a rattling coughing fit, and Annie waited.

"You can tell me the story behind that another time," she said.

He sighed, the shake of his head the slightest of movements. "I'm dying this time."

She squeezed his hand and thought he'd dozed off, but then his fingers flexed. She had to bend to hear him. "Do you believe in God?"

"Not sure I do, ducks. Seen too much."

"I do. Got to be something better." He lapsed into silence. His breath a rasp, before quietening again. "But what if there's not?"

Annie bent close. "Soldier, would you like to speak to the padre?"

His eyes fluttered again, and his chin dropped in a nod.

"Righto. I'll send for him. Be right back." She smoothed his forehead then went to the sluice room where a junior nurse sterilized bed pans. "Nurse, nip down to the Chapel, please, and get the padre."

"What if he's not there, Sister?"

"Then find him."

"Yes, Sister."

Silent in rubber-soled shoes, Annie checked patients as she made her way back to the soldier, who now lay with his eyes open, staring, barely blinking. "The padre's on his way, Soldier." She sat down again and held his hand. Too young to die. Hell for so many: Ernie; Iris; Verna's sister Ruth. And Bill. What a waste.

"Good evening, Sister."

Brought back to the ward by the calm affable voice, Annie glanced up and noted the dog collar below heavy stubble.

"Oh, evening, Padre. Sorry, miles away." She stroked the patient's hand as he refocused, his jaw slack. "The padre's here." Annie swapped places, then said, "This is Stanley Moore. He's had a tough few years. Changi. The railway." She watched as the padre leant close to the dying man, but couldn't hear his murmured words, then she manoeuvered screens around the bed before going back to her desk, sad, doubting Stanley would be alive in the morning.

Chapter 25
Summer Returns, 1950

After the unexpected snowfall of late April, Annie wondered if the sun ever shone in England. Flo had confirmed it never did in Glasgow but, apart from the weather, which, she told Annie, the Scots called 'dreich', she loved the city, her studies, her life.

As if to defy both of them, Flo's visit to London in early June coincided not only with Annie's three nights off, but glorious weather too. They spent their days happily wandering the city, and the nights talking.

The tip of Annie's cigarette glowed. Funny how such a simple thing could trigger memories of the war. "Do you ever get lonely, Flo?"

"Not really. Although I do sometimes wonder, particularly at exam time, if I'm mad. I can't tell you, Annie, how glad I am that, for once, I listened." Flo put the kettle on, then turned to Annie. "When Dr. Callwood suggested I should train as a psychologist rather than in psychiatry, my initial reaction was that he didn't think I had the chops to earn a medical degree. It wasn't that. He really felt I was better suited to psychology because he knew I'd much rather listen to the patient than dish out drugs. And he was right. Not to mention it saved years at medical school."

"But in the quiet moments, Flo. Do you?"

"Get lonely? I suppose I do, but I'm too busy for it to last long." She poured water on top of the tealeaves in the pot. "What's this about, Annie?"

"Don't know really." Annie shook the bottle of nail varnish.

"Do you know what I think?" Flo ignored Annie's eye roll. "You need to meet some new people. You work. You come home. And now that Joe has left, you're festering."

"Festering?" Annie tossed the tea towel across the table. "Charming! Thanks, Flo!"

"You know what I mean. Why don't you join a club or something."

"I'll do the 'or something'." Annie handed Flo the bottle. "Can you do my right hand? You know I'm hopeless. Then I'll do yours."

Florence painted Annie's nails, then returned to the lonely question. "No, really, Annie. Remember Joe said there was one around the corner. On St. James. The Over-Seas Club." Flo sat back and looked satisfied. "Join that!"

"I don't think so. I'm not clubby material." Annie waggled her feet, "Maybe they're just itchy."

Flo smiled. "Well, they have been in one place for a whole year."

"I don't know. Perhaps I'm envious of Verna. She sounds utterly content being at home with Ruthie and Mark. And now Trisha and Edmund, with her three." Annie pushed her mug across the table. "That sounds jealous, not envious!"

"You don't have a jealous jot in you."

Annie gave a wry chuckle. "You're my friend, you have to say that."

"No, I don't." Flo strained tea into mugs. "Don't get cross, Annie, but could it be the baby timer going off?" She hurried on. "We've never really talked about having children. But I have decided that I really do not want any."

Annie's head jerked up as she stubbed out her cigarette.

"Don't misunderstand me. I love Ruthie to bits. A few of the friends I've made in Glasgow have children and I enjoy seeing them, but to have my own—not interested." Flo paused. "And I have thought about it a lot. That's the trouble with studying psychology, one tends to delve deep. Even if a man appeared who interested me, I wouldn't change my mind."

"It's not fair is it?" Annie sighed. "I mean we have this brief window and if we miss the opening, for whatever reason, it slams shut and that's it. No second chance."

Flo searched her face, "Have you met someone? Is this what this is about? Bill? Guilt?"

Annie shook her head. "No."

"Righto, ducks, what gives then?"

"I had a patient who died. Been on the Death Railway in Thailand. Never recovered."

Flo groaned. "Oh, God, what hell that must've been. Was he young?"

"Yeah, younger than us. Strongyloides stercoralis. Lungs, intestines. I sat with him, holding his hand, and all I could think of was Ernie, Iris, Ruth, Bill, all of them. Such a waste." Annie wiped her eyes with the back of her hands, then rubbed her temples. "He asked me if I believed in a God."

"And?"

"You know I don't, Flo. But I can't stop thinking about him. He never had a chance at life. It's silly. Other patients have died, but this chap—his name was Stanley Moore—really got to me."

"Some do, ducks. I don't know why some do more than others, but they do. Did the padre come?"

"Yeah. Gentle man. I suppose they have to be. He sat with Stanley till the end. About five hours. Then we had a cup of tea. Life goes on."

"Have you seen him since? This padre?"

"He popped in the next night to check up on me."

"That was kind. And?"

"And what?"

"Have you seen him again?"

"He wanders by sometimes."

Flo watched Annie's face. "Do you like him?"

"Sure. He has to be nice, it's his job." Annie snorted. "Oh, my God, Flo, he's a padre!"

"But not a priest."

"Righto, this conversation has got completely out of hand. Enough. Practice your psychology on some other sucker." Annie looked at the mantel clock. "Come on, it's your last night. Let's go to The Goat? I'll leave a note for Betty. She might like to join us. She'll be home soon."

—

A puff of steam, then a sharp whistle and more steam announced the departure of the Royal Scot from Euston next morning. Flo leant out of the window and blew Annie a kiss as the train chuffed out of the station. She waited until Flo's waving arm disappeared from view, then ambled along Euston Road to King's Cross Tube station, and got the Piccadilly Line to Green Park. Faster than the bus, and she wanted to watch the world go by from a deckchair in the park, before tidying the flat and going back on duty. And who knew how long summer would last?

"Morning, luv, 'aven't seen you round for a while." Albert, his hands knotty and misshapen, held out a copy of The Daily Telegraph, "Workin' nights?"

"Yup. Thanks, Albert. Is this warmer weather helping your arthritis?"

His shoes a couple of sizes too big to accommodate his swollen feet, did a little jig. "What d' think you? Fancy goin' dancin' with me, Annie?"

She grinned. "Love to, ducks, but I don't think your wife'd be too impressed!"

"Probably not. Never mind, eh? Be seein' ya!"

"Hooroo, Bert." Annie branched off the Broadwalk and found an empty deckchair and settled down with a sigh. Shuffling through the paper, she glanced at headlines, read a few stories that caught her attention, then folded the pages to the cryptic crossword. Rootling around in her handbag for a pencil, she settled down. 'Sea salt eroded navigational aids (7)' "Hah, easy one to start with!" She wrote 'ATLASES', then noted her crimson nails. Must remember to take off the varnish. Matron would have a fit.

Lost in the black and white squares of the crossword, she didn't notice the figure strolling along the path stop, then head towards her.

"Sister Cutler?"

Annie squinted up at the bulk blocking the sun. "Oh, g'day, Padre. What are you doing here?"

"The same as you, I assume. Enjoying the sunshine before a night at work." He looked at the empty chair next to her and raised his eyebrows in question.

"Sure." She laid the newspaper on her lap.

"Don't let me stop you."

"I'm stuck anyway."

"36 down stymied me this morning." He glanced over at the crossword. "And you, it seems."

"I think they have different setters on different days. Sometimes it's a doddle, other days I haven't a clue," Annie broke off with a laugh, "no pun intended, what I'm meant to be looking for. Today is the latter."

"Did you know The Daily Telegraph's contribution to the war effort involved the crossword?" At Annie's shake of the head, he continued. "Irked by complaints it had got easier, the editor got a chap, can't remember his name, to set a crossword that had to be completed in under twelve minutes by a select group. Only a handful succeeded. Then it was run in the paper sometime in January '42, I think it was, and entries could be sent in. Those who got the answers correct received a letter from the War Office wondering if they would care to come in for a chat."

"Why?"

"Bletchley! And code breaking."

"Good story, Padre." Annie laughed.

"True story, Sister. And actually, I'm a chaplain these days, although during the war I did wear a padre's badge. RAF."

"Sorry. Force of habit, I suppose."

"Some are hard to lose. That young man, Stanley, told me you'd served in Singapore too."

She nodded. "You?"

"Started at RAF Duxford in Cambridgeshire, then Malta."

They lapsed into silence. A comfortable one. Annie closed her eyes and allowed the warmth on her face to tease away memories of faces lost to the war. She might have dozed, and sat up with a start. "Oh, God, am I drooling?"

A deep chuckle followed her question. "Are you asking God, or me?"

"You're his spokesperson."

"Then, no, you're not." The chaplain checked his watch. "Could I tempt you with a pot of tea? Or coffee, Sister? There might even be a currant bun on offer. There's a little café on the south side of the park that I frequent."

"Only if you stop calling me Sister. I'm Annie."

"Happy to. I'm David Rowland." He held out his hand and hauled Annie out of the low-slung deck chair. "Come on, then."

They dawdled along under the plane trees whose shadows dappled the paths that led down to Constitution Hill, then on towards Victoria Station. Sometimes talking. Sometimes not.

David broke their silence. "I moonlight at St. Stephen's, so I know this area well."

Annie nodded. Her mind flew to the nurses slaughtered in St. Stephen's in Hong Kong, then shifted back to London. "I thought you worked nights at the hospital. You can't moonlight during the day."

"Shift work, same as you. Though, I suppose more on call rather than regular shifts."

"Do you live in the area too?"

"I do, Ebury Street."

"Sounds grand." Annie's curiosity got the better of her. "Family home?"

"Not really. I've got the basement. My brother and his brood have the rest of the house. Richard's wife's familial home. One of. Eve is a lovely woman who puts up with her brother-in-law's odd hours and occasional even odder guests."

Annie looked at the man walking by her side. "You're going to have to explain that," she said, as David held the door to the café open for her.

"There are a great many affected by the war. Some of them land on my doorstep. Usually pilots." He held a chair for her. "Now, tea or coffee? Sometimes the latter is passable. My recommendation would be tea. No one in this country can get away with a bad pot."

They talked over their steaming mugs and currant buns, about the war, the country, Australia, words flowing as easily as the tea. A clock struck three, reminding Annie she had to get back to Cork Street, tidy up and prepare for work. A brisk walk back through Green Park gave her time to clear her head. And give herself a stern talking to. Get a grip Sister Cutler. He's a kind man who stumbled upon you in the park. But she couldn't stop smiling. Until she got home and saw the splodge of dried breakfast jam on her skirt.

"Really?" Perhaps he hadn't noticed. He'd have to be blind to have missed it. She shrugged. "Oh, well." Taking her nail polish off, she had a wash, then set the alarm and lay on the bed hoping for a nap before work. After the wash of loneliness from waving Flo off at the station, the day had turned out better than expected. Sleep did not come.

Chapter 26
August, 1950

By the end of August, Annie felt ready to get on the next ship back to Sydney. Not because of the job, or London, but the weather.

Albert, the newspaper vendor at Green Park grinned, as Annie, walking home from night duty, wrestled with an umbrella and asked the same question as the previous morning. "Does it ever stop raining?"

"What you need, luv, is some flowers." He nodded across to the barrow. "Go on, buy yourself some. 'Enry'll give you a deal, won't you?" He called over to the capped chap wearing a thick overcoat and mittens.

Annie looked at the buckets filled with the rainbow-colored flowers, and shrugged. "Why not? No one else will."

"Good on yer, luv."

Putting the dahlias in a milk jug immediately cheered up the sitting room. How silly to wait for a man to buy me flowers. She raised her mug of tea, "Thanks, Albert!"

Dear Verna, James, Ruthie and Mark,

It's been ages, sorry. And thanks for your letter, Verna—wonderful to hear how the children are doing, and you. And that rogue you married. I was surprised he changed his mind about plastic surgery, but I am so very glad he enjoys private practice. I always thought he'd make a great G.P.

I'm on a treadmill of work, sleep and back to work. It has been so bloody miserable, weather-wise, that on days off I tend to curl up with a book or the radio. However, Albert, and before you get excited, he's the bloke from whom I buy my newspaper and is about as old as Methuselah and for good measure has a wife, told me to buy myself flowers and to cheer up. Isn't that silly? But that is actually what I needed.

I suppose some of my glums are due to Korea. It's a civil war, for God's sake, but I guess that's what the United Nations is all about. Stopping any kind of war. But with guns? I dunno, I can't bear to think of our boys, as in Brits and Aussies, and the Yanks, going back to war. The Argyll and Sutherland Highlanders—remember them, Verna, the last regiment to get back to Singapore before it all went to hell in a hand basket—are being sent from Hong Kong. Doubt it'll be long before the Diggers join them. Doom and sodding gloom.

Annie looked at the dahlias, sunshine in a vase.

Righto, time to cheer up. Again. Verna, you are not to laugh. Promise? I have joined a club! It's no good, I can almost hear you sniggering as I write—-which is also good for my mood, so thank you. Where was I? Flo suggested it when she was here and I pooh-poohed the idea, but she's right. I do need to meet some new people. Now I really can hear you! The Over-Seas Club is close to the flat, just south of Piccadilly—it 'fosters international connections', but unlike The Queen's Club in Sydney, it has both men and women members. And, even more importantly, has accepted women since its inception. What a concept! I popped in for tea for the first time the other day and met a pleasant woman from India, so my social life might be looking up, if I can stay awake long enough after my shift. She, her name is Samira, is studying at the London School of Economics. Anyway, she told me the Indian government gave, or sponsored, one of the reception rooms, the Hall of India, and that during the war the BBC used it as a wartime broadcasting studio to send messages to the troops overseas. Somehow that seems to make it all less frivolous.

I also gave myself a good talking to. Actually, I think it was Auntie May sending me a message. Because it's thanks to her I can do things like join a ritzy club and afford a lovely flat. Betty has turned out to be the perfect housemate. We don't see a lot of each other, different shifts, but when we do, we have a laugh.

Sleepy now. Will finish later.

"Good morning, Sister."

Annie looked up from the patient chart to see David Rowland's raffish smile. "G'day, Padre." She clipped the chart back on the end of the bed. "What brings you here?"

"Same as you, doing my rounds."

"Saving souls?"

"Trying to give comfort." His correction held no rancour.

"Fair enough." Annie moved along the ward, to be stopped by a soft touch to her arm.

With a lowered voice, David asked, "Would you care to join me for a drink? Perhaps next week sometime?"

"Go for it, Vicar," a cheeky voice from the next bed called out.

Annie glared at the wan face, "Shht, you're meant to be sick."

"Nah, not me. Just 'ere for you, Sister. You make me 'eart pound."

"Oh, for God's sake, Jimmy, behave." Annie smiled as she held his wrist, and with the other hand checked the watch pinned to her uniform. She had a soft spot for the lad. Just old enough to be on the men's ward and not the children's, his records showed he'd been in and out of hospital for five years. His pulse raced. War wounds weren't just from bombs and guns. "How's the chest pain, ducks?"

"Better now you're 'olding me 'and." Jimmy winked at David. "You should give it a try, Vicar."

Annie blushed at David's soft chuckle. "I'm trying my best, lad, trying my best."

Jimmy's breath hissed and he paused. "I could give yer a couple of tips."

"I'll be back. But for now, do as the sister tells you." David patted Jimmy's feet hidden under the blanket then carried on down the ward.

"Is your mum coming to see you today, Jimmy?"

"Nah, told 'er not to. She's busy with the others, an' she gets all weepy-like." Jimmy turned his head away, and Annie waited. "I can't 'elp 'er now, Sister. You know, cos me dad got it in the war. It's been me and me mum trying to look after the little 'uns. Now it's jus' 'er."

Annie squeezed his thin hand. "You can't help this, Jimmy. It's not your fault."

"Yeah, I know. Deep down. But that doesn't always 'elp, does it?"

"No, ducks, it doesn't." She tucked his hand under the covers. "Have a doze now. Lunch won't be long." Jimmy stayed quiet. No energy left for humour.

Then his weak voice followed her. "'Ave a drink with the Vicar, Sister. 'E's a good 'un, and 'e likes ya!"

—

The doors to Annie's wardrobe stood open. Clothes lay strewn across her bed as if a tornado had lifted the hangers and flung them across the room. Two white uniforms remained on hangers, the only things to survive the storm. Annie, shivering in her petticoat, picked up a beige dress and held it against her. Too dull. Just like the weather. Rain trickled paths down the window panes. The yellow looked too summery. "Come on, choose one." Not the pink, too girly. The blue will have to do. "Nope. Too like a WAAF uniform." Or the green. She nodded. Fighting with the back zipper, she buckled the wide skirt with a black patent belt, and matched it with a black handbag and heels.

Her hair curled any way it chose. "Hah, he's only seen me without a veil once before." Green Park. Ages ago. Brown eyeshadow, a lick of mascara and a soft coral lipstick. "Too pale!" Annie smudged some of the lipstick across her cheeks. "Better. A bit!" She slipped the lipstick into her handbag. "It's only a drink, Annie. Settle down. Don't even know the bloke."

She heard voices on the landing, and Betty calling. "I'll get it!" Then murmurs from the sitting room.

Annie, with a last glance in the mirror, hurried in to find both Betty and Mrs. Bellows chatting to the vicar. David Rowland turned with a smile that deepened the creases around his mouth. Relieved, she saw he had changed his dog collar for a tie.

"Good evening, Annie."

"Hello." Annie's stomach did a nervous flip. "I see you've met both my housemate and my landlady!"

Mrs. Bellows simpered. "Oh, I had to show him up, dear."

"Of course you did, Mrs. B. Thank you." Annie turned to David, "Would you like a drink before we go?"

"No, thanks, we should head off." He turned to the other women with a slight bow, "Delightful to meet you both, goodbye." He helped Annie on with her coat then ushered her out and down the stairs. As she pushed open the front door he said, "That was quite the welcome committee."

"I know, I'm sorry, David." Annie paused, "They're looking out for me. It's a novelty for them to see me go out."

"Really?"

"Really." She popped up the umbrella. "Is it far?"

"In my head I thought it would be a pleasant evening stroll. Sorry! I'll try for a cab."

"Where are we going?"

"Jermyn Street."

"Oh, for heaven's sake, that's just around the corner. We don't need a cab."

"You're sure?"

"Yes. Come on, let's not dawdle though." She avoided a puddle. "I didn't know Jermyn Street had a pub."

"Aah, it doesn't." He took her elbow as they crossed Piccadilly. "I thought we'd go to Franco's. It's a little Italian place I rather like. Perhaps have some dinner too?" They ducked between two cabs. "I didn't have time to eat, so I'm rather hoping you didn't either."

Annie glanced up at his open face. "You must have heard my tummy growling. I'd love to have dinner." She laughed at his beaming face. "And I've never eaten Italian food."

"Then you're in for a treat, I hope. Franco opened just after the war and swears his is the first Italian restaurant in London." David guided her down St. James's Street and left onto Jermyn Street. "Here we are." He brushed droplets of water from her shoulders. "And not too drowned."

Warm air and the smell of summer tomatoes, garlic and some other scent Annie didn't recognise greeted them as the door opened. "Buonasera, signora." The smiling man took her coat. "And, Padre. It is good to see you, my friend."

"Evening, Franco."

"I 'ave your usual table, come, come."

They followed the owner to the banquette halfway down the narrow and dimly lit restaurant. "Prego," Franco pulled the table out so Annie could slide in. She nodded her thanks. "You would like the house wine?"

David looked at her. "Would you prefer red or white, Annie?"

"I'm not much of a wine drinker, so I don't mind. Whatever you usually have." She leant back as Franco placed the napkin on her lap, then took the menu and watched him disappear behind the bar. "This is charming, David."

"I'm glad. The food is excellent, and I like the casual atmosphere."

"You're obviously a regular." Annie looked around. "Do you bring all your girlfriends here?" She blushed. "I didn't mean to sound nosy. Sorry."

David laughed. "Two other women, Annie. My mother and my sister-in-law!" He paused. "The dog collar tends to put women off."

"Oh. I didn't think of that." She looked down at the menu. "You are going to have to order for me, otherwise God knows what I'll end up with." She coloured again. "I mean, goodness knows."

"Annie, can we get something straight, right now?" David's smile crinkled his eyes. "Just because I'm a vicar, it does not mean you have to watch what you say. Alright?"

She nodded. "Righto." She liked his laugh. Warm, friendly. "I can't always be relied upon to say the right thing anyway. Just ask Joe."

"Who's Joe?"

"My brother. He's the reason I've got that lovely flat. It was his, then I took it over when I returned from Berlin, and he went back to Sydney."

"Do you miss him?"

"Yes, I do. He's a lovely bloke." Annie watched Franco pour the wine.

"Eccoci qui. Here. You try." It was not a request.

The taste of summer tingled her tongue as she sipped the crisp cold white wine. "Oh, that really is delicious!"

Both men beamed. Annie sat back whilst David and Franco discussed the menu.

"I have no idea what he's saying, but it sounds wonderful. And you speak Italian. I'm impressed. I struggle with English."

"Not really. I understand a bit. A lot of Italian is spoken on Malta. I seem to remember reading somewhere it was one of the official languages until 1934. But don't quote me."

"Is it like Maltese—is that what they call it, Maltese?"

"It is. No, not really. It's more guttural, and is similar to Arabic. Which, before you ask, I don't speak."

Annie looked around the restaurant. "I like hearing the different languages." She smiled at the voluble stream of Italian coming from the next table. "In Berlin, you only ever heard English in restaurants. They were full of Brits, Yanks, with a smattering of French and Aussies. Not that I went to many. The blockade started a month after I arrived."

"Did you stay the entire time?"

"Yes, we did. I was nannying for a diplomatic family. We couldn't be seen to be deserting the Berliners. My God, they went through a lot." Annie blushed again. She hadn't realised she called on the man she didn't believe in quite so much.

"Annie, relax." David touched her hand. "Tell me more about Berlin. I've never been."

She gathered her thoughts, making order of words she'd never expressed before. "I learnt a lot there." She paused. "Singapore and New Guinea both fought against the enemy. In Berlin, it was different. Land of the vanquished. Does that make sense?"

David nodded and stayed silent.

"When we arrived, in 1948, the horror of the bombing surrounded us. I mean, London wasn't great, but Berlin was a whole other story. Better than immediately after the war but Berliners still lived in rat-infested basements. Food remained scarce. Hot water was a luxury for most. Then we, the victors, waltzed in and requisitioned any houses still standing and intact." Annie sipped her wine. "Sorry. A bit heavy for a first date."

"No. It's called getting to know each other. Go on."

"I felt terribly guilty. But I suppose we can always justify our existence." Annie swirled the wine in her glass. "I told myself, actually, Joe made me see it this way, that we were there to help. Well, not me exactly. But my employer. And even Joe, who flitted in and out. His, and Edmund's role, involved getting technical and scientific knowledge out of Germany."

"Who's Edmund? A boyfriend?"

"Oh, God, no!" Annie laughed. "I mean, he's a delight. But no. He's actually about to marry my employer's ex-wife. That's sounds awful. It isn't. She's a lovely woman who was married to an unlovely man. Edmund is perfect for her and adores her children."

"Will I get to meet them?"

"After all my yakking I doubt you'll want to have anything to do with me." Annie groaned. "That sounded like a fishing expedition. It wasn't."

David's rumbling laugh relaxed her. "You do have an interesting turn of phrase!"

They watched as a waiter placed a platter between them.

"I thought we'd start with an antipasti plate." He pointed, "salami, olives, and I asked Franco to include those crostini, slices of French bread—or maybe Italian." David grinned. "It's a white bean dip kind of thing with anchovy and lemon sauce."

"Kind of thing? Is that the technical term?"

"Of course. Ask Franco!" He put a piece on her plate. "Try it."

Annie took a mouthful, allowing the flavours to fill her senses. "Oh, that is good. It reminds me of sunshine. I think I'd like Italy."

"I'll take you there!" He bit his lip.

"You will, will you?"

"My turn to speak out of line." He looked sheepish. "I'm sorry, Annie. Getting carried away with myself."

"That's alright. Makes me feel better." She took another bite. "Righto, your turn."

"What do you want to know?"

"Everything."

"Well, that won't take long."

"Go on then." Annie grinned. "It just means I can eat and not worry about talking with my mouth full, because you'll be doing the talking." She liked to hear his laugh.

"I grew up in Dorset. Farming. Sheep and apples. If that doesn't sound an odd combination."

"A bit," Annie said. "Our property was sheep and wheat. Go on."

"I knew I didn't want to be a farmer. Got into university. Read Philosophy and English, then did a post graduate degree in Theology. Then the war."

Annie wiped her mouth. "Why did you join the RAF?"

"May I please have a bite?" David took a piece of crostini. "It is good, isn't it?"

She nodded and picked up an olive. "I've only ever had these in a martini."

"Hah, a cocktail girl!"

"Not really, I had one in Sydney, once I think. A tad strong for me."

She took another. "Hmmm, nice. Go on. Why the RAF?"

"I suppose because my father flew with the Royal Flying Corps in the Great War. Then Bill, my middle brother, joined. I thought I might as well keep it in the family." David looked up at Annie's stillness. "What's wrong?"

"Nothing." She shook her head and looked down.

"Please don't do that, Annie. We're both too old for evasions. What's wrong?"

She sighed, then took a deep breath. "Bill. The man I thought I'd marry. He died in New Guinea. Of all things, of dengue. In 1944."

"I'm sorry," David reached for her hand, "of all the names. Are you alright?"

"It was a long time ago. It just brought me up short. I'm fine."

"Which, in my limited experience of women, means you're not."

Her smile tight she said, "No, David, I am. Really." She nodded. "Go on. I like hearing your story."

"Not much more. Posted to RAF Duxford, not far from Cambridge. Rather nice. I knew the area well because of university."

Annie interrupted his flow. "You kept that snippet out. You went to Cambridge University?"

He nodded.

"Now I'm really intimidated."

"Don't be." He said with a laugh. "I had to work very hard to get there and stay there."

"If you say so. Keep going," Annie grinned, "because then I can snaffle the last olive!"

"Right. So Duxford. Then Malta. As I said."

"Not a barrel of laughs."

"You could say that!" David leant back as Franco produced two plates of steaming pasta.

"Pasta con funghi," he announced. "Mushrooms, with fresh basil. I grow. Simple, but very, very good, eh?"

"Certainly is, Franco," David agreed, and watched as he poured more wine.

"Is that what I can smell. Basil? A combo of peppermint and eucalyptus?"

Franco nodded, pleased.

Annie sat back with a sigh, having turned down a dessert even though they looked delicious. Far more appetizing than the war cake still usually offered. They finished the bottle of wine and as David settled the bill, she watched him and realised she was happy, and not just from the unaccustomed wine.

"You're a hit with Franco," David said, as he drew Annie's hand through his arm. It felt a comfortable fit. The rain had finally stopped, and they sauntered back to Cork Street. As they neared her front door, Annie tensed and she hoped Mrs. Bellows had gone to bed and not positioned herself behind the net curtains.

"Would you like to come up for a whisky? I haven't any coffee, I'm afraid."

David looked down at her with a smile. "Yes, I'd like to, but no, I'm not going to. Thank you."

"Oh, righto." Annie felt a tug of disappointment.

"You've got work in the morning, and so do I. Although I happen to have learnt you have a couple of days off at the end of the week."

Her laughter circled them. "I do, do I?"

"You do. It might surprise you to know that Sunday is my busy day. But how about Friday? If it's a pleasant evening, we could go down to the Thames."

"I'd like that. And thank you. I've had a lovely time. And Italian cuisine is now a firm favourite." Annie rummaged in her bag for her keys, which David took to unlock the door. She paused, then reached up and kissed his cheek. "Thank you for a lovely, evening. Good night."

Chapter 27
Falling

An autumn cold put Annie's next date with David on hold. That and a sadness she couldn't shake. And an anger. Jimmy, the cheeky lad who'd encouraged her to go out with the padre, died. The invasive aspergillosis, probably caused by spending hours in a damp, mouldy basement during the Blitz, had caused irreparable damage to his heart muscle. Matron, in a rare breaking of the rules, had allowed his younger siblings a brief visit, along with his mother, when it became obvious his body had had enough. He had died that night. Yet one more war death, five years after the Armistice.

"Come on, love. We can't save them all." Betty brought a hot lemon drink to Annie, with a red nose and a scratchy throat, propped up in bed with Auntie May's Paisley shawl around her shoulders.

"I know. But, damn it, he was eighteen." She took a sip. "He'd been sick more than half his life. How is that fair? Where is God when he's needed?"

Betty gave a sad smile. "That's a question for your vicar."

"I don't want to see him."

"Don't be barmy, Annie."

"No, I don't. I can't understand someone who doesn't get angry about death, of a child, someone who hasn't even had a chance at life. Who believes it's God's will." She thumped the mug down. "I'm sorry, Betty. I'm just grumpy." She took her hand, "Thanks for listening."

Betty sighed. "Aah, love, it's tough. And some are tougher than others. We just have to keep going."

"I dunno. Maybe it's time I had a change. Went back to midwifery."

"And that's not hard? To lose a baby?"

"Yeah, I know." Annie snuggled down under the eiderdown with a sniff. "I'm just out of sorts."

A strange aroma drifted into her disjointed dreams. As consciousness came Annie opened her eyes to a mug of something on the bedside table, then heard the rustle of clothes. Confused, she sat up.

"Hello, sleepy head." Samira, sitting in the chair by the window, dim light from outside creating a kind of halo, smiled and nodded to the mug. "Try that. My mother always made it when we were ill." She laughed. "Actually she made it all the time. But being in bed with a mug of it was only allowed if sickness was in the house."

Annie shimmied up and plumped the pillows. "What is it?"

"Masala chai. Try it."

After a cautious sip, Annie asked, "Can I taste pepper?"

A delighted laugh followed her question as Samira nodded. "Yes, masala means spices in Hindi. Chai is just tea. So, it is spicy black tea. Do you like it?"

"I'm not sure." Annie sipped again. "I think I do." She looked across the deepening shadows of her bedroom. "What time is it? And what are you doing here?"

"Four-ish. Finished exams, and stopped by on the off chance you weren't working. I caught Betty as she left. She said you weren't well, so I nipped home, got my magic ingredients and came back. Mrs. B. let me in."

"Huh," Annie breathed in the swirling scents, "I'll have to speak to her about letting roaming miscreants into my home." It felt good to laugh. "Thanks, ducky. It's really kind of you." She sneezed. "It's alright. My cold's gone. The spices tickled my nose. And," Annie waved her hand at the bed, "I'm just being a wombat."

"Truly, Annie," Samira frowned, "I have no idea what you're saying half the time. And I grew up speaking English."

"You see, that's your problem. English is not Australian!" She sipped again, still not sure whether she liked the taste. "A wombat is a slow-moving marsupial, so it just means I'm being lazy. Although," Annie said, "they can run fast in short bursts. Which is not something I can do!"

The Indian girl shook head. "Crazy."

"Give me a couple of minutes to wash up and get dressed, and we can have a proper natter." Splashing her face with water, Annie thanked Flo for pushing her to get out more. Meet new people. She frowned, her mind flitting back to when she'd first opened her eyes. Samira had looked miserable. Her usual straight back, slumped.

"Righto, ducks, into the kitchen." Annie, now wearing trousers and a baggy jumper, looked at the slight girl gazing out of the sitting room window, her hair glossy in a stream of late afternoon sun.

"What do you mean?"

"The kitchen is always the best place to talk." Annie opened a round tin, images of teddy bears just visible on its battered surface. "Mrs. B. brought up a cake the other day. Let's have a slice, another cup of tea, although I might stick to builders if that's okay, and we'll put the world to rights. Because, Samira, I know something is up."

"No. No, nothing is wrong." Samira nodded her thanks as Annie slid a plate across the table.

"Ducky, I've seen and heard a lot of things. There's not much that ruffles me."

They sat in silence. Street sounds drifted up. A car horn sounded followed by a shout. A door slamming. A policeman's whistle. Annie waited.

Samira, her voice hesitant, began. "Do you know much about Indian culture?"

"Not a thing, I'm sorry to say." Her thoughts flashed to the hospital in Lae. "We nursed some Sikh POWs in New Guinea. And we learnt a little of their beliefs—especially about cutting their hair."

"Sikhism is very different to Hinduism."

Annie nodded and waited.

"We believe the soul is immortal." Samira paused. "Have you heard of karma?"

Annie shook her head.

"So, karma means the effect, or consequence, of any action. We both believe in that." Her smile wan, Samira continued. "We Hindus also love our image worship, our caste system. Sikhs don't. And although they sometimes have arranged marriages, it is not like that for us. We must marry in our caste."

"Whoa! Arranged marriages?"

"It happens in many cultures. Look at your kings and queens. Were their marriages not arranged for the good, or greed, of respective countries?"

"Never thought about it. But yes, I suppose so." Annie looked at her friend. "Are you telling me you're being told who to marry?"

With tears in her eyes, Samira nodded.

"Oh hell, ducks." Annie reached across for Samira's hand. "Do you like the bloke?"

Samira's tears fell in a steady stream as she shook her head again. "His name is Manish. He is old. Traditional. I would not be allowed to work."

"But why would your parents agree you could study here, if you can't use your degree?"

"It is better to have an educated child, particularly when there is no son." Samira stood and looked down into the street.

"Sami, what would happen if you absolutely refuse to marry Manish?"

"My mother and sisters will wail. Pressure to conform will be immense. There would be massive loss of face for my family. And his. My place in society would be at risk. I am lucky, though, because I would not be beaten, many are." Samira gave a sad smile and sat down again. "If I refuse Manish, no one else will marry me." Her eyes filled again. "And, if I return to Delhi, I would be expected to live out my life in my parent's house, and to look after them in their old age." She shrugged. "Which I would have to do anyway, but at least I'd have my own home."

"What are you going to do?"

"Stretch out my time in London for as long as possible." Samira wiped her eyes. "Now, enough. I'm bored with my story. But thank you for listening, Annie. I must go now."

With another cup of tea, again builder's, Annie sat at the table a long time, mulling over Sami's words. She couldn't image being ordered to marry someone. Bill's words floated in about the different beliefs, particularly surrounding death, among the tribes in New Guinea. Tambaran. Annie couldn't believe she'd remembered the word. Everything has a spirit, so death is not the end, more a stepping stone, similar to Aborigines. Annie spoke to the empty room, remembering the woman who had helped her mother feed the shearers. "I wonder what happened to Ani."

—

A toot toot sent Annie scurrying, tea in hand, to the sitting room window. It seemed as if the blue moon of a couple of nights earlier had also brought some rare October warmth, and David. She couldn't help but smile. Three days off, which had coincided with the end of night duty, had given her time to recover both her health and her equilibrium.

Clutching her dressing gown, she pushed open the sash window and called down, "G'day, what are you doing here so early? Actually, at all?"

"Someone happened to mention your mood had lightened so I thought I'd be brave and see if you'd like to go for a drive." He grinned.

"Bloody cheek!" Annie felt her spirits lifting. Betty had mentioned she'd seen him at the hospital. She nodded at the car behind David. "Is that yours?"

"It is."

"Then I can be bought." She put a hand to her hair. "You'll have to wait. I'm not decent."

She pulled the window down before he could answer then ran to her bedroom. Sports car meant casual. A pair of tangerine trousers with a double panel of buttons at the front, a plain cream mock turtleneck sweater and the Liberty scarf, rolled and tied. Flatties. Annie dithered over makeup and settled for mascara and her favourite coral lipstick. She grabbed her navy coat, glanced in the mirror by the door and untied the scarf. More useful over her head than around her neck.

"Good morning, dear." Mrs. Bellows happened to be in the hallway. "Is that the Reverend I see outside?" She tssked. "He really shouldn't have just beeped his horn, you know. A gentleman comes to the door."

"It's alright, Mrs. B. I told him he couldn't come up." Annie ducked her chin to hide a grin. "It wouldn't have been proper. I wasn't dressed."

"Well, all right then." She nudged the silver salver on the hall table an inch. "Where are you off to?"

"Not a clue, Mrs. B." Annie edged past her to the door. "See you later, maybe."

"Well, that didn't take long," David smiled and held the car door open. "You look lovely, by the way."

"I would've been quicker but Mrs. Bellows had to tell me your manners were lacking. No tooting in the street!" She laughed as she watched David climb over the door on his side of the mallard-green Morgan and slide behind the wheel. "The beauty of long legs, huh?"

The engine growled as he turned the ignition and said, "I have a feeling you could do the same!"

Annie felt her colour rise. "Hmm." She watched as he pulled away from the kerb. "Golly, it's got a long bonnet, hasn't it?"

"It has. It used to be my father's, but he finds it too difficult to get in and out of now, and Mother never liked it, so I bought it from him. A 1937 beauty."

"It is. I love it." She stroked the wood panelling. "Where are we going, by the way?"

"I promised you a trip to the river. Henley-on-Thames."

"Isn't that miles?" Annie tied the scarf over her hair and put on her sunglasses, her eyes already watering as they nipped through London with the roof down.

David glanced across at her. "A couple of hours. Alright with that?"

"Long as I'm back in time for work tomorrow I'm fine."

He laughed. "I see!"

"Oh, hell," she blushed again, "I didn't mean that."

"I'm teasing, Annie." His grin made his face boyish. "You'll be back by nightfall. Well before Mrs. Bellows can make a fuss." He lapsed into silence, concentrating on the traffic.

Annie didn't feel the need to talk, it was something she liked about David's company. Her thoughts drifted to Bill and their drive to the beach in New Guinea. She shook her head. Different time, different place, Annie. She looked at David's profile. A strong face. Kind. She liked his eyes, somewhere between blue and grey. A speck of blood showed where he'd nicked his neck shaving. No tie today.

"Do you never wear your dog collar when you're not on duty?"

He laughed. "Isn't that a double negative?"

"Well?"

He rubbed his chin. "Actually, Annie, only when I'm seeing you."

"Why?"

He looked straight ahead. "Because I think it's going to be hard enough to woo you, without having the Church breathing down my neck."

"Woo me, huh?"

"Uh huh! That is what I am trying to do."

"David," Annie paused, choosing her words carefully, "this is the second time we have been out together. Don't you think 'wooing' is a bit soon?"

"No, I don't," he replied, keeping his eyes on the road. "To put it bluntly, Annie, neither of us are as young as we'd like to believe. I haven't felt like this since …" He stopped, glanced across at her, then continued, "… since I was about twenty-one."

She studied him. "Do you want to tell me now, or when you're not driving?"

"Not much to tell. No desperate lovelorn story. I fell in love with a girl around the same time I decided I wanted to be a vicar." He gave a chuckle. "It was not to be a marriage made in Heaven."

"I'm sorry, David."

"Oh, God, I'm not! It would've been disastrous. At the time I went through all sorts of conflicting emotions. God won. And that, Annie, is something I have never regretted." He paused, again. "This is a conversation I thought we'd have on date number five or six."

"Well, you brought up age."

"I did. Right. What do you want to know?"

"Nothing." She watched a bus disgorge its passengers. "Not true. What happened to her?"

"Elizabeth married a man destined for great things. A chum of mine. He's in the Foreign Office. They have two children and currently reside in Cairo. He will be an ambassador or high commissioner one day, which will suit her perfectly. They are dear friends, whom I hope you will one day meet." He glanced across at Annie. "Anything else?"

"No, I think that just about covers it." She looked down at her bare hands. "I'm thirty-eight."

"I'm forty-three. Just."

"David," she smiled, "I do like you. It's just that this is moving pretty fast. And I don't just mean the car." She grabbed her scarf, sliding off as they picked up speed. Annie touched his arm, her grin tempering her words. "Let's not talk for a while."

She put her hand over the door and let the wind trail through her fingers.

—

Crossing the bridge into Henley itself, Annie smiled. "Please tell me we're having lunch in that pub." She pointed to a white building that looked as if it had grown out of the bridge. "You know, I haven't seen much of England. I went almost immediately to Berlin, and haven't done much exploring outside London since I got back. This is lovely. So," she searched for the word, "so English!"

"Thank goodness we're in England then!"

"Very funny."

David parked and guided her along the riverbank, dropping dollops of history into their walk. "Seems incredible, doesn't it," he nodded along the serene waterway, a couple of mallards swanning along, "that this used to be a busy internal port. Flat-bottomed barges took grain, timber, wool, and malt, I think, to London. Salt, silk and wine came back."

"Wonder how long each trip took?"

"Four or five days, I believe. Bit before my time!"

She laughed. "So not that old." She looked up at him. "How do you know so much about the place?"

"Spent quite a lot of time here. Rowing."

"Next you'll tell me you've been in the Oxford and Cambridge Boat Race. I read about it."

David looked bashful. "Uh huh."

"Really?"

"Just once. Long time ago."

"My God, is there no end to your talents?"

"There will be if I don't get a pint soon. Come on, let's find the pub."

It felt natural that David should take her hand.

—

I'm ashamed to say, I completely forgot I hadn't finished this letter. I'm so sorry, Verna. And I can't blame work, or the glums, for my bad correspondence. I've been busy. Falling in love. And no, it's not Albert or the flower seller.

His name is David Rowland. And, believe it or not, he's a vicar. But not a holier than thou sort. Very down to earth. Very tall. Very handsome. Very wonderful. I introduced him to Trisha and Ed, and the children and they all liked him. Molly wouldn't stop climbing over him—that's a good sign, isn't it? And, most importantly, my landlady approves so that's all you need to know.

I'm going to sign off here, as otherwise who the hell knows when I'll remember to post it.

Promise to write more, soon, soon, soon. Just know I'm happy, in a way I never I thought I would be again.

With big cuddles to Ruthie and Mark, even though he doesn't know me, and I'm sure she's forgotten me, and to you and your galoot of a husband,

All love,

Your walking-on-air mate, Annie X

A chortle escaped Annie's lips as she pushed the envelope through the red pillar box at the end of Cork Street. It wouldn't take long for a return letter. She looked up at the sky. Even the November drizzle couldn't dampen her spirits.

Annie hugged herself. Two days off in the middle of the week meant God did not interfere with her time with David. She kept walking until she came to the fishmonger tucked in on the south side of Oxford Street.

With a piece of cod, a couple of potatoes, carrots and a tin of peas she could fashion a dinner of sorts. An apple pie with a trellis of pastry eked out of her rations of sugar, butter and flour would have to do for a pudding. And tinned cream.

They hadn't talked about money, but Annie got the impression David came from a monied background. He drove a Morgan, for Heaven's sake. And Franco's was a favourite. Most people she knew did not have a regular restaurant. He probably thought the same about her. I mean, how many nurses had membership at the Over-Seas Club? Thank you, Auntie May. Her giggle drew a curious look from a passing woman, laden with a shopping basket and a pram. And wine. He had said he'd bring a bottle to dinner.

The fish cakes sat under a tea towel ready to be fried, carrots peeled. Apple pie ready to be popped in the oven, Annie scraped her hair back with combs and washed. Then came the perennial conundrum. What to wear? Casual, trousers? Cocktail, green silk? Day, skirt and jumper. No, not that. She pulled out a pair of charcoal coloured wide-leg woollen trousers and a cream cashmere sweater that Joe had given her. She clipped Ma's pearls on her ears and surveyed her reflection. Too severe. She swapped the trousers for a cherry red pair. Better. The sweater needed lifting. She added Auntie May's long string of pearls then wondered, not for the first time, who had given them to her. Perhaps she'd bought them for herself. Annie laughed. Made her flower buying tame in comparison.

The doorbell rang and she nearly poked her eye with the mascara wand. "Bugger, he's early." She dragged a brush through her hair, then dabbed crimson lipstick over her cheeks and lips, slid her feet into flats and ran for the door. Too late. Mrs. B's less-than-dulcet tones echoed up the stairs. Did the woman never go out?

"Lovely to see you, Mrs. Bellows. It's fine. I'll save you the climb." Then David's footsteps leaping up the stairs.

Annie had the door open for him to fall through. "G'day!"

"G'day to you too!" He brushed her lips. "I made it without interrogation."

"So I heard. Well done." She closed the door firmly on any intrusion from downstairs. "Come on through. Let me take your coat."

"Sorry, I haven't been home to change." He gestured to his neck and unwound his scarf, "I came straight from a meeting."

"That's alright. Would you like a glass of sherry?" Annie realised she had started to gabble. "I've only got dry, I'm afraid."

"Dry would be perfect, thank you." He followed her into the kitchen carrying a wicker basket. "I'll open this now. Let it breathe."

Annie groaned. "Oh, God, I don't have a corkscrew."

"How fortunate that I do." He lifted the towel off the basket. "I thought I should hide the evidence. I'm not sure Mrs. B. holds me in very high esteem."

"She does keep asking me if I'm sure you really are a vicar. And why don't you wear the clothes of your office." She chuckled. "I think those were her words. I was trying hard to swallow a laugh!"

"I should have taken my scarf off downstairs." He fingered the dog collar. "I can take it off now."

"David, it's fine." Annie smiled. "It's who you are. Like my veil. Although I hear rumours they are soon to be ditched!" She passed him a glass of sherry.

"This is an unusual glass." David held it up to the light.

"I found them in Portobello Road. The bloke told me Early Victorian."

"Lovely. As are you, Annie." David drew her to him, his lips finding hers. "Delicious. Slightly almondy!"

She pushed against his chest. "I should be getting supper ready." His arms tightened and, with a sigh, she raised her head again and their kiss deepened.

"You know I want you, Annie." His voice murmured in her mouth.

She broke away, picked up her glass and went to the kitchen window. David waited. She sighed again and turned. "David, I have slept with a man before. Bill."

"For Heaven's sake, Annie. You're thirty-eight. Of course you have." He moved towards her. "I just don't want you to think this is casual. It's not. I am in love with you." His smile gleamed white against the stubble beginning to show.

Her gaze intent, she sipped her sherry, then took his hand and led him to her bedroom.

David held back a moment. "Annie, are you sure?"

"Oh yes. Very. Because, you see, Reverend Rowland, I happen to love you too."

Chapter 28
Back to Sydney, 1951

An insistent knocking penetrated Annie's sleep. She groaned and rolled over, but the noise continued. She heard Betty grumble as she went to open their front door. Then a gasp. Then murmurs.

The January chill rose up from the floor and through the windows. No light filtered around the edges. Annie reached for the bedside lamp, shoved her arms into the dressing gown serving double duty as an extra blanket, and shuffled her feet into slippers. She opened the door to the sitting room as Betty's hand raised to rap. Annie could see Mrs. B. behind her, hair pinned and hidden under a floral wrap.

"What's up?"

"A telegram, love." Betty held out the brown envelope.

"Oh!" Annie's thoughts went straight to David. An accident. In that damn car. He'd gone down to see his family in Dorset. She took the envelope and turned it over.

"Would you like me to open it, Annie?" asked Betty.

"No. I'm right." Annie turned away and rotated her neck. Her nail sliced the fold and she pulled out the terse words.

Father dead Stop Can you come Stop Things complicated Stop Love Joe Stop

"Annie, what is it?" Betty's voice brought her back.

"My father. Joe wants me to go home. Says things are complicated."

Mrs. B. asked, "Is he ill? Your dad?"

"No. Dead."

"Oh, my dear," Mrs. Bellows went to hug Annie as she moved into the kitchen.

"It's alright, Mrs. B. We were estranged."

Betty touched her arm. "He was still your father."

"Yeah. I suppose." Annie plopped down on the table and watched her landlady fill the kettle.

"A cup of tea. That's what we all need."

Annie's smile was tight. "The universal panacea!"

"I know, dear. But it works."

—

The interview with Matron went without drama. Annie wondered why she thought it wouldn't. Probably because she wasn't leaving the hospital for another. She had been assured her job would be awaiting her return. "It might be a while."

"Now, Sister Cutler, I doubt that."

Annie had looked quizzical.

"I happen to know a certain vicar and one of my nurses have become close."

"How could you possibly know, Matron?"

"It's my job, Sister. To know everything that happens in my hospital." The stern face relaxed. "And I am delighted. For you both. Just come back soon."

From there everything went in a swirl of activity. The minuscule bedroom in the flat became what it really was—a box room—now filled with Annie's accumulated stuff.

Samira, who had passed the Mrs. Bellows test with the help of her gift of cardamom milk cake—no eggs required—needed a place to stay for a few months while she finished her course at the London School of Economics. Annie wondered how long after that her friend would be able to keep putting off her return to India.

And David. Kind. Patient. Loved. They spent the night before she left at Dukes Hotel, discreetly tucked into a corner of St. James's Place.

"I feel deliciously wanton," Annie said as she stole his olive from the martinis they sipped at the bar. "But," she looked at David through her lashes, "should you really be here? With a woman? A man of the cloth?"

He ignored her question, and asked, "What am I going to do without you, Annie May Cutler?"

Annie's hand faltered as she reached for her cocktail glass. What was it about the men in her life, that prompted the use of her full name? She shook her head.

"What's wrong, my love?"

"Not a thing." Annie turned a dazzling smile on him, and the barman.

"Good. Because I have something to say." He picked up both their drinks and moved to a corner table. "And," he continued as he put the glasses down and sat with his back to the room, "it would not do to be overheard."

"Is it naughty?" She touched her finger to her lips.

"Don't do that. It is most provocative." David took her hand and slid a ring over her finger and with a low voice said, "With this ring I thee wed. Not just for tonight, but forever. Will you marry me?"

Annie's eyes glistened. She looked down at the gold band set with five diamonds. "Oh, darling, I think you got things around the wrong way. You ask before you put the ring on the finger!"

"We've done a few things the wrong way. Will you? Will you marry me the moment you get back from Australia? I don't care—no that's not true—no matter how long you have to be away, just tell me you'll marry me."

"I do. And then I will!" She laughed and leant across the table to kiss him. "I don't care who sees. I will, I will, I will."

He eased away and looked down at Annie's hand still in his. "I know it's not an engagement ring, but I decided if you wore a ring that looked like a wedding band, it might keep those Aussie chaps away from you. Not to mention protect your reputation tonight." He smiled. "You'll have a proper engagement ring when you get back." David stroked her hand. "Do you like it?"

"I love it. Thank you, darling."

"I'm so glad. It was my grandmother's. And she would've loved you."

Tears trembled on Annie's lashes. "I'll be back as soon as I can. I promise."

"And then we are going to be married." David smiled. "I have one more thing to ask."

"Only one?"

"For now." He looked down at her hand. "Would you mind leaving London?"

"No. As long as I'm with you, then no. I don't care where we go." She watched the smile spread across David's face.

"How about our room, right now?"

—

Boarding Orcades next morning, David carrying her overnight case, they followed the purser's directions to her cabin.

"Have I told you how much I loathe sailing?"

David took the key from her hand, "Yes, my love. But," he looked around the spotless cabin, "this does not look too uncomfortable."

Annie peered around his bulk. "Oh, yes, it's alright. This'll be the first time I've had a cabin to myself. I suppose it is a bit different to travelling in wartime. Or just after."

"And it's not one of the dedicated migration ships. Although I believe there are some Ten Pound Poms aboard." He kicked the door shut and pulled Annie into his arms. "This is the bit I hate. So, Annie May Cutler, I'm going to kiss you, hard, then leave. All right? Don't go up on deck until I've gone. And, my darling girl, come back as soon as you can. I'll be waiting."

They embraced, Annie's face damp with tears. David kissed the diamond band then the palm of her hand and closed her fist over the kiss. The door closed firmly behind him as the mournful single sound from the ship's horn gave the going ashore warning.

—

Misery gave way to a tingle of excitement as the Orcades left the Mediterranean after a stop at Port Said before navigating the Suez Canal. It surprised her, all over again, how the air smelt different the moment a ship either left or reached the Mediterranean. Spicy almost. Annie, grateful not to be dipping below South Africa and around the unpredictable Cape of Good Hope, watched from the deck as bumboats selling wares clustered around their ship. Entering the Canal, she was again taken by the flatness of the desolate landscape stretching away on either side, and the swirling sandstorms turning the air gritty as they entered the Red Sea. Most passengers stayed indoors reading, playing cards or writing letters to be posted from Aden.

Dear Flo,

Here I am, once again on board a bloody ship! I'm sorry I only had time to send a quick note about my trip home, although ducks, to be honest, Australia doesn't feel like home anymore. I am though travelling in rather more style than our other sea-going adventures. Something I can recommend. I even have my own cabin. How's that for luxury?

We're currently chugging through the Red Sea. Remember the sandstorms? Still horrendous. It is a constant source of amazement how sand can get into every crevice no matter how secure one thinks one's clothing, or the ship. That always reminds me of Coogee Beach with our gal!

The gentlemen have ditched their evening jackets and donned Red Sea Rig, and I must admit I rather like it. Bow ties and cummerbunds don't seem so pompous somehow without evening jackets every night. Though I'd like to see David in one. I wonder if he'd have to wear a dog collar. Oh, my God, Flo, I've just realized I haven't told you. We are engaged. David proposed, sort of, on my last night. We stayed in a ritzy hotel not far from the Ritz, but far more discreet. I am wearing the most gorgeous gold and diamond band—looks like a wedding ring really, which David says should keep the wolves away. Sweet man. He seems to think I am far more alluring than I really am. I shall not dissuade him. Flo, I adore him. Anyway, back to dog collars. I have to learn about being a vicar's wife. I'm still grinning. He knows all about Bill. And my heart is singing. How lucky I am.

My dining companions are a delightful Australian couple returning to Sydney after being in England to settle family affairs—not sure what, maybe it's something scandalous; an affable and mustachioed bloke who does, however, suffer from roving hands despite my flashy gold ring, and who is returning to a Malayan tin mine after home leave. He has a pronounced bottom jaw, which does not add to his attraction. Then there's the wet-behind-the-ears bloke, who looks about sixteen but assures us he is twenty-three, going to Ceylon as an assistant tea planter. He can scarcely take his eyes off the final occupant of the table, a nineteen-year-old debutante, Susanna, delighted to be free of the constraints of a divorced and hovering mother, and who is joining her diplomat father, also in Malaya. I gather she is on the hunt for a white rajah—a rich husband. I haven't had the heart to dissuade her. They all make entertaining dinner companions and help pass the time.

I'm not entirely sure what awaits me in Armidale and have a feeling a letter from Joe probably arrived in London after I left. It was too good an opportunity to miss, and very lucky getting a ticket on the Orcades leaving so soon after the telegram arrived. I am assuming it's something to do with the property. I wonder whether Father left it to Helen. She's deserves it. Putting up with the miserable bugger all these years. But honestly, I don't care. Thanks to Auntie May, I'm not in financial distress, and I rather think David is comfortably off. Funny, that's about the only thing we haven't talked about. Oh, and children. But I don't believe either will be an issue. Because, ducky, I do want them. And, as you so succinctly pointed out, time is a ticking. We plan to marry as soon as I return, so don't go buggering off anywhere. I have to have some representation from home at my wedding, even though I said Aus doesn't really feel like home. When am I returning, you ask? Not a clue. But as soon as humanly possible.

Before I get too wrapped up in myself, ducks, how did the exams go? Honestly, I don't know why you get so panicky. You always do well. Better than well. And, just remember, Flo, age equals experience, particularly when dealing with the mind. And especially all the experiences we've had. And I'm not even a psychiatric nurse!

I hope you know how incredibly proud of you I am. Your ears will be burning when I see Verna and her mob. Your praises will be sung on high. You see, I can be a vicar's wife. Got the lingo! I would like to think you're being a bit wicked too. There is a lot to be said for it!

Pep talk over. We now return to me!

Matron was a darl about me leaving so suddenly. Said I'd have a job waiting. I didn't have the heart to tell her I'm going back to midwifery. Thought I'd apply to St. Teresa's, the new maternity hospital. Mind you, it's been a while since I delivered a baby. I might have to understudy someone for a couple of births. They're still crying out for nurses in London. Is it the same in Glasgow?

I'm so pleased about your new flat. Above ground is much nicer, and your land-

lady sounds altogether pleasanter. The Scottish equivalent to Mrs. B. I worried about you being in that basement flat. All I ever seem to hear about Glasgow is the damp and fog, and TB. Maybe with their share of the exhibitions for the Festival of Britain, the city is being gussied up.

Gossip now. Trisha and Edmund are still not married but are very happy. She feels she should leave a respectable amount of time before jumping into another marriage. I can't really see the point. The children love E, and he them. Such a change for them to be seen as little people and not an inconvenience, except when they were to be trotted out for inspection. Rupert is, I believe in South America. No one misses him.

Flo, I can say this to you, but hovering on the outer rim of my mind is a concern about Joe. Perhaps that is why he wanted me home. He is such a dear man but no hint of a woman in his life. Nor has there ever been, as far as I know. Lots of female friends but no one special. Then I give myself a severe talking to and look at David. He's been fairly woman-free, certainly no one of any consequence, since he was a young man. I just want him, Joe, to be happy. I don't care. My over-active imagination again, I'm sure. Another reason to be lucky—to have such dear friends I can say or write anything to without fear of judgement—particularly one who's almost a psychologist.

I am so looking forward to seeing Verna. And I thought I'd go and see Iris's mother. She didn't want to see anyone before we left, but perhaps with another couple of years distance she would enjoy talking about her wonderful, somewhat scatterbrained daughter. Those bloody Japs have a lot to answer for. So do the Russkies. Some of the stories I heard when I was in Berlin were just as terrible. And they were on our side. Oh, God, maybe I'm not vicar's wife material. I find that kind of forgiveness difficult, if not impossible. I have a lot to learn. A good thing David loves my body, maybe he can forget about my terrible mind and soul.

And on that cheerful note, I'm going to finish … I found a letter I started to Verna then left for about three months, I am not to be trusted … this will leave my hands in Aden.

Look after yourself, ducks, don't wear your brain to a frazzle, I know you can do this,

All love,

Annie X

P.S. He, David, did say something that pulled me up a bit. Not straight away because I was lost in the euphoria of being engaged, but now I've had lots of thinking time on board. He asked how I felt about leaving London. I said something gooey along the lines of not caring as long as I was with him. Now I'm wondering where he'd like to go! I suppose I could ask. But I think it's more a face-to-face kind of thing, don't you? A X

Annie ducked the tin miner's reaching hands as he tried to bid a fond farewell before he departed the Orcades at Port Swettenham in Malaya. She did promise though to stay in touch with the debutante whose buoyancy had diminished the closer they got to Malay waters, and after the want-to-be-planter disembarked in Colombo. It would be strange to be living with a parent she hadn't seen for over five years, and Annie felt for her. Two couples joined their table who seemed pleasant enough, but the closer the ship got to Sydney the more Annie felt a sense of misgiving. Until Hornby Lighthouse came into view and they sailed around South Head and started the final leg into the magnificence of Sydney Harbour. Nothing compared to it. The sun shone, the water shimmered like fine crystal, and as they passed under the Bridge and eased next to one of the finger piers at Darling Harbour, Annie felt her heart expanding.

Australia was still home. How could it not be? All the unique aspects. 'Roos and koalas. And the birds. She couldn't wait to see the rosellas and cockatoos at Gunida.

Chapter 29
Home, 1951

Verna, her arm waving madly, with James standing behind her, met Annie after she cleared the immigration line. Tears streamed with the hugs and laughter as James shepherded them into his car for the journey to Coogee, where they had a house not far from Verna's childhood home.

"I can't wait to see Ruthie, and meet Mark," Annie said, leaning forward between her two friends on the front seat. "And your mum, Verna. How's she doing?"

"Not bad, all things considered. Of course she misses Dad, but with all the grandchildren nearby there's always something happening. She's turned Dad's shed into a sewing room."

"A sewing room? That must be strange for you."

"'Tis a bit. It's not like there isn't space in the house, but she says it makes him feel closer. Funny really. She used to get so cross when he'd disappear down there, when it all got too chaotic."

After the flutter of activity with the children, and once the sun dipped into the ocean in a halo of gold, Annie and Verna sat on the verandah with a cigarette and a mug of tea catching up on the last three years. The bedroom windows upstairs were open so they'd hear the children if they woke. James had been called out to a patient.

Verna wafted the smoke away. "How do you feel about your father, ducky?"

"I don't. I feel a fraud for rushing back and only came because, for the first time in his life, Joe asked for help."

"Is it to do with the property?"

"I've no idea." She sipped her tea. "I'll know soon enough. If it's alright with you, I'll get the train to Armidale the day after tomorrow."

—

The Gunida sign had been painted, as had the wooden railings to the side of the cattle ramp. Annie couldn't remember when the entrance to the family property had looked so sharp.

"Did you do that, Joe?"

"No, all Helen's work." He grinned. "She's a tough one. But kind."

Sitting on the bench seat of the old Ute, Annie looked across Taffy's head at her brother. "Yeah, I've always liked her." Their talk from the Armidale railway station to the property had been a catch up. Nothing of any consequence although Annie was itching to ask what had prompted the enigmatic cable.

As if Joe could read her mind he said, "I know you've got questions, Annie, but let's leave them until after supper. Words with whisky, eh?"

"Righto." She laughed as the Corgi tried to sit on her lap.

"You're in his spot."

"Too bad. He's a dog."

"Shh, don't tell him that."

"I didn't even know you had a dog." Annie tickled Taffy's chin.

"Good company.

Pushing open the screen door to the back porch, then through to the kitchen, Annie drew in her breath. She hadn't known what she'd feel. Certainly not the lightness of spirit that embalmed her. She smelt lavender and immediately thought of her mother and Auntie May.

Joe smiled. "I decided the smell of pipe smoke had to go."

"And you've painted."

"Yup. That was me, not Helen. Years of nicotine yellow gone in a few strokes." He carried the suitcases into her old bedroom.

Annie followed. "You know what, Joe, it's as if Ma's here. And as if Father never was. It's the oddest thing."

He nodded. "And even stranger, is that some evenings, when I sit with a drink and watch the sun go down, I swear I can feel Ernie."

"Oh, Joe!" Tears swelled and Annie leant her head on her brother's shoulder. "I'm so glad I've come home."

"I am, too. Thank you! Especially as you are now an engaged woman. I want to hear all about David. I'm not sure I approve of you marrying someone I haven't met but I suppose at least Edmund, and Trisha have, and like him." Joe took her hand and led her down the hall. "Come on. One more surprise."

"My God, a shower! No more tub on the back porch!" She looked around the cheerful bathroom, and an indoor dunny." She laughed. "Do you know one of the things I hate most about living in England, apart from the weather, is having to slide into lukewarm water in a cold porcelain bath."

"Hey, at least Cork Street has a bathroom. You wouldn't believe how many places didn't when I first arrived in London." They moved back to the kitchen. "And how is the delightfully nosy Mrs. Bellows."

"She's fine. I couldn't really ask for a better landlady. And she approves of David." Annie punched Joe's arm. "See, another good reference."

A lamb stew, mashed potatoes and carrots, eaten, and the plates washed up and left to dry on the draining board, Joe picked up the bottle of single malt and two glasses. I've been saving this for a special occasion." He waved the bottle at her. "I brought this from England, much better than the stuff produced here. Let's sit on the front porch, it's still warm enough."

Annie lit a cigarette and watched as Joe released the spring cap and pour two fingers into each glass.

"To the remaining Cutlers!"

"I'll drink to that," Annie said, taking a sip. "That is delicious."

"Glenlivet," Joe told her, "from Speyside. If you ever go and see Flo in Glasgow, you should keep going and explore Scotland."

"Maybe we could honeymoon there." Annie looked out at the evening shadows casting a blue tinge across the home paddock, then at the man next to her. "Righto, time to talk, ducks. What's going on? I imagine it's to do with the property. Ian left it to the Church? To Helen?"

Joe sighed and watched the amber whisky swirl before taking another sip. "Yes, and no."

Annie bent to stroke Taffy's head. "Clarification, please. Don't believe Father found God."

"Definitely no to that. And to Helen." Joe took a slug. "He left it to us both. You and me."

"Good grief. I rather thought, if I ever really thought about it, that after Auntie May left me everything, he'd think that was enough for one girl." Annie chuckled. "And, Joe, he'd have been right."

He didn't laugh with her. Annie waited. Quiet. Breathing in the scent of the bush. Listening to the owlet-nightjars and other sounds of the bush settling for the night. She watched the flare of her cigarette and realized she had finally stopped equating it with streaming strafe-fire from warplanes. When did that happen?

Joe broke the silence. "I'm not sure where to start." He put his glass down and reached for a cigarette. He exhaled and watched the smoke curl through the porch screens. "Alright, here goes. I handed in my notice, about four months ago. Before Dad died. Not because of him. He died the way he wanted. He'd been out in the paddocks, checking sheep. Fed the dogs and locked them in their enclosure, walked towards the house and collapsed. Heart attack. Helen found him a little later. She'd come over to get some eggs."

"Good way to go."

"Yeah." Joe looked at his glass, as if surprised it was empty. He poured more, and raised the bottle to Annie, who shook her head.

"I thought you loved your job. Although I never really understood what you did. Always seemed under the radar."

"In the war, yes. Not afterward. And yes, I did enjoy my work. But," Joe paused, "I had been thinking of a change."

Annie waited, then asked, "Why?"

"Because, Annie, I fell in love with the wrong person."

"Oh." Her neck tightened. Did she really want to know.

"That's it? Oh?" A sorrowful smile tempered his words. "Don't you want to know who with?"

"Only if you want to tell me, ducks." Taffy pressed his nose against the screen watching the gum at the side of the house with an intensity that relieved Annie's tension and made her smile. "Silly dog, it's only a possum." The silence stretched until her nerves twanged, and she wanted to shout, just tell me!

The nightjar screeched again, and Joe leant forward to scratch Taffy's head. Not turning to look at Annie, he spoke, his voice soft, to the bush reaching beyond the home paddock. "His name is Martin."

Annie relaxed. There it was. What she had suspected, confirmed. She chose her words with care. "Does he love you?"

Joe shrugged. "No. I don't know. It doesn't matter."

"Of course it matters." A snatch of irritation made her snap.

"No, it doesn't."

"Why not?"

"Because, Annie," Joe, his eyes closed, said, "he is married. He has children. And he holds—what's the term—an eminent position.

"Ducks, I'm so sorry."

Joe continued, as if now the words had been spoken the spigot could not be replaced. "Not to mention, of course, and probably, of most significance, homosexuality is illegal."

"Oh, what a bugger!" Annie buried her head in her hands and gasped. "I don't believe I said that, I'm sorry." She looked across at Joe to see tears pouring down his face. She reached for his hand.

His shoulders shaking, Joe said, "God, Annie, only you could make me cry with laughter. Really? Bugger?"

"You know I'm hopeless, Joe. I'm sorry."

"No, it's wonderful. No wonder I asked you to come home. For once Father did us a favour." He snorted. "Flo would classify us as damaged children. For all sorts of reasons."

"She wouldn't, you know. She'd say humour is often the best way to deal with issues." Annie lit another cigarette. "And," she continued, all levity gone, "this is an issue."

"Don't I know it." Joe pushed his hand through his hair.

"Does anyone else know? Apart from Martin."

"A few rumours. Nothing definitive. Like I said, he's a powerful man."

"Do you still love him?"

"Who knows? First love, eh?" Joe sighed. "And, naturally enough, he wants nothing to do with me."

She couldn't bear to think he'd been hurt. "Joe?" Annie stopped, not sure how to continue.

"You can ask me anything. Anything at all.

With a deep breath Annie plowed on. "Righto. Who started the affair?"

"He did. But I probably gave off signals. Not deliberately. But I'm sure they were there. I was in thrall to him."

She held out her glass. "I'll have another now, please." Annie waited until Joe refreshed his own drink, again. "To lost loves!"

"That's it? That's all you're going to say?"

"Yup! What else is there? You fell in love with the wrong person. And I'm sad." She sipped her whisky, arranging her thoughts. "Not because of who you love, but because you're not allowed to love."

"Thanks, Annie." He clinked his glass to hers. "Good thing Dad has died, eh? Can you imagine his reaction?"

Her smile contrite, Annie agreed. "But, Joe, I do want to know what you're going to do. You can't bury yourself at Gunida. You're only thirty-two."

"I know." Joe looked across the paddock to where a light from Helen's cottage shimmered between the copse of gums, then took a deep breath. "What do you know about homosexuality?"

"Not much. The mechanics, I imagine."

"I meant the laws."

"Nothing. Apart from the fact it is illegal and that the law is iniquitous."

Joe nodded. "Well, for some odd reason, to be a lesbian is not."

"Not what?"

"Illegal." Joe gave a sad smile. "I suppose the act of love between women does not seem so reprehensible to many of the population as the act of sodomy."

"Oh, Joe. What a mess."

"But, Annie," a smile radiated from his set mouth, "there is a plan."

She waited, watching Joe sort his thoughts. No wonder he was a good lawyer. His words invariably tempered.

"A question, first." He paused, again. "Do you and David plan to live in England?"

"Yeah. Although I felt such a surge of affection and loss when the ship sailed into the Harbour." David's words echoed back to her. If not London, where? Presumably not Australia. "But, no, I won't be coming back to stay."

"Alright. In that case, I'd like to buy you out? Fair price. We'd do it all properly. Legally" He rushed on. "It might take a few years, but I've got a nice pot squirrelled away, and I should be able to get a loan."

"Nope." Annie put her hand up. "Not happening."

"Oh." Joe looked stunned.

"No, you galah, I mean I'm not selling my half. You can have it. I don't need the money. We haven't talked about it, but I don't believe David is struggling. Not filthy rich, but comfortable. And, God love her, I have Auntie May in my back pocket. And I've always worked. And been careful." She smiled. "So, no, I'm not selling. I'll sign whatever you want. But Gunida is yours."

Joe sniffed and wiped his eyes. "Oh, Annie." He squeezed her hand. "We'll talk more about that another time."

"But what are you going to do, Joe? You're not a grazier. You couldn't wait to get to the City."

"War changed us all. I relish being here, now." He looked down at Taffy, nose still pressed against the mesh. "Do you want to go out and see?" He let the dog out. "Have you the energy to hear the rest?"

"Of course."

"You asked if anyone else, apart from Martin—whose name will not be mentioned again—knows. The answer is yes. Helen."

Annie gasped. "I didn't see that coming."

"I know you've always liked her, as have I. She has been wonderful, when Dad was alive, and since." Joe paused. "Anyway, I was a mess when I arrived here. Got blind drunk. With her, and it all came out." He sipped his whisky, no longer slugging it back. "Have you ever wondered about her? Living in the bush alone?"

"Not really. She had the other Land Girls for company during the war, and she always said she'd never go back to Sydney. I suppose I assumed she'd meet someone here and settle in the country."

"Helen is the female equivalent of me." Joe laughed at Annie's face. "You had no idea?"

"Not an iota."

"Does it bother you?"

"That wouldn't be very fair, would it? Alright for you, but not her?" Annie looked at the end of her cigarette. "I suppose what I feel is sad. Sad neither of you can be loved without censure."

"But look at the symmetry, Annie."

She looked at Joe, puzzled. "What do you mean?"

"She lives in the cottage. I'll stay here. It will become known that we are both a little eccentric. Rumours will circulate that we are lovers but have no desire to live together. People might frown, but we're not rubbing anyone's nose in our Bohemian ways." He paused again. "Perhaps, one day, occasionally, a 'friend' might come to stay with either of us. It would raise no eyebrows."

"You've thought of everything. You should be a lawyer! "Annie's laughter filtered around the porch and out into the night. "Ingenious. And she's in with it all?"

"Absolutely. Are you?"

"None of my business, ducks. But, yes. I am absolutely behind it." She laughed again. "Oh, my God."

Joe's shoulders slumped in relief and his laugh joined hers. "You know you're going to have to stop saying that, don't you? The vicar's wife can't be heard to blaspheme." He turned to her, his face serious again. "Annie, will you tell David?"

"Of course."

"How will he feel?"

"The same as me."

"Really?"

"Yup. He's a good man, Joe. Seen as much, if not more than me, to make him accept people for who they are, not who they love." Annie frowned. "But you still haven't told me what you're going to do. Don't say farm."

"No. Well," Joe corrected himself, "I'll help out at lambing and with harvesting, like we did as kids, but no, the day-to-day work is up to Helen.

I'm going to write, and maybe paint. I've always loved the former and want to try the latter."

"Wow!" Annie shook her head. "A night of surprises! Although, I suppose, not all of them."

"What do you mean?"

"I did wonder. You've never, to my knowledge, had a girlfriend."

"You never said anything."

"Why would I? I love you. I want you to be happy, and if," she waved her hand around, "this works for you, then good on ya!" She patted Joe's hand. "Now, pour me the tiniest bit more, then I'm going to bed."

Lying in her room, the door open to the porch, Annie watched shadows dance. She flinched when a door clattered as the wind picked up. She'd meant everything she said, but concern nagged her, stopping sleep. Would Joe, and Helen, really be able to pull it off? Nothing stayed secret in the bush for long, aided and abetted by Mrs. Somers and the party line. She'd have to get David to ask his God to keep an eye on them both.

Chapter 30
Another Home, England

The dress, a dove grey silk shot with moss green, fell in soft swirls over Annie's hips. The bodice with the sweetheart neckline followed the swell of her breasts to cinch at her waist then fell into a ballerina length skirt. A simple dress that complimented her neat figure and long legs. The cobbler behind Victoria Station had dyed a pair of pumps a deeper shade of grey and Flo helped her fix the soft green satin leaf band to her head, lowering the short broad netting veil to cover her eyes.

"Damn, Annie, you look gorgeous." Flo stood back to admire her handiwork. "David is one lucky man."

"You look spiffy, too, ducks. We've run the gamut of clothing, haven't we? From uniforms to boiler suits in New Guinea to wedding finery." She smiled at her friend in an elegant navy shirt-waister that hugged her now sturdier figure. "God, haven't we come a long way, Flo?"

"Yup, now come on, a surprise for you in the kitchen, courtesy of your husband-to-be. Then we need to get a scoot on. You are not going to be late for your wedding. The cab will be here in just over half-an-hour."

A shot made Annie recoil as she turned towards the door. "What the hell was that?"

"Champagne, ducky, champagne. You are leaving spinsterhood with a pop!"

"From David?"

Flo nodded. "He told me to make sure you didn't make a run for it." She held Annie back a moment, her eyes searching her face. "Ducks, he knows you're anxious about being a vicar's wife. He loves you and, maybe even more importantly, he understands you."

Annie felt tears bubble.

"No, don't you dare cry, Captain Cutler. Your mascara will run." Flo hugged Annie, careful not to dislodge the headpiece or crush her dress. "He's a good man, and you are the best friend anyone could have. And you will make beautiful babies ..." Flo smirked, "... if you haven't already!" She ducked from Annie's swat. "Come on, a drink, a cab, a wedding."

Annie waited for Betty, Mrs. Bellows and Flo to clamber out of the cab, then joined them on the pavement, aware of smiling passers-by. The bells from St. Stephen's peeled in welcome. The ragstone, no longer honey-coloured but blackened by bombs, looked austere in the crisp early February sunshine. Annie glanced up at the figure of the saint kneeling in prayer in the niche above the porch, and smiled, happy and sure, although she wished Joe were here to give her away.

She straightened her shoulders and looked down at the simple bouquet put together by 'Enry, the flower seller at the entrance to Green Park. With, Albert had assured her the day before, help from him. Roses with a hint of pink, white ranunculi, berries and, by special request and as a nod to her heritage, eucalyptus leaves, whose scent of mint with a touch of honey reminded her of Gunida, Ma, Ernie, and Joe. Then, as the notes from the organ began Vivaldi's Largo from Winter, Annie entered the church where David moonlighted, and walked down the aisle, alone.

Heads turned to watch her. David's family, thankfully smiling, and a smattering of friends, including Trisha, Edmund and the children, Janet, Peter and Molly. Annie had considered asking them to be her attendants but in the end decided to keep everything simple. Samira, still in London, wearing a shimmering peacock blue sari, winked as Annie passed. An intimate gathering of people who cared.

And David, wearing his clerical collar, standing straight and sure. This felt right, and Annie smiled as she saw love beaming from his eyes as she approached the altar.

—

With the news on February 6th that King George had died, David and Annie had been glad of their decision to postpone their honeymoon until the winter weather had abated in Scotland. They wanted to be in London to pay their respects to the reluctant monarch who lay in state at Westminster Hall, the King who had lived through the Blitz with the rest of the city.

Upon her return from Australia, Annie, thrilled to be back, but unable to dislodge her concern for Joe, also needed to understand just where David wanted to be. She'd meant what she'd said about not caring as long as they were together, but a little more insight would set her mind at ease. Was he talking about rejoining the RAF, perhaps being stationed in Germany? Where?

"Nothing so dramatic, my love," he'd answered. "Just out of London. I know you come from the country, but the English countryside is rather different, I imagine, to what you're used to."

"I suppose," Annie had paused, "I suppose, it depends where. I'm not sure how well I'd do in a hamlet. With a Mrs. Somers equivalent knowing everything about me."

"That wouldn't happen." David said with certainty.

"Why not?"

"Because a hamlet doesn't have a church!"

"Oh! Fair enough. But you get my meaning?"

"I do'," he'd hugged Annie tight. "You do understand, my love, I have no desire to climb the Church hierarchy, don't you? I just want to know my parishioners, to be part of their lives." David had looked out the window of their basement flat to his brother's garden. "I'd like to see green fields."

"Definitely different to Australia then!" Annie had snaked her arms around him, "in drought time, at least."

"It could take years to get a living."

"Then we'll be just fine here," Annie had assured him.

Having decided the trek out to St. Teresa's Maternity Hospital in Wimbledon would eat into her time with David, Annie became a district midwife. It made no difference, their time together was limited, with twenty-four hours off one week and forty-eight the next. But the long hours, sometime a whole night spent with a woman in labour, did not lessen Annie's determination to work until a country parish became available.

—

After the wedding, Samira, once again, took over her room at Cork Street, much to Betty and Mrs. Bellows' delight. She became a regular visitor to the basement flat on Ebury Street, which would become wreathed in the peppery scents of cinnamon, cardamom, nutmeg, ginger and cloves as she made masala chai. David had come to love the aromatic tea and had been delighted when she gave him the requisite spices.

"Now I don't have to carry them with me whenever I visit," she said with a smile, when he bussed her cheek goodbye before he left to officiate at the Sunday morning service.

Samira watched him kiss Annie at the door. "That is what I want."

Annie laughed. "What, a husband and wife whose work schedules mean they don't see enough of each other?"

"No, a husband who loves me. Who is proud of my work."

"I know, ducks." Annie blew on her regular builder's tea, finding chai too sweet. "Any change?"

Samira shook her. "What is the point of an education if I am not allowed to work?"

Annie looked at her friend's glum face. "Could you stay here?"

"Of course. Indian and Pakistani citizens, as part of the British Commonwealth and Colonies, have the right to settle in Britain. I'm sure it will change at some point, but for now I'm the same as you! Just more beautiful!"

Samira's tinkling laugh, her eyes still glistening with unshed tears, made Annie smile. "No argument there, ducky. But I hate that this is all hanging over your head." She pushed the cigarette pack over the table. "Would it be worth getting a job?"

"Actually, I've started looking. I don't know what's going to happen but I'm not going to just sit and wait for the family's strong-arm tactics." Samira looked at the tip of her cigarette. "And smoking would be frowned upon. Certainly in public. Now, let's talk about something else."

"Sami," Annie looked across the rim of her mug, "what if you met a man here?"

All trace of the cultivated voice disappeared as Samira replied in a heavily accented Indian accent, "He would need to be a very nice, very rich Indian boy."

"Are there any?"

"For sure. But they are promised to girls back in India."

—

The sun shone, a welcome change from the previous soggy month, and David walked between Annie and Samira, their arms linked. Unrecognizable from the derelict, bombed-out crater that had been the area around Waterloo after the war, the lavish Dome of Discovery, part of the Festival of Britain soared overhead. The austerity of the previous six years seemed a thing of the past, if only in the confines of the Festival grounds. Gentle curves, colour and space had replaced the drab khaki of uniforms, grime-encrusted buildings and sharp lines of pillboxes and Nissen huts. The choking smell of dust and death banished. Frivolity appeared to have taken over London, despite grumbles about the expense of staging the event, the entrance fee, and a cup of coffee costing ninepence.

Annie didn't care. People smiled. Women and girls wore summer frocks. She felt a moment's pang for the men in suits but soon forgot in the excitement of the day. They gazed up at a futuristic structure with aluminium louvres supported by cables.

"It looks like a giant pick-up stick!" Annie said, thinking of the interminable games she had played with Janet and Peter in the kitchen in Berlin.

"Or a floating cigar," Sami suggested. "I read somewhere that it mirrored the British economy in that it has no clear means of support."

"You are both peasants." David said, with a laugh. "It is meant to represent hope for the future."

"Well, I'm hoping for a very expensive cup of coffee before we head along the river to the Pleasure Gardens at Battersea."

Stepping off the boat an hour later, Annie said, "Let's find the Guinness Festival Clock. I read that it strikes on the quarter hour with all sorts of moving parts, and a toucan pops out of the doors."

"A South American bird in a Swiss cuckoo clock advertising an Irish drink!" David's laugh turned heads. "Perhaps I should have a Guinness to go with it."

"Whoever came up with that idea is a genius," said Samira, shrugging a cardigan over her dress as the sun sidled behind the fun-fair attractions and lights began to flicker.

At the end of the long day and night, they said goodbye to Sami as she stayed in the cab they had shared and carried on to Cork Street. Tired but exhilarated, Annie and David took the stairs down to their basement flat on Ebury Street, and after a cup of tea fell asleep, curled together.

—

Annie had worried how she would feel sharing space with someone. Of course, she'd lived with people all her life—home, nurses' homes, military camps, then the flat on Cork Street—but certainly for the last few years, she'd had the privacy of a bedroom. Surely, she told herself, David would have the same anxiety. And since being de-mobbed, he'd been entirely on his own.

Instead, she found their lives fell into an easy rhythm. He allowed her space to stew if someone had riled her, and could usually jolly her out of a mood. She gave him his space with God, even on the rare Sundays she had off. They made the most of any shared free time, exploring the surrounding countryside in the Morgan, or picnics on Hampstead Heath, or wandering along The Embankment watching the river and stopping for a pub lunch. Annie had enjoyed their three-day break down in Sherborne, in Dorset, staying with David's parents, who she liked, if feeling a little overawed by his mother, who appeared to run every function in the town.

Life was busy, they delighted in each other, and Annie loved living in London, quite happy that a parish had not materialized yet, although she knew David longed for one.

Chaining her bicycle to the railings, Annie lifted the gas and air cylinder slung over the handlebars, then the leather case in which she carried forceps, syringes, and all the paraphernalia required for a delivery. She had summoned the energy to smile at Eve, her sister-in-law, looking out the morning room window upstairs as she opened the gate, but shook her head with a weary smile at the hand waving her in. She glanced at the watch ticking over her heart, and groaned. Bed. Her legs felt like lead as she stumbled down the steps to the basement. The night, and labour, had been long but finally a robust baby had appeared without the need to call the doctor out to assist. Apart from the hours, she loved district nursing, getting to know the women, and sometimes their children, at the ante-natal clinic.

Annie was well aware some of her patients considered her brusque but, on the whole, knew she did a good job. She couldn't help her impatience showing at the ignorance, and arrogance, of some of the fathers. Their wives churning out babies like a sausage-making machine. Other times, it would be the mothers in grand houses who irritated her with their airs and graces. But mostly she loved the role, and the sense of community that it fostered. And tea. Always cups of tea.

The smell of toast met her as she pushed open the door.

"G'day!" she called. Nothing. David must have only just left. She shrugged off her grey uniform coat and hat and hung them by the door. Then she cleaned out her case, boiled the instruments and put clean linings in the case, ready for whatever came next.

But first, she hoped, tea, toast, bed. Maybe just bed. The room spun and Annie clutched the chair nearest her. She concentrated on deep breathing until her equilibrium returned. Definitely bed. She smiled as she snuggled down under the quilt with a sigh.

She woke to the pressure of the mattress sinking.

"Hello, my love." David's lips brushed her cheeks. "Are you awake?"

"I am now!"

He grinned, his face creasing above the dog collar.

"What time is it?"

"About eleven-thirty." He leant past her to the bedside table, "Here, have some tea?"

"I'm going to be resurrected as tea-leaves, I drink so much of it. But thank you!" Annie shuffled up in bed and pulled the Paisley shawl around her, then took the mug. "What are you doing home?"

"What would you say to Cambridge?

"University? City? County?"

"The last one. A parish. A vicarage. A garden."

"Oh, darling. I say, when?"

"As soon as possible. Their vicar died. Old age, nothing sinister. No ghosts. But rather unexpected."

Annie put down her cup and reached for her husband. "Lie down with me."

"What would the parishioners say?"

"Don't care." She nestled into his arms. "But I do have a question." Annie felt his nod. "Could we add a baby to the list?"

Chapter 31
Cambridgeshire, 2003

Annie tweaked her neck as her head nodded back. "Ouch!" A dribble of gin and lemonade spilt onto her lap as the glass tipped. "Oh, for God's sake!" The sun had eased behind the eucalyptus and a nip had crept into the air. She rubbed her face. "What time is it, Eartha?" She asked the somnolent cat, who ignored her. "There is something I am meant to be doing." She put the glass down at the sunroom door, then ambled over to the Pilgrim Roses and deadheaded a few with browned edges with the secateurs she'd left on the low wall. "Bugger. Prescription." Annie looked down at her jeans. She couldn't be bothered changing, and even she couldn't drive into town looking like a hobo or a tramp. She rather liked both words. Somehow, they seemed more romantic than vagrant. And who wouldn't want to be tramp-like at some stage of their life?

Perhaps she had been. Sleeping with Bill and David before a ring touched her finger. She tittered. She'd better make sure that little nugget didn't escape in a chat with Gemma. Her mother already felt Annie was a bad influence. Silly woman. How could she possibly think a ninety-something-year-old could sway a teenager?

Prescription. Pills. How many left? Annie did a mental count of tablets in the bottles by the bed, next to the despised safety alarm on a cord. Enough. She'd drive in on Monday. Decision made, she plunked down on the wall, the scent of the roses wafting her in memories.

Joe had loved roses. He'd turned the homestead garden into a sweet-smelling bower of hundreds of different varieties. Dear Joe. She smiled.

She hadn't seen him since David's funeral when he had surprised her by arriving on the doorstep. Three years. Annie had been right. Joe and David had always got on well. Not that they'd seen a lot of each other. She remembered David's anxiety about meeting her brother the first time they'd gone to Australia together. By plane. No more ships. Not because Joe was gay, but because he was her only relative. He needn't have worried. Gunida had felt more of a home then, than even when Ma had been alive. The brooding spectre of their father expelled from every aspect of the place. Jake and Hugh had loved the freedom of the property, thriving under Helen's care. She'd had them riding out in the paddocks with her from the first day.

Annie sighed. The boys had been fascinated by the 'roos. So had David. And the shy koala who had taken up residence in a gum tree near the back door, a carpet of poo pellets around the tree. She had never regretted leaving Australia. How could she, when her life had been spent with a man she loved deeply. But she did miss elements, perhaps more now. And Joe and Donald.

David's initial anxiety had been matched by her own, when Joe and his partner had visited them. What if she didn't like him? This man with whom Joe had fallen in love. Over thirty years after that first disastrous liaison.

She looked down at Eartha eeling herself around Annie's ankles. "Out of the way, cat. If you trip me up you'll never get your supper." Making her way to the kitchen, Annie noticed a blinking light on the phone. "I must've been asleep, or a deep daydream, not to have heard the phone." She tipped kibble into Eartha's bowl, then listened to the message.

Hello, Mrs. Rowland. It's Kathy. From the surgery. I'm just leaving now. I noticed you hadn't picked up your prescription, so I checked with Dr. Yeo and he said it was okay for me to drop it off in the morning on my way to Church. There was a pause. *Erm, okay, then, hope you get this message, I'll see you tomorrow. Bye.*

How kind.

Annie returned to the kitchen and watched Eartha delicately choosing which piece of kibble to eat next. It made Annie feel peckish. She tipped olives out of a jar, then cubed some cheese. An image of martinis at Dukes flashed up, and she looked down at the gold band with five diamonds. She'd convinced David she didn't need or want an engagement ring. She'd never taken the band off. Not true. Annie grinned. When delivering babies she had. Then she'd worn it on a chain around her neck.

Perhaps it was diamonds that made Annie think of the Queen's Golden Jubilee celebrations the year before. Fifty years on the throne. She and David had almost made that many years of marriage—not too shabby, with the few cross words, usually, she had to admit, started by her. Annie wriggled her fingers. Did the Queen ever take off her diamonds?

She took down a crystal tumbler, then the Glenmorangie. She had always preferred whisky to wine, although champagne was a different story. It was her whisky of choice since their much delayed honeymoon, taken a year after Jake's birth. Annie liked the more creamy vanilla and honey tastes of the Highland single malts, whereas David had preferred the Speyside whiskies, much like Joe. Dear Flo. She had travelled down to Umbleford to look after her godson while his parents ran away to Scotland. Annie raised her glass to her friend of sixty years. She'd drunk a lot of whisky the night she had died.

"Right. No maudlin thoughts Annie May Rowland." She picked up the bowl of olives and cheese and went out to the sunroom. An evening for music. She switched on a lamp, then pushed in the Andrea Boccelli CD Hugh had given her at Christmas. She loved the timbre of the Italian's voice and the romance of the music. *Vivo per lei* drifted from the player and she turned it up loud enough to scatter doves pecking around on the patio.

Funny how she could remember song lyrics, even in Italian, but not to pick up a prescription. 'Non mi ricordo come, ma, mi è entrata dentro c'è restata'—recalling Hugh's translation—I don't remember how, but she entered into me and stayed there. The song reminded her of David and his deep faith, even though the words referred to music as 'she' and not to any god. A conversation early in their relationship came back to her as if yesterday.

"When," Annie had asked, playing with her fork as they waited for Franco to bring their pasta, "did you know you believed?" She hadn't waited for a response before asking, "And how?"

David had picked up his glass and gazed at the wine, a vivid crimson in the candle light. "I can't answer either definitively." He took a sip, and smiled at her. "There was no sudden awakening. I suppose the more I read, not just the Bible, but things like *Beyond Good and Evil* by Nietzsche, or *Leviathan* by Thomas Hobbes, the more I questioned. He argued, and I'll have to paraphrase, that without a central figure of power we would be brutish and nasty, and probably solitary. Which to me," he had reached across the table and taken her hand, "doesn't sound a particularly pleasant way to live."

Annie remembered looking down at their joined hands. "But, David, what made you want to devote your life to Him?"

He had stroked her fingers. "Again, no sudden revelation. The more news came of what was happening in Asia, with Japan entering Manchuria, then the anti-Jewish sentiment coming out of Germany, the more the word 'brutish' resonated. Fair play, civility, morality I suppose, seemed to be disappearing. And when that goes, war comes."

"And everyone thought the Great War was the last." The candle spluttered, for an instant like tracer fire. She shivered.

David had tried to lighten the mood. "Sadly that pesky Greek, Plato, was right. He said, 'Only the dead have seen the end of war.'"

"You know," Annie persisted, "you still haven't answered my question. Why?"

David had leant back in his chair. "Goodness, this is not a light conversation over an Italian dinner, is it?"

"No, I'm sorry." Annie frowned. "But, David, I really want to know. I want to understand."

"Alright," he paused, "there was a sense of something looming. Young men at university late-night talking over whisky. We all sounded terribly earnest. But there was some truth to what we said. What we felt. That another war could happen."

"You were right about that."

"Sadly. And if that was to happen, I knew I did not want to fight. Nor be a conscientious objector." He paused. "My father rarely talked about his war, but that entire lost generation prayed on his mind. And those who did come back were also lost." David sipped his wine. "I thought I might be able to offer something—not conversion—but a chance for those men fighting to have somewhere to go to talk, maybe rant, or be silent. Not necessarily in a church. Just for them to have someone to listen to their fears. Sometimes hopes. Sometimes beliefs."

"Is that why you always had whisky in your room at the air force base?"

David laughed. "It is. At Duxford, anyway. Hidden in my gumboots. Alcohol only in the Mess. Malta was a whole other story."

"And they came?"

"Some. Sometimes late at night. After a sortie. Or a night of drinking. Or after an argument with a girl. Or after falling in love." David poured more wine. "For some bomber pilots, despite wanting to destroy munitions factories and the Nazi war machine, and payback for the Blitz, the knowledge they also bombed civilians invoked an almost unbearable sense of guilt."

As Franco delivered their dinner, David had thanked him, then said, "Now, enough of that. Let's talk of something else."

Annie remembered thanking David for his honesty, her mind still swirling with questions that would have to wait for another day.

Honesty. There had been a lot of omission in honesty from the Australian military records. Flo's phone call had come one evening. The boys had just gone to bed, and Annie was waiting for David to get home from seeing a parishioner so they could have their evening drink.

"It's me." Flo's voice, slurred by tears and whisky, had set Annie's heart racing.

"Ducky, what's wrong?"

"Just had a letter from Thelma. Remember her?"

"Of course. I saw her for tea—before we came to England. But we haven't stayed in touch."

"She'll never recover from the prison camps."

Annie, impatience rising, asked again, "Flo, what's happened?" At Flo's renewed tears, her stomach curdled. "Oh Christ, it's Iris, isn't it?"

"I can't bear to think of it."

"What?" Annie shouted.

"Before those bastards shot them on the beach, they were tortured and raped."

Annie sank to the kitchen floor, the phone clutched in her hand, tears and rage silencing her.

"Are you there?" Flo, calmer now, asked.

"Yeah." Annie wiped her dripping nose on her apron. "How does Thelma know?"

"She's always stayed in touch with Vivian Bullwinkel. They became close when on Sumatra." The sound of Flo gulping a drink came through the phone. "I sense she already knew. I remember her telling me, years ago, that Vivian was in the camp hospital for weeks with boils on her thighs, and her feet were in a mess." Flo's voice broke again. "And you know what that could be."

From her position on the floor, Annie nodded, as if Flo were in the room with her. She whispered, "Secondary syphilis."

"Thelma said Vivian had been ordered not to mention it in her statement for the war crimes tribunal, back in 1946."

"Why the hell not?"

"To protect the families from the shame of rape."

"Dear God, what about the truth? Honesty? Those bastards on Radji beach should be held accountable. Charged."

"All dead. Killed in New Guinea. I suppose the Army couldn't see the point."

"What a terrible secret to have." Tears fell in a steady stream. "Flo, why has Thelma told you this, now?"

"I don't know. She doesn't sound in a very good state. She's back living with her parents. Doesn't go out. Sees Vivian occasionally, but she's busy, still nursing."

"And we have to stay quiet because it's not our story. Just another thing locked away."

Annie sighed, repeating the words from years before. "Just another thing locked away, Eartha Kitty," she said as the cat returned from the garden. She sipped her whisky then sucked the pimento out of an olive before popping the whole thing in her mouth and chewing the firm flesh. Yummy.

The smell of smouldering pine in someone's fire drifted through the late summer evening air. She hoped they'd dried the wood properly. David had always insisted on oak. Less spitting, he'd said.

She remembered getting horribly drunk that night. Sitting at the kitchen table as David scrambled some eggs as she had railed at the authorities, the nurses' dedication and adherence to the following orders, and at God.

"Explain to me, David" she'd asked, belligerence in every spat word, "how you can accept the Bible and God as good and true?" She'd cried again, and he hadn't even tried. Instead, he had helped her up to bed, sat stroking her hair until she finally fell into a whisky-induced sleep then, in the morning, appeared with a mug of tea to help her hangover. She had reached for his hand, accepting his kindness and love was the only way he could answer unanswerable questions.

Annie loved watching shapes change from her seat in the sunroom. Shadows swathed the sitting room in mystery. They had arrived at the Vicarage a couple of months before Jake's birth. In a way it had eased Annie into English village life. Expecting to be in the parish a few years before being moved on, Annie and David had been pleased they had been able to stay until he officially retired at seventy. Never one to play politics, David had been happy to be in a rural backwater, allowed to tend his flock, and sometimes, during lambing, their flocks. Annie, too, had on occasion been called out to help with a difficult ovine birth.

She remembered asking David not long after they arrived in Umbleford, how he felt being so near to RAF Duxford, with the reminders of war.

"Actually, my love," he'd replied, "it's rather nice. Some sad echoes but, in a way, it's where my faith truly guided me. Taught me to be silent sometimes, to absorb another's pain without words."

Annie raised her glass to David's memory. The newer breed of clergymen had less desire to live in draughty old Victorian piles, so when the Church had started selling off their vicarages and rectories, David and Annie had jumped at the chance to purchase the renamed 'Old' Vicarage. Years of love, some blood and at times, a lot of tears, had dissolved into the fabric of the building. It was their story.

Chapter 32
The Vicarage, 1952

Annie, her belly straining against her coat, heaved herself out of the Morgan before David had a chance to help. She stood, her hands rubbing her back, and looked up at the ivy-covered walls, trails covering some of the windows too. The grass had been cut but weeds had taken over the beds, and poked up through the crazy-paving path. An air of general neglect permeated the property.

She felt David's arms go around her. "It just needs some love."

"And elbow grease!"

Before she could say more the front door opened and a woman with tight grey curls, a floral apron covering a sensible twill skirt and an ample bosom, smiled from the doorstep. "Welcome, Vicar, Mrs. Rowland. The kettle's on, and Fred is just bringing in some more wood."

"Hello, you must be Mrs. Winters." David moved to the door, then turned to Annie with his hand outstretched. "Shall we?"

Annie swallowed her disappointment at not being able to see their home on their own. "We shall," she replied, reaching for him. "How kind of you, Mrs. Winters, to open up for us."

"I've been looking after The Vicarage nigh on thirty years. All through the war." She moved aside to let David and Annie through the door. "And my Fred, well, he's a bit slow these days what with his troubles, but he helped the old vicar sometimes. There's not much I don't know about this house," she paused for breath, "or the village. Ask me anything you like, dear. And I know how to keep a closed lip. Now, come along. I've set up in the kitchen. Then I can show you the house."

Before Annie could say anything, David spoke. "That's very good of you, Mrs. Winters, but I think a cup of tea first, as you suggested, then," he glanced at Annie, "if you don't mind, I think my wife and I would like to explore our new home together." He smiled. "Alone."

"Oh!" Mrs. Winters looked downcast. "Well, as I said, I know the ins and outs of this place, but if you're sure."

"You will be the first person I turn too," Annie said, with a forced smile.

"Right then. Of course." She poured from a brown pot then offered milk and sugar. "I made a cake. With eggs."

David, sitting on the other side of the pine table, winked at Annie. "How delicious, and how generous."

"You're not from England then?" Mrs Winters nodded at Annie.

"No, Australia."

"Hmph." Before she could say more, a bang on the back door startled them, and Mrs. Winters's cup chinked down on her saucer. "That'll be Fred."

"I'll get it," David said, opening the door, then taking some of the logs balanced on the shrivelled man's arms. "You must be Fred," he said. "I'm David Rowland. It's good of you to bring these in, thank you."

Fred, his eyes down, looked confused as he limped in.

"You remember, Fred? I told you the new vicar and his wife was arriving today." Mrs. Winters poured another cup of tea and pushed it across the table. "Sit down, dear, and have your tea." She looked at Annie. "He doesn't say much. The war, you know. He's not been the same since he came back."

"That's alright, Mrs. Winters. New people can be upsetting." Annie finished her tea, refused another cup, then stood.

"When's the little one due?"

"About two months," Annie replied.

"I've got three grandchildren." Mrs. Winters sniffed. "Never see them, mind."

"That's a pity." David said. "Do they live a long way away?"

"London. With their mother. She took them back."

"Oh." David looked at Annie for help.

"The war?" She asked, her voice gentle.

The grey head bowed. "The week before the Armistice."

"I'm so sorry."

"Oh well, we all lost someone." Mrs. Winters looked at her husband. "I'm lucky my Fred came home." She stood, her eyes damp, as she reached for the tea things. "But I would like to see the children sometimes."

Annie moved around the table to help, "I'm sure you would."

"No, no, you sit down, dear." Plonking the cups and saucers in the sink with a clatter, she added as she started washing up, "I'll be round tomorrow to help you settle."

This time it was Annie signalling for help from David. "Thank you, Mrs. Winters, but I think we'll need a few days to find our feet, but then perhaps you could come around for coffee," he said. "Shall we say Thursday morning?"

Her hands in soap suds stilled, then with a nod Mrs. Winters resumed the washing up. "Of course, Vicar."

—

"This has got to go!" Annie, her hands on her hips, stood at the foot of the bed they had shared until David moved to the sofa downstairs. "It's not big enough for one, let alone three!" She rubbed her tummy. "Honestly, darling, I'd rather sleep on the floor, and that's saying something."

"I know, I know." He rubbed his eyes. "Look, let's make an inventory of what we need. Starting with the bed."

"Will the Church provide us with furniture?"

"The basics."

"Should be all. This stuff is as old as God!" Annie flicked her fingers at the mattress. "I'm not being unreasonable, David. This is awful." She paused. "And, while I'm on a rant, I do not want Mrs. Winters to work here."

"That could be tricky."

Annie snuggled into David's side. "I know, but there has to be a way."

"Can we ease in first? I don't even know who pays her. The Church, or the old vicar."

"Righto, but I mean it, David. She'll drive me demented, and there's not a chance in Hell she'd keep her lips sealed." Annie looked at the cobwebs across the windows. "It'll be easier if it was the vicar."

"My love, you will try to temper your language, won't you?"

"I'm sorry. I promise. I will be the model vicar's wife."

"You don't need to go that far!" David hugged her and planted a kiss on her forehead.

Determined not to be a mother caught out by an early birth, Annie set to work on the nursery—in reality little more than another box room but perfect for a rocking chair and a crib. She scrubbed the walls and painted three of them a light stone colour, the perfect backdrop for the prints of the May Gibbs' Gumnut babies that Joe had mailed. An Australian element for his first niece or nephew. The fourth she covered in a forest-like wallpaper of greens and blues. Flo, always better with a sewing machine than her, made striped curtains of blue and green which she posted down from Glasgow, and Betty sent a green baby blanket. Annie draped Auntie May's shawl over the rocking chair.

Everything, except their bed, had been piled into a van and brought from the basement flat on Ebury Street. What had seemed plenty there soon became swallowed up in the meandering rooms of the Vicarage. Their first purchase, a bed with a mattress that didn't sag, was followed by a sofa long enough for three to cuddle on. Stone floors gave way to wood floors upstairs—both cold, some covered with thread-bare rugs.

Searching for his slippers in the half-light, David said, "We have to get some more rugs. It's freezing."

"Hmmm. It's cosy in here," Annie peeked out from under the eiderdown.

"Well, wife, some of us have work to do." He bent to kiss her. "Shall I bring you a cup of tea?"

"Yes, please." She watched him dress. "We could get that wall-to-wall carpeting in this room, and the baby's. It's not too expensive."

"What would Mrs. Winters say to that?" David ducked out of the room as Annie threw a pillow.

Most days, Annie walked. Either across the railway line to the wetlands along the River Cam or along the High Street to the shops. Those she chatted with proved friendly and welcoming, particularly when it became known she had been a nurse. Although she had no doubt an element of distrust grumbled among the Church-going of the village—a vicar whose wife did not attend services on a regular basis.

After fidgety hours spent sitting in the front pew, trying not to glance at her watch, or wriggle with pleasure in a stream of sunlight that filtered through the stained glass, a compromise had been reached. Annie would attend the family service one Sunday a month but was exempted from all others.

More than happy to help tend the practical and physical needs of his parishioners, she wanted nothing to do with their spiritual requirements. That was his job. She cared though. It helped her decide that once the baby had been weaned, she would go back to work. A shortage of nurses remained, despite many arriving from the Caribbean, but they stayed mainly in the cities. And she missed the contact, the sense of community it gave, becoming part of a family's life, even for a few hours. And the endless cups of tea.

"What do you think?" Annie asked David, as she warmed soup for their supper at the end of his busiest day of the week.

"I know you're feeling restless at the moment, my love, but ..." he shushed her as she began to speak, "... how will you manage? I mean, with a baby."

"I don't mean right away. But once I'm not feeding him, or her, and once a routine is established."

"They still take time. Look at Richard's lot, and Bill's. They're always on about how busy they are."

Annie thought of her brothers-in-law. "I know, darling, but it can be done, with some help." Annie, at the stove, looked at David over her shoulder. "I thought I'd ask Mrs. Winters to help me find someone."

"That, my love, is a low blow."

"I know. But a good blow." Annie laughed and ladled potato and leek soup into bowls. "It would be good for the village, although it would probably be a few villages. The current district nurse is due to retire next year. I could work with her for a while, ease into it. She walks everywhere, but I could cycle which would be quicker."

"What if she gets sick?"

"Or he. Whatever it is, boxes like a kangaroo." Annie rubbed her belly. "And you do most of your paperwork here. We'd manage, darling. With some help, of course. Think of it as an extension to your pastoral duties."

"What depths to which you will sink!" David laughed. "You really want to do this? You know we don't need the money."

"I do, and I know. But first the baby."

—

Tears fell in a steady stream as Annie stared out of the nursery window. She scrubbed her eyes as she gazed at the wintery landscape. Snow drifted like petals from the pine tree to add more depth to the white carpet.

Sound deadened by both the snow and the wall-to-wall carpet meant she didn't hear David enter. His arms went around her and she leant back with a sigh.

"Are these the tears you warned me about?" he asked, his voice hushed.

"Yup." She sniffed. "You know we're not told about it at nursing school, but every midwife will tell you lots of women get the weeps a few days after delivering."

"So why are you surprised?"

"I don't know." Annie's shoulders shook with her sobs. She moved away to look down at the sleeping baby, swaddled tight in the green blanket. "Isn't he beautiful?"

"He takes after his father." David kissed Annie.

She gave a tearful laugh. "I'm glad he's got hair."

The new father nodded. "He doesn't have the wrinkly old man look I'd expected."

"He's beautiful." Annie repeated. She took David's hand. "Come on, let's have a cup of tea while it's quiet. He'll wake soon enough."

"He looks like a Jake."

Dearest Verna and James, Ruthie and Mark,

Jake Edward Rowland arrived six days ago, weighing in at 8 lbs 2 oz, and 20 inches long. You probably already know, as we did send Joe a cable and he said he'd telephone you. Jake has lots of black hair and is absolutely beautiful. David has not stopped grinning. Even when I was having my weeps. They only lasted a couple of days, and this morning I woke up feeling wonderful—and that's after a thrice-disturbed night.

He's feeding well and seems remarkably content. Jake, not David! But, oh my God, the nappies. Which I know will only get worse. It's a whole different thing trying to keep up with washing. I take everything back I said about Mrs. Winters. She is being terrific. Thankfully I listened to David, and didn't ditch her straight away. You see, I can still listen and learn! Stop laughing, ducks.

Anyway, we'll see how things go. Some days I think I want someone younger to help care for him, on others I love having someone older, perhaps wiser, even if a little bossy. Did I tell you Mrs. W.'s grandchildren all live in London, and she rarely sees them, so Jake delights her. And us.

It was an easy birth. Not too long and delivered by the local midwife—the one I want to take over from at some stage. No doctors involved. Sorry, James. I'm sure it helped that I kept moving right up until the day. Long solo walks, which towards the end sent David into a spin. Dear, silly man.

I hear a peep—amazing how keen my ears have become—so must dash,

All love,

Annie X

—

"Shashthi is the Hindu goddess of children, among other things." Samira explained the silver spinning baby rattle she held out for Jake to grasp. "I couldn't find one that was actually Indian, so this will have to do!"

"It's gorgeous, thank you. I'm so glad you came, Sami." Annie watched her friend's delight as she played with the baby on her lap. "And Flo arrives tomorrow."

"Weddings and christenings. Of course we all gather. I've been to a church twice more in the last two years than a temple."

"Is there even one in London?"

"Not really. One day perhaps. But Hinduism is more a way of life than a religion."

"Praise be! Do I hear my wife discussing theology?" David kissed the top of Annie's head, then their guest's cheek. "Welcome to the countryside, Samira!"

"I'm not a total philistine, darling. More an agnostic."

"I know, my love." David pulled out a chair and reached for Jake. "Can I join in?"

"I was just saying Hinduism is more a way of life. We have six enemies, what we call shadripu." Samira ticked them off on her fingers. "Lust, anger, jealousy, laziness, greed and ego."

"Our seven deadly sins, to which we've added gluttony."

Samira laughed. "We don't have gluttony because we don't eat beef."

"Neither do we much, these days!" Annie looked at the skinny chicken waiting to be roasted. "I can't wait for rationing to be over."

"At least your parents can attend, David," Samira said, chucking Jake under the chin. "It has made life easier not having to worry about petrol. Speaking of which, what do you think of my car?"

David glanced out of the kitchen window at the Morris Minor. "Nifty!"

"I didn't think you drove." Annie said. "When did you get your license?"

"Not long after you left London. Actually," Samira looked down, then met their eyes, "I decided to use my final allowance to get it, and a car, before my parents cut me off. If I'm going to be considered a wild woman, I might as well be one! By Indian standards, at least."

"Oh, Sami," Annie got up to hug her friend. "You've decided."

"Decided for me. I couldn't keep putting off my return to Delhi. Manish gave an ultimatum. I missed it."

"Why didn't you say something?"

"I was tired of my own story, Annie. Yours is a much a happier one."

"What's happened?" David, ever practical, asked.

"A lot of teeth gnashing by mail. Loss of face. Gossip about how my parents can't control their daughter. My mother wrote to a friend of the family in London to speak to me." Samira grimaced. "Screech, not speak. Which is what I would get from my mother, and sisters if I were at home. So, to be expected."

Jake, grizzled, wanting to be fed.

"Sorry, pumpkin," Annie said, hurriedly preparing a bottle of Cow & Gate formula, questions swirling in her head.

"May I feed him, please?"

"Of course you can, ducks." She handed Samira the bottle and watched as her friend settled Jake into the crook of her arm.

"This is probably as close to having a baby as I get," she said, once he was feeding, his eyes on Samira's face.

"You don't know that," Annie said, looking at the exquisite woman cradling Jake.

"Sami," David asked, concern etched on his face, "would you rather I weren't here for this conversation?"

Her smile grateful, she responded, "No, it's alright. It's nice to talk to a man who doesn't judge me."

"What has your father said?" Annie asked.

"I've tried to reason with him. Say I'll go back as long as I don't have to marry Manish. And can work. I even said I'd agree to an arranged marriage, if I can have a say in the decision. But he has written of his disappointment in me. How he regrets encouraging me to go to London. How my mother warned him I would become corrupted. And I have." She gave a dispirited laugh, "Look at me, driving!"

David, elbows on the table, his chin resting on his clasped hands, looked at their friend. "What I'm not sure I understand, is why encourage a girl to get an education then take it away from her."

"It's a caste, or if you like, a class thing. Allowing me to travel to England for education showed people my family are modern, can afford it, and that their daughter is clever."

"Didn't Nehru's daughter go to Oxford? Before the war?" David asked, scratching his neck.

"Yes. But Indira followed the rules."

"She had an arranged marriage?" asked Annie.

"Yes, but to a man of a similar age. And someone she knew, and liked. Feroze Gandhi—no relation to the Mahatma—went to the LSE, same as me. And being in England at the same time, they had a chance to get to know one another away from prying eyes." She eased the teat away from Jake, and patted his back until the required burp erupted and they all laughed.

"Sami," David looked at the woman holding his baby with such care, "are you absolutely sure? It sounds as if the bridges will be well and truly burned. Is Manish really so unbearable?"

"He is twenty-four years older than me. Which in itself isn't too awful, I suppose." She blinked hard. "No, David, it's what would await me that I can't bear. Manish comes from a religious household so I would be expected to wear the veil. Not the hijab, like a Muslim, but the palu—you know, the end of the sari. No freedom to go out without my husband. Certainly not work."

"What would happen if, no, when he dies? I mean, he's much older than you," Annie ignored David's glare, "would you be allowed greater freedom then?"

Samira's harsh laugh bounced around the kitchen, startling the dozing baby. She calmed him before answering. "No chance. I would be expected to remove my jewellery, wear mourning clothes for the rest of my life, and certainly never remarry."

"I'm not sure I understand, Sami." David looked puzzled.

"I would become a source of shame."

"It wouldn't be your bloody fault if he died—well, unless you knocked him off."

David glared again. "Annie!"

Samira gasped, then laughed. "I'm sure that is sometimes considered, in a cruel household." She shook her head. "I did try to ask, through my father, whether I'd even be able to help my husband with his business."

"And?"

"No, of course not. I doubt Pita even asked. That would imply a failing on my husband's part. No, I'd be expected to look after the household, any children, his parents."

Annie looked at David, thinking about their recent conversation about her returning to work. And, despite her rocky relationship with her father, knew Ian would never have forced her into marriage and, had it ever come to it, would have taken her side in any unpleasantness. Annie sighed. "What a waste of your brain, your talents."

"You know the silly thing?" Samira's eyes watered as she put the bottle back to Jake's mouth. "All the time I've been here I've missed simple things, like my mother oiling my hair."

"Oh, ducks, what a mess. I'm so sorry. It just seems so cock-eyed."

Samira nodded. "Anyway, it is all immaterial. It is too late. I missed Manish's deadline. I have written to him, trying to explain, but he is furious. There will be no dowry given. He has also lost face. His first wife is old. He has no sons, which I was supposed to provide."

"What if you didn't?" David asked.

"He would take another wife."

"Good grief, one's enough!" David gave a short laugh, and this time, it was Annie who glared. "I'm not making light of it, Sami."

"I know. But that is India." Samira shrugged, looked at her friends and smiled. "Thank you for listening. It feels better to talk, but now that is enough. Like I said, I am tired of my story."

Chapter 33
Cambridgeshire, 2003

A whisper of wind slithered through the open patio doors and sent a shiver across Annie's shoulders. Eartha felt it as well and jumped from her position on the arm of the chair to saunter out into the garden. Twilight had always been a special time—that magical half-hour wherein day and night merge, and creatures scurry either home or start their nightly foraging.

Annie rose. Dusk also heralded the closing-of-the-garage-doors routine. Another tell-tale for her neighbours to know she'd survived another day. Kicking a semi-eaten apple from the path sent a flurry of bees over to the purply-pink sedum growing in an undisturbed clump under the kitchen windows. She watched a big bumbler for a moment, admiring his yellow and black coat—rather like David's favourite scarf from Clare College, Cambridge.

As she approached the garage she eyed the navy Ford Fiesta with dislike. David had been delighted with his brand new car when he bought it in 1995, and had driven it up until the day he died five years later. Not quite the Morgan in which he had wooed Annie, and which Hugh now cared for with reverence, and occasionally drove on rare sunny days when he happened to be in England. Annie chuckled and patted the bonnet. Not entirely Fifi's fault! Having only ever driven a Ute on Gunida, where the only thing to worry about were sheep who soon moved, then not driving again until they moved to Umbleford, Annie had no love of driving. It had become a necessary evil when district nurses' areas became larger and cars took over from bicycles; then because the boys had needed to be transported to various activities.

Still, Fifi, the name she had given the car and which David had refused to use, allowed her freedom from reliance on others for day-to-day needs for which she was grateful. She patted the bonnet again, then hauled the garage door down.

Pulling her cardigan tighter, Annie ambled back into the Old Vicarage. Time for supper.

Nothing too filling, otherwise she wouldn't be hungry for lunch at The Swan with the family. Such a treat that Hugh would join them. She loved seeing Jake and Hugh together, the bond still as tight as when they'd been children, just two years apart.

Another celebration that drew the whole family together, even Joe from Australia, had been present when Hugh had been christened. Her brother had missed Jake's, his own godson's, christening but happily looked on at Hugh's. Annie had never forgotten Sami's delight at being asked to be his godmother. Although technically, as David had explained, not allowed in the eyes of the Church to be a godparent because Hindus are not baptised, she nevertheless was part of the ceremony as an honorary godmother. Annie and David had decided two bona fide godparents for their second born would be plenty, and so David's middle brother, Bill, had been chosen. And Edmund, finally married to Trisha.

The Vicarage had echoed with joy as old and new friends mingled. Trisha's children, particularly Janet, had decided their role involved junior parental supervision of the little ones, even if Molly had only just turned six.

"So," Sami had said, holding Hugh in her arms after the christening at which David officiated, and after most people had left the gathering at the house, "I would like, with your permission, to give Hugh a Hindi name—our equivalent of a baptism is called namakarana."

She had looked at David and Annie with hope. "Would you mind? It would just be my name for him?" And so, to Sami, Hugh had always been Suraj, sun. With his blond hair it had seemed doubly appropriate. Perhaps that was why Hugh had always been fascinated by other religions.

Annie smiled at the memories rolling in. The day Sami had married Rahul had been another happy one. So many of them over the years. But that especially so. They hadn't gone to India for the wedding but held a celebration in the garden on the couple's return. Annie had always found it remarkable that Samira had been able to forgive the ten years of exile from her family with so little bitterness, and delight in her return to the fold. Annie doubted she would have been so charitable. Hugh had remained Sami's Suraj, and in turn had been a very young 'godfather' to their only child, a daughter.

The boys and Chahna had run riot in the garden. Her adoration of the boys had continued, and one of both Annie's and Samira's enduring delights had been the closeness of the three that followed them into adulthood. She must give Sami a call in the morning, it had been ages since they'd caught up.

"And so life turns, like the sun." Annie said aloud as she mixed mayonnaise with left-over baked salmon. Next she rinsed lettuce leaves, and peeled some cucumber, then crumbled feta over the salad. Perfect! Ever since David's death, she had made it part of her evening ritual to sit at the dining table, set properly. Otherwise, she had told her sons, I might be in danger of becoming rather sloppy. A mad, cantankerous, old harpy.

A giggle erupted as grinding pepper on her supper, David's words drifted in, "You are turning into a peppery and splenetic shrew!"

One of the few times he had been truly angry. She had been so stunned at his description that she had burst out laughing. "Rather defeated the whole argument, Eartha," Annie told the cat. Greenham Common. Annie tapped her head trying to remember the year. "1982!" David had been livid when she announced she would be joining the throngs of women planning to encircle the airbase where nuclear armed cruise missiles were to be deployed. She'd nearly clocked him when he'd said, "For God's sake, Annie, you're almost seventy."

"Does that make it okay to sit back and let the bloody Americans use us as a staging post?"

"They have to be somewhere," he'd tried to argue.

"Well, not in my backyard! And," Annie had been on a roll, "shouldn't you be more concerned? What with God, and everything. You know what war does." Definitely a NIMBY moment. Annie remembered applauding the person who came up with the acronym.

She'd gone, despite David's reservations.

Bocelli had stopped singing. Annie considered leaving the dishes for the new housekeeper, Mary. She chuckled. New? Really? Mary had taken over from Mrs. Winters about thirty-five years ago. Dear Mrs. Mabel Winters, although neither Annie nor David ever called her anything but Mrs. Winters, or occasionally Mrs. W. Even now, Annie wondered how she could have wanted to slough her off. The housekeeper, particularly after Fred died a few months after their arrival in Umbleford, had become an integral part of the family—called Bel by the boys. They had become her adopted grandsons, helping salve the hurt at not being a part of her own grandchildren's lives.

Annie pushed her chair back, her mind roving from memory to memory. The boys and their music. A lot of which she'd liked, although not the screaming mayhem caused by any mention of The Beatles. And Hugh, a boy of twelve. Just older than the twins now. Trying not to cry tears of elation when England won the World Cup in 1966. They'd all, including Mrs. W., crowded around and watched it on the black and white television in the sitting room.

The dishes could wait. Annie slipped a new CD into the player, skipped down to the eighth track and turned it up loud. She took the rest of her whisky and sat on the garden wall singing along to Metallica's *Nothing Else Matters*. The lyrics and music had always resonated, *Trust I seek and I find in you, Every day for us something new, Open mind for a different view, And nothing else matters.* "That was our life, darling," she said, her voice a murmur. "Trust. And love."

She sipped the last of her whisky and watched the cat slink off into the shadows. "Please, no mice tonight, Eartha Kitty," Annie called, going inside to put the house to bed before climbing the stairs. The red alarm light still blinked on the bedside table where she'd left it that morning. Where she left it every morning. She glanced out at the church, the spire just visible through the gum tree, before drawing the curtains, then smoothed the Paisley shawl flung on the chair.

Annie lay in the soft semi-darkness surrounded by the subtle scent of eucalyptus wafting through the open window. It had been a good day. As she drifted off she saw David standing at the end of the bed smiling down at her. She focused more sharply. Behind David, she could clearly see Bill, his eyebrow raised, holding out his hand.

Acknowledgements

My mother, Ida Arundel Morse, to whom this book is dedicated along with her great grandchildren, was in the Australian Army Nursing Service and served, as Annie did, in both Singapore and New Guinea. She did evacuate from Singapore on the Empire Star. She did not speak about it much, and it is one of my regrets that I did not push more for her stories. Like many involved in wars, her memories were locked away. Annie's postings during the war are based on Mum's army records which I got from the Australian War Memorial Archives—a wonderful resource for all things pertaining to Australia at war. Mum was also in Berlin during the Airlift, although she spoke even less about that period.

People often ask about how I research my books. I am fortunate to have lived in many countries—Singapore, Papua New Guinea, and Australia being three of them. I had fun adding NEGS into the story—it was where I was educated. And lots of reading. The internet is always a good starting point but can send the writer down rabbit holes from which it is hard to escape. The Imperial War Museum in England is a fantastic resource. A few books I should mention are: *D-Day in New Guinea* by Phillip Bradley; *Our War Nurses* by Rupert Goodman; *Australian Women at War* by Patsy Adam-Smith; *Checkmate in Berlin* by Giles Milton, and *Life and Death in the Battle of Britain* by Guy Maysfield—the whisky in the gumboot is his story.

People are very generous with their knowledge, and I would like to thank four in particular.

Reverend Lydia Smith of the Hinkledux Churches, a benefice of three churches in the Cambridgeshire villages of Hinxton, Ickleton and Duxford, graciously answered many questions, both practical and theoretical, about life as a country vicar.

Pooja Vacchani, a friend, allowed me to bombard her with questions about Hindu culture, particularly with regard to arranged marriages. Samira's words about missing her hair being oiled by her mother come directly from Pooja.

And Max Uechritz, a chap I knew fifty years ago while living in Papua New Guinea. His knowledge of PNG is prodigious and, when I contacted him out of the blue, he kindly pointed me in a number of directions when I asked for clarifications about the war years.

Paul Andrews kindly produced the maps of New Guinea and Berlin which, I hope, help the reader follow some of Annie's moves.

Once again my Beta readers, Kay Chapman, Sandy Lease, Val Miller and Mary Cadell have been invaluable in their honesty—I don't think they recognize how much I appreciate their comments. Sarah Burson joined their ranks for *Annie's Day*. I thank them all!

Vine Leaves Press are again my publisher. What can I say? They are wonderful in their support and match me and my words to remarkable editors, from whom I learn so much. I have been thrilled to once again work with Ann S. Epstein as my developmental editor, herself a talented author, and she was also the evaluation editor who recommended taking me on. Karen Jones honed my grammar, and made insightful comments during the copy edit phase. Amie McCracken nurtures the book through the production process, and Jessica Bell comes up with outstanding covers, time and time again.

It is a grind getting onto the shelves when a writer is with a small press. So I truly thank those independent bookshops that support me—three in particular: Undercover Books on St. Croix, in the US Virgin Islands; Hart's Books in Saffron Walden, and Boobooks in Armidale, Australia. Book clubs are also a hugely important to writers, and I thank them, and hope that the reading questions are helpful.

In our living room is a portrait of my mother in uniform when she was in New Guinea, sketched by Nora Heyson, the first Australian woman war artist. Mum always admired strong women, and I like to think she'd have approved of Annie.

Annie's Day is not my mother's story, but she gave me the kernel for this book—I wish she could have read it, because it speaks to my pride in her, and to the bravery and resilience of so many army nurses; the fact that many returned from war to find that strength and resilience were not necessarily attractive traits in the eyes of many men. These women were, in some ways, another lost generation—a generation of spinsters, not prepared to settle for just 'any' man.

Burying oneself away in a study is not always conducive to a happy marriage, and I am so grateful to John for giving me the space and time to write. He appears with refreshments and encouragement at just the right times. I am a lucky woman.

Reading Group Questions

One theme in *Annie's Day* is the power of female friendships. Do you think they are still as important now as they were during wartime?

Annie's father, despite his prickly manner and not just because of the inconvenience to him, did not want his children enlisting. How would you feel if your son or daughter wanted to join any branch of the armed forces? Do you think some young men and women enlist because of peer pressure, as perhaps Iris did?

Singapore was considered a "citadel" by the British government. Why?

The subject of collaboration comes up in three places—Singapore, New Guinea and Berlin. Where, or what, is the line between active collaboration, and collaboration in order to survive?

The Australian Government withheld information, and sometimes censored information, about some wartime deaths "to spare the families." Do you think that is right?

Cultural differences with regard to death are mentioned—tambaran, in New Guinea—a sense of perpetual community. Discuss other countries wherein death is handled in a different way to Western norms?

Annie's brother, Joe, is gay. In some ways her attitudes were ahead of the times. Why do you think this is?

Samira's family want her to marry a man of their choosing. What are your thoughts on arranged marriages? Do you think they have a place in today's society?

Annie infuriates David when she tells him she is joining the Greenham Common demonstrations. Do you think Britain should have been willing to house nuclear weapons for the United States?

Annie is an expatriate in England, where she lives for many years. Do you think expatriates ever, or always, long to return to their passport country?

Glossary

AAMWS: Australian Army Medical Women's Services
AANS: Australian Army Nursing Service
AGH: Army General Hospital
AIF: Australian Imperial Force (2nd) the volunteer force formed following the declaration of war on Nazi Germany
ANZAC: Australian and New Zealand Army Corps
CCS: Casualty Clearing Station
CMF: Citizen Military Force, the Australian home defence force
Batavia: The Dutch colonial name for Jakarta
Dalforce Company: aka Singapore Overseas Chinese Anti-Japanese Volunteer Army Formed in 1942 by Colonel John Dalley, previously responsible for counter-intelligence operations in Malaya
Dunny: Lavatory (Australian slang)
FCO: Foreign and Commonwealth Office (UK)
Galah: Australian cockatoo
MIA: Missing in action
NEGS: New England Girls School
Pita: Father (Hindi)
QA: Nurse with the Queen Alexandra Royal Army Nursing Corps
RAAF: Royal Australian Air Force
Sheila: Girl / woman (Australian slang)
TAS: The Armidale School (brother school to NEGS)
VAD: Voluntary Aid Detachments
WAAF: Women's Auxiliary Air Force

Vine Leaves Press